The Darkest Road

The young heroes from our world have gained power and maturity from their sufferings and adventures in Fionavar. Now they must bring all the strength and wisdom they possess to the aid of the armies of Light in the ultimate battle against the evil of Rakoth Maugrim and the hordes of the dark. On a ghost-ship the legendary Warrior, Arthur Pendragon, and Pwyll Twiceborn, Lord of the Summer Tree, sail to confront the Unraveller at last. Meanwhile, Darien, the child within whom Light and Dark vie for supremacy, must walk the darkest road of any child of earth or stars.

Guy Gavriel Kay was born and raised in Canada. In 1974-5 he spent a year in Oxford assisting Christopher Tolkien in his editorial construction of JRR Tolkien's posthumously published *The Silmarillion*. Widely regarded as one of the pre-eminent fantasy novelists currently writing, he has subsequently published nine books, which have been translated into twenty-two languages and appeared on bestseller lists around the world.

Visit the authorized website for Guy Gavriel Kay: www.brightweavings.com

By Guy Gavriel Kay

The Fionavar Tapestry:

THE SUMMER TREE
THE WANDERING FIRE
THE DARKEST ROAD

TIGANA
A SONG FOR ARBONNE
THE LIONS OF AL-RASSAN

The Sarantine Mosaic:

SAILING TO SARANTIUM
LORD OF EMPERORS

THE LAST LIGHT OF THE SUN

BEYOND THIS DARK HOUSE (POETRY)

Voyager

GUY GAVRIEL KAY

THE DARKEST ROAD

The Fionavar Tapestry
Book Three

HarperCollins*Publishers*

Voyager
An Imprint of HarperCollins*Publishers*
77–85 Fulham Palace Road,
Hammersmith, London W6 8JB

www.voyager-books.co.uk

This paperback edition 2006
1

First published in Great Britain by
Unwin Hyman Ltd 1987

ISBN-13 978 0 00 721726 7
ISBN-10 0 00 721726 9

Set in Times

Printed and bound in Great Britain by
Clays Limited, St Ives plc

At the end of this road
as at the beginning of all roads
are my parents

Sybil and Sam Kay

This tapestry is theirs.

CONTENTS

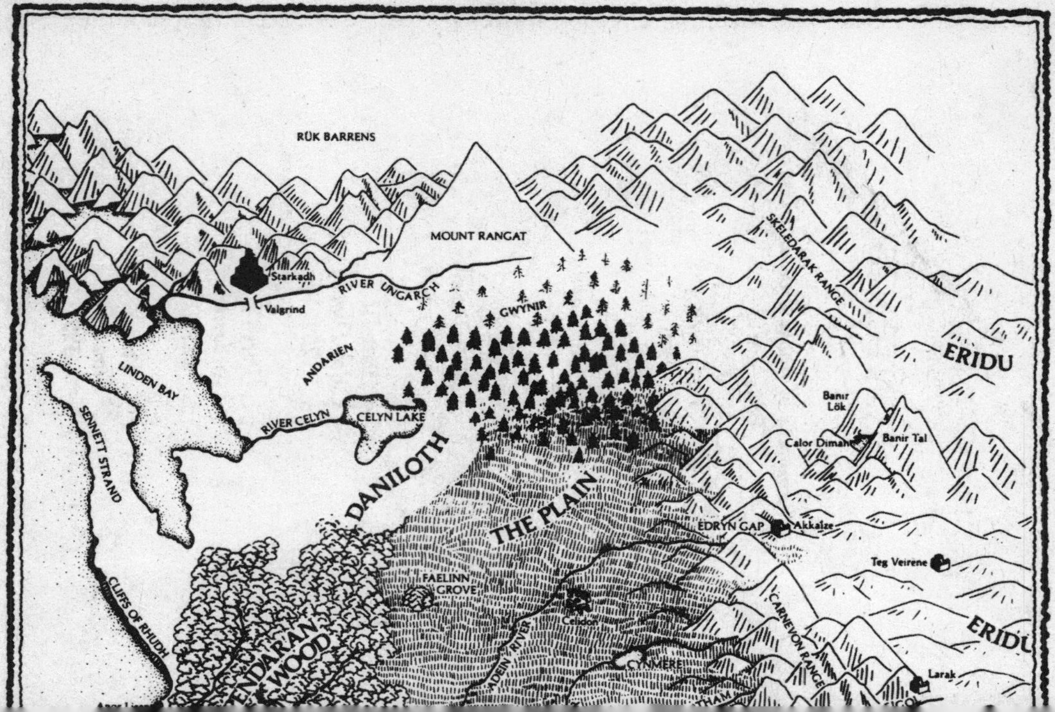
RŪK BARRENS
MOUNT RANGAT
Starkadh
RIVER UNGARCH
Valgrind
GWYNIR
SKELEDARAK RANGE
ERIDU
ANDARIEN
LINDEN BAY
SENNETT STRAND
RIVER CELYN
CELYN LAKE
DANILOTH
THE PLAIN
Banir Lök
Calor Diman
Banir Tal
EDRYN GAP
Akkaize
Teg Veirene
FAELINN GROVE
Celidon
ADEIN RIVER
CARNEVON RANGE
CYNMERE
ERIDU
Larak
CLIFFS OF RHUDH
ENDARAN WOOD

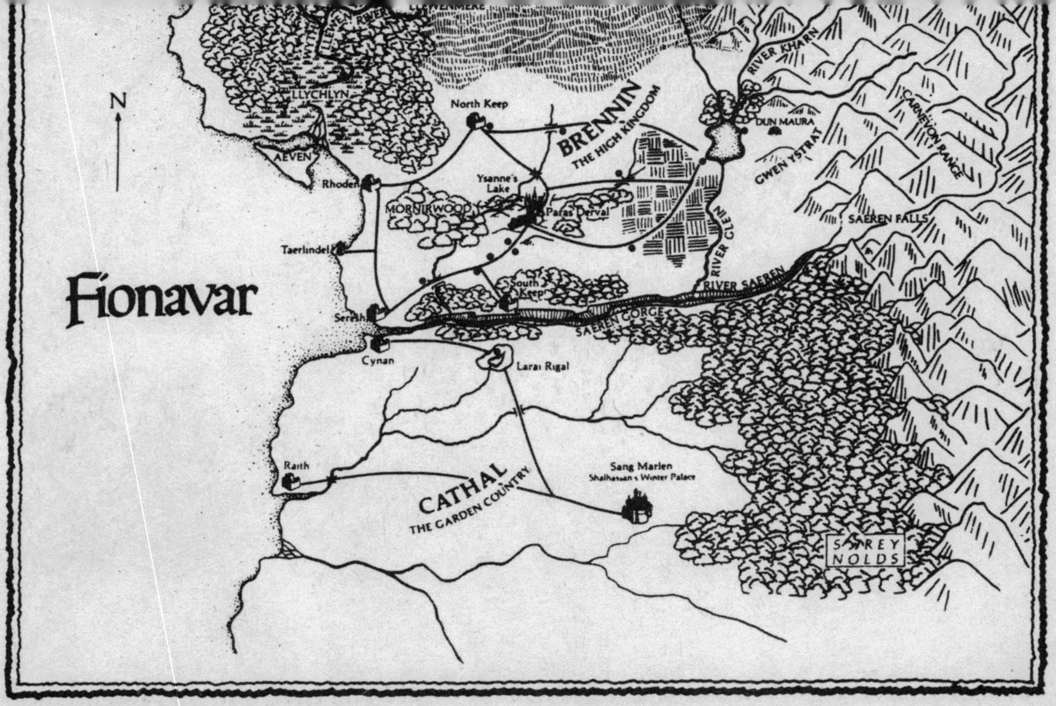
Fionavar
N
LLYCHLYN
AEVEN
North Keep
BRENNIN
THE HIGH KINGDOM
Ysanne's Lake
Paras Derval
MORNIRWOOD
Rhoden
Taerlindel
Seresh
South Keep
Cynan
Larai Rigal
Raith
CATHAL
THE GARDEN COUNTRY
Sang Marlen
Shalhassan's Winter Palace
RIVER KHARN
DUN MAURA
GWEN YSTRAT
CARNEVON RANGE
SAEREN FALLS
RIVER CLEIN
RIVER SAEREN
SAEREN GORGE
NOLDS

Summary of Books One and Two

In *The Summer Tree* it was told how Loren Silvercloak and Matt Sören, a mage and his magical source from the High Kingdom of Brennin in the world of Fionavar, induced five people from our own world to "cross" with them to Fionavar. Their ostensible purpose was to have the five participate in the festivities attendant on the celebration of the fiftieth year of the reign of Ailell, the High King. In fact, there were darker premonitions underlying the mage's actions.

In Brennin, a brutal drought was afflicting the kingdom. Ailell's older son, Aileron, had already been exiled for cursing his father's refusal to allow him to sacrifice himself on the Summer Tree in an effort to end the drought.

In Fionavar, the five strangers quickly found themselves drawn into the complex tapestry of events. Kim Ford was recognized by the aged Seer, Ysanne, as the successor she had prophetically dreamt. Kim was initiated into the knowledge of the Seers by the water spirit, Eilathen, and presented with the Baelrath, the "Warstone" that Ysanne had been guarding. Kim was also shown the Circlet of Lisen, a gem that shone with its own light. The beautiful Lisen, a power of Pendaran Wood, had been the magical source and the beloved companion of Amairgen Whitebranch, the first of the mages. She had killed herself, leaping into the sea from her Tower, upon learning that Amairgen had died. Ysanne told Kim the prophecy that accompanied the Circlet: "Who shall wear this next, after Lisen, shall have the darkest road to walk of any child of earth or stars." Later, as a last gesture of ultimate sacrifice of the eve of war, Ysanne, knowing Kim would have need of the old Seer's power in the days to come, used Lökdal, the magic dagger of the Dwarves, to kill herself—but not before tracing a symbol on the brow of the sleeping Kim, which action enabled her to make of her own soul a gift for Kimberly.

Meanwhile, Paul Schafer and Kevin Laine were initiated in quite a different way. Paul played—and lost—a night game of chess with the High King in the palace of Paras Derval, during which an unexpected bond of sympathy was forged between the two. The next morning he and Kevin joined the band of the reckless Prince Diarmuid, Ailell's younger son, in a raid across the River Saeren to Cathal, the Garden Country. There, Diarmuid achieved his intended seduction of Sharra, the Princess of Cathal. After the company's return to Brennin, they passed a wild night in the Black Boar tavern. Late at night a song Kevin sang reminded Paul too acutely of the death in a car accident of Rachel Kincaid, the woman he had loved. Paul, blaming himself for the accident, which had occurred moments after Rachel had announced she was going to wed someone else, took a drastic step: he approached the High King and received Ailell's sanction to sacrifice himself in the King's stead on the Summer Tree.

The next night, the glade of the Summer Tree in the Godwood saw an epic battle. As Paul, bound on the Tree, watched helplessly, Galadan the Wolflord, who had come to claim Paul's life, was opposed and driven back by a mysterious grey dog. The following night—Paul's third on the Tree—a red full moon shone in the sky on a new moon night, as Dana, the Mother Goddess, granted Paul release from his guilt, by showing that he had not, in fact, subconsciously willed the accident that had killed Rachel. As Paul wept, rain finally fell over Brennin. Paul, though, did not die. He was taken down from the Tree alive by Jaelle, the High Priestess of Dana. Henceforth Paul would carry another name: Pwyll Twiceborn, Lord of the Summer Tree.

By now it was clear that an epochal confrontation was at hand: Rakoth Maugrim, the Unraveller, defeated a thousand years before and bound under the great mountain, Rangat, had freed himself and had caused the mountain to explode with a hand of fire to proclaim that fact.

His freedom was to have immediate consequences for

Jennifer Lowell, the fourth of the strangers. In Paras Derval she had witnessed an unsettling incident during a children's counting game. A young girl, Leila, had "called" a boy named Finn to "take the Longest Road" for the third time that summer. No one, not even Jaelle, who had also been watching, knew exactly what that meant, though Jaelle was quick to enlist Leila as an acolyte in the Temple. The next day, riding outside the town walls, Jennifer met Brendel of the lios alfar—the Children of Light—and a party of his people. She spent the night in the woods with them, and in the darkness they were attacked. Concerned about the arrival of the five strangers, Rakoth Maugrim had Galadan and Metran—the traitorous First Mage of Brennin—abduct Jennifer. She was bound to the back of the black swan, Avaia, and borne north to Rakoth's fortress of Starkadh.

Meanwhile, the terrifying explosion of the mountain had caused the death of the aged High King. This led to a tense confrontation between Diarmuid and his brother, Aileron—who had been disguised as Ysanne's servant since his exile. The potentially violent situation was ended by Diarmuid's voluntarily relinquishing his claim to the throne, but not before he'd received a knife in the shoulder, courtesy of Sharra of Cathal, who had come to Brennin to seek vengeance on him for the deception that had led to her seduction.

In the meantime, Dave Martyniuk, the last of the five strangers, had been separated from the others in the crossing to Fionavar. He ended up far to the north among the Dalrei, the "Riders," on the Plain, and found himself drawn into the life of the third tribe, led by Ivor, their Chieftain.

Ivor's young son, Tabor, fasting in the forest for a vision of his totem animal, dreamt a seemingly impossible creature: a winged, chestnut unicorn. Three nights later, at the edge of the Great Wood, Pendaran, he met and flew upon this creature of his fast, Imraith-Nimphais—a double-edged gift of the Goddess, born of the red full moon.

Meanwhile, Dave was escorted toward Brennin by a party of Dalrei led by Ivor's older son, Levon. The company was ambushed by a great number of the evil svart alfar, and only Dave, Levon, and a third Dalrei, Torc, survived by riding into the darkness of Pendaran Wood. The trees and spirits of Pendaran, hating all men since the loss of the beautiful Lisen of the Wood a thousand years before, plotted the death of the three men, but they were saved by the intervention of Flidais, a diminutive forest power, who claimed, among other things, to know the answers to all the riddles in all the worlds, save one: the name by which the "Warrior" could be summoned. As it happened, the search for this name was one of the tasks Ysanne had left with Kimberly.

Flidais sent word to Ceinwen, the capricious, green-clad goddess of the Hunt, who had taken a special liking to Dave. The goddess arranged for the three friends to awaken safely on the southern edge of the Great Wood in the morning.

She did more. She also caused Dave to find a long-lost object of power: Owein's Horn. Levon, who had been taught by wise old Gereint, the blind shaman of his tribe, then found the Cave of the Sleepers nearby—a cave wherein Owein and the kings of the Wild Hunt lay asleep.

The three friends rode south with this knowledge to Paras Derval, in time to arrive for the first council of Aileron's reign. The council was interrupted twice. The first time, by the arrival of Brock, a Dwarf from Banir Tal who knelt before Matt Sören—once King of the Dwarves—and proffered the terrible tidings that the Dwarves, under the leadership of two brothers, Kaen and Blöd, had helped the Unraveller to free himself by treacherously breaking the wardstone of Eridu, thus preventing any warning of Rakoth's stirring under the mountain. They had also found and delivered to Rakoth the Cauldron of Khath Meigol, which had the power to raise the newly dead.

In the midst of this terrifying recitation, Kimberly suddenly saw—in a vision shaped by the Baelrath—Jennifer being raped and tortured by Rakoth in his fortress of Starkadh. She gathered Dave, Paul, and Kevin around her, reached out for Jennifer with the wild power of her ring, and drew the five of them out of Fionavar back to their own world.

And so ended *The Summer Tree*.

The Wandering Fire picked up the story some six months later, in November and back in Toronto, with Kimberly waiting for the dream that would give her the Warrior's summoning name. Jennifer, badly scarred in her soul and carrying the child of Rakoth Maugrim—having vowed to give birth to that child as her answer to the Dark—was brought early to her time by a sudden crossing back to Fionavar. The crossing was achieved by Paul when the two of them were threatened by Galadan, who had crossed to their world in pursuit of Paul.

In Fionavar, Jennifer's child, Darien, was left to be secretly fostered in the house of Vae and Shahar, the parents of Finn—the boy called by the children's counting game to "take the Longest Road." The only persons informed of the secret were the priestesses of Dana, because Paul and Jennifer needed Jaelle's magic to send them home.

The following spring Kim finally had the dream for which she had been waiting. As a result, the five traveled to Stonehenge where Kim raised the spirit of Uther Pendragon by the power of the Baelrath and compelled him to name his son's resting place. Kim then went alone, by the magic she carried, to Glastonbury Tor and there—having first sent the others ahead to Fionavar—she drew the Warrior, Arthur, from his rest by the summoning name: Childslayer. The name was an echo of the sin Arthur had committed in his youth after discovering his inadvertent incest with his sister. Kim and the Warrior followed the others to Paras Derval.

An icy winter gripped Fionavar, even as midsummer approached—a winter so terrible that Fordaetha, the Ice Queen of Rük, was able to come as far south as Paras Derval. She almost killed Paul in the Black Boar tavern before he succeeded in driving her back north. It was decided in council that Jaelle and the mages and Kimberly would join with Gereint, the old shaman, in an attempt to magically probe the source of the killing winter—a necessary prelude to trying to end it.

In the meantime the dimensions of Arthur Pendragon's tragedy were beginning to take shape as it became clear (to Brendel of the lios alfar, first of everyone) who Jennifer Lowell really was: Guinevere, beloved of Arthur and of Lancelot. Marred by her suffering in Starkadh, Jennifer withdrew to the sanctuary of Dana with Jaelle. It was Jaelle who explained that Vae and Finn had taken Darien (who was growing with the unnatural rapidity of all the andain—

children of mortals and gods) to Ysanne's cottage by the lake. There, Darien, seeming now to be a child of five years old, was growing up in the loving care of his foster mother and brother, who were troubled by two things: a power which caused his blue eyes to flash red, and an awareness that the child was drawn by voices in the storms of winter.

On the Plain the Dalrei were hard-pressed. The winter had rendered the graceful eltor—the creatures the Dalrei hunted and depended upon—awkward and ungainly in the snow, which made them easy prey for Galadan's wolves. Ivor—now Aven, or "Father" of all the Dalrei—had herded the eltor down to the southeastern corner of the vast Plain, and there the gathered tribes guarded them as best they could. Until one attack included great numbers of the hideous urgach mounted upon six-legged monsters called slaug. Only the intervention of Diarmuid of Brennin, with Dave and Kevin in his company, saved the Dalrei from the first wave of the mounted urgach. And only the appearance of Ivor's son Tabor, riding Imraith-Nimphais, his deadly, winged mount with the shining horn, saved them from the second, larger wave. Ivor was painfully aware of the effect such flight had on Tabor, drawing him ever farther from the world of men.

Shortly after, back in Brennin, another new strand entered the Tapestry. At the urging of Levon, Ivor's older son—and having the reluctant agreement of Loren—Kim and Dave, the bearers of what Levon thought to be the elements of an ancient verse that spoke of the waking of the Wild Hunt, went with a number of companions to the place at the edge of Pendaran Wood where the Cave of the Sleepers lay. The Baelrath shattered the stone at the cave mouth and then Dave's horn summoned forth Owein and the seven kings of the Hunt. With the shadowy sky kings wailing "Where is the child?" a child did, indeed, step forth to become one of the Wild Hunt: it was Finn, and this was the Longest Road to which he had been called.

Most of the company, including Shalhassan the Supreme Lord of Cathal, and Sharra, his daughter, who had arrived from the south with reinforcements, made their way the next morning to Gwen Ystrat, the province of the Goddess; partly to meet Gereint, the shaman, there, partly in response to a report from Audiart, Jaelle's second in command, that the province was being beset by wolves. The company was led by the grey dog that had saved Paul on the Summer Tree, and who turned out to be Cavall, Arthur's hunting dog. They passed into the province of the Mother amid ice and snow on the day before Maidaladan—Midsummer's Eve—with all the ancient, erotic, blood magic such a night implied. That evening, with the aid of the other magic wielders, Kim descended into the designs of Maugrim and found a clue that enabled Loren to deduce that the winter was being shaped by Metran, the treacherous mage, using the Cauldron of Khath Meigol, and basing himself on the unholy island of Cader Sedat. Kim herself would have died in her quest, had she not been saved by an unexpected source: Ruana of the Paraiko, one of the Giants, the people who had shaped the Cauldron in the first place. They were a race long thought to be dead and haunting the mountain passes with their "blood curse." Ruana reached Kim telepathically and told her that his people were alive but were slowly being put to death—bloodlessly—by the urgach and svart alfar.

The next day, during the wolf hunt, Kevin—who had been feeling useless through all the combats—had nearly fatal injury added to insult when he was gored by a white boar. He was saved by the healing magic of the mages, but this last symbolic portent finally brought home to him what his own fate and task were to be. Amid the unbridled eroticism of Midsummer's Eve in Gwen Ystrat (on a night when Prince Diarmuid told Sharra of Cathal that he loved her), Kevin slipped away alone to the east and, guided by Cavall in the snow, came to the cave of Dun Maura where he sacrificed his life to the Goddess, that she might intercede and break the winter—thus enabling the others to sail to Cader Sedat and battle with Metran.

In the meantime, Paul had remained behind with Vae and Darien. Earlier that same day he had taken Darien to the Summer Tree. His plan was to summon Cernan, the stag-horned god of the forests (and Galadan's father) to help accelerate Darien's progression to his maturity—a maturity desperately needed, for the ambivalent child was growing steadily in power. As it happened, Darien needed no such aid in an oak grove on Midsummer's Eve. He propelled himself forward in years to much the same age as his brother Finn had been before he left. Having overheard Cernan ask Paul why the child had even been allowed to live, Darien departed, vowing to seek out his father, Rakoth Maugrim.

Not long after, it was decided that Diarmuid's men, with Loren and Arthur and Paul, would sail for Cader Sedat. Kimberly had remained in the east, with only Brock the Dwarf as her companion on a journey to the mountain pass where the Paraiko were being slain. The two of them had scarcely entered the mountains, however, when they were attacked and captured by a band of brigands.

With Kevin's sacrifice ending the winter, war became a reality. From the borders of Daniloth, the Shadowland, where dwelt the lios alfar, an army of the Dark was seen sweeping south toward the Plain. Ra-Tenniel, Lord of the lios alfar, sent warning to the Dalrei. In response, Ivor led his whole army—save for Tabor, left behind to guard the camp—in a wild, full-tilt ride across half the length of the Plain to meet the enemy by the banks of the Adein River. The battle that followed was on the verge of being lost—despite the appearance of Ra-Tenniel and the lios alfar—when Dave Martyniuk sounded Owein's Horn to summon the Wild Hunt. The kings of the Hunt, led by the child who had once been Finn, began slaughtering the forces of the Dark—and then, without discrimination, those of the Light as well. They were only diverted from their kill by the intercession of the goddess Ceinwen. Much later, Dave awoke in the darkness on the mound beneath which Ceinwen had gathered the dead, and she made love with him on the grass that night.

Back in Brennin, on the morning before the voyage to Cader Sedat, Jennifer emerged from the Temple at the urging of Matt Sören. For the space of a single day she was reunited with Arthur. Then, after the ship sailed she set out in turn, with only Brendel of the lios alfar to accompany her, to watch for its return from the Anor Lisen: the Tower at the westernmost edge of Pendaran Wood where Lisen, a thousand years ago, had waited for Amairgen.

At sea, the ship *Prydwen* was attacked by a monstrous

creature, the Soulmonger of Maugrim. Amid the sound of unearthly music, Loren and Matt defended the ship while Paul desperately sought the power to summon Liranan, the god of the sea, to battle the monster. At the last instant he was reached by Gereint the shaman, who had sent his soul traveling out to sea in search of Paul to give him the aid that would make the summoning possible. Thus compelled, the sea god came and drove the monster into the deeps, killing it—but not before Diarmuid had leaped to the Soulmonger's enormous head and plucked the white staff of Amairgen Whitebranch from where it was embedded between its eyes.

And so two tragic mysteries were made clear. Amairgen, who had disappeared after sailing for Cader Sedat a thousand years ago, had evidently been slain by this creature. Even worse, the music they had heard was the glorious singing of all the lios alfar who had set sail west toward the hidden island the Weaver had shaped for them alone. Not one of them had reached it in a thousand years; all had been slain in this place.

With Arthur's guidance and Loren's power the ship came to Cader Sedat. There they discovered that Metran had been using his mage's power, augmented by the Cauldron, to shape a death rain over the eastern land of Eridu and was preparing to bring the rain westward over the mountains. On that island a titanic mages' battle was fought by Loren and Matt against Metran, who was sourced in the power of a myriad of svart alfar who—drained to death by the power he sucked from them—were being revived by the Cauldron of Khath Meigol. In the end Loren prevailed, killing Metran and shattering the Cauldron, but only by drawing upon a depth of power that also killed his source, Matt Sören.

In the aftermath of that duel, Paul and Diarmuid followed Arthur into the Chamber of the Dead beneath Cader Sedat. There they watched the Warrior wake Lancelot du Lac from his bed of stone to join in the war against the Dark. And so all three members of that triangle were now in Fionavar. Back in the shattered Hall of Cader Sedat, Lancelot's first action was to use his own particular gifts (exercised once before, in Camelot) to bring Matt Sören back to life. Unfortunately, during the brief time that Matt had lain lifeless, the bond of mage and source had been irrevocably broken, and Loren Silvercloak had lost his magical powers. *The Wandering Fire* ended as the company prepared to leave the island and sail back to war.

The Characters

The Five:

KIMBERLY FORD, Seer of Brennin
JENNIFER LOWELL, who is also GUINEVERE
DAVE MARTYNIUK ("Davor")
PAUL SCHAFER, Lord of the Summer Tree ("Pwyll Twiceborn")

KEVIN LAINE ("Liadon"), the sacrifice come freely on Midsummer's Eve

From Brennin:

AILERON, High King of Brennin
DIARMUID, his brother

LOREN SILVERCLOAK, once First Mage of Brennin
MATT SÖREN, once his source: King of the Dwarves
TEYRNON, a mage
BARAK, his source

JAELLE, High Priestess of the Goddess
AUDIART, her second in command, in the province of Gwen Ystrat
LEILA, a young priestess, mind-linked to Finn dan Shahar
SHIEL, a priestess in Paras Derval

COLL of Taerlindel, lieutenant to Diarmuid, captain of the ship PRYDWEN
CARDE, ERRON, TEGID, ROTHE, AVERREN — the men of South Keep, members of Diarmuid's band

GORLAES, Chancellor of Brennin
MABON, Duke of Rhoden
NIAVIN, Duke of Seresh

VAE, a craftswoman in Paras Derval
SHAHAR, her husband
FINN, their son, now riding with the Wild Hunt upon ISELEN
DARIEN, their foster child, son of Jennifer Lowell and Rakoth Maugrim

BRENDEL, a lord of the lios alfar, from Daniloth
BROCK, a Dwarf, from Banir Tal

From Cathal:

SHALHASSAN, Supreme Lord of Cathal
SHARRA, his daughter and heir ("the Dark Rose"); betrothed to Diarmuid

From the Plain:

IVOR, Aven of the Plain, Chieftain of the third tribe of the Dalrei
LEITH, his wife
LEVON, his older son
CORDELIANE ("LIANE"), his daughter
TABOR, his younger son, rider of IMRAITH-NIMPHAIS

TORC, a Rider of the third tribe

GEREINT, shaman of the third tribe

From Daniloth:

RA-TENNIEL, Lord of the lios alfar
GALEN, LYDAN } twin brother and sister, of the Brein Mark
LEYSE of the Swan Mark

In the Mountains:

DALREIDAN, an exile from the Plain
FAEBUR of Larak, exiled from Eridu
CERIOG, leader of the mountain outlaws

RUANA of the Paraiko, in the caves of Khath Meigol

MIACH, First of the Dwarfmoot, in Banir Lök

The Dark:

RAKOTH MAUGRIM the UNRAVELLER

GALADAN, Wolflord of the andain, his lieutenant
UATHACH, the urgach in white, commander of the army of Maugrim

FORDAETHA OF RÜK, Ice Queen of the Barrens
AVAIA, the Black Swan
BLÖD, a Dwarf, servant to Rakoth
KAEN, brother to Blöd, ruling the Dwarves in Banir Lök

The Powers:

THE WEAVER at the Loom

MÖRNIR of the Thunder
DANA, the Mother
CERNAN of the Beasts
CEINWEN of the Bow, the HUNTRESS
LIRANAN, god of the sea
MACHA, NEMAIN } the goddesses of war

OWEIN, Lord of the Wild Hunt, rider of CARGAIL
FLIDAIS ("Taliesin") of the andain, a power of Pendaran Wood
CURDARDH, the Oldest One, guardian of Pendaran's sacred grove

From the Past:

ARTHUR PENDRAGON, the Warrior, with CAVALL, his dog
LANCELOT du LAC, from the Chamber of the Dead in Cader Sedat

IORWETH FOUNDER, first High King of Brennin
CONARY, High King during the Bael Rangat
COLAN, his son, High King after him ("the Beloved")

AMAIRGEN WHITEBRANCH, first of the mages; slain by the Soulmonger
LISEN of the Wood, a deiena, source and wife to Amairgen

RA-TERMAINE, greatest of the Lords of the lios alfar; slain by Galadan in the Bael Rangat
RA-LATHEN ("Lathen Mistweaver"), his successor, who shaped the mists that made Daniloth into the Shadowland
LAURIEL, the White Swan, slain by Avaia in the Bael Rangat

REVOR, ancestral hero of the Dalrei; first Aven of the Plain
SEITHR, King of the Dwarves during the Bael Rangat
CONNLA, mightiest of the Paraiko, who bound the Wild Hunt and forged the Cauldron of Khath Meigol

PART I

The Last Kanior

Chapter 1

"Do you know the wish of your heart?"

Once, when Kim Ford was an undergraduate, young for university and young for her age, someone had asked her that question over cappuccino on a first date. She'd been very impressed. Later, rather less young, she'd often smiled at the memory of how close he'd come to getting her into bed on the strength of a good line and a way with waiters in a chic restaurant. The question, though, had stayed with her.

And now, not so much older but white-haired nonetheless, and as far away from home as she could imagine being, Kim had an answer to that question.

The wish of her heart was that the bearded man standing over her, with the green tattoos on his forehead and cheeks, should die an immediate and painful death.

Her side ached where he had kicked her, and every shallow breath was a lancing pain. Crumpled beside her, blood seeping from the side of his head, lay Brock of Banir Tal. From where Kim lay she couldn't tell if the Dwarf was alive or not, and if she could have killed in that moment, the tattooed man would be dead. Through a haze of pain she looked around. There were about fifty men surrounding them on the high plateau, and most of them bore the green tattoos of Eridu. Glancing down at her own hand she saw that the Baelrath lay quiescent, no more than a red stone set in a ring. No power for her to draw upon, no access to her desire.

It didn't really surprise her. The Warstone had never, from the first, brought anything but pain with its power, and how could it have been otherwise?

"Do you know," the bearded Eridun above her said, with harsh mockery, "what the Dalrei have done down below?"

"What? What have they done, Ceriog?" another man asked, moving forward a little from the circle of men. He was older than most of them, Kim saw. There was grey in his dark hair, and he bore no sign of the green tattoo markings.

"I *thought* you might be interested," the one named Ceriog said, and laughed. There was something wild in the sound, very near to pain. Kim tried not to hear it, but she was a Seer more than she was anything else, and a premonition came to her with that laughter. She looked at Brock again. He had not moved. Blood was still welling slowly from the wound at the side of his head.

"I am interested," the other man said mildly.

Ceriog's laughter ended. "They rode north last night," he said, "every man among them, except the blind ones. They have left the women and children undefended in the camp east of the Latham, just below us."

There was a murmur among the listening men. Kim closed her eyes. *What had happened?* What could have driven Ivor to do such a thing?

"What," the older man asked, still quietly, "does any of that have to do with us?"

Ceriog moved a step toward him. "You," he said, contemptuously, "are more than a fool. You are an outlaw even among outlaws. Why should any of us answer questions of yours when you won't even give us your name?"

The other man raised his voice very slightly. On the windless plateau it carried. "I have been in the foothills and the mountains," he said, "for more years than I care to remember. For all of those years, Dalreidan is what I have offered as my name. Rider's Son is what I choose to call myself, and until this day no man has seen fit to question it. Why should it matter to you, Ceriog, if I choose not to shame my father's grave by keeping his name as part of my own?"

Ceriog snorted derisively. "There is no one here who has not committed a crime, old man. Why should you be different?"

"Because," said Dalreidan, "I killed a mother and child."

Opening her eyes, Kim looked at him in the afternoon

sunlight. There was a stillness on the plateau—broken by Ceriog's laughter. Again Kim heard the twisting note in it, halfway between madness and grief.

"Surely," Ceriog mocked, "that should have given you a taste for more!" He flung his arms wide. "Surely we should all have a taste for death by now! I had come back to tell you of women and boys for sport down below. I had not thought to see a Dwarf delivered into my hands so soon."

He did not laugh again. Instead, he turned to look down on the figure of Brock, sprawled unconscious on the sun-baked stone of the plateau.

A sick foreboding swept over Kimberly. A recollection, though not her own: Ysanne's, whose soul was a part of her now. A memory of a legend, a nightmare tale from childhood, of very great evil done, very long ago.

"What happened?" she cried, wincing with pain, desperate to know. "What did they do?"

Ceriog looked at her. They all did. For the first time she met his eyes and flinched away from the raw grief she read in them. His head jerked up and down convulsively. "Faebur!" he cried suddenly. A younger light-bearded Eridun stepped forward. "Play messenger again, Faebur. Tell the story one more time. See if it improves with age. She wants to know what the Dwarves have done. *Tell her!*"

She was a Seer. The threads of the Timeloom shuttled for her. Even as Faebur began his flat-voiced recitation, Kim cut straight past his words to the images behind them and found horror.

The background of the tale was known to her, though not less bitter for that: the story of Kaen and Blöd, the brothers who had led the Dwarves in search, forty years ago, of the lost Cauldron of Khath Meigol. When the Dwarfmoot had voted to aid them, Matt Sören, the young King, had thrown down his scepter and removed the Diamond Crown and left the twin mountains to find another fate entirely, as source to Loren Silvercloak.

Then, a year ago, the Dwarf now lying beside her had come to Paras Derval with tidings of great evil done: Kaen and Blöd, unable to find the Cauldron on their own and driven near to madness by forty years of failure, had entered into an unholy alliance. With the aid of Metran, the treacherous mage, they had finally unearthed the Cauldron of the Giants—and had paid the price. It had been twofold: the Dwarves had broken the wardstone of Eridu, thus severing the warning link of the five stones, and then they had delivered the Cauldron itself into the hands of their new master, the one whose binding under Rangat was to have been ensured by the linked wardstones—Rakoth Maugrim, the Unraveller.

All this she had known. Had known, too, that Metran had used the Cauldron to lock in the killing winter that had ended five mornings ago, after the night Kevin Laine had sacrificed himself to bring it to a close. What she hadn't known was what had happened since. What she now read in Faebur's face and heard him tell, feeling the images like lashes in her soul.

The death rain of Eridu.

"When the snow began to melt," Faebur was saying, "we rejoiced. I heard the bells ring in walled Larak, though I could not return there. Exiled in the hills by my father, I too gave thanks for the end of the killing cold." So had she, Kim remembered. She had given thanks even as she mourned, hearing the wailing of the priestesses at dawn outside the dark cave of Dun Maura. *Oh, my darling man.*

"For three days," Faebur went on, in the same detached, numb tones, "the sun shone. The grass returned overnight, and the flowers. When the rain came, on the fourth day, that too seemed natural, and cause for joy.

"Until, looking down from the high hills west of Larak, I heard the screaming begin. The rain did not reach the hills, but I could see herdsmen not far away on the slopes below, with their goats and kere, and I heard them scream when the rain fell, and I saw huge black blisters form and break on animals and men as they died."

Seers could go—were forced by their gift to go—behind the words to the images suspended in the coils of time. Try as she might, Kim's second, inner sight would not let her look away from the vision caught in Faebur's words. And being what she was, twinned soul with two sets of memories, she knew more, even, than Faebur knew. For Ysanne's childhood memories were hers, and clearer now, and she

knew the rain had been shaped once before in a distant time of dark, and that the dead were deadly to those who touched them, and so could not be buried.

Which meant plague. Even after the rain stopped.

"How long did it last?" she asked suddenly.

Ceriog's harsh laughter told her her mistake and opened a new, deeper vein of terror, even before he spoke. "How long?" he snapped, his voice swirling erratically. "White hair should bring more wisdom. Look east, foolish woman, up the valley of the Kharn. Look past Khath Meigol and tell me how long it lasted!"

She looked. The mountain air was thin and clear, the summer sun bright overhead. She could see a long way from that high plateau, almost to Eridu itself.

She could see the rain clouds piled high east of the mountains.

The rain hadn't ended. And she knew, as surely as she knew anything at all, that, if unchecked, it would be coming their way: Over the Carnevon Range, and the Skeledarak, to Brennin, Cathal, the wide Plain of the Dalrei, and then, of course, to the place where undying Rakoth's most undying hatred lay—to Daniloth, where dwelt the lios alfar.

Her thoughts, shrouded in dread, winged away west, far past the end of land, out over the sea, where a ship was sailing to a place of death. It was named *Prydwen*, she knew. She knew the names of many things, but not all knowledge was power. Not in the face of what was falling from that dark sky east of them.

Feeling helpless and afraid, Kim turned back to Ceriog. As she did, she saw that the Baelrath was flickering on her hand. That, too, she understood: the rain she had just been shown was an act of war, and the Warstone was responding. Unobtrusively she turned the ring inward and closed her palm so it would not be seen.

"You wanted to know what the Dwarves had done, and now you know," Ceriog said, his voice low and menacing.

"Not all the Dwarves!" she said, struggling to a sitting position, gasping with the pain that caused. "Listen to me! I know more of this than you. I—"

"Doubtless, you know more, traveling with one of them.

And you shall tell me, before we are done with you. But the Dwarf is first. I am very pleased," said Ceriog, "to see he is not dead."

Kim whipped her head around. A cry escaped her. Brock moaned, his hands moved slightly. Heedless of risk, she crawled over to help him. "I need clean cloths and hot water!" she shouted. "Quickly!"

No one moved. Ceriog laughed. "It seems," he said, "that you haven't understood me. I am pleased to see him alive, because I intend to kill him with great care."

She did understand and, understanding, could no longer hate—it seemed that clear, uncomplicated wishes of the heart were not allowed for her. Which wasn't all that surprising, given who she was and what she carried.

She could no longer hate, nor could she hold back her pity for one whose people were being so completely destroyed. But neither could she allow him to proceed. He had come nearer, had drawn a blade. She heard a soft, almost delicate rustle of anticipation among the watching outlaws, most of whom were from Eridu. No mercy to be expected there.

She twisted the ring back outward on her finger and thrust her hand high in the air.

"Harm him not!" she cried, as sternly as she could. "I am the Seer of Brennin. I carry the Baelrath on my hand and a magegift vellin stone about my wrist!"

She was also hellishly weak, with a brutal pain in her side, and no idea whatsoever of how she could hold them off.

Ceriog seemed to have an intuition about that, or else was so goaded by the presence of the Dwarf that he was beyond deterrence. He smiled thinly, through his tattoos and his dark beard.

"I like that," he said, gazing at the Baelrath. "It will be a pretty toy to carry for the hours we have left before the rains come west and we all turn black and die. First, though," he murmured, "I am going to kill the Dwarf very slowly, while you watch."

She wasn't going to be able to stop him. She was a Seer, a summoner. A storm crow on the winds of war. She could wake power, and gather it, and sometimes to do so she could flame red and fly between places, between worlds. She had two souls within her, and she carried the burden of the

Baelrath on her finger and in her heart. But she could not stop a man with a blade, let alone fifty of them, driven mad by grief and fury and awareness of coming death.

Brock moaned. Kim felt his life's blood soaking through her clothing as she held his head in her lap. She glared up at Ceriog. Tried one last time.

"Listen to me—" she began.

"While you watch," he repeated, ignoring her.

"*I think not*," said Dalreidan. "Leave them alone, Ceriog."

The Eridun wheeled. A twisted light of pleasure shone in his dark face. "You will stop me, old man?"

"I shouldn't have to," Dalreidan said calmly. "You are no fool. You heard what she said: the Seer of Brennin. With whom else and how else will we stop what is coming?"

The other man seemed scarcely to have heard. "For a Dwarf?" he snarled. "You would intercede, now, for a Dwarf?" His voice skirled upward with growing incredulity. "Dalreidan, this has been coming between us for a long time."

"It need not come. Only hear reason. I seek no leadership, Ceriog. Only to—"

"Only to tell the leader what he may or may not do!" said Ceriog viciously. There was a frozen half second of stillness, then Ceriog's arm whipped forward and his dagger flew—

—over the shoulder of Dalreidan, who had dived and rolled and was up again in a move the Plain had seen rehearsed from horseback for past a thousand years. No one had seen his own blade drawn, nor had they seen it thrown.

They did see it, all of them, buried in Ceriog's heart. And an instant later, after the shock had passed, they saw also that the dead Eridun was smiling as might one who has found release from overmastering pain.

Kim was suddenly aware of the silence. Of the sun overhead, the finger of the breeze, the weight of Brock's head in her lap—details of time and place made unnaturally vivid by the explosion of violence.

Which had come and was gone, leaving this stillness of fifty people in a high place. Dalreidan walked over to retrieve his blade. His steps were loud on the rocks. No one spoke. Dalreidan knelt and, pulling the dagger free, cleaned it of blood on the dead man's sleeve. Slowly he rose again and looked around the ring of faces.

"First blade was his," he said.

There was a stir, a loosening of strain, as if every man there had been holding his breath.

"It was," said an Eridun quietly, a man older even than Dalreidan himself, with his green tattoos sunken deep in the wrinkles of his face. "Revenge lies not in such a cause, neither by the laws of the Lion nor the code of the mountains."

Slowly, Dalreidan nodded his head. "I know nothing of the former and too much of the latter," he said, "but I think you will know that I had no desire for Ceriog's death, and none at all to take his place. I will be gone from this place within the hour."

There was another stir at that. "Does it matter?" young Faebur asked. "You need not go, not with the rain coming so soon."

And that, Kim realized, brought things back round to her. She had recovered from the shock—Ceriog's was not the first violent death she'd seen in Fionavar—and she was ready when all their eyes swung to where she sat.

"It may not come," she said, looking at Faebur. The Baelrath was still alive, flickering, but not intensely so.

"You are truly the Seer of Brennin?" he asked.

She nodded. "On a journey for the High King with this Dwarf, Brock of Banir Tal. Who fled the twin mountains to bring us tidings of the treachery of others."

"A Dwarf in the service of Ailell?" Dalreidan asked.

She shook her head. "Of his son. Ailell died more than a year ago, the day the Mountain flamed. Aileron rules in Paras Derval."

Dalreidan's mouth crooked wryly. "News," he said, "is woven slowly in the mountains."

"Aileron?" Faebur interjected. "We heard a tale of him in Larak. He was an exile, wasn't he?"

Kim heard the hope in his voice, the unspoken thought. He was very young; the beard concealed it only partially. "He was," she said gently. "Sometimes they go back home."

"If," the older Eridun interposed, "there is a home to go back to. Seer, can you stop the rain?"

She hesitated, looking beyond him, east to where the clouds were piled high. She said, "I cannot, not directly. But the High King has others in his service, and by the Sight I have I know that some of them are sailing even now to the place where the death rain is being shaped, just as the winter was. And if we stoped the winter, then—"

"—then we can end the rain!" a deep voice rumbled, low and fierce. She looked down. His eyes were open.

"Oh, Brock!" she cried.

"Aboard that ship," the Dwarf went on, speaking slowly but with clarity, "will be Loren Silvercloak and my lord, Matt Sören, true King of the Dwarves. If any people alive can save us, it is the two of them." He stopped, breathing heavily.

Kim held him close, overwhelmed for an instant with relief. "Careful," she said. "Try not to talk."

He looked up at her. "Don't worry so much," he said. "Your forehead will set in a crease." She gave a little gasp of laughter. "It takes a great deal," he went on, "to kill a Dwarf. I need a bandage to keep the blood out of my eyes, and a good deal of water to drink. Then, if I can have an hour's rest in the shade, we can go on."

He was still bleeding. Kim found that she was crying and clutching his burly chest far too hard. She loosened her grip and opened her mouth to say the obvious thing.

"Where? Go where?" It was Faebur. "What journey takes you into the Carnevon Range, Seer of Brennin?" He was trying to sound stern, but the effect was otherwise.

She looked at him a long moment, then, buying time, asked, "Faebur, why are *you* here; why are you exiled?"

He flushed but, after a pause, answered, in a low voice. "My father unhoused me, as all fathers in Eridu have the right to do."

"Why?" she asked. "Why did he do that?"

"Seer—" Dalreidan began.

"No," said Faebur, gesturing at him. "You told us your reason a moment ago, Dalreidan. It hardly matters any more. I will answer the question. There is no blood on the Loomweft with my name, only a betrayal of my city, which in Eridu is said to be red on the Loom, and so the same as blood. It is simply told. Competing at the Ta'Sirona, the

Summer Games, at Teg Veirene a year ago, I saw and loved a girl from high-walled Akkaïze, in the north, and she . . . saw and loved me, as well. In Larak again, in the fall of the year, my father named to me his choice for my wife, and I . . . refused him and told him why."

Kim heard sympathetic sounds from the other Eriduns and realized they hadn't known why Faebur was in the mountains; nor Dalreidan either, for that matter, until, just now, he'd told of his murders. The code of the mountains, she guessed: you didn't ask.

But she had, and Faebur was answering. "When I did that, my father put on his white robe and went into the Lion's Square of Larak, and he called the four heralds to witness and cursed me west to Carnevon and Skeledarak, unhoused from Eridu. Which means"—and there was bitterness now—"that my father saved my life. That is, if your mage and Dwarf King can stop Rakoth's rain. You cannot, Seer, you have told us so. Let me ask you again, where are you going in the mountains?"

He had answered her, and with his heart's truth. There were reasons not to reply, but none seemed compelling, where they were, with the knowledge of that rain falling east of them.

"To Khath Meigol," she said, and watched the mountain outlaws freeze into silence. Many of them made reflexive signs against evil.

Even Dalreidan seemed shaken. She could see that he had paled. He crouched down on his haunches in front of her and spent a moment gathering and dispersing pebbles on the rocks. At length, he said, "You will not be a fool, to be what you are, so I will say none of what first comes to me to say, but I do have a question."

He waited for her to nod permission, then went on.

"How are you to be of service in this war, to your High King or anyone else, if you are bloodcursed by the spirits of the Paraiko?"

Again, Kim saw them making the sign against evil all around her. Even Brock had to suppress a gesture. She shook her head. "It is a fair question—" she began.

"Hear me," Dalreidan interrupted, unable to wait for her answer. "The bloodcurse is no idle tale, I know it is not.

Once, years ago, I was hunting a wild kere, east and north of here, and so intent on my quarry that I lost track of how far I had gone. Then the twilight came, and I realized I was on the borders of Khath Meigol. Seer of Brennin, I am no longer young, nor am I a tale-spinning elder by a winter fire stretching truth like bad wool: I was there, and so I can tell you, there *is* a curse on all who go into that place, of ill fortune and death and souls lost to time. It is true, Seer, it is not a tale. I felt it myself, on the borders of Khath Meigol."

She closed her eyes.

Save us, she heard. Ruana. She opened her eyes and said, "I know it is not a tale. There is a curse. I do not think it is what it is believed to be."

"You do not think. Seer, do you know?"

Did she know? The truth was, she didn't. The Giants went back beyond Ysanne's learning or Loren's or that of the Priestesses of Dana. Beyond, even, the lore of the Dwarves, or the lios alfar. All she had was her own knowledge: from the time in Gwen Ystrat when she'd made that terrible voyage into the designs of the Unraveller, shielded by the powers of her friends.

And then the shields had fallen, she had gone too far, had lost them and was lost, burning, until another one had come, far down in the Dark, and had sheltered her. The other mind had named himself as Ruana of the Paraiko, in Khath Meigol, and had begged for aid. They were alive, not ghosts, not dead yet. And this was what she knew, and all she knew.

On the plateau she shook her head, meeting the troubled gaze of the man who called himself Dalreidan. "No," she said. "I know nothing with certainty, save one thing I may not tell you, and one thing I may."

He waited. She said, "I have a debt to pay."

"In Khath Meigol?" There was a real anguish in his voice. She nodded. "A personal debt?" he asked, straining to deal with this.

She thought about that: about the image of the Cauldron she had found with Ruana's aid, the image that had told Loren where the winter was coming from. And now the death rain.

"Not just me," she said.

He drew a breath. A tension seemed to ease from within him. "Very well," he said. "You speak as do the shamans on the Plain. I believe you are what you tell me you are. If we are to die in a few days or hours, I would rather do so in the service of Light than otherwise. I know you have a guide, but I have been in the mountains for ten years now and have stood on the borders of the place you seek. Will you accept an outlaw as companion for this last stage of your journey?"

It was the diffidence that moved her, as much as anything else. He had just saved their lives, at risk of his own.

"Do you know what you are getting into? Do you—" She stopped, aware of the irony. None of them knew what they were getting into, but his offer was freely made, and handsome. For once she had not summoned nor was she compelled by the power she bore. She blinked back tears.

"I would be honored," she said. "We both would." She heard Brock murmur his agreement.

A shadow fell on the stone in front of her. The three of them looked up.

Faebur was there, his face white. But his voice was manfully controlled. "In the Ta'Sirona, the Games at Teg Veirene, before my father exiled me, I came . . . I placed third of everyone in the archery. Could you, would you allow—" He stopped. The knuckles of the hand holding his bow were as white as his face.

There was a lump in her throat and she could not speak. She let Brock answer this time.

"Yes," said the Dwarf gently. "If you want to come we will be grateful for it. A bowman is never a wasted thread."

And so, in the end, there were four of them.

Later that day, a long way west, Jennifer Lowell, who was Guinevere, came to the Anor Lisen as twilight fell.

With Brendel of the lios alfar as her only companion, she had sailed from Taerlindel the morning before in a small boat, not long after *Prydwen* herself had dipped out of sight in the wide, curving sea.

She had bidden farewell to Aileron the High King, to

Sharra of Cathal, and Jaelle, the Priestess. She had set out with the lios alfar that she might come to the Tower built so long ago for Lisen. And so that, coming there, she might climb the spiraling stone stairs to the one high room with its broad seaward balcony and, as Lisen had done, walk upon that balcony, gazing out to sea, waiting for her heart to come home.

Handling the boat easily in the mild seas of that first afternoon, sailing past Aeven Island where the eagles were, Brendel marveled and sorrowed, both, at the expressionless beauty of his companion's face. She was as fair as were the lios, with fingers as long and slender, and her awakened memories, he knew, went back almost as far. Were she not so tall, her eyes not held to green, she might have been one of his people.

Which led him to a strange reflection, out among the slap of waves and the billow of the single sail. He had not made or found this boat, which would ultimately be required when his time came, but it was a trim craft made with pride, and not unlike what he would have wanted. And so it was easy to imagine that they had just departed, not from Taerlindel but from Daniloth itself. To be sailing west and beyond west, toward that place made by the Weaver for the Children of Light alone.

Strange thoughts, he knew, born of sun and sea. He was not ready for that final journey. He had sworn an oath of vengeance that bound him to this woman in the boat, and to Fionavar and the war against Maugrim. He had not heard his song.

He did not know—no one did—the bitter truth. *Prydwen* had just set sail. She was two nights and a dawn yet from the sound of singing in the sea, from the place where the sea stars of Liranan did not shine and had not shone since the Bael Rangat.

From the Soulmonger.

As darkness came on that first night, Brendel guided their small craft toward the sandy shore west of Aeven and the Llychlyn Marshes and beached it in the gentle evening as the first stars appeared. With the provisions the High King had given them, they made camp and took an evening meal.

Later, he laid out a sleeping roll for each of them, and they lay down close to each other between the water and the woods.

He did not make a fire, being too wise to burn even fallen driftwood from Pendaran. They didn't need one, in any case. It was a beautiful night in the summer shaped by Kevin Laine. They spoke of him for a time as the night deepened and the stars grew more bright. They spoke, softly, of the morning's departures, and where the next evening would see them land. Looking at the night sky, glorying in it, he spoke to her of the beauty and the peace of Daniloth, and lamented that the dazzle of the stars was so muted there since Lathen Mistweaver, in defense of his people, had made their home into the Shadowland.

After that they fell silent. As the moon rose, a shared memory came to both of them of the last time they had lain beside each other under the sky.

Are you immortal? she had asked, before drifting to sleep.

No, Lady, he had answered. And had watched her for a time before falling asleep himself, beside his brothers and sisters. To wake amid wolves, and svart alfar, and red mortality in the presence of Galadan, Wolflord of the andain.

Dark thoughts, and too heavy a silence for the quicksilver leader of the Kestrel Mark. He lifted his voice again, to sing her to sleep as one might a cherished child. Of seafaring he sang, a very old song, then one of his own, about aum trees in leaf and sylvain flowering in spring. And then, as her breathing began to slow, his voice rode her to rest with the words of what was always the last song of a night: Ra-Termaine's Lament, for all those who had been lost.

When he finished, she was asleep. He remained awake, though, listening to the tide going out. Never again would he fall asleep while she was in his care, not ever again. He sat up all night watching, watching over her.

Others watched as well, from the dark edgings of Pendaran: eyes not welcoming, but not yet malevolent, for the two on the sands had not entered the forest nor burned wood of the Wood. They were very near, though, and so were closely observed, for Pendaran guarded itself and nurtured its long hate.

They were overheard as well, however low their voices, for the listening ears were not human and could discern speech at the very edge of unspoken thought. So their names became known. And then a drumming sound ran through that part of the Wood, for the two of them had named their destination, and that place had been built for the one who had been most loved and then most bitterly lost: Lisen, who would never have died had she not loved a mortal and been drawn into war outside the shelter of the Wood.

An urgent message went forth in the wordless rustle of leaves, the shadowed flicker of forms half seen, in a vibration, quick as a running pulse, of the forest floor.

And the message came, in very little time as such things are measured, to the ears of the only one of all the ancient powers of the Wood who wholly grasped what was at work, for he had moved through many of the Weaver's worlds and had played a part in this story when it first was spun.

He took thought, deliberate and unhurried—though there was a surge in his blood at the tidings, and a waking of old desire—and sent word back through the forest, by leaf and quick brown messenger and by the pulse that threaded through the roots of the trees.

Be easy, he sent, calming the agitation of the Wood. *Lisen herself would have made this one welcome in the Tower, though with sorrow. She has earned her place by the parapet. The other is of the lios alfar and they built the Anor, forget it not.*

We forget nothing.

Nothing, rustled the leaves coldly.

Nothing, throbbed the ancient roots, twisted by long hate. *She is dead. She need never have died.*

In the end, though, he put his will upon them. He had not the power to compel them all, but he could persuade, sometimes, and this night, and for this one, he did.

Then he went out from the doors of his house and he traveled at speed by ways he knew and so came to the Anor just as the moon rose. And he set about making ready a place that had stood empty for all the years since Lisen had seen a ghost ship passing and had leaped from her high balcony into the darkness of the sea.

There was less to be done than might have been supposed,

for that Tower had been raised with love and very great art, and magic had been bound into its stones that they should not fall.

He had never been there before; it was a place too sharp with pain. He hesitated on the threshold for a moment, remembering many things. Then the door swung open to his touch. By moonlight he looked at the rooms on the lower level, made for those who had stood guard. He left them as they were and passed upward.

With the sound of the sea always in his ears, he climbed the unworn stone stairs, following their spiral up the single turret of the Tower, and so he came to the room that had been Lisen's. The furnishings were sparse but exquisite and strange, crafted in Daniloth. The room was wide and bright, for along the western curve of it there was no wall; instead, made with the artifice of Ginserat of Brennin, a window of glass stretched from floor to ceiling, showing the moonlit sea.

There was salt staining the outside of the glass. He walked forward and slid the window open. The two halves rolled easily apart along their tracks into recesses hidden in the curving wall. He stepped out on the balcony. The sea sound was loud; waves crashed at the foot of the Tower.

He remained there a long time, claimed by griefs too numerous to be isolated or addressed. He looked to his left and saw the river. It had run red past the Anor for a year from the day she had died, and it did so yet, every year, when the day came around again. It had had a name once, that river. Not any more.

He shook his head and began to busy himself. He pulled the windows closed and, having more than power enough to deal with this, made them clean again. He slid them open a second time and left them so, that the night air might come into a room that had been closed a thousand years. He found candles in a drawer and then torches at the bottom of the stairs—wood of the Wood vouchsafed for burning in this place. He lit the torches in the brackets set into the wall along the stairwell, and then placed the candles about the one high room, and lit them all.

By their light he saw that there was a layer of dust on the

floor, though not, curiously, on the bed. And then he saw something else. Something that chilled even his wise, knowing blood.

There were footsteps in the dust, not his own, and they led over to that bed. And on the coverlet—woven, he knew, by masters of the art in Seresh—lay a mass of flowers: roses, sylvain, corandiel. But it was not the flowers that held his gaze.

The candles flickered in the salt breeze off the sea, but they were steady enough for him to clearly see his own small footprints in the dust and, beside them, those of the man who had walked into the room to lay those flowers on the coverlet.

And those of the giant wolf that had walked away.

His heart beating rapidly, fear shadowed by pity within him, he walked over to that bright profusion of flowers. There was no scent, he realized. He reached out a hand. As soon as he touched them they crumbled to dust on the coverlet. Very gently, he brushed the dust away.

He could have made the floor shine with a trace assertion of his power. He did not; he never did in his own rooms under the forest floor. Going down the stairs one more time, he found a sturdy broom in one of the lower chambers and then, with strong domestic motions, proof of long habit, Flidais swept out Lisen's chamber by candlelight and moonlight, to make it ready for Guinevere.

In time, for his was a spirit of play and laughter even in darkest times, he began to sing. It was a song of his own weaving, shaped of ancient riddles and the answers he had learned for them.

And he sang because he was filled with hope that night—hope of the one who was coming, that she might have the answer to his heart's desire.

He was a strong presence and a bright one, and there were torches and candles burning all through the Anor. The spirit of Gereint could not fail to sense him, singing, sweeping the dust with wide motions of the broom, as the shaman's soul went past overhead, leaving the known truths of the land to go spinning and tumbling out over the never-seen sea, in search of a single ship among all the waves.

* * *

As the sun went down on their left the following evening, Brendel guided the boat across the bay and past the river mouth toward the small dock at the foot of the Tower.

They had seen the upper lights come on as they swung into the bay. Now, drawing near, the lios alfar saw a portly, white-bearded, balding figure, smaller even than a Dwarf, waiting on the dock for them, and being of the lios alfar and more than six hundred years old himself, he had an idea who this might be.

Gentling the small craft up to the dock, he threw a rope as they approached. The small figure caught it neatly and tied the end to a peg set in the stone dock. They rested there in silence a moment, bobbing with the waves. Jennifer, Brendel saw, was looking up at the Tower. Following her gaze, he saw the reflection of the sunset sparkle off the curved glass beyond the parapet.

"Be welcome," said the figure on the dock in a voice unexpectedly deep. "Bright be the thread of your days."

"And of yours, forest one," said the lios alfar. "I am Brendel of the Kestrel Mark. The woman with me—"

"I know who she is," the other said. And bowed very low.

"By what name shall we call you?" Brendel asked.

The other straightened. "I am pied for protection, dappled for deception," he said reflexively. Then, "Flidais will do. It has, for this long while."

Jennifer turned at that and fixed him with a curious scrutiny. "You're the one Dave met in the woods," she said.

He nodded. "The tall one, with the axe? Yes, I did meet him. Green Ceinwen gave him a horn, after."

"I know," she said. "Owein's Horn."

To the east just then, under a darkening sky, a battle was raging along the bloodied banks of the Adein, a battle that would end with the blowing of that horn.

On the dock, Flidais looked up at the tall woman with the green eyes that he alone in Fionavar had cause to remember from long ago. "Is that the only knowledge you have of me?" he asked softly. "As having saved your friend?"

In the boat Brendel kept silent. He watched the woman reach for a memory. She shook her head. "Should I know you?" she asked.

Flidais smiled. "Perhaps not in this form." His voice went even deeper, and suddenly he chanted, "I have been in many shapes. I have been the blade of a sword, a star, a lantern light, a harp and a harper, both." He paused, saw something spark in her eyes, ended diffidently, "I have fought, though small, in battle before the Ruler of Britain."

"*I remember!*" she said, laughing now. "Wise child, spoiled child. You liked riddles, didn't you? I remember you, Taliesin." She stood up. Brendel leaped to the dock and helped her alight.

"I have been in many shapes," Flidais said again, "but I was his harper once."

She nodded, very tall on the stone dock, looking down at him, memory playing in her eyes and about her mouth. Then there came a change. Both men saw it and were suddenly still.

"You sailed with him, didn't you?" said Guinevere. "You sailed in the first *Prydwen.*"

Flidais' smile faded. "I did, Lady," he said. "I went with the Warrior to Caer Sidi, which is Cader Sedat here. I wrote of it, of that voyage. You will remember." He drew breath and recited:

> "*Thrice the fullness of* Prydwen *we went with Arthur,*
> *Except seven, none returned from—*"

He stopped abruptly, at her gesture. They stood so a moment. The sun sank into the sea. With the dark, a finger of wind arose. Brendel, watching, only half understanding, felt a nameless sorrow come over him as the light faded.

In the shadows, Jennifer's face seemed to grow colder, more austere. She said, "You were there. So you knew the way. Did you sail with Amairgen?"

Flidais flinched, as from an actual blow. He drew a shaken breath, and he, who was half a god and could induce the powers of Pendaran to accede to his will, said in a voice of humble supplication, "I have never been a coward, Lady, in any guise. I sailed to that accursed place once, in another form. But this is my truest shape, and this Wood my true home in this first world of all. How should a forest warden go to sea, Lady? What good would I have done? I told him, I told Amairgen what I knew—that he would have to sail north into a north wind—and he said he would know where to do so, and when. I did that, Lady, and the Weaver knows that the andain seldom do so much for men."

He fell silent. Her regard was unresponsive, remote. Then suddenly she said:

"I will not allow praise to the men with trailing shields,
They know not on what day the chief arose,
When we went with Arthur of mournful memory—"

"*I wrote that!*" Flidais protested. "My lady Guinevere, I wrote that."

It was quite dark now on the path, but with the keen sight of the lios alfar Brendel saw the coldness leave her face. Voice gentle now, she said, "I know, Taliesin. Flidais. I know you did, and I know you were there with him. Forgive me. None of this makes for easy memory."

On the words she brushed past both of them and went up the pathway toward the Tower. Over the darkened sea the evening star now shone, the one named for Lauriel the White.

He had done it completely wrong, Flidais realized, watching her walk away. He had meant to turn the conversation to the name, the summoning name of the Warrior, the one riddle left in all the worlds for which he had no answer. He was clever enough, and to spare, to have led the talk anywhere he wanted, and the Weaver knew how deep his desire for that answer was.

The thing he had forgotten, though, was what happened in the presence of Guinevere. Even though the andain cared little for the troubles of mortal men, how could one be sly in the face of so ancient a sorrow?

The lios alfar and the andain, each with his own thoughts, gathered the gear from the boat and followed her into the Anor and up the winding stair.

It was strange, thought Jaelle, to feel so uneasy in the place of her own power.

She was in her rooms in the Temple in Paras Derval, surrounded by the priestesses of the sanctuary and by the brown-robed acolytes. She could mind-link at a moment's need or desire with the Mormae in Gwen Ystrat. She even had a guest-friend in the Temple: Sharra of Cathal, escorted to the doors, but not beyond, by the amusing Tegid of Rhoden—who, it seemed, was taking his duties as Intercedent for Diarmuid with unwonted seriousness.

It was a time for seriousness, though, and for disquiet. None of the familiar things, not even the bells ringing to summon the grey ones to sunset invocation, were enough to ease the thoughts of the High Priestess.

Nothing was as clear as it once had been. She was here and she belonged here, would probably have scorned any request, let alone command, to be anywhere else. Hers was the duty and the power, both, to shape the spun webs of Dana's will, and to do so in this place.

Even so, nothing felt the same.

For one thing, hers also, as of yesterday, was half the governing of Brennin, since the High King had gone north.

The summonglass of Daniloth had blazed yestereve—two nights ago, in truth, but they had only learned of it on their return from Taerlindel. She had seen, with Aileron, the imperative coiling of light in the scepter the lios alfar had given to Ailell.

The King had paused only long enough to snatch a meal as he gave terse commands. In the garrisons, the captains of the guard were mobilizing every man. It took very little time; Aileron had been preparing for this moment since the day she had crowned him.

He had done everything properly. Had appointed her with Gorlaes the Chancellor to govern the realm while he was away at war. He had even paused beside her in front of the palace gates and quickly, but not without dignity, besought her to guard their people as best her powers allowed.

Then he had been up on his black charger and galloping away with an army, first to North Keep to collect the garrison there, and then north, at night, over the Plain toward Daniloth and Dana alone knew what.

Leaving her in this most familiar of places, where nothing seemed familiar at all.

She had hated him once, she remembered. Hated them all: Aileron, and his father, and Diarmuid, his brother, the one she called the "princeling" in response to his mocking, corrosive tongue.

Faintly to her ears came the chanting from the domed chamber. It was not the usual twilight invocation. For eight more nights, until Midsummer's moon was gone, the evening chants would begin and end with the Lament for Liadon.

And so much power lay in this, so magnificent a triumph for the Goddess, and thereby for herself, as first High Priestess in uncounted, unknowable years to have heard the voice from Dun Maura cry out on Maidaladan, in mourning for the sacrifice come freely.

And with that, her thoughts circled back to the one who had become Liadon: Kevin Laine, brought from another world by Silvercloak to a destiny both dark and dazzlingly bright, one that not even the Seer could have foreknown.

For all Jaelle's knowledge, all her immersion in the nature of the Goddess, Kevin's had been an act so overwhelming, so consummately gallant, it had irrevocably blurred the clarity with which once she'd viewed the world. He was a man, and yet he had done this thing. It was, since Maidaladan, so much harder to summon the old anger and bitterness, the hate. Or, more truly, so much harder to summon them for anything and anyone but Rakoth.

The winter was over. The summonglass had blazed. There was war, somewhere north, in the dark.

And there was a ship sailing west.

That thought carried her back to a strand of beach north of Taerlindel, where she had watched the other stranger, Pwyll, summon and speak to the sea god by the water's edge in an inhuman light. Nothing was easy for any of them, Dana and the Weaver knew, but Pywll's seemed such a harsh, demanding power, taking so much out of him and not giving, so far as she could see, a great deal back.

Him too she remembered hating, with a cold, unforgiving fury, when she had taken him from the Summer Tree to this very room, this bed, knowing that the Goddess had spoken to him, not knowing what she had said. She had struck him, she remembered, drawing the blood all men should give, but hardly in the manner prescribed.

"*Rahod hedai Liadon,*" the priestesses sang under the dome, ending the lament on the last long, keening note. And after a moment she heard Shiel's clear voice begin the antiphonal verses of the evening invocation. There was some peace there, Jaelle thought, some comfort to be found in the rituals, even now, even in time of darkness.

Her chamber door burst open. Leila stood in the doorway.

"What are you doing?" Jaelle exclaimed. "Leila, you should be in the dome with—"

She stopped. The girl's eyes were wide, staring, focused on nothingness. Leila spoke, in a voice tranced and uninflected. "They have blown the horn," she said. "In the battle. He is in the sky now, above the river. Finn. And the kings. I see Owein in the sky. He is drawing a sword. Finn is drawing a sword. They are—they are—" Her face was chalk white, her fingers splayed at her sides. She made a thin sound.

"They are killing," she said. "They are killing the svarts and the urgach. Finn is covered in blood. So much blood. And now Owein is—he is—"

Jaelle saw the girl's eyes flare even wider then, and go wild with terror, and her heart lurched.

Leila screamed. "*Finn, no! Stop him! They are killing us!*"

She screamed again, wordlessly, and stumbling forward, falling, buried her head in Jaelle's lap, her arms clutching the Priestess, her body racked convulsively.

The chanting stopped under the dome. There were footsteps running along the corridors. Jaelle held the girl as tightly as she could; Leila was thrashing so hard, the High Priestess was genuinely afraid she would hurt herself.

"What is it? What has happened?"

She looked up and saw Sharra of Cathal in the doorway.

"The battle," she gasped, fighting to hold Leila, her own body rocking with the force of the girl's weeping. "The Hunt. Owein. She is tuned to—"

And then they heard the voice.

"*Sky King, sheath your sword! I put my will upon you!*"

It seemed to come from nowhere and from everywhere in the room, clear, cold, utterly imperative.

Leila's violent movements stopped. She lay still in Jaelle's arms. They were all still: the three in the room and those gathered in the corridor. They waited. Jaelle found it difficult to breathe. Her hands were blindly, reflexively stroking Leila's hair. The girl's robe was soaked through with perspiration.

"What is it?" whispered Sharra of Cathal. It sounded loud in the silence. "Who said that?"

Jaelle felt Leila draw a shuddering breath. The girl—fifteen, Jaelle thought, only that—lifted her head again. Her face was splotchy, her hair tangled hopelessly. She said, "It was Ceinwen. It was Ceinwen, High Priestess." There was wonder in her voice. A child's wonder.

"Herself? Directly?" Sharra again. Jaelle looked at the Princess, who despite her own youth had been trained in power and so evidently knew the constraints laid by the Weaver on the gods.

Leila turned to Sharra. Her eyes were normal again, and very young. She nodded. "It was her own voice."

Jaelle shook her head. There would be a price demanded for that, she knew, among the jealous pantheon of goddesses and gods. That, of course, was far beyond her. Something else, though, was not.

She said, "Leila, you are in danger from this. The Hunt is too wild, it is the wildest power of all. You must try to break this link with Finn, child. There is a death in it."

She had powers of her own, knew when her voice was more than merely hers. She was High Priestess and in the Temple of Dana.

Leila looked up at her, kneeling still on the floor. Automatically, Jaelle reached out to push a snarl of hair back from the girl's white face.

"I can't," Leila said quietly. Only Sharra, nearest to them, heard. "I can't break it. But it doesn't matter any more. They will never call them again, they dare not—there will be no way to bind them if they do. Ceinwen will not intercede twice. He is gone, High Priestess, out among the stars, on the Longest Road."

Jaelle looked at her for a long time. Sharra came up and

laid a hand on Leila's shoulder. The tangle of hair fell down again, and once more the Priestess pushed it back.

Someone had returned to the dome. The bells were ringing.

Jaelle stood up. "Let us go," she said. "The invocations are not finished. We will all do them. Come."

She led them along the curving corridors to the place of the axe. All through the evening chants, though, she was hearing a different voice in her mind.

"*There is death in it.*" It was her own voice, and more than her own. Hers and the Goddess's.

Which meant, always, that what she said was true.

Chapter 2

The next morning at the greyest hour, just before dawn, *Prydwen* met the Soulmonger far out at sea. At the same time, on the Plain, Dave Martyniuk woke alone on the mound of the dead near Celidon.

He was not, never had been, a subtle man, but one did not need deep reserves of subtlety to apprehend the significance of Ceinwen's presence beneath him and above him on the green grass tinted silver in the night just past. There had been awe at first, and a stunned humility, but only at first, and not for very long. In the blind, instinctive assertion of his own lovemaking Dave had sought and found an affirmation of life, of the living, after the terrible carnage by the river.

He remembered, vividly, a moonlit pool in Faelinn Grove a year ago. How the stag slain by Green Ceinwen's arrow had split itself in two, and had risen, and bowed its head to the Huntress, and walked away from its own death.

Now he had another memory. He sensed that the goddess had shared—had engendered, even—his own compelling desire last night to reaffirm the absolute presence of the living in a world so beleaguered by the Dark. And this, he suspected, was the reason for the gift she had given him. The third gift, in fact: his life, in Faelinn that first time, then Owein's Horn, and now this offering of herself to take away the pain.

He was not wrong in any of this, but there was a great deal more to what Ceinwen had done, though not even the most subtle of mortal minds could have apprehended it. Which was as it should be, as, indeed, it had always been. Macha knew, however, and Red Nemain, and Dana, the Mother, most surely of all. The gods might guess, and some of the andain, but the goddesses would know.

The sun rose. Dave stood up and looked around him under a brightening sky. No clouds. It was a beautiful morning. About a mile north of him the Adein sparkled, and there were men and horses stirring along its bank. East, somewhat farther off, he could make out the standing stones that surrounded and defined Celidon, the mid-Plain, home of the first tribe of the Dalrei and gathering place of all the tribes. There were signs of motion, of life, there as well.

Who, though, and how many?

Not all need die, Ceinwen had said to him a year ago, and again last night. Not all, perhaps, but the battle had been brutal, and very bad, and a great many *had* died.

He had been changed by the events of the evening and night before, but in most ways Dave was exactly what he had always been, and so there was a sick knot of fear in his stomach as he strode off the mound and began walking swiftly toward the activity by the riverbank.

Who? And how many? There had been such chaos, such muddy, blood-bespattered confusion: the wolves, the lios arriving, Avaia's brood in the darkening sky, and then, after he'd blown the horn, something else in the sky, something wild. Owein and the kings. And the child. Carrying death, manifesting it. He quickened his pace almost to a run. *Who?*

Then he had part of an answer, and he stopped abruptly, a little weak with relief. From the cluster of men by the Adein two horses, one dark grey, the other brown, almost golden, had suddenly wheeled free, racing toward him, and he recognized them both.

Their riders, too. The horses thundered up to him, the two riders leaping off, almost before stopping, with the unconscious, inbred ease of the Dalrei. And Dave stood facing the men who'd become his brothers on a night in Pendaran Wood.

There was joy, and relief, and all three showed it in their own ways, but they did not embrace.

"Ivor?" Dave asked. Only the name.

"He is all right," Levon said quietly. "Some wounds,

none serious." Levon himself, Dave saw, had a short deep scar on his temple, running up into the line of his yellow hair.

"We found your axe," Levon explained. "By the riverbank. But no one had seen you after . . . after you blew the horn, Davor."

"And this morning," Torc continued, "all the dead were gone, and we could not find you. . . ." He left the thought unfinished.

Dave drew a breath and let it out slowly. "Ceinwen?" he said. "Did you hear her voice?"

The two Dalrei nodded, without speaking.

"She stopped the Hunt," Dave said, "and then she . . . took me away. When I awoke she was with me, and she said that she had . . . gathered the dead." He said nothing more. The rest was his own, not for the telling.

He saw Levon, quick as ever, glance past him at the mound, and then Torc did the same. There was a long silence. Dave could feel the freshness of the morning breeze, could see it moving the tall grass of the Plain. Then, with a twist of his heart he saw that Torc, always so self-contained, was weeping soundlessly as he gazed at the mound of the dead.

"So many," Torc murmured. "They killed so many of us, of the lios. . . ."

"Mabon of Rhoden took a bad shoulder wound," Levon said. "One of the swans came down on him."

Mabon, Dave remembered, had saved his life only two days before, when Avaia herself had descended in a blur of death from a clear sky. He swallowed and said, with difficulty, "Torc, I saw Barth and Navon, both of them. They were—"

Torc nodded stiffly. "I know. I saw it too. Both of them."

The babies in the wood, Dave was thinking. Barth and Navon, barely fourteen when they died, had been the ones that he and Torc had guarded in Faelinn Grove on Dave's first night in Fionavar. Guarded and saved from an urgach, only to have them . . .

"It was the urgach in white," Dave said, bitterness like gall in his mouth. "The really big one. He killed them both. With the same stroke."

"Uathach." Levon almost spat the name. "I heard the others calling him. I tried to go after him, but I couldn't get—"

"No! Not that one, Levon," Torc interrupted, his voice fiercely intense. "Not alone. We will defeat them because we must, but promise me now that you will not go after him alone, ever. He is more than an urgach."

Levon was silent.

"*Promise me!*" Torc repeated, turning to stand squarely before the Aven's son, disregarded tears still bright in his eyes. "He is too big, Levon, and too quick, and something more than both of those. Promise me!"

Another moment passed before Levon spoke. "Only to the two of you would I say this. Understand that. But you have my word." His yellow hair was very bright in the sun. He tossed it back with a stiff twist of his head and spun sharply to return to the horses. Over his shoulder, not breaking stride, he snapped, "Come. There is a Council of the tribes in Celidon this morning." Without waiting for them, he mounted and rode.

Dave and Torc exchanged a glance, then mounted up themselves, double, on the grey, and set out after him. Halfway to the standing stones they caught up, because Levon had stopped and was waiting. They halted beside him.

"Forgive me," he said. "I am a fool and a fool and a fool."

"At least two of those," Torc agreed gravely.

Dave laughed. After a moment, so did Levon. Ivor's son held out his hand. Torc clasped it. They looked at Dave. Wordlessly, he placed his own right hand over both of theirs.

They rode the rest of the way together.

"Weaver be praised, and the bright threads of the Loom!" venerable Dhira, Chieftain of the first tribe, said for the third time.

He was beginning to get on Dave's nerves.

They were in a gathering hall at Celidon. Not the largest hall, for it was not a very large assembly: the Aven, looking alert and controlled despite a bandaged arm and a cut, much like Levon's, above one eye; the Chieftains of the other eight tribes with their advisers; Mabon, Duke of Rhoden, lying on a pallet, obviously in pain, as obviously determined to be present; and Ra-Tenniel, the Lord of the lios alfar, to whom all eyes continually returned, in wonder and awe.

There were people absent, Dave knew, people sorely missed. Two of the Chieftains, Damach of the second tribe and Berlan of the fifth, were new to their titles, the son and brother, respectively, of men who had died by the river.

Ivor had, to Dave's surprise, left control of the gathering to Dhira. Torc whispered a terse explanation: the first tribe was the only one that never traveled the Plain; Celidon was their permanent home. They remained here at the mid-Plain, receiving and relaying messages through the auberei of all the tribes, preserving the records of the Dalrei, providing the tribes with their shamans, and always taking command of the gatherings here at Celidon. Always—even in the presence of an Aven. So it had been in Revor's time, and so it was now.

Checks and balances, Dave thought. It made some sense in the abstract but did little to reconcile him now, in the aftermath of battle, to Dhira's quavering voice and laggard pace.

He had made a rambling, discursive speech, half mournful, half in praise, before finally calling upon Ivor. Levon's father had then risen to tell, for the benefit of Ra-Tenniel, the story of their wild, improbable ride—a night and a day across half the length of the Plain—to just beat the forces of Maugrim to the river.

He had then deferred, with grace, to the Lord of Daniloth, who in turn told of how he had seen the army of the Dark crossing Andarien; how he had set his summonglass alight on Atronel, that it might flare a warning in Paras Derval, had sent two messengers on the magnificent raithen to alert the Dalrei, and, finally and most gallantly, had led his own army out of the protected Shadowland to battle by the Adein.

His voice carried music, but the notes were shaped by sorrow as he spoke. A very great many from Daniloth had died, and from the Plain and Brennin as well, for Mabon's five hundred men from Rhoden had fought their way to the thick of the battle.

A battle that had seemed lost, utterly, for all the courage

on profligate display, until a horn had sounded. And so Dave, who was Davor here on the Plain, rose at Ivor's request and told his own story: of hearing a voice in his mind reminding him of what he carried (and in his memory it *still* sounded like Kevin Laine, chiding him for being so slow), and then blowing Owein's Horn with all the strength he had left in that hour.

They all knew what had happened. Had seen the shadowy figures in the sky, Owein and the kings, and the child on the palest horse. Had seen them descend from a great height, killing the black swans of Avaia's brood, the svart alfar, the urgach, the wolves of Galadan . . . and then, without pause or discrimination, without mercy or respite, turning on the lios alfar and the men of the Plain and Brennin.

Until a goddess had come, to cry, "Sky King, sheath your sword!" And after that only Davor, who had blown the horn, knew anything more until dawn. He told of waking on the mound, and learning what it was, and hearing Ceinwen warn him that she could not intercede another time if he blew Owein's Horn again.

That was all he told them. He sat down. He had, he realized, just made a speech. Once, he would have been paralyzed by the very thought. Now now, not here. There was too much at stake.

"Weaver be praised, and the bright threads of the Loom!" Dhira intoned once more, raising both his wrinkled hands before his face. "I proclaim now, before all of this company, that it shall henceforth be the duty and the honor of the first tribe to tend that mound of the dead with fullest rites, that it remain forever green, and that—"

Dave had had more than enough of this. "Don't you think," he interrupted, "that if Ceinwen can raise the mound and gather the dead, she can keep it green if she wants?"

He winced, as Torc landed a punishing kick on his shin. There was a small, awkward silence. Dhira fixed Dave with a suddenly acute glance.

"I know not how these matters are dealt with in the world from which you come, Davor, and I would not presume to comment." Dhira paused, to let the point register. "In the same way," he went on, "it ill behooves you to advise us about one of our own goddesses."

Dave could feel himself flushing, and an angry retort rose to his lips. He bit it back, with an effort of will, and was rewarded by hearing the Aven's voice. "He has seen her, Dhira; he has spoken to Ceinwen twice, and received a gift of her. You have not, nor have I. He is entitled, and more than that, to speak."

Dhira considered it, then nodded. "It is so," he admitted quietly, to Dave's surprise. "I will unsay what last I said, Davor. But know this: if I speak of tending the mound, it is as a gesture of homage and thanksgiving. Not to cause the goddess to do anything, but to acknowledge what she has done. Is that inappropriate?"

Which left Dave feeling sorry in the extreme for having opened his mouth. "Forgive me, Chieftain," he managed to say. "Of course it is appropriate. I am anxious and impatient, and—"

"And with cause!" Mabon of Rhoden growled, raising himself on his cot. "We have decisions to make and had best get to them!"

Silvery laughter ran through the chamber. "I had heard," Ra-Tenniel said, amused, "of the urgency of mankind, but now I hear it for myself." The tenor of his voice shaded downward; they all listened, entranced by his very presence among them. "All men are impatient. It is woven into the way time runs for you, into the shortness of your threads on the Loom. In Daniloth we say it is a curse and a blessing, both."

"Are there not times when urgency is demanded?" Mabon asked levelly.

"Surely," Dhira cut in, as Ra-Tenniel paused. "Surely, there are. But this must, before all else, be a time of mourning for the dead, or else their loss goes unremembered, ungrieved, and—"

"No," said Ivor.

One word only, but everyone present heard the long-suppressed note of command. The Aven rose to his feet.

"No, Dhira," he repeated softly. He had no need to raise his voice; the focus of the room was his. "Mabon is right, and Davor, and I do not think our friend from Daniloth will disagree. Not one man who died last night, not one of the brothers and sisters of the lios who have lost their song, will lie ungrieved beneath Ceinwen's mound. The danger," he said, and his voice grew stern, implacable, "is that they may yet have died to no purpose. This must not while we live, while we can ride and carry weapons, be suffered to come to pass. Dhira, we are at war and the Dark is all about us. There may be time for mourning, but only if we fight through to Light."

There was nothing even slightly prepossessing about Ivor, Dave was thinking. Not beside Ra-Tenniel's incandescence or Dhira's slow dignity, or even Levon's unconscious animal grace. There were far more imposing men in the room, with voices more compelling, eyes more commanding, but in Ivor dan Banor there was a fire, and it was matched with a will and a love of his people that, together, were more than any and all of these other things. Dave looked at the Aven and knew that he would follow this man wherever Ivor asked him to go.

Dhira had bowed his head, as if under the conjoined weight of the words and his long years.

"It is so, Aven," he said, and Dave was suddenly moved by the weariness in his voice. "Weaver grant we see our way through to that Light." He lifted his head and looked at Ivor. "Father of the Plain," he said, "this is no time for me to cling to pride of place. Will you allow me to yield to you, and to your warriors, and sit down?"

Ivor's mouth tightened; Dave knew that he was fighting the quick tears for which he took so much abuse from his family. "Dhira," the Aven said, "pride of place is always, always yours. You cannot relinquish it, to me or anyone else. But Dhira, you are Chieftain of the first tribe of the Children of Peace—the tribe of the shamans, the teachers, loremasters. My friend, how should such a one be asked to guide a Council of War?"

Incongruous sunshine streamed through the open windows. The Aven's pained question hung in the room, clear as the motes of dust where the slanting sunlight fell.

"It is so," said Dhira a second time. He stumbled toward an empty chair near Mabon's pallet. Obscurely moved, Dave began rising to offer his arm as aid, but then he saw that Ra-Tenniel, with a floating grace, was already at Dhira's side, guiding the aged chieftain to his seat.

When the Lord of the lios alfar straightened up, though, his gaze went out the western window of the room. He stood very still a moment, concentrating, then said, "Listen. They are coming!"

Dave felt a quick stab of fear, but the tone had not been one of warning, and a moment later he too heard sounds from the western edge of Celidon—and the sounds were cries of welcome.

Ra-Tenniel turned, smiling a little, to Ivor. "I doubt the raithen of Daniloth could ever come among your people without causing a stir."

Ivor's eyes were very bright. "I know they could not," he said. "Levon, will you have their riders brought here?"

They were on their way, in any case. Moments later Levon returned, and with him were two more—a man and a woman—of the lios alfar. The air in the room seemed brighter for their presence as they bowed to their Lord.

For all that, they were hardly noticed.

It was the third of the new arrivals who claimed the absolute attention of every person in the room, even in the company of the lios alfar. Dave was suddenly on his feet. They all were.

"Brightly woven, Aven," said Aileron dan Ailell.

His brown clothing was stained and dusty, his hair tousled, and his dark eyes lay sunken in deep pools of weariness. He held himself very straight, though, and his voice was level and clear. "They are making songs outside, even now. About the Ride of Ivor, who raced the army of the Dark to Celidon, and beat them there, and drove them back."

Ivor said, "We had aid, High King. The lios alfar came out from Daniloth. And then Owein came to the horn that Davor carries, and at the last Green Ceinwen was with us, or we would all have died."

"So I have just been told," said Aileron. He fixed Dave with a brief, keen glance, then turned to Ra-Tenniel. "Bright the hour of our meeting, my lord. If Loren Silvercloak, who taught me as a child, said true, no Lord of Daniloth has ventured so far from the Shadowland since Ra-Lathen wove the mist a thousand years ago."

Ra-Tenniel's expression was grave, his eyes a neutral grey. "He said true," he replied calmly.

There was a little silence; then Aileron's dark bearded face was lit by the brightness of his smile. "Welcome back, then, Lord of the lios alfar!"

Ra-Tenniel returned the smile, but not with his eyes, Dave saw. "We were welcomed back last night," he murmured. "By svart alfar and urgach, by wolves and Avaia's brood."

"I know it," said Aileron, swiftly changing mood. "And there is more of that welcome to come. I think we all know it."

Ra-Tenniel nodded without speaking.

"I came as soon as I saw the summonglass," Aileron went on after a pause. "There is an army behind me. They will be here tomorrow evening. I was in Taerlindel the night the message was sent to us."

"We know," Ivor said. "Levon explained. Has *Prydwen* sailed?"

Aileron nodded. "She has. For Cader Sedat. With my brother, and the Warrior, and Loren and Matt, and Pwyll also."

"And Na-Brendel, surely?" Ra-Tenniel asked quickly. "Or is he following with your army?"

"No," said Aileron, as the two lios alfar behind him stirred. "Something else has happened." He turned then, surprisingly, to Dave, and told of what Jennifer had said when *Prydwen* was out of sight, and what Brendel had said and done, and where the two of them had gone.

In the silence that followed they could hear the sounds of the camp through the windows; there were still cries of wonder and admiration from the Dalrei gathered about the raithen. The sounds seemed to be coming from far away. Dave's thoughts were with Jennifer, and with what—and who—she seemed to have become.

Ra-Tenniel's voice slid into the silence of the room. His eyes were violet now as he said, "It is well. Or as well as could be in such a time as this. Brendel's weaving was twined with hers since the night Galadan took her from him. We may have greater need of him in the Anor than anywhere else."

Only half understanding, Dave saw the diamond-bright lios alfar woman let slip a sigh of relief.

"Niavin of Seresh and Teyrnon the mage are bringing up the army," Aileron said, crisply coming back to solid facts. "I brought almost all of my forces, including the contingent from Cathal. Shalhassan is levying more men in his country even now. I have left word that those should remain in Brennin as a rear guard. I came here alone, riding through the night with Galen and Lydan, because I had to let the army have some rest; they had been riding for more than twenty-four hours."

"And you, High King?" Ivor asked. "Have you rested?"

Aileron shrugged. "There may be time after this meeting," he said, almost indifferently. "It doesn't matter." Dave, looking at him, thought otherwise, but he was impressed all the same.

"Whom did you ride behind?" Ra-Tenniel asked suddenly, an unexpected slyness in his voice.

"Do you think," Galen answered, before Aileron could speak, "that I would let a man so beautiful ride with anyone else?" She smiled.

Aileron flushed red beneath his beard as the Dalrei burst into sudden, tension-breaking laughter. Dave, laughing too, met Ra-Tenniel's eyes—silver now—and caught a quick wink from the lios alfar. Kevin Laine, he thought, would have appreciated what Ra-Tenniel had just done. A sorrow, there. The deepest among many, he realized, with a twist of surprise.

There was no time to even try to deal with the complexities of that sort of thought. It was probably just as well, Dave knew. Emotions on that scale, running so deep, were dangerous for him. They had been all his life, and he had no room now for the paralysis they caused, or the pain that would follow. Ivor was speaking. Dave forced his thoughts sharply outward again.

"I was about to initiate a Council of War, High King. Will it please you to take charge now?"

"Not in Celidon," Aileron said, with unexpected courtesy. He had recovered from his momentary embarrassment and was once again controlled and direct. Not entirely without tact, however.

Dave, out of the corner of his eye, saw Mabon of Rhoden nod quiet approval, and a look of gratitude suffused the features of old Dhira, sitting beside the Duke. Dhira, Dave decided, was all right after all. He wondered if he'd have a chance to apologize later, and if he'd be able to handle it.

"I have my own thoughts," the High King said, "but I would hear the counsel of the Dalrei and of Daniloth before I speak."

"Very well," said Ivor, with a crispness that matched Aileron's. "My counsel is this. The army of Brennin and Cathal is on the Plain. We have Daniloth here with us, and every fit Dalrei of fighting age. . . ."

Except for one, Dave thought involuntarily, but kept silence.

"We are missing the Warrior and Silvercloak and have no word from Eridu," Ivor continued. "We know that there will be no aid for us from the Dwarves. We do not know what has happened or will happen at sea. I do not think we can wait to find out. My counsel is to linger here only so long as it takes Niavin and Teyrnon to arrive, and then to ride north through Gwynir into Andarien and force Maugrim into battle there again."

There was a little silence. Then, "Ruined Andarien," murmured Lydan, Galen's brother. "Always and ever the battleground." There was a bittersweet sadness in his voice. Echoes of music. Memories.

Aileron said nothing, waiting. It was Mabon of Rhoden who spoke up, raising himself on his one good arm. "There is good sense in what you say, Aven. As much good sense as we are likely to find in any plan today, though I would dearly love to have Loren's counsel here, or Gereint's, or our own Seer's—"

"Where are they, Gereint and the Seer? Can we not bring them here now—with the raithen, perhaps?" It was Tulger of the eighth tribe.

Ivor looked at his old friend, worry deep in his eyes. "Gereint has left his body. He is soul-traveling. He did not say why. The Seer went into the mountains from Gwen Ystrat. Again, I know not why." He looked at Aileron.

The High King hesitated. "If I tell you, it must not leave this chamber. We have fear enough without summoning more." And into the stillness, he said, "She went to free the Paraiko in Khath Meigol."

There was a babble of sound. One man made the sign against evil, but only one. These were Chieftains and their hunt leaders, and this was a time of war.

"They live?" Ra-Tenniel whispered softly.

"She tells me so," Aileron replied.

"Weaver at the Loom!" Dhira murmured, from the heart. This time it didn't sound inappropriate. Dave, comprehending little, felt tension in the room like an enveloping presence.

"So we have no access to the Seer either," Mabon continued grimly. "And we must accept, given what you have said, that we may never have her or Gereint or Loren again. We will have to decide this using what wisdom we have among ourselves, and so I have one question for you, Aven." He paused. "What assurance do we have that Maugrim will fight us in Andarien when we get there? Could his army not sweep around us among the evergreens of Gwynir and so run south to destroy what we have left behind: the mid-Plain here? The Dalrei women and children? Gwen Ystrat? All of Brennin and Cathal, open to him with our army so far away? Could he not do that?"

There was total silence in the room. After a moment, Mabon went on, almost whispering.

"Maugrim is outside of time, not spun on the Loom. He cannot be killed. And he has shown, with the long winter, that he is in no hurry this time to bring us to battle. Would he not glory and his lieutenants exult to watch our army waiting uselessly before impregnable Starkadh while the svarts and urgach and Galadan's wolves were ravaging all we loved?"

He stopped. Dave felt a weight like an anvil hanging from his heart. It was painful to draw breath. He looked at Torc for reassurance and saw anguish in his face, saw it mirrored deeply in Ivor's and, somehow most frighteningly, in the normally unreadable features of Aileron.

"*Fear not that,*" said Ra-Tenniel.

A voice so very clear. Blurring forever, Ivor dan Banor thought, the borders between sound and light, between music and spoken word. The Aven turned to the Lord of the lios alfar as might one desperate for water in a rainless land.

"Fear Maugrim," said Ra-Tenniel, "as must any who name themselves wise. Fear defeat and the dominion of the Dark. Fear, also, the annihilation that Galadan purposes and strives for, ever."

Water, Ivor was thinking, as the measured words flowed over him. Water, with sorrow like a stone at the bottom of the cup.

"Fear any and all of these things," Ra-Tenniel said. "The tearing of our threads from the Loom, the unsaying of our histories, the unraveling of the Weaver's design."

He paused. Water in time of drought. Music and light.

"But do not fear," said the Lord of the lios alfar, "that he will avoid a battle with us, should we march to Andarien. I am your surety for that. I and my people. The lios alfar are out from Daniloth for the first time in a thousand years. He can see us. He can reach us. We are no longer hidden in the Shadowland. *He will not pass us by.* It lies not in his nature to pass us by. Rakoth Maugrim will meet this army if the lios alfar go into Andarien."

It was true. Ivor knew that as soon as he heard the words, and he knew it as deeply as he had known any single thing in all his life. It reinforced his own counsel and offered complete answer to Mabon's terrifying question, an answer wrought from the very essence of the lios alfar, the Weaver's chosen ones, the Children of Light. What they were and had always been; and the terrible, bitter price they paid. The other side of the image. The stone in the cup.

Most hated by the Dark, for their name was Light.

Ivor wanted to bow, to kneel, to offer grief, pity, love, heart's gratitude. Somehow none of them, nor all of them together, seemed adequate in the face of what Ra-Tenniel had just said. Ivor felt heavy, clodlike. Looking at the three lios alfar he felt like a lump of earth.

And *yes*, he thought. Yes, he was exactly that. He was prosaic, unglamorous, he *was* of the earth, the grass. He was of the Plain, which endured, which would endure this too if they proved equal to the days ahead, but not otherwise.

Reaching back into his own history, as Ra-Tenniel had just

done, the Aven cast aside all thoughts, all emotions save those that spoke of strength, of resistance. "A thousand years ago the first Aven of the Plain led every Dalrei hunter who could ride into the woven mists and the skewed time of Daniloth, and the Weaver laid a straight track for them. They came out onto a battlefield by Linden Bay that would otherwise have been lost. Revor rode from there beside Ra-Termaine across the River Celyn into Andarien. And so, Brightest Lord, will I ride beside you, should that be our decision when we leave this place."

He paused and turned to the other King in the room. "When Revor rode, and Ra-Termaine, it was in the army and at the command of Conary of Brennin, and then of Colan, his son. It was so then, and rightly so—for the High Kings of Brennin are the Children of Mörnir—and it will be so again, and as rightly, should you accept this counsel, High King."

He was utterly unaware of the ringing cadences, the up-welling power of his own voice. He said, "You are heir to what Conary was, as we are the heirs of Revor and Ra-Termaine. Do you accede to this counsel? Yours is governance here, Aileron dan Ailell. Will you have us to ride with you?"

Bearded and dark, devoid of ornament, a soldier's sword in a plain sheath at his side, Aileron looked the very image of a war king. Not bright and glittering as Conary had been, or Colan, or even as his own brother was. He was stern and expressionless and grim, and one of the youngest men in the room.

"I accede," he said. "I would have you ride with me. When the army comes tomorrow, we set out for Andarien."

In that moment, halfway and a little more to Gwynir, a lean and scarred figure, incongruously aristocratic atop one of the hideous slaug, slowed and then dragged his mount to a complete stop. Motionless on the wide Plain, he watched the dust of Rakoth's retreating army settle in front of him.

For most of the night he had run in his wolf form. In

careful silence he had observed as Uathach, the giant urgach in white, had enforced an orderly withdrawal out of what had begun as blind flight. There had been a question of precedence there, to be resolved eventually, but not now. Galadan had other things to think about.

And he thought more clearly in his human shape. So a little before dawn he had taken his own form again and commandeered one of the slaug, even though he hated them. Gradually through the greyness of dawn he had let the army pass him by, making sure that Uathach did not notice.

He was far from afraid of the white-clad urgach, but he knew too little about him, and knowledge, for the Wolflord, had always been the key to power. It mattered almost not at all that he was reasonably certain he could kill Uathach; what was important was that he *understand* what had made him what he was. Six months ago Uathach had been summoned to Starkadh, an oversized urgach, as stupid as any of the others, a little more dangerous because of quickness and size.

He had come out again four nights ago, augmented, enhanced in some unsettling way. He was clever now, vicious and articulate, and clad by Rakoth in white—a touch that Galadan appreciated, remembering Lauriel, the swan the lios had loved. Uathach had been given command of the army that issued over the Valgrind Bridge. That, in the inception, Galadan had no quarrel with.

The Wolflord himself had been away, engaged in tasks of his own devising. It had been he, with the knowledge that came with being one of the andain, son of a god, and with the subtlety that was his own, who had conceived and led the attack on the Paraiko in Khath Meigol.

If attack it could be called. The Giants by their very nature had no access to anger or violence. No response to war, save the single inviolate fact that shedding their blood brought down any curse the injured Giant chose to invoke. *That* was the true, the literal concept of the bloodcurse; it had nothing to do with the superstitions about roaming, fanged ghosts haunting Khath Meigol.

Or so the Wolflord had continually reminded himself in the days he spent there while the Paraiko were penned like helpless sheep in their caves by the svarts and urgach, breathing the clever, killing smoke of the fires he'd ordered to be made.

He had only lasted a few days, but the true reason was his own secret. He had tried to convince himself of what he had told those he left behind—that his departure was dictated by the demands of war—but he had lived too long and too searchingly to really deceive himself.

The truth was that the Paraiko unsettled him deeply in some subconscious way his mind could not grasp. In some fashion they lay in his path, huge obstacles to his one unending desire—which was for annihilation, utter and absolute. How they could oppose him he knew not, for pacifism was woven into their very nature, but nonetheless they disturbed him and rendered him uneasy as did no one else in Fionavar or any other world, with the single exception of his father.

So, since he could not kill Cernan of the Beasts, he set about destroying the Paraiko in their mountain caves. When the fires were burning properly and the svarts and urgach made relentlessly aware of the need not to shed blood—as if they had to be reminded, for even the stupid svarts lived in abject terror of the bloodcurse—Galadan had withdrawn from the bitter cold of the mountains and the incessant chanting that came from the caves.

He had been in east Gwynir when the snow had, shockingly, melted. Immediately he had begun massing his wolves among the evergreens, waiting for the word of attack. He had just garnered tidings of his contingent slaughtered in Leinanwood by the High King when Avaia herself had swooped, glorious and malevolent, to hiss that an army had issued forth across the Valgrind Bridge, heading for Celidon.

At speed he had taken his wolves down the eastern edge of the Plain. He had crossed Adein near the Edryn Gap, unseen, unanticipated, and then, timing it flawlessly, had arrived at the battlefield to fall on the exposed right flank of the Dalrei. He hadn't expected the lios to be there, but that was only a source of joy, a deepening of delight: they were going to slaughter them all.

They would have, had the Wild Hunt not suddenly flashed in the heavens above. Alone among the army of the

Dark he knew who Owein was. Alone, he grasped a hint of what had happened. And alone, he comprehended something of what lay beneath the cry that stopped the killing. Alone in that army he knew whose voice it was.

He was, after all, her brother's son.

There had been a great deal to assimilate, and a very immediate danger as well. And through all the pandemonium a thought, inchoate, little more than a straining toward a possibility, was striving to take shape in his mind. Then, above and beyond all this, as if it had not been enough and more than enough, there came an intuition he had learned to trust, a vibration within the part of him that was a god, Cernan's son.

As the cold rage of battle passed, and then the chaos of flight, Galadan became increasingly aware that something was happening in the forest realm.

There was suddenly a very great deal to consider. He needed solitude. He always needed that—as being nearest to his long desire—but now his mind craved it as much as his soul. So he had detached himself from the army, unseen in the dawn shadows, and he was riding alone when the morning sunlight found him.

Shortly after sunrise he stopped, surveying the Plain. He found it deeply pleasing to his heart. Except for the cloud of dust, settling now, far to the north, there was no sign of life beyond the insentient grass he did not care about. It was almost as if the goal for which he had striven for past a thousand years had come.

Almost. He smiled thinly. Irony was nearly at the center of his soul and would not let him dream for very long. The striving had been too lengthy, too deeply ingrained, for dreams to ever be remotely adequate.

He could remember the very instant his designs had taken shape, when he had first aligned himself with the Unraveller—the moment when Lisen of the Wood had sent word running through Pendaran that she had merged her fate and given her love to Amairgen Whitebranch, the mortal.

He had been in the Great Wood that morning, ready to celebrate with all the other powers of Pendaran her slaying of the man for his presumption in the sacred grove.

It had turned out otherwise. Everything had.

He had gone into Starkadh, once and once only, for in that place he, who was mightiest by far of the andain and arrogant with that strength, had been forced to humble himself before an obliterating magnitude of power. He had not even been able to mask his own mind from Maugrim, who had laughed.

He was made to realize that he was entirely understood and, notwithstanding that, had been accepted, with amusement, as lieutenant by the Dark. Even though Rakoth knew precisely what his own purposes were and how they differed from Maugrim's own, it hadn't seemed to matter.

Their designs marched together a very long way, Galadan had told himself, and though he was not—no one was—remotely an equal to the Unraveller, he might yet, ere the very end, find a way to obliterate the world Maugrim would rule.

He had served Rakoth well. Had commanded the army that cut Conary off by Sennett Strand so long ago. He had killed Conary himself, in his wolf shape, and he would have won that battle, and so the war, had Revor of the Plain not come, somehow, impossibly soon, through the mists of Daniloth to turn the tide of battle north to Starkadh itself, where it ended. He himself, badly wounded, had hardly escaped with his life from Colan's avenging sword.

They had thought he'd died, he knew. He almost had. In an icy cave north of the Ungarch River he had lain, bitterly cold, nursed only by his wolves. For a very long time he'd huddled there, damping his power, his aura, as low as he could, while the armies of the Light held parley before the Mountain and Ginserat made the wardstones and then shaped, with aid of the Dwarves, the chain that bound Rakoth beneath Rangat.

Through all the long waiting years he had continued to serve, having made his choice and set his own course. He it was who had found Avaia, half dead herself. The swan had been hiding in the frigid realm of Fordaetha, Queen of Rük, whose icy touch was instant death to a spirit less strong than one of the andain. With his own hands he had nursed the swan back to health in the court of that cold Queen. Fordaetha had wanted to couple with him. It had pleased him to refuse her.

His, too, had been the stratagem, subtle and infinitely slow, whereby the water spirit of Llewenmere, innocent and fair, had been lured into surrendering her most handsome swans. He had given her a reason that sufficed: his earnest desire, in the identity he had dissembled with, to bring swans north to Celyn Lake, on the borders of devastated Andarien. And she had released her guardianship and had, all unsuspecting, let him take them away.

He had only needed some of them: the males. North, indeed, they had been carried, but far past Celyn into the glacier-riven mountains beyond Ungarch, where they had been bred to Avaia. Then, when they had died, she, who could not die unless slain, had coupled with her children, and had continued doing so, year after year, to bring forth the brood that had stained the skies on the evening just past.

The spirit of Llewenmere never knew for certain what she had done or who, indeed, he really was. She may have guessed, though, for in after years, the lake, once benign and inviting, had turned dark and weedy, and even in Pendaran, which knew a darkness of its own, it was said to be haunted.

It brought him no joy. Nothing had, since Lisen. A long, long life, and a slow, single purpose guiding it.

He it was who had freed Rakoth. Orchestrating, with infinite patience, the singling out and then the corruption of the Dwarf brothers, Kaen and Blöd; bringing into play the festering hatred of Metran of the Garantae, First Mage of Brennin; and, finally, cutting off, with his own sword, the hand of Maugrim when Ginserat's chain could not be made to break.

He had run then with Rakoth—a wolf beside a cloud of malice that dripped, and would forever drip, black blood—to the rubble of Starkadh. There he had watched as, inexorably, Rakoth Maugrim had showed forth his might—greater here than anywhere in any of the worlds, for here had he first set down his foot—and raised anew the ziggurat that was the first and the last seat of his power.

When it reared upward again, complete, even to the green flickering of its lights, an obliterating presence among the ice, Galadan had stopped before the mighty doors, though they stood open for him. Once had been enough. Everywhere else his mind was his own. In one way, he knew, this resistance was meaningless, for Maugrim, in that one instant a thousand years ago, had learned everything of Galadan he would ever need to know. But in another way, the sanctity of his thoughts was the only thing that had any meaning left for the Wolflord.

So he had halted before the doors, and there had he received his reward, the offered image, never before seen, never known, of Maugrim's revenge against the lios alfar for being what they were: the Soulmonger at sea. Waiting for the lios as they sailed west in search of a promised world and destroying them, singly and in pairs, to claim their voices and their songs as a lure for those who followed. *All* of those who followed.

It was perfect. It was beyond perfection. A malevolence that used the very essence of the Children of Light to shape their doom. He could never have bound to his service a creature so awesome, Galadan knew. He could never even, for all his own guile, have thought of something so encompassing. The image was, among other things, a reminder to him of what Rakoth, now free again, was and could do.

But it was also a reward, and one that had nothing at all to do with the lios alfar.

The vision had been clear in his mind. Rakoth had made it clear. He had seen the Soulmonger vividly: its size and color, the flat, ugly head. He could hear the singing. See the lidless eyes. And the staff, the white staff, embedded uselessly between those eyes.

The staff of Amairgen Whitebranch.

And so, for the very first time, he learned how that one had died. There was no joy. There could never again be joy, he had no access to such a thing. But that day, before the open doors of Starkadh, there had come an easing within him for a moment, a certain quiet, which was as much as he could ever have.

Alone now on the Plain he tried to summon up the image again, but he found it blurred and unsatisfying. He shook his head. There was too much happening. The implications of Owein's return with the Wild Hunt were enormous. He had to find a way to deal with them. First, though, he knew he would have to address the other thing, the intuition from the Wood that went deeper than anything else.

This was why he had stopped. To seek out the quiet that would allow the thing, whatever it was, to move from the edge of his awareness to the center, to be seen.

For a while he thought it was his father, which would make a great deal of sense. He never ventured near Cernan, and his father had never, since a certain night not long before the Bael Rangat, tried to contact him. But this morning's sensation was intense enough, so laden with overtones and shadings of long-forgotten emotions, that he thought it had to be Cernan calling him. The forest was, somehow, part of this. It had—

And in that instant he knew what it was.

Not, after all, his father. But the intensity was suddenly explained, and more. With an expression on his face no one living had ever been allowed to see, Galadan leaped from the back of the slaug. He put his hand to his chest and made a gesture. Then, a moment later, in his wolf shape, covering ground faster than even the slaug might, he set out west, running as swiftly as he could, the battle forgotten, the war, almost.

West, to where lights were burning and someone stood in the Anor, in the room that had been Lisen's.

Chapter 3

They had been climbing all morning, and the rough going was not made easier by the pain in Kim's side where Ceriog had kicked her. She was silent, though, and kept going, head down, watching the path and the long legs of Faebur climbing in front of her. Dalreidan was leading them; Brock, who had to be hurting far more than she was, brought up the rear. No one spoke. The trail was difficult enough without wasting breath on words, and there was, really, not a great deal to say.

She had dreamt again the night before, in the outlaw camp not far from the plateau where they had been captured. Ruana's deep chanting ran through her sleep. It was beautiful, but she found no comfort in that beauty—the pain was too great. It twisted through her and, what was worse, a part of it came from her. There was smoke in the dream again, and the caves. She saw herself with lacerations on her arms but, again, no blood was flowing. No blood in Khath Meigol. The smoke drifted in the starlit, firelit night. Then there was another light, as the Baelrath blazed into life. She felt it as a burning, as guilt and pain, and in the midst of that flaming she watched herself looking up into the sky above the mountains and she saw the red moon ride again and she heard a name.

In the morning, heavily wrapped in her thoughts, she had let Brock and Dalreidan make arrangements for their departure, and in silence all morning and into the afternoon she had climbed upward and east toward the sun.

Toward the sun.

She stopped abruptly. Brock almost ran into her from behind. Shielding her eyes, Kim gazed beyond the mountains as far as she could, and then a cry of joy escaped her. Dalreidan turned, and Faebur. Wordlessly, she pointed. They spun back to look.

"Oh, my King!" cried Brock of Banir Tal. "I knew you would not fail!"

Over Eridu the rain clouds were gone. Sunlight streamed from a sky laced only with the thin, benevolent cirrus clouds of a summer's day.

Far to the west, in the spinning place of Cader Sedat, the Cauldron of Khath Meigol lay shattered in a thousand pieces and Metran of the Garantae was dead.

Kim felt the shadows of her dream dissolve as hope flared within her like the brilliant sun. She thought of Kevin in that moment. There was sorrow in the memory, there always would be, but now there was joy as well, and a burgeoning pride. The summer had been his gift—the green grass, the birdsong, the mild seas that had allowed *Prydwen* to sail and the men who sailed her to do this thing.

There was a keen brightness in Dalreidan's face as he turned back to look at her. "Forgive me," he said. "I doubted."

She shook her head. "So did I. I had terrible dreams of where they had to go. There is a miracle in this. I do not know how it was done."

Brock had come up to stand beside her on the narrow trail. He said nothing, but his eyes were shining beneath the bandage Kim had wrapped about his wound. Faebur, though, had his back to them, still gazing to the east. Looking at him, Kim sobered quickly.

At length he, too, turned to look at her, and she saw the tears in his eyes. "Tell me something, Seer," he said, sounding older, far, than his years. "If an exiled man's people are all dead, does his exile end or does it go on forever?"

She struggled to frame a reply and found none. It was Dalreidan who answered. "We cannot unsay the falling of that rain, or lengthen the cut threads of those who have died," he said gently. "It is in my heart, though, that in the face of what Maugrim has done no man is an exile any more. Every living creature on this side of the mountains has received a gift of life this morning. We must use that gift, until the hour comes that knows our name, to deal such blows as we can against the Dark. There are arrows in your quiver, Faebur. Let them sing with the names of your loved ones as they fly. It may not seem like a true recompense, but it is all we can do."

"It is what we must do," said Brock softly.

"Easy for a Dwarf to say!" snarled Faebur, rounding on him.

Brock shook his head. "Harder by far than you could know. Every breath I draw is laden with the knowledge of what my people have done. The rain will not have fallen under the twin mountains, but it fell in my heart and it is raining there still. Faebur, will you let my axe sing with your arrows in mourning for the people of the Lion in Eridu?"

The tears had dried on Faebur's face. His chin was set in a hard, straight line. He had aged, Kim thought. In a day, in less than a day he seemed to have aged so much. For what seemed to her a very long time he stood motionless, and then slowly and deliberately he extended a hand to the Dwarf. Brock reached up and clasped it between both of his own.

She became aware that Dalreidan was looking at her.

"We go on?" he asked gravely.

"We go on," she said, and even as she spoke the dream came back, with the chanting and the smoke, and the name written in Dana's moon.

To the south and far below, the Kharn River flashed through its gorge in the evening light. They were so high that an eagle hovering over the river was below them, its wings shining in the sunlight that slanted down the gorge from the west. All around them lay the mountains of the Carnevon Range, the peaks white with snow even in midsummer. It was cold, this high up and with the day waning; Kim was grateful for the sweater they had given her in Gwen Ystrat. Lightweight and wonderfully warm, it was a testimonial to the value accorded all the cloth arts in this, the first of all the Weaver's worlds.

Even so, she shivered.

"Now?" Dalreidan asked, his voice carefully neutral. "Or would you like to camp here until morning?"

The three of them looked at her, waiting. It was her

decision to make. They had guided her to this place, had helped her through the hardest parts of the climb, had rested when she had needed to rest, but now they had arrived, and all the decisions were hers.

She looked past her companions to the east. Fifty paces away the rocks looked exactly as they did where she was standing now. The light fell upon them the same way, with the same softening as evening came to the mountains. She had expected something different, some sort of change: a shimmering, shadows, a sharpening of intensity. She saw none of these, yet she knew, and the three men with her knew, that the rocks fifty paces to the east lay within Khath Meigol.

Now that she was here she longed with all her heart to be anywhere else. To be graced with the wings of the eagle below, that she might sweep away on the evening breeze. Not from Fionavar, not from the war, but far from the loneliness of this place and the dream that had led her here. Within herself she reached for, and found, the tacit presence that was Ysanne. She took comfort in that. She was never truly alone; there were two souls within her, now and always. Her companions had no such solace, though, had no dreams or visions to guide them. They were here because of her, and only because of her, and they were looking now for her to lead them. Even as she stood, hesitating, the shadows were slowly climbing the slopes of the ravine.

She drew a breath and slowly let it out. She was here to repay a debt, and one that was not hers alone. She was also here because she bore the Baelrath in a time of war, and there was no one else in any world who could make manifest the Seer's dream she'd had, however dark it was.

However dark. It had been night in the dream, with fires in front of the caves. She looked down and saw the stone flickering like a tongue of flame on her hand.

"Now," she said to the others. "It will be bad in the dark, I know, but it won't be that much better in the morning, and I don't think we should wait."

They were very brave, all three of them. Without a word spoken they made room for her to fall into line after Faebur, with Brock behind; and Dalreidan led them into Khath Meigol.

Even with the vellin shielding her she felt the impact of magic as they passed into the country of the Giants, and the form the magic took was fear. They are not ghosts, she told herself, over and over. They are alive. They saved my life. Even so, even with the vellin, she felt terror brushing her mind with the quick wings of night moths. The two men and the Dwarf with her had no green vellin bracelets to guard them, no inner voices to reassure, yet none of them made a sound and none broke stride. Humbled by their courage, she felt her own heart flame with resolution, and as it did the Baelrath burned brighter on her hand.

She quickened her pace and moved past Dalreidan. She had brought them to this place, a place where no man should ever have had to come. It was her turn to lead them now, for the Warstone knew where to go.

For almost two hours they walked in the gathering darkness. It was full night under the summer stars when Kim saw smoke and the distant blaze of bonfires and heard the raucous laughter of svart alfar. And with the brutal mockery of that sound she found, suddenly, that her fears, which had walked with her until now, were gone. She had arrived, and the enemy ahead of her was known and hated, and in the caves beyond those ridges of stone the Giants were imprisoned and were dying.

She turned and saw by starlight and the glow of her ring that her companions' faces were grim now, not with strain but with anticipation. Silently Brock unslung his axe, and Faebur notched an arrow to his bow. She turned to Dalreidan. He had not yet drawn a sword or unslung his own bow. "There will be time," he whispered, answering her unspoken question, scarcely a breath in the night air. "Shall I find us a place where we can look?"

She nodded. Calmly, silently, he moved past her again and began picking his way among the strewn boulders and loose rocks toward the fires and the laughter. Moments later the four of them lay prone above a plateau. Sheltered by upthrust teeth of rock, they looked down, sickened, on what the glow of the bonfires revealed.

There were two caves set into the mountainside, with high vaulted entrances and runic lettering carved over the arches. It was dark in the caves and they could not see within. From one of them, though, if they strained to hear past the laughter of the svart alfar, they could make out the sound of a single deep voice chanting slowly.

The light came from two huge fires on the plateau, set directly before each of the caves in such a fashion that the smoke of their burning was drawn inward. There was another fire just over the ridge east of them, and Kim could make out the glow and the rising smoke of a fourth about a quarter of a mile away, to the northeast. There were no others to be seen. Four caves then, four sets of prisoners dying of starvation and smoke.

And four bands of svart alfar. Around each of the bonfires below them, about thirty of the svarts were gathered, and there were a handful of the nightmare urgach as well. About a hundred and fifty of them, then, if the same numbers held true beyond the ridges. Not a very great force, in truth, but more than enough, she knew, to subdue and hold the Paraiko, whose pacifism was the very essence of their being. All that the svarts had to do, under the guidance of the urgach, was keep the fires burning and refrain from shedding blood. Then they could claim their reward.

Which they were doing now, even as she watched. On each of the pyres below lay the huge body, charred and blackened, of a Paraiko. Every few moments one of the svart alfar would dart close enough to the roaring flames to thrust in a sword and cut for himself a piece of roasted flesh.

Their reward. Kim's stomach heaved in revulsion and she had to close her eyes. It was an unholy scene, a desecration in the worst, the deepest sense. Beside her she could hear Brock cursing under his breath in a steady invocation, bitter and heartfelt.

Meaningless words, whatever scant easing they might afford. And the curses of the Paraiko themselves, which might have been unleashed had any one of them been killed directly, had been forestalled. Rakoth was too clever, too steeped in the shaping of evil, his servants too well trained, for the bloodcurse to have been set free.

Which meant that another sort of power would have to be invoked. And so here she was, drawn by a savesong chanted and the burden of a Seer's dream, and what, in the Weaver's name, was she to do? She had three men beside her, three men alone, however brave they might be. From the moment she and Brock had left Morvran, everything in her had been focused on getting to this plateau, knowing that she had to do so, with never a thought until now about what she could do when she arrived.

Dalreidan touched her elbow. "Look," he whispered.

She opened her eyes. He wasn't looking at the caves or the fires or the ridges beyond with their own smoke. Reluctantly, as always, she followed his gaze to the ring on her own hand and saw the Baelrath vividly aflame. With a real grief she saw that the fire at the heart of the Warstone was somehow twinned to the hue and shape of the hideous fires below.

It was deeply unsettling, but when had there been anything reassuring or easy about the ring she bore? In every single thing she had ever done with the Baelrath there was pain. In its depths she had seen Jennifer in Starkadh and carried her, screaming, into the crossing. She had awakened a dead King at Stonehenge against his will. She had summoned Arthur on the summit of Glastonbury Tor to war and bitterest grief again. She had released the Sleepers by Pendaran on the night Finn took the Longest Road. She was an invoker, a war cry in darkness, a storm crow, truly that, on the wings of a gathering storm. She was a gatherer indeed, a summoner. She was—

She was a summoner.

There was a scream, and then a raucous burst of laughter down below. An urgach, for sport, had hurled a svart alfar, one of the smaller green ones, onto the blazing fire. She saw, but hardly registered it. Her eyes went back to the stone, to the flame coiled in the depths of it, and there she read a name, the same name she had seen written across the face of the moon in her dream. Reading it, she remembered something: how the Baelrath had blazed in answering light on the night that Dana's red full moon had ridden through the sky over Paras Derval.

She was a summoner, and now she knew what she had to do. For with the name written in the ring had come knowledge that had not lain in the dream. She knew who this was and knew, also, what the price of her calling would be. But this was Khath Meigol in a time of war, and the Paraiko were dying in the caves. She could not harden her heart, there was too much pity there, but she could steel her will to do what had to be done and shoulder the grief as one more among many.

She closed her eyes again. It was easier in darkness, a way of hiding, almost. Almost, but not truly. She drew a breath and then within her mind, not aloud, she said, *Imraith-Nimphais.*

Then she led her companions back down and away from the fires to wait, knowing it would not be long.

Tabor's watch was not until the end of the night, and so he had been asleep. Not any more. She was in the sky over the camp, and she had called his name, and for the first time ever he heard fear in the creature of his fast.

He was wide awake, instantly, and dressing as quickly as he could.

Wait, he sent. *I do not want to frighten them. I will meet you on the Plain.*

No, he heard. She was truly afraid. *Come now. There is no time!*

She was descending, even as he went outside. He was confused, and a little afraid himself, for he had not summoned her, but even with that, his heart lifted to see the beauty of her as she came down, her horn shining like a star, her wings folding gracefully as she landed.

She was trembling. He stepped forward and put his arms about her, laying his head against hers. *Easy, my love,* he sent, projecting all the reassurance he could. *I am here. What has happened?*

I was called by name, she sent, still trembling.

A shocked surge of anger ran through him, and a deeper fear of his own that he fought to master and conceal. He could conceal nothing from her, though, they were bonded too deeply. He drew a ragged breath. *Who?*

I do not know her. A woman with white hair, but not old. A red ring on her hand. How does she know my name?

His own hands moved ceaselessly, gentling her. Anger was still there, but he was Ivor's son and Levon's brother, both of whom had seen her, and so he knew who this was. *She is a friend,* he sent. *We must go to her. Where?*

The wrong question, though it had to be asked. She told him, and with the naming of that place fear was in both of them again. He fought it and helped her do the same. Then he mounted her, feeling the joy of doing so in the midst of everything else. She spread her wings, and he prepared to fly—

"Tabor!"

He turned. Liane was there, in a white shift brought back from Gwen Ystrat. She seemed eerily far away. Already. And he had not even taken flight. "I must go," he said, forming the words carefully. "The Seer has called us."

"Where is she?"

He hesitated. "In the mountains." His sister's hair, snarled in tangles of sleep, lay loose on her back. Her feet were bare on the grass; her eyes, wide with apprehension, never left his own.

"Be careful," she said. "Please." He nodded, jerkily. Beneath him, Imraith-Nimphais, restless to be gone, flexed her wings. "Oh, Tabor," whispered Liane, who was older than he but didn't sound it, "please come back."

He tried to answer that. It was important that he try; she was crying. But words would not come. He raised one hand, in a gesture that had to encompass far too much, and then they were in the sky and the stars blurred before their speed.

Kim saw a streak of light in the west. She raised her hand, with the ring glowing on her finger, and a moment later the power she had summoned descended. It was dark, and the clearing where they waited was rough and narrow, but nothing could mar the grace of the creature that landed beside her. She listened for alarms raised east of them but heard nothing: why should a falling star in the mountains be cause for concern?

But this was not a falling star.

It was a deep red through the body, the color of Dana's moon, the color of the ring she carried. The great wings folded now, it stood restlessly on the stones, seeming almost to dance above them. Kim looked at the single horn. It was shining and silver, and the Seer in her knew how deadly it was, how far beyond mere grace this gift of the Goddess was.

This double-edged gift. She turned her gaze to the rider. He looked very much like his father, only a little like Levon. She had known he was only fifteen, but seeing it came as a shock. He reminded her, she realized abruptly, of Finn.

Very little time had passed since the summoning. The waning moon had barely risen above the eastern reaches of the range. Its silver touched the silver of the horn. Beside Kim, Brock stood watchfully, and Faebur, his tattoos glowing faintly, was on her other side. Dalreidan had withdrawn a little way, though, back into the shadows. She was not surprised, though she sorrowed for that, too. This meeting would have to be a hard thing for the exiled Rider. She'd had no choice though. Just as she had none now, and there was deeper cause for sorrow written in the eyes of the boy.

He sat quietly, waiting for her to speak.

"I'm sorry," she said, and meant it with all her heart. "I have some idea of what this does to you."

He tossed his head impatiently, in a gesture like his brother's. "How did you know her name?" he asked, low, because of the laughter nearby, but challenging. She heard both the anger and the anxiety.

She shouldered her own power. "You ride a child of Pendaran's grove and the wandering moon," she said. "I am a Seer and I carry the Wandering Fire. I read her name in the Baelrath, Tabor." She had dreamt it too, but she didn't tell him that.

"No one else is to know her name," he said. "No one at all."

"Not so," she replied. "Gereint does. The shamans always know the totem names."

"He's different," Tabor said, a little uncertainly.

"So am I," said Kim, as gently as she could. He was very young, and the creature was afraid. She understood how they felt. She had come crashing, she and her wild ring, into the midst of an utterly private communion the two of them shared. She understood, but the night of which she had dreamt was passing, and she didn't know if she had time to assuage them properly, or even what to say.

Tabor surprised her. He might be young, but he was the Aven's son, and he rode a gift of Dana. With calm simplicity he said, "Very well. What are we to do in Khath Meigol?"

Slay, of course. And take the consequences upon themselves. Was there an easy way to say it? She knew of none. She told them who was here, and what was taking place, and even as she spoke she saw the head of the winged creature lift and her horn begin to shine more brightly yet.

Then she was done. There was nothing more to tell. Tabor nodded to her, once; then he and the creature he rode seemed to change, to coalesce. She was near to them, and a Seer. She caught a fragment of their inner speech. Only a fragment, then she took her mind away. *Bright one,* she heard and, *We must kill,* and, just before she pulled away, . . . *only each other at the last.*

Then they were in the air again and Dana's creature's wings were spread and she turned, killingly bright, to flash down on the plateau and suddenly the servants of the Dark were not laughing any more. Kim's three companions were already running for their vantage point again and she followed them as quickly as she could, stumbling over the rocks and loose stones.

Then she was there and watching how stunningly graceful death could be. Again and again Imraith-Nimphais descended and rose, the horn—with a cutting edge now—stabbing and slashing until the silver was so coated with blood it looked like the rest of her. One of the urgach rose before her, enormous, a two-handed sword upraised. With the preternatural skill of the Dalrei, Tabor veered his mount at full speed, up and to one side in the air, and the sharp edge of the horn sliced through the top of the urgach's head. It was all like that. They were elegant, blindingly swift, utterly lethal.

And it was destroying them both, Kim knew.

A myriad of griefs, and no time to deal with them: even as she watched, Imraith-Nimphais was soaring again, east to the next bonfire.

One of the svart alfar had been shamming death. Quickly it rose and began running west across the plateau.

"Mine," said Faebur quietly. Kim turned. She saw him draw an arrow and whisper something over its long shaft.

She saw him notch it to his bow and draw, and she saw the moonlit arrow, loosed, flash into the throat of the running svart and drop it in its tracks.

"For Eridu," said Brock of Banir Tal. "For the people of the Lion. A beginning, Faebur."

"A beginning," Faebur echoed softly.

Nothing else moved on the plateau. The fires still roared; their crackling was the only sound. Over the ridge a distant screaming could be heard, but even as she picked her way down the loose slope toward the caves those sounds, too, abruptly ceased. Kim glanced over, instinctively, in time to see Imraith-Nimphais rise and flash north toward the last of the bonfires.

Making her way carefully amid the carnage and around the searing heat of the two fires she stopped before the larger of the caves.

She was here, and had done what she'd come to do, but she was weary and hurting, and it was not a time for joy. Not in the face of what had happened, in the presence of those two blackened bodies on the pyres. She looked down at the ring finger of her right hand: the Baelrath lay quiescent, mute. It was not finished, though. In her dream she had seen it burning on this plateau. There was more to come in the weaving of this night. What, she knew not, but the workings of power were not yet ended.

"Ruana," she cried, "this is the Seer of Brennin. I have come to the savesong chanted and you are free."

She waited, and the three men with her. The fires were the only sound. A flaw of wind blew a strand of hair into her eyes; she pushed it back. Then she realized that the wind was Imraith-Nimphais descending, as Tabor brought her down to stand behind the four of them. Kim glanced over and saw the dark blood on the horn. Then there was a sound from the cave and she turned back.

Out of the blackness of the archway and through the rising smoke the Paraiko came. Only two of them at first, one carrying the body of the other in his arms. The figure that moved out from the smoke to stand before them was twice the height of long-legged Faebur of Eridu. His hair was as white as Kimberly's, and so was his long beard. His robe, too, had been white once, but it was begrimed now with smoke and dust and the stains of illness. Even so, there was a gravity and a majesty to him that surmounted time and the unholy scene amid which they stood. In his eyes as he surveyed the plateau Kim read an ancient, ineffable pain. It made her own griefs seem shallow, transitory.

He turned to her. "We give thanks," he said. The voice was soft, incongruously so for one so enormous. "I am Ruana. When those of us who yet live are gathered we must do kanior for the dead. If you wish you may name one of your number to join us and seek absolution for all of you for this night's deeds of blood."

"Absolution?" growled Brock of Banir Tal. "We saved your lives."

"Even so," said Ruana. He stumbled a little as he spoke. Dalreidan and Faebur sprang forward to help him with his burden. "Hold!" Ruana cried. "Drop your weapons, you are in peril."

Nodding his understanding, Dalreidan let fall his arrows and his sword, and Faebur did the same. Then they went forward again and, straining with the effort, helped Ruana lower the other Giant gently to the ground.

There were more coming now. From Ruana's cave two women emerged supporting a man between them. Six, in all, came out from the other cave, sinking to the earth as soon as they were clear of the smoke. Looking east, Kim saw the first of the contingent from over the ridge coming to join them on the plateau. They moved very slowly, and many were supported and some were carried by others. None of them spoke.

"You need food," she said to Ruana. "How can we aid you?"

He shook his head. "After. The kanior must be first, it has been so long delayed. We will do the rites as soon as we are gathered." Others appeared now, from the northeast, from the fourth fire, moving with the same slow, strength-conserving care and in absolute silence. They were all clad in white, as Ruana was. He was neither the oldest nor the largest of them, but he was the only one who had spoken, and the others were gathering around the place where he stood.

"I am not leader," he said, as if reading Kim's thoughts. "There has been no leader among us since Connla transgressed in the making of the Cauldron. I will chant the kanior, though, and do the bloodless rites." His voice was infinitely mild. But this, Kim knew, was someone who had been strong enough to find her in the very heart of Rakoth's designs, and strong enough to shield her there.

He scanned the ranks of those who had come. "This is full numbering?" he asked. Kim looked around. It was hard to see amid the shadows and the smoke, but there were perhaps twenty-five of the Paraiko gathered on the plateau. No more than that.

"Full numbering," a woman said.

"Full."

"Full numbering, Ruana," a third voice echoed, plangent with sorrow. "There are no more of us. Do the kanior, too long delayed, lest our essence be altered and Khath Meigol shed its sanctity."

And it was in that moment that Kim had her first premonition, as the dark webs of her Seer's dream began to spin clear. She felt her heart clench like a fist and her mouth go dry.

"Very well," Ruana said. And then, to her again, with utmost courtesy, "Do you want to choose someone to join with us? For what you have done it will be allowed."

Kim said shakily, "If expiation is needed, it is mine to seek. I will do the bloodless rites with you."

Ruana looked down on her from his great height, then he glanced at each of the others in turn. She heard Imraith-Nimphais move nervously behind her under the weight of the Giant's gaze.

"Oh, Dana," Ruana said. Not an invocation. The words were addressed as to a coeval. Words of reproach, of sorrow. He turned back to Kimberly. "You speak truly, Seer. I think it is your place. The winged one needs no dispensation for doing what Dana created her to do, though I must grieve for her birthing."

Again, Brock challenged him, looking up a long way. "You summoned us," the Dwarf said. "You chanted your song to the Seer, and we came in answer. Rakoth is free in

Fionavar, Ruana of the Paraiko. Would you have us all lie down in caves and grant him dominion?" The passionate words rang in the mountain air.

There came a low sound from the assembled Paraiko.

"Did you summon them, Ruana?" It was the voice of the first woman who had spoken, the one from the cave over the ridge.

Still looking at Brock, Ruana said, "We cannot hate. Were Rakoth, whose voice I heard in my chanting, obliterated utterly from the tale of time, my heart would sing until I died. But we cannot make war. There is only passive resistance in us. It is part of our nature, the way killing and grace are woven into the creature that flew to save us. To change would be to end what we are and to lose the bloodcurse, which is the Weaver's gift to us in compensation and defense. Since Connla bound Owein and made the Cauldron we have not left Khath Meigol."

His voice was still low, but it was deeper now than when he had first walked from the cave; it was halfway to the chanting that Kim knew was coming. Something else was coming too, and she was beginning to know what it would be.

Ruana said, "We have our own relationship with death, have had it since first we were spun on the Loom. You know it means death, and a curse, to shed our blood. There is more that you do not know. We lay down in the caves, because there was nothing else we could do, being what we are."

"Ruana," came the woman's voice again, "did you summon them?"

And now he turned to her, slowly, as if bearing a great burden.

"I did, Iera. I am sorry. I will chant it in the kanior and seek absolution with the rites. Failing which, I will leave Khath Meigol as Connla did, that the transgression might lie on my shoulders alone."

He raised his hands then, high over his head in the moonlight, and no more words were spoken, for the kanior began.

It was a chant of mourning and a woven spell. It was unimaginably old, for the Paraiko had walked in Fionavar long before the Weaver had spun even the lios alfar or the Dwarves into the Tapestry, and the bloodcurse had been a part of them from the beginning, and the kanior which preserved it.

It began with a low humming, almost below the threshold of hearing, from the Giants gathered around Ruana. Slowly, he lowered his hands and motioned Kim to come forward beside him. As she did so she saw that room had been made for Dalreidan, Faebur, and Brock in the circle surrounding them. Tabor and his winged creature remained outside the ring.

Ruana sank to his knees and motioned for Kim to do the same. He folded his hands in his lap and then, suddenly, he was in her mind.

I will carry the dead, she heard him say within. *Whom would you give to me?*

Her pulse was slowing, dragged by the low sounds coming from those around them. Her hands shook a little in her lap. She clasped them together, very tightly, and gave him Kevin and then Ysanne: who they were and what they had done.

Ruana's expression did not change, nor did he move, but his eyes widened a little as he absorbed what she sent to him, and then, within her mind, not speaking aloud, he said, *I have them, and they are worthy. Grieve with me.*

Then he lifted his voice in lament.

Kim never forgot that moment. Even with what followed after, the memory of the kanior stayed clear within her, the sorrow and the cleansing of sorrow.

I will carry the dead, Ruana had said, and now he proceeded to do so. With the textured richness of his voice he gathered them both, Kevin and then Ysanne, and drew them into the circle to be mourned. As the humming grew stronger, his own chanting twined through it and about it, a thread on a loom of sound, names offered to the mountain night, and into the ring began to come the images of the Paraiko who had died in the caves: Taieri, Ciroa, Hinewai, Caillea, and more, so many more. All of them approached to be gathered there, to stand in the place where Kim knelt, to be reclaimed for this moment by the woven power of the song. Kim was weeping, but the tears of her heart fell soundlessly, that nothing might mar what Ruana shaped.

And in that moment he went even deeper; he claimed more. His voice growing stronger yet, he reached back through the tumbling ribbon of years and began to gather the Paraiko from the very beginning of days, all of them who had lived in their deep peacefulness, shedding no blood, and had, in the fullness of their time, died to be mourned.

And to be mourned now, again, as Ruana of Khath Meigol reached back for them, spreading the ambit of his mighty soul to encompass the loss of all the dead amid the carnage and the fires of that night. Kneeling so near, Kim watched him do it through her falling tears. Watched him try to shape a solace for sorrow, to rise above what had been done to them, with this majestic affirmation of what the Paraiko were. It was a kanior of kaniors, a lament for every single one of the dead.

And he was doing it. One after another they came, the ghosts of all the Paraiko in all the years, crowding into the wide circle of mourning for one last time on this night of deepest grief for deepest wrong done to their people. Kim understood, then, the source of the tales of ghosts in Khath Meigol, for there *were* ghosts in this place when the kanior rites were done. And on this night the pass in the mountains became a realm, truly, of the dead. Still they came, and still Ruana grew, forcing his spirit to grow great enough to reach for them, to carry them all with his song.

Then his voice went deeper yet, with a new note spun within it, and Kim saw that one had come into the circle who was taller than any Giant there, whose eyes, even from beyond the world, were brighter than any other's, and she knew from Ruana's song that this was Connla himself, who had transgressed in binding Owein, and again in making the Cauldron. Connla, who had gone forth from Khath Meigol alone in voluntary exile from his people—to be reclaimed on this night when every one of them was being reclaimed and mourned anew.

Kim saw Kevin there, honored among those gathered. And she saw Ysanne, insubstantial even among ghosts, for she had gone farther away than any of them, had gone so far, with her own sacrifice, that Kim scarcely grasped how

Ruana had managed to bring even her shadow back to this place.

And at length there came a time when no new figures were drifting into the ring. Kim looked at Ruana as he swayed slowly back and forth, his eyes closed with the weight of all he was carrying. She saw his hands close tightly in his lap as his voice changed one last time, as it went deeper yet, found access to even purer sorrow.

And one by one, into the humbling amplitude of his soul, he summoned the dead svart alfar and the urgach who had imprisoned his people and slain them and devoured them when they were dead.

Kim had never known an act to match the grandeur of what Ruana did in that moment. It was an assertion, utter and irrefutable, of his people's identity. A clear sound in the wide dark of the night, proclaiming that the Paraiko were still without hate, that they were equal to and greater than the worst of what Rakoth Maugrim could do. That they could endure his evil, and absorb it, and rise above it in the end, continuing to be what they had always been, never less than such and never slaves of the Dark.

Kim felt purified in that moment, transfigured by what Ruana was shaping, and when she saw his eyes open and come to rest upon her, even as he sang, she knew what was to come and fearing nothing in his presence she watched him lift a finger and, using it like a blade, lay open the skin on his face and arms in long, deep cuts.

No blood flowed. None at all, though the skin curled back from the gashes he had made and she could see the nerves and arteries exposed within.

He looked at her. With no fear in her, none at all, in a spirit of mourning and expiation, Kim raised her own hands and drew her fingernails along her cheeks and then down the veins of her forearms, feeling the skin slice open to her touch. She was a doctor, and she knew that this could kill.

It did not. No blood welled from her wounds either, though her tears were falling still. Tears of sorrow and now of gratitude as well, that Ruana had offered her this, had been strong enough to shape a magic so profound that even she, who was not one of the Paraiko, and who carried grief and guilt running so deep, might find absolution in the bloodless rites amid the presence of the dead.

Even as Ruana's voice lifted in the last notes of his kanior, Kim felt her gashes closing, and looking down on her arms she saw the skin knit whole and unscarred, and she gave thanks from the wellspring of her being for what he had given her.

Then she saw the Baelrath burning.

Nothing had ever been worse, not even the summoning of Arthur from his rest in Avalon among the summer stars. The Warrior had been doomed by the will of the Weaver to his long fate of summoning and grief, to restitution through all the years and worlds for having the children slain. She had shattered his rest with that terrible name cried out upon the Tor, and her own heart had almost shattered with the pain of it. But she had not shaped his doom; that had been done long ago. She and the Baelrath had created nothing, had changed nothing. She had only compelled him, in sorrow, to do what he was bound by his destiny to do.

This was different, and unimaginably worse, for with the flaming of the ring the image of her dream was made real, and Kim finally knew why she was here. To free the Paraiko, yes, but not only for that. How could it have been so, in time of war, and being who she was? She had come here drawn by the ring, and the Baelrath was a summoning power. It was wild, allowing no compunction or pity, knowing only the demands of war, the dictates of absolute need.

She was in Khath Meigol to draw the Giants forth. In the most transcendent moment of their long history, the hour of their most triumphant assertion of what they were, she had come to change them: to strip them of their nature and the defenses that came with it; to corrupt them; to bring them out to war. Notwithstanding the peace woven into their essence. Notwithstanding the glory of what Ruana had just done, the balm he had offered her soul, the honor he had bestowed upon her two loved ones among the dead.

Notwithstanding everything. She was what she was, and the stone was wild, and it demanded that the Paraiko be undone so they might come to war against Maugrim. What they could do, she knew not. Such healing clarity was not granted her. That would, she thought, with corrosive bitterness, have made things too easy, wouldn't it?

Nothing was to be made easy for her—or for any of them, she amended inwardly. She thought of Arthur. Of Paul on the Summer Tree. Of Ysanne. Of Kevin in the snow before Dun Maura. Of Finn, and Tabor behind her now. Then she thought of Jennifer in Starkadh, and Darien, and she spoke.

"Ruana, only the Weaver, and perhaps the gods, know whether I will ever be granted forgiveness for what I now must do." After the sonority of the kanior her voice sounded high and harsh. It seemed to bruise the silence. Ruana looked down on her, saying nothing, waiting. He was very weak; she could see the weariness etched into his features.

They would all be ravaged by weakness and hunger, she knew. Easy prey, the inward bitterness added. She shook her head, as if to drive those thoughts away. Her mouth was dry when she swallowed. She saw Ruana look at the Baelrath. It was alive, driving her.

She said, "You may yet wish you had never chanted the savesong to bring me here. But it might be that the Warstone would have drawn me to this place, even had you kept silent. I do not know. I do know that I have come not only to set you free, *but to bring you down, by the power I bear, to war against Rakoth Maugrim.*"

There was a sound from the Paraiko gathered around them, but watching only Ruana, she saw that his grave eyes did not change. He said, very softly, "We cannot go to war, Seer. We cannot fight, nor can we hate."

"Then I must teach you!" she cried, over the grief rising within her, as the Warstone blazed more brilliantly than it ever had before.

There was real pain. Looking at her hand she saw it as within a writhing nest of flame, brighter than the bonfires, too fierce, almost, to look upon. Almost. She had to look, and she did. The Baelrath was her power, wild and merciless, but hers was the will and the knowledge, the Seer's wisdom needed to turn the power to work. It might seem as if the stone were compelling her, but she knew that was not truly so. It was responding—to need, to war, to the half-glimpsed intuitions of her dreams—but it needed her will to unleash its power. So she shouldered the weight, accepted the price of power, and looking into the heart of the fire enveloping her hand she cast a mental image into it and watched as the Baelrath threw it back, incarnate, suspended in the air within the circle of the Paraiko. An image that would teach the Giants how to hate and so break them of their sanctity.

An image of Jennifer Lowell, whom they knew now to be Guinevere, naked and alone in Starkadh before Maugrim. They saw the Unraveller then, huge in his hooded cloak, faceless save for his eyes. They saw his maimed hand, they watched him hold it over her body so that the black dripping blood might burn her where it fell, and Kimberly's own burning seemed as nothing before what she saw. They heard Jennifer speak, so blazingly defiant in that unholy place that it could break the heart to hear, and they heard him laugh and fall upon her in his foulness. They watched him begin to change his shapes, and they heard what was said and understood that he was tearing her mind apart to find avenues for torture.

It went on for a very long time. Kim felt wave after wave of nausea rising within her, but she forced herself to watch. Jennifer had been there, had lived through this and survived it, and the Paraiko were being stripped of their collective soul through the horror of this image. They could not look away, the power of the Baelrath compelled them, and so she would watch it too. A penance, in the most trivial sense she knew. Seeking expiation where none could possibly come. But she watched. She saw Blöd the Dwarf when he was drawn into the image, and she grieved for Brock, being forced to see this ultimate betrayal.

She saw it all, through to the end.

Afterward, it was utterly silent in Khath Meigol. She could not hear anyone breathe. Her own numbed, battered soul longed for sound. For birdsong, water falling, the laughter of children. She needed light. Warmer, kinder light than the red glow of the fires, or the mountain stars, or the moon.

She was granted none of these. Instead she was made

conscious of something else. From the moment they had entered Khath Meigol there had been fear: an awareness of the presence of the dead in all their inviolate sanctity, guarding this place with the bloodcurse that was woven into them.

Not any more.

She did not weep. This went too far beyond sorrow. It touched the very fabric of the Tapestry on the Loom. She held her right hand close to her breast; it was blistered and painful to the touch. The Baelrath smoldered, embers seeming to glow far down in its depths.

"Who are you?" Ruana asked, and his voice broke on the words. "Who are you to have done this deed unto us? Better we had died in the caves."

It hurt so much. She opened her mouth, but no words came.

"Not so," a voice replied for her. It was Brock, loyal, steadfast Brock of Banir Tal. "Not so, people of the Paraiko." His voice was weak when he began, but grew in strength with every word. "You know who she is, and you know the nature of what she carries. We are at war, and the Warstone of Macha and Nemain summons at need. Would you value your peacefulness so highly that you granted Maugrim dominion? How long would you survive if we went away from here and were destroyed in war? Who would remember your sanctity when all of you and all of us were dead or slaves?"

"The Weaver would," Ruana replied gently.

It stopped Brock, but only for a moment. "So too would Rakoth," he said. "And you have heard his laughter, Ruana. Had the Weaver shaped your destiny to be sacrosanct and inviolate, could you have been changed by the image we have seen tonight? Could you hate the Dark as now you do? Could you have been brought into the army of Light, as now you are? Surely this is your true destiny, people of Khath Meigol. A destiny that allows you to grow when the need is great, however bitter the pain. To come forth from hiding in these caves and make one with all of us, in all the Weaver's worlds afflicted by the Dark."

He ended ringingly. There was silence again. Then: "We are undone," came a voice from the circle of the Giants.

"We have lost the bloodcurse."

"And the kanior." A wailing rose up, heartrending in its grief and loss.

"Hold!" Another voice. Not Ruana. Not Brock. "People of the Paraiko," said Dalreidan, "forgive me this presumption, but I have a question to ask of you."

Slowly, the wailing died away. Ruana inclined his head toward the outlaw from the Plain. "In what you did tonight," Dalreidan asked, "in the very great thing you did tonight did you not sense a farewell? In the kanior that gathered and mourned every Paraiko that ever was, could you not find a sign from the Weaver who shaped you that an ending to something had come?"

Holding her breath, clutching her burned hand, Kim waited. And then Ruana spoke.

"I did," he said, as a sigh like a wind in trees swept over the bare plateau. "I did sense that when I saw Connla come, how bright he was. The only one of us who ever stepped forward to act in the world beyond this pass, when he bound the Hunt to their long sleep, which our people called a transgression, even though Owein had asked him to do so. And then he built the Cauldron to bring his daughter back from death, which was a wrong beyond remedy and led him to his exile. When I saw him tonight, how mighty he was among our dead, I knew that a change was come."

Kim gasped, a cry of relief torn from her pain.

Ruana turned to her. Carefully he rose, to tower over her in the midst of the ring. He said, "Forgive me my harshness. This will have been a grief for you, as much as for us."

She shook her head, still unable to speak.

"We will come down," he said. "It is time. We will leave this place and play a part in what is to come. But hear me," he added, "and know this for truth: *we will not kill.*"

And with that, finally, words came to her. She too rose to her feet. "I do know it for truth," she replied, and it was the Seer of Breenin who spoke now. "I do not think you are meant to. You have changed, but not so much as that, and not all your gifts, I think, are lost."

"Not all," he echoed gravely. "Seer, where would you have us go? To Brennin? Andarien? To Eridu?"

"Eridu is no more." Faebur spoke for the first time. Ruana turned to him. "The death rain fell there for three days, until this morning. There will be no one left in any of the places of the Lion."

Watching Ruana, Kim saw something alter deep in his eyes. "I know of that rain," he said. "We all do. It is a part of our memories. It was a death rain that began the ruin of Andarien. It only fell for a few hours then. Maugrim was not so strong."

Fighting his weariness with a visible effort, he drew himself up very straight.

"Seer, this is the first role we will play. There will be plague with the rain, and no hope of return to Eridu until the dead are buried. But the plague will not harm the Paraiko. You were not wrong: we have not lost all of what the Weaver gave to us. Only the bloodcurse and the kanior, which were shaped of the peace in our hearts. We have other magics, though, and most of them are ways of dealing with death, as Connla's Cauldron was. We will go east from this place in the morning, to cleanse the raindead of Eridu, that the land may live again."

Faebur looked up at him. "Thank you," he whispered. "If any of us live through the dark of these days, it will not be forgotten." He hesitated. "If, when you come to the largest house in the Merchant's Street of Akkaïze, you find lying there a lady, tall and slender, whose hair would once have gleamed the color of wheat fields in sunlight . . . her name will have been Arrian. Will you gather her gently for my sake?"

"We will," said Ruana, with infinite compassion. "And if we meet again, I will tell you where she lies."

Kim turned and walked from the circle. They parted to make way for her, and she went to the edge of the plateau and stood, her back to everyone else, gazing at the dark mountains and the stars. Her hand was blistered and painful to the touch, and her side ached from yesterday. The ring was utterly spent; it seemed to be slumbering. She needed sleep herself, she knew. There were thoughts chasing each other around in her head, and something else, not clear enough yet to be a thought, was beginning to take shape.

She was wise enough not to strain for the Sight that was coming, so she had walked toward darkness to wait.

She heard voices behind her. She did not turn, but they were not far away, and she could not help but hear.

"Forgive me," Dalreidan said, and coughed nervously. "But I heard a story yesterday that the women and children of the Dalrei had been left alone in the last camp by the Latham. Is this so?"

"It is," Tabor replied. His voice sounded remote and thin, but he answered the exile with courtesy. "Every Rider on the Plain went north to Celidon. An army of the Dark was seen sweeping across Andarien three nights ago. The Aven was trying to outrace them to the Adein."

Kim had known nothing of this. She closed her eyes, trying to calculate the distance and the time, but could not. She offered an inner prayer to the night. If the Dalrei were lost, everything the rest of them did might be quite meaningless.

"The Aven!" Dalreidan exclaimed softly. "We have an Aven? Who?"

"Ivor dan Banor," Tabor said, and Kim could hear the pride. "My father." Then, after a moment, as the other remained silent, "Do you know him?"

"I knew him," said Dalreidan. "If you are his son, you must be Levon."

"Tabor. Levon is my older brother. How do you know him? What tribe are you from?"

In the silence that followed, Kim could almost hear the older man struggle with himself. But, "I am tribeless," was all he said. His footsteps receded as he walked back toward the circle of Giants.

She was not alone, Kim thought, in carrying sorrows tonight. The conversation had disturbed her, stirring up yet another nagging thread at the corner of her awareness. She turned her thoughts inward again, reaching for quiet.

"Are you all right?"

Imraith-Nimphais moved silently; Tabor's voice coming so near startled her. This time she did turn, grateful for the kindness in the question. She was painfully aware of what she had done to them. And the more so when she looked at

Tabor. He was deathly pale, almost another ghost in Khath Meigol.

"I think so," she said. "And you?"

He shrugged, a boy's gesture. But he was so much more, had been forced to be so much more. She looked at the creature he rode and saw that the horn was clean again, shining softly in the night.

He followed her glance. "During the kanior," he said, wonder in his voice, "while Ruana chanted, the blood left her horn. I don't know how."

"He was absolving you," she said. "The kanior is a very great magic." She paused. "It was," she amended, as the truth hit home. She had ended it. She looked back toward the Paraiko. Those who could walk were bringing water from over the ridge—there had to be a stream or a well—to the others. Her companions were helping them. As she watched, she began, finally, to cry.

And suddenly, astonishingly, as she wept, Imraith-Nimphais lowered her beautiful head, careful of the horn, and nuzzled her gently. The gesture, so totally unexpected, opened the last floodgates of Kim's heart. She looked up at Tabor through her tears and saw him nod permission; then she threw her arms about the neck of the glorious creature she had summoned and ordered to kill, and laying her head against that of Imraith-Nimphais, she let herself weep.

No one disturbed them, no one came near. After some time, she didn't know how long, Kim stepped back. She looked up at Tabor. He smiled. "Do you know," he said, "that you cry as much as my father does?"

For the first time in days she laughed, and Ivor's son laughed with her. "I know," she gasped. "I know I do. Isn't it terrible?"

He shook his head. "Not if you can do what you did," he said quietly. As abruptly as it had surfaced, the boyishness was gone. It was Imraith-Nimphais' rider who said, "We must go. I am guarding the camps and have been too long away."

She had been stroking the silken mane. Now she stepped back, and as she did so, the Sight that had been eluding her, drifting at the edges of her mind, suddenly coalesced enough for her to see where she had to go. She looked at the Baelrath; it was dulled and powerless. She wasn't surprised. This awareness came from the Seer in her, the soul she shared with Ysanne.

She hesitated, looking up at Tabor. "I have one thing more to ask of you. Will she carry me? I have a long way to travel, and not enough time."

His glance was distanced already, but it was level and calm. "She will," he said. "You know her name. We will carry you, Seer, anywhere you must go."

It was time, then, to make her farewells. She looked over and saw that her three guides were standing together, not far away.

"Where shall we go?" Faebur asked.

"To Celidon," she answered. A number of things were coming clearer even as she stood here, and there was urgency in her. "There was a battle, and it is there that you will find the army, those who survived."

She looked at Dalreidan, who was hesitating, hanging back. "My friend," she said, in the hearing of all of them, "you said words to Faebur this morning that rang true: no one in Fionavar is an exile now. Go home, Dalreidan, and take your true name on the Plain. Tell them the Seer of Brennin sent you."

For a moment he remained frozen, resisting. Then he nodded slowly. "We will meet again?" he asked.

"I hope," she said, and stepped forward to embrace him, and then Faebur as well. She looked at Brock. "And you?" she asked.

"I will go with them," he answered. "Until my own King comes home I will serve the Aven and the High King as best I can. Will you be careful, Seer?" His voice was gruff.

She moved closer and out of habit checked the bandage she'd wrapped about his head. Then she bent and kissed him on the lips. "You too," she whispered. "My dear."

At the very last she turned to Ruana, who had been waiting for her. They said nothing aloud.

Then in her mind she heard him murmur: *The Weaver hold your thread fast in his hand, Seer.*

It was what, more than anything else, she had needed to

hear—this last forgiveness where she had no right to any. She looked up at his great, white-bearded patriarch's head, at the wise eyes that had seen so much. *And yours,* she replied, in silence. *Your thread, and that of your people.*

Then she walked slowly back to where Tabor waited, and she mounted behind him upon Imraith-Nimphais, and told him where it was she had to go, and they flew.

There were hours yet before dawn when he set her down. Not at a place of war but in the one place in Fionavar where she had known a moment's peace. A quiet place. A lake like a jewel, with moonlight glancing along it. A cottage by the lake.

He was in the air again, hovering, as soon as she dismounted. He wanted to be back, she knew. His father had given him a task and she had drawn him from it, twice now.

"Thank you," she said. There was nothing more she could think of to say. She raised a hand in farewell.

As he did the same she saw, grieving, that the moonlight and the stars were shining through him. Then Imraith-Nimphais spread her wings, and she and her rider were gone. Another star for a moment, and then nothing at all.

Kim went into the cottage.

PART II

Lisen's Tower

Chapter 4

Leaning back against the railing of the afterdeck, Paul watched Lancelot dueling with his shadow. It had been going on for most of yesterday, from the time they sailed from Cader Sedat, and had continued for much of this second morning and into the afternoon. The sun was behind them now. Lancelot stood with his back to it and advanced and retreated along the deck, his feet sliding and turning intricately, his sword a blur of thrusts and parries, too fast to follow properly.

Almost every man on *Prydwen* had spent some time watching him, either covertly or, as Paul was, with open admiration. He had finally begun to pick out some of the disciplined patterns in what Lancelot was doing. And as he watched it go on and on, Paul understood something else.

This was more than merely training on the part of someone newly wakened from the Chamber of the Dead. In these relentless, driven repetitions Paul had finally begun to see that Lancelot was masking, as best he could, the emotions rising within himself.

He watched the dark-haired man go through his systematic drills without fuss or wasted motion of any kind. Now and always there was a quiet to Lancelot, a sense of a still pool wherein the ripples of turbulent life were effortlessly absorbed. On one level it was deeply reassuring, and that reassurance had been present from the moment he had come among them, rising from his bed of stone to bring Matt Sören back from the dead as well.

Paul Schafer was too wise, though, for that to be the only level on which he perceived what was happening. He was

Pwyll Twiceborn, had spoken to gods and summoned them, had lived three nights on the Summer Tree, and the ravens of Mörnir were never far from him. *Prydwen* was sailing back to war, and Lancelot's training was apt and fit for the role he would play when they landed again.

They were also sailing back to something else, to someone else: to Guinevere.

In Lancelot's compulsive physical action, however disciplined it might be, Paul read that truth as clearly as in a book, and the themes of the book were absolute love and absolute betrayal, and a sadness that could bind the heart.

Arthur Pendragon, at the prow with Cavall, gazing east, was the only man on the ship who had not taken a moment to watch Lancelot duel his shadow's sword. The two men had not spoken since walking from the wreckage of Cader Sedat. There was no hatred between them, or even anger, or manifest rivalry that Paul could see. He saw, instead, a guarding, a shielding of the self, a tight rein kept on the heart.

Paul remembered—knew he would never forget—the few words they had spoken to each other on the island: Lancelot, newly wakened, asking with utmost courtesy, *Why have you done this, my lord, to the three of us?*

And Arthur, at the very end, the last doorway of that shattered, bloody hall: *Oh, Lance, come. She will be waiting for you.*

No hatred or rivalry there but something worse, more hurtful: love, and defenses thrown up against it, in the sure foreknowledge of what was to come. Of the story to be played out again, as it had been so many times, when *Prydwen* came again to land.

Paul took his eyes from that fluid, mesmerizing form moving up and down the deck, repeating and repeating the same flawless rituals of the blade. He turned away, looking out to sea over the port railing. He would have to defend his own heart, he realized. He could not afford to lose himself in the woven sorrow of those three. He had his own burdens and his own destiny waiting, his own role to play, his own terrible unspoken anxiety. Which had a name, the name of a child who was no longer a child, of the boy who had taken himself, in the Godwood just a week ago, most of the way to his adulthood and most of the way to his power. Jennifer's son. And Rakoth Maugrim's.

Darien. He was not Dari any more, not since that afternoon by the Summer Tree. He had walked into that place as a little boy who had just learned to skip pebbles across a lake and had gone forth as someone very different, someone older, wilder, wielding fire, changing shape, confused, alienated, unimaginably powerful. Son of the darkest god. The wild card in the deck of war.

Random, his mother had called him, knowing more, perhaps, than any of them. Not that there was reassurance in that. For if Darien was random, truly so, he could do anything. He could go either way. Never, Brendel of the lios alfar had said, never had there been any living creature in any of the worlds so poised between Light and Dark. Never anyone to compare with this boy on the brink of manhood, who was graceful and handsome, and whose eyes were blue except when they were red.

Dark thoughts. And there was no light, or approach to it, at the memory of Brendel, either: Brendel, to whom he was going to have to tell, or stand by while others told the story of the Soulmonger and the fate of all the lios alfar who had sailed west in answer to their song since the Bael Rangat. Paul sighed, looking out at the sea curling away from the motion of the ship. Liranan was down there, he knew, the elusive sea god moving through his element. Paul had a longing to summon him again, questions to ask, comfort, even, to seek, in the knowledge of sea stars shining again in the place where the Soulmonger had been slain. Wishful thinking, that. He was far too distant from the source of whatever power he had, and far too unsure of how to channel that power, even when it was ready to hand.

Really, when it came down to it, there was only one thing he knew for certain. There was a meeting in his future, a third meeting, and it drifted through his sleep and his daytime reveries. Along the very tracings of his blood, Paul knew that he would meet Galadan one more time, and not again. His fate and the Wolflord's were warp and weft to each other, and the Weaver alone knew whose thread was marked to be cut when they crossed.

Footsteps crossed the deck behind him, cutting against the

rhythm of Lancelot's steady advance and retreat. Then a light, utterly distinctive voice spoke clearly.

"My lord Lancelot, if it would please you, I think I might test you somewhat better than your shadow," said Diarmuid dan Ailell.

Paul turned. Lancelot, perspiring slightly, regarded Diarmuid with grave courtesy in his face and bearing. "I should be grateful for it," he said, with a gentle smile. "It has been a long time since I faced someone with a sword. Have you wooden ones then, training swords aboard ship?"

It was Diarmuid's turn to smile, eyes dancing under the fair hair bleached even paler by the sun overhead. It was an expression most of the men aboard knew very well. "Unfortunately not," he murmured, "but I would hazard that we are both skilled enough to use our blades without doing harm." He paused. "Serious harm," he amended.

There was a little silence, broken by a third voice, from farther up the deck. "Diarmuid, this is hardly the time for games, let alone dangerous ones."

The tone of command in Loren Silvercloak's voice was, if anything, even stronger since the mage had ceased to be a mage. He looked and spoke with undiminished authority, with, it seemed, a clearer sense of purpose, ever since the moment Matt had been brought back from his death and Loren had vowed himself to the service of his old friend, who had been King under Banir Lök before he was source to a mage in Paras Derval.

At the same time, the ambit of his authority—of anyone's, for that matter—seemed always to come to a sharp terminus at the point where Diarmuid's own wishes began. Especially this kind of wish. Against his will, Paul's mouth crooked upward as he gazed at the Prince. Out of the corner of his eye he saw Erron and Rothe handing slips of paper to Carde. Wagers. He shook his head bemusedly.

Diarmuid drew his sword. "We are at sea," he said to Loren with exaggerated reasonableness, "and at least a day's sailing, perhaps more, depending on the winds and our marginally competent captain"—a fleeting glance spared for Coll, shirtless at the helm—"from reaching land. There may never be a more felicitous occasion for play. My lord?"

The last question was directed at Lancelot, with a salute of the sword, angled in such a way that the sun glinted from it into Lancelot's eyes—who laughed unaffectedly, returned the salute, and moved neatly to the side, his own blade extended.

"For the sacred honor of the Black Boar!" Diarmuid said loudly, to whistles and cheers. He flourished his steel with a motion of wrist and shoulder.

"For my lady, the Queen," said Lancelot automatically.

It shaped an immediate stillness. Paul looked instinctively toward the prow. Arthur stood gazing outward toward where land would be, quite oblivious to all of them. After a moment, Paul turned back, for the blades had touched, ritually, and were dancing now.

He'd never seen Diarmuid with a sword. He'd heard the stories about both of Ailell's sons, but this was his initial encounter at first hand and, watching, he learned something else about why the men of South Keep followed their Prince with such unwavering loyalty. It was more than just the imagination and zest that could conjure moments like this out of a grim ship on a wide sea. It was the uncomplicated truth—in a decidedly complex man—that he was unnervingly good at everything he did. Including swordplay, Paul now saw, with no surprise at all.

The surprise, though thinking about it later Paul would wonder at his unpreparedness, was how urgently the Prince was struggling, from the first touch of blades, to hold his own.

For this was Lancelot du Lac, and no one, ever, had been as good.

With the same economic, almost abstract precision with which he had dueled his shadow, the man who had lain in a chamber undersea among the mightiest dead in all the worlds showed the men of *Prydwen* why.

They were using naked blades and moving very fast on a swaying ship. To Paul's untutored eye there was real danger in the thrusts and cuts they leveled at each other. Looking past the shouting men, he glanced at Loren and then at Coll and read the same concern in both of them.

He thought about interceding, knew they would stop for him, but even with the thought he became aware of his own racing pulse, of the degree to which Diarmuid had just lifted him—all of them—into a mood completely opposite to the hollow silence of fifteen minutes before. He stayed where he was. The Prince, he realized, knew exactly what he was doing.

In more ways than one. Diarmuid, retreating before Lancelot's blurred attack, managed to angle himself toward a coil of rope looped on the deck. Timing it perfectly, he quick-stepped backward, spun around the coil, and, bending low, scythed a cut at Lancelot's knees, a full, crippling cut.

It was blocked by a withdrawn blade, a very quickly withdrawn blade. Lancelot stood up, stepped back, and with a bright joy in his dark eyes cried, "Bravely done!"

Diarmuid, wiping sweat from his own eyes with a billowing sleeve, grinned ferociously. Then he leaped to attack, without warning. For a few quick paces Lancelot gave ground but then, again, his sword began to blur with the speed of its motion, and he was advancing, forcing Diarmuid back toward the hatchway leading belowdeck.

Engrossed, utterly forgetful of everything else, Paul watched the Prince give ground. He saw something else as well: even as he retreated, parrying, Diarmuid's eyes were darting away from Lancelot to where Paul stood at the rail—or past him, actually—beyond his shoulder, out to sea. Just as Paul was turning to see what it was, he heard the Prince scream, "*Paul! Look out!*"

The whole company spun to look, including Lancelot. Which enabled Diarmuid effortlessly to thrust his blade forward, following up on his transparent deception—

—and have it knocked flying from his hand, as Lancelot extended his spin into a full pirouette, bringing him back to face Diarmuid but down on one knee, his sword sweeping with the power of that full, lightning-quick arc to crash into Diarmuid's and send it flying, almost off the deck.

It was over. There was a moment's stunned silence, then Diarmuid burst into full-throated laughter and, stepping forward, embraced Lancelot vigorously as the men of South Keep roared their approval.

"Unfair, Lance," came a deep voice, richly amused. "You've seen that move before. He didn't have a chance."

Arthur Pendragon was standing halfway up the deck.

Paul hadn't seen him come. None of them had. With a lifting heart, he saw the smile on the Warrior's face and the answering gleam in Lancelot's eyes, and again he saluted Diarmuid inwardly.

The Prince was still laughing. "A chance?" he gasped breathlessly. "I would have had to tie him down to have a chance!"

Lancelot smiled, still composed, self-contained, but not repressively so. He looked at Arthur. "You remember?" he asked. "I'd almost forgotten. Gawain tried that once, didn't he?"

"He did," Arthur said, still amused.

"It almost worked."

"Almost," Arthur agreed. "But it didn't. Gawain could never beat you, Lance. He tried all his life."

And with those words, a cloud, though the sky was still as blue, the afternoon sun as bright as before. Arthur's brief smile faded, then Lancelot's. The two men looked at each other, their expressions suddenly unreadable, laden with a weight of history. Amid the sudden stillness of *Prydwen* Arthur turned again, Cavall to heel, and went back to the prow.

His heart aching, Paul looked at Diarmuid, who returned the gaze with an expression devoid of mirth. He would explain later, Paul decided. The Prince could not know: none of the others except, perhaps, Loren could know what Paul knew.

Knowledge not born of the ravens or the Tree but from the lore of his own world: the knowledge that Gawain of the Round Table had, indeed, tried all his life to defeat Lancelot in battle. They were friendly battles, all of them, until the every end—which had come for him at Lancelot's own hand in a combat that was part of a war. A war that Arthur was forced to fight after Lancelot had saved Guinevere from burning at the stake in Camelot.

Diarmuid had tried, Paul thought sadly. It was a gallant attempt. But the doom of these two men and the woman waiting for them was far too intricately shaped to be lifted, even briefly, by access to laughter or joy.

"Look sharp, you laggards!" Coll's prosaic, carrying voice broke into his reverie. "We've a ship to sail, and it may need some sailing yet. Wind's shifting, Diar!"

Paul looked back, south and west to where Coll's extended arm was pointing. The breeze was now very strong, he realized. It had come up during the swordplay. As he looked back he could discern, straining, a line of darkness at the horizon.

And in that moment he felt the stillness within his blood that marked the presence of Mörnir.

Younger brothers were not supposed to ride creatures of such unbridled power. Or to sound or look as had Tabor last night, before he took flight toward the mountains. True, she'd overheard her parents talking about it many times (she managed to overhear a great deal), and she'd been present three nights ago when her father had entrusted the guarding of the women and children to Tabor alone.

But she'd never seen the creature of his fast until last night, and so it was only then that Liane had truly begun to understand what had happened to her younger brother. She was more like her mother than her father: she didn't cry often or easily. But she'd understood that it was dangerous for Tabor to fly, and then she'd heard the strangeness in his voice when he mounted up, and so she had wept when he flew away.

She had remained awake all night, sitting in the doorway of the house she shared with her mother and brother, until, a little before dawn, there had been a falling star in the sky just west of them, near the river.

A short time later Tabor had walked back into the camp, raising a hand to the astonished women on guard. He touched his sister lightly on the shoulder before he passed inside, unspeaking, and fell into bed.

It was more than weariness, she knew, but there was nothing she could do. So she had gone to bed herself, to a fitful sleep and dreams of Gwen Ystrat, and of the fair-haired man from another world who had become Liadon, and the spring.

She was up with the sunrise, before her mother even, which was unusual. She dressed and walked out, after checking to see that Tabor still slept. Aside from those on guard at the gates, the camp was quiet. She looked east to the foothills and the mountains, and then west to see the sparkle of the Latham, and the Plain unrolling beyond. As a little girl she'd thought the Plain went on forever; in some ways she still did.

It was a beautiful morning, and for all her cares and the shallow sleep she'd had, her heart lifted a little to hear the birds and smell the freshness of the morning air.

She went to check on Gereint.

Entering the shaman's house, she paused a moment to let her eyes adjust to the darkness. They had been checking on him several times a day, she and Tabor: a duty, and a labor of love. But the aged shaman had not moved at all from the moment they had carried him here, and his expression had spoken of such terrible anguish that Liane could hardly bear to look at him.

She did though, every time, searching for clues, for ways of aiding him. How did one offer aid to someone whose soul was journeying so far away? She didn't know. She had her father's love of their people, her mother's calm stability, her own headstrong nature, and not a little courage. But where Gereint had gone, none of these seemed to matter. She came anyhow, and so did Tabor: just to be present, to share, in however small a way.

So she stood on his threshold again, waiting for the darkness to clear a little, and then she heard a voice she'd known all her life say, in a tone she'd also known all her life, "How long does an old man have to wait for breakfast these days?"

She screamed a little, a girlish habit she was still trying to outgrow. Then she seemed to have covered the distance into the room very fast, for she was on her knees beside Gereint, and hugging him, and crying just as her father would have and, for this, perhaps even her mother too.

"I know," he said patiently, patting her back. "I know. You are deeply sorry. It will never happen again. I know all that. But Liane, a hug in the morning, however nice, is *not* breakfast."

She was laughing and crying at the same time, and trying to hold him as close as she could without hurting his brittle bones. "Oh Gereint," she whispered, "I'm so glad you're back. So much has happened."

"I'm sure," he said, in a different voice entirely. "Now be still a moment and let me read it in you. It will be quicker than the telling."

She did. It had happened so many times before that it no longer felt strange. This power was at the heart of what the shamans were; it came with their blinding. In a very little time Gereint sighed and leaned back a little, deep in thought.

After a moment, she asked, "Did you do what you went to do?"

He nodded.

"Was it very difficult?"

Another nod. Nothing more, but she had known him a long time, and she was her father's daughter. She had also seen his face as he journeyed. She felt an inner stirring of pride. Gereint was theirs, and whatever he had done, it was something very great.

There was another question in her, but this one she was afraid to ask. "I'll get you some food," she said, preparing to rise.

With Gereint, though, you seldom had to ask. "Liane," he murmured, "I can't tell you for certain, because I am not yet strong enough to reach as far as Celidon. But I think I would know already if something very bad had happened there. They are all right, child. We will have fuller tidings later, but you can tell your mother that they are all right."

Relief burst within her like another sunrise. She threw her arms around his neck and kissed him again.

Gruffly he said, "This is still not breakfast! And I should warn you that in my day any woman who did that had to be prepared to do a good deal more!"

She laughed breathlessly. "Oh, Gereint, I would lie down with you in gladness any time you asked."

For once, he seemed taken aback. "No one has said that particular thing to me for a very long time," he said after a moment. "Thank you, child. But see to breakfast, and bring your brother to me instead."

She was who she was, and irrepressible.

"Gereint!" she exclaimed, in mock astonishment.

"I knew you would say that!" he growled. "Your father never did teach his children proper manners. That is not amusing, Liane dal Ivor. Now go get your brother. He has just awakened."

She left still giggling. "And breakfast!" he shouted after her.

Only when he was quite sure she was out of earshot did he allow himself to laugh. He laughed a long time, for he was deeply pleased. He was back on the Plain where he'd never thought to be again, once having ventured out over the waves. But he had, indeed, done what he'd set out to do, and his soul had survived. And whatever had happened at Celidon, it was not too bad, it could not be, or, even weakened as he was, he would have known from the moment of his return.

So he laughed for several moments and allowed himself—it wasn't hard—to look forward to his meal.

Everything changed when Tabor came. He entered the mind of the boy and saw what was happening to him, and then read the tale of what the Seer had done in Khath Meigol. After that his food was tasteless in his mouth, and there were ashes in his heart.

She walked in the garden behind the domed Temple with the High Priestess—if, Sharra thought to herself, this tiny enclosure could properly be said to constitute a garden. For one raised in Larai Rigal and familiar with every pathway, waterfall, and spreading tree within its walls, the question almost answered itself.

Still, there were unexpected treasures here. She paused beside a bed of sylvain, silver and dusty rose. She hadn't known they grew so far south. There were none in Cathal; sylvain was said to flourish only on the banks of Celyn Lake, by Daniloth. They were the flower of the lios alfar. She said as much to Jaelle.

The Priestess glanced at the flowers with only mild attention. "They were a gift," she murmured. "A long time ago, when Ra-Lathen wove the mist over Daniloth and the lios began the long withdrawal. They sent us sylvain by which to remember them. They grow here, and in the palace gardens as well. Not many, the soil is wrong or some such thing—but there are always some of them, and these seem to have survived the winter and the drought."

Sharra looked at her. "It means nothing to you, does it?" she said. "Does anything, I wonder?"

"In flowers?" Jaelle raised her eyebrows. Then, after a pause, she said, "Actually, there *were* flowers that mattered: the ones outside Dun Maura when the snow began to melt."

Sharra remembered. They had been red, blood red for the sacrifice. Again she glanced at her companion. It was a warm morning, but in her white robe Jaelle looked icily cool, and there was a keen, cutting edge to her beauty. There was very little mildness or placidity about Sharra herself, and the man she was to wed would carry all his life the scar of a knife she'd thown at him, but with Jaelle it was different, and provoking.

"Of course," the Princess of Cathal murmured. "Those flowers would matter. Does anything else, though? Or does absolutely everything have to circle back to the Goddess in order to reach through to you?"

"Everything *does* circle back to her," Jaelle said automatically. But then, after a pause, she went on, impatiently. "Why does everyone ask me things like that? What, exactly, do you all expect from the High Priestess of Dana?" Her eyes, green as the grass in sunlight, held Sharra's and challenged her.

In the face of that challenge, Sharra began to regret having brought it up. She was still too impetuous; it often took her out beyond her depth. She was, after all, a guest in the Temple. "Well—" she began apologetically.

And got no further. "Really!" Jaelle exclaimed. "I have no idea what people want of me. I am High Priestess. I have power to channel, a Mormae to control—and Dana knows, with Audiart that takes doing. I have rituals to preserve, counsel to give. With the High King away I have a realm to govern with the Chancellor. How should I be other than I am? What do you all *want* from me?"

Astonishingly, she had to turn away toward the flowers,

to hide her face. Sharra was bemused, and momentarily moved, but she was from a country where subtlety of mind was a necessity for survival, and she was the daughter and heir of the Supreme Lord of Cathal.

"It isn't really me you're talking to, is it?" she asked quietly. "Who were the others?"

After a moment Jaelle, who had, it seemed, courage to go with everything else, turned back to look at her. The green eyes were dry, but there was a question in their depths.

They heard a footstep on the path.

"Yes, Leila?" Jaelle said, almost before she turned. "What is it? And why do you continue to enter places where you should not be?" The words were stern, but not, surprisingly, the tone.

Sharra looked at the thin girl with the straight, fair hair who had screamed in real pain when the Wild Hunt flew. There was some diffidence in Leila's expression, but not a great deal.

"I am sorry," she said. "But I thought you would want to know. The Seer is in the cottage where Finn and his mother stayed with the little one."

Jaelle's expression changed swiftly. "Kim? Truly? You are tuned to the place itself, Leila?"

"I seem to be," the girl replied gravely, as if it were the most ordinary thing imaginable.

Jaelle looked at her for a long time, and Sharra, only half understanding, saw pity in the eyes of the High Priestess. "Tell me," Jaelle asked the girl gently, "do you see Finn now? Where he is riding?"

Leila shook her head. "Only when they were summoned. I saw him then, though I could not speak to him. He was . . . too cold. And where they are now it is too cold for me to follow."

"Don't try, Leila," Jaelle said earnestly. "Don't even try."

"It has nothing to do with trying," the girl said simply, and something in the words, the calm acceptance, stirred pity in Sharra as well.

But it was to Jaelle that she spoke. "If Kim is nearby," she said, "can we go to her?"

Jaelle nodded. "I have things to discuss with her."

"Are there horses here? Let's go."

The High Priestess smiled thinly. "As easily as that? There is," she murmured with delicate precision, "a distinction between independence and irresponsibility, my dear. You are your father's heir, and betrothed—or did you forget?—to the heir of Brennin. And I am charged with half the governance of this realm. And—or did you forget that too?—we are at war. There were svart alfar slain on that path a year ago. We will have to arrange an escort for you if you intend to join me, Princess of Cathal. Excuse me, if you will, while I tend to the details."

And she brushed smoothly past Sharra on the pebbled walkway.

Revenge, the Princess thought ruefully. She had trespassed on very private terrain and had just paid the price. Nor, she knew, was Jaelle wrong. Which only made the rebuke more galling. Deep in thought, she turned and followed the High Priestess back into the Temple.

In the end, it took a fair bit of time to get the short expedition untracked and on the road to the lake, largely because the preposterous fat man, Tegid, whom Diarmuid had elected as his Intercedent in the matter of their marriage, refused to allow her to ride forth without him, even in the care of the Priestess and a guard from both Brennin and Cathal. And since there was only one horse in the capital large enough to survive martyrdom under Tegid's bulk, and that horse was quartered in the South Keep barracks on the other side of Paras Derval . . .

It was almost noon before they got under way, and as a consequence they were too late to do anything at all about what happened.

In the small hours of that morning, Kimberly, asleep in the cottage by the lake, crossed a narrow bridge over a chasm filled with nameless, shapeless horrors, and when she stood on the other side a figure approached her in the dream, and terror rose in her like a mutant shape in that lonely, blighted place.

On her pallet in the cottage, never waking, she tossed

violently from side to side, one hand raised unconsciously in rejection and denial. For the first and only time she fought her Seer's vision, struggling to change the image of the figure that stood there with her on the farther side. To alter—not merely foresee—the loops spun into time on the Loom. To no avail.

It was to dream this dream that Ysanne had made Kim a Seer, had relinquished her own soul to do so. She had said as much. There were no surprises here, only terror and renunciation, helpless in the face of this vast inevitability.

In the cottage the sleeping figure ceased her struggling; the uplifted, warding hand fell back. In the dream she stood quietly on the far side of the chasm, facing what had come. This meeting had been waiting for her from the beginning. It was as true as anything had ever been true. And so now, with the dreaming of it, with the crossing of that bridge, the ending had begun.

It was late in the morning when she finally woke. After the dream she had fallen back into the deeper, healing sleep her exhausted body so desperately needed. Now she lay in bed a little while, looking at the sunlight that streamed in through the open windows, deeply grateful for the small grace of rest in this place. There were birds singing outside, and the breeze carried the scent of flowers. She could hear the lake slapping against the rocks along the shore.

She rose and went out into the brightness of the day. Down the familiar path she walked, to the broad flat rock overhanging the lake where she had knelt when Ysanne threw a bannion into the moonlit waters and summoned Eilathen to spin for her.

He was down there now, she knew, deep in his halls of seaweed and stone, free of the binding flowerfire, uncaring of what happened above the surface of his lake. She knelt and washed her face in the cool, clean waters. She sat back on her heels and let the sunlight dry the drops of water glistening on her cheeks. It was very quiet. Far out over the lake a fishing bird swooped and then rose, caught by the light, flashing away south.

She had stood on this shore once, most of a lifetime ago, it seemed, throwing pebbles into the water, having fled from the words Ysanne had spoken in the cottage. Under the cottage.

Her hair had still been brown then. She had been an intern from Toronto, a stranger in another world. She was white-haired now, and the Seer of Brennin, and on the far side of a chasm in her dream she had seen a road stretching away, and someone had stood before her on that road. Sparkling brilliantly, a speckled fish leaped from the lake. The sun was high, too high; the Loom was shuttling even as she lingered by this shore.

Kimberly rose and went back into the cottage. She moved the table a little to one side. She laid her hand on the floor and spoke a word of power.

There were ten steps leading down. The walls were damp. There were no torches, but from below the well-remembered pearly light still shone. On her finger the Baelrath began to glow in answer. Then she reached the bottom and stood in the chamber again, with its woven carpet, single desk, bed, chair, ancient books.

And the glass-doored cabinet on the farther wall wherein lay the Circlet of Lisen, from which the shining came.

She walked over and opened the cabinet doors. For a long time she stood motionless, looking down at the gold of the Circlet band and the glowing stone set within: fairest creation of the lios alfar, crafted by the Children of Light in love and sorrow for the fairest child of all the Weaver's worlds.

The Light against the Dark, Ysanne had named it. It had changed, Kim remembered her saying: the color of hope when it was made, since Lisen's death it shone more softly, and with loss. Thinking of Ysanne, Kim felt her as a palpable presence; she had the illusion that if she hugged herself, she'd be putting her arms about the frail body of the old Seer.

It was an illusion, nothing more, but she remembered something else that was more than illusory: words of Raederth, the mage Ysanne had loved and been loved by, the man who had found the Circlet again, notwithstanding all the long years it had lain lost.

Who wears this next, after Lisen, Raederth had said, *shall have the darkest road to walk of any child of earth or stars.*

The words she had heard in her dream. Kim reached out a hand and with infinite care lifted the Circlet from where it lay.

She heard a sound from the room above.

Terror burst inside her, sharper even than in the dream. For what had been only foreknowing then, and so removed a little, was present, now, and above her. And the time had come.

She turned to face the stairway. Keeping her voice as level as she could, knowing how dangerous it would be to show fear, she said, "You can come down if you like. I've been waiting for you."

Silence. Her heart was thunder, a drum. For a moment she saw the chasm again, the bridge, the road. Then there were footsteps on the stairs.

Then Darien.

She had never seen him. She endured a moment of terrible dislocation, over and above everything else. She knew nothing of what happened in the glade of the Summer Tree. He was supposed to be a child, even though a part of her had known he wasn't, and couldn't be. In the dream he had been only a shadowed presence, ill defined, and a name she'd learned in Toronto even before he was born. By the aura of the name she had known him, and by another thing, which had been the deepest source of her terror: his eyes had been red.

They were blue now and he seemed very young, though he should have been even younger. So much younger. But Jennifer's child, born less than a year ago, stood before her, his eyes uneasy, darting about the chamber, and he looked like any fifteen-year-old boy might look—if any boy could be as beautiful as this one was, and carry as much power within himself.

"How did you know I was here?" he said abruptly. His voice was awkward, underused.

She tried to will her heartbeat to slow; she needed to be calm, needed all her wits about her for this. "I heard you," she said.

"I thought I was being quiet."

She managed to smile. "You were, Darien. I have very good ears. Your mother used to wake me when she came in late at night, however quiet she was."

His eyes came to rest on hers for a moment. "You know my mother?"

"I know her very well. I love her dearly."

He moved a couple of paces into the room but stayed between her and the stairway. She wasn't sure if it was to keep an exit for himself or block it from her. He was looking around again.

"I never knew this room was here."

The muscles of her back were corded with tension. "It belonged to the woman who lived here before you," she said.

"Why?" he challenged. "Who was she? Why is it underground?" He was wearing a sweater and trousers and fawn-colored boots. The sweater was brown, too warm for summer, and too large for him. It would have been Finn's, she realized. All the clothing was. Her mouth was dry. She wet her lips with her tongue.

"She was a very wise woman, and she had many things she loved in this room, so she kept it hidden to guard them." The Circlet lay in her hand; it was slender and delicate, almost no weight at all, yet she felt as if she carried the weight of worlds.

"What things?" said Darien.

And so the time, truly, was upon them.

"This," said Kim, holding it out to him. "And it is for you, Darien. It was meant for you. It is the Circlet of Lisen." Her voice trembled a little. She paused. He was silent, watching her, waiting. She said, "It is the Light against the Dark."

Her voice failed her. The high, heroic words went forth into the little chamber and fell away into silence.

"Do you know who I am?" asked Darien. His hands had closed at his side. He took another step toward her. "Do you know who my father is?"

So much terror. But she had dreamt this. It was his. She nodded. "I do," she whispered. And because she thought she had heard a diffidence in his voice, not a challenge, she said, "And I know your mother was stronger than him." She didn't, really, but that was the prayer, the hope, the gleam of light she held. "He wanted her to die, so you wouldn't be born."

He withdrew the one step he had advanced. Then he laughed a little, a lonely, terrible laugh. "I didn't know that," he said. "Cernan asked why I was allowed to live. I heard him. Everyone seems to agree." His hands were opening and closing spasmodically.

"Not everyone," she said. "Not everyone, Darien. Your mother wanted you to be born. Desperately." She had to be so careful. It mattered so much. "Paul—Pwyll, the one who stayed with you here—he risked his life guarding her and bringing her to Vae's house the night you were born."

Darien's expression changed, as if his face had slammed shut against her. "He slept in Finn's bed," he said flatly. Accusingly.

She said nothing. What could she way?

"Give it to me," he said.

What could she do? It all seemed so inevitable, now that the time had come. Who but this child should walk the Darkest Road? He was already on it. No other's loneliness would ever run so deep, no other's dangerousness be so absolute.

Wordlessly, for no words could be adequate to the moment, she stepped forward, the Circlet in her hands. Instinctively he retreated, a hand raised to strike her. But then he lowered his arm, and stood very still, and suffered her to place it about his brow.

He was not even as tall as she. She didn't have to reach up. It was easy to fit the golden band over his golden hair and close the delicate clasp. It was easy; it had been dreamt; it was done.

And the moment the clasp was fitted the light of the Circlet went out.

A sound escaped him; a torn, wordless cry. The room was suddenly dark, lit only by the red glow of the Baelrath, which yet burned, and the thin light that streamed down the stairs from the room above.

Then Darien made another sound, and this time it was laughter. Not the lost laugh of before, this was harsh, strident, uncontrolled. "Mine?" he cried. "The Light against the Dark? Oh, you fool! How should the son of Rakoth Maugrim carry such a light? How should it ever shine for me?"

Kim's hands were against her mouth. There was so much unbridled torment in his voice. Then he moved, and her fear exploded. It doubled, redoubled itself, outstripped any measure she'd ever had, for by the light of the Warstone she saw his eyes flash red. He gestured, nothing more than that, but she felt it as a blow that drove her to the ground. Thrusting past her, he strode to the cabinet against the wall.

In which lay the last object of power. The last thing Ysanne had seen in her life. And lying on the ground, helpless at his feet, Kim saw Rakoth's son take Lökdal, the dagger of the Dwarves, and claim it for his own.

"No!" she gasped. "Darien, the Circlet is yours, but not the dagger. It is not for you to take. You know not what it is."

He laughed again and drew the blade from its jeweled sheath. A sound like a plucked harpstring filled the room. He looked at the gleaming blue thieren running along the blade and said, "I do not need to know. My father will. How should I go to him without a gift, and what sort of gift would this dead stone of Lisen's make? If the very light turns away from me, at least I now know where I belong."

He was past her then, and by the stairs; he was climbing them and leaving, with the Circlet lifeless upon his brow and Colan's dagger in his hand.

"Darien!" Kim cried with the voice of her heart's pain. "He wanted you dead. It was your mother who fought to let you be born!"

No response. Footsteps across the floor above. A door opening, and closing. With the Circlet gone the Baelrath slowly grew dim, so it was quite dark in the chamber below the cottage, and in the darkness Kim wept for the loss of light.

When they came an hour later, she was by the lake again, very deep in thought. The sound of the horses startled her, and she rose quickly to her feet, but then she saw long red hair and midnight black, and she knew who had come and was glad.

She walked forward along the curve of the shore to meet them. Sharra, who was a friend and had been from the first day they'd met, dismounted the instant her horse came to a stop, and enfolded Kim in a fierce embrace.

"Are you all right?" she asked. "Did you do it?"

The events of the morning were so vivid that for a moment Kim didn't realize it was Khath Meigol that Sharra was talking about. The last time the Princess of Cathal had seen her, Kim had been preparing to leave for the mountains.

She managed a nod and a small smile, though it was difficult. "I did," she said. "I did what I went to do."

She left it at that for the moment. Jaelle had dismounted as well and stood a little way apart, waiting. She looked as she always did, cool and withdrawn, formidable. But Kim had shared a moment with her in the Temple in Gwen Ystrat on the eve of Maidaladan, so, walking over, she gave the Priestess a hug and a quick kiss on the cheek. Jaelle stood rigid for an instant; then, awkwardly, her arms went around Kim in a brief, transient gesture that nonetheless conveyed a great deal.

Kim stepped back. She knew her eyes were red from weeping, but there was no point in dissembling, not with Jaelle. She was going to need help, not least of all in deciding what to do.

"I'm glad you're here," she said quietly. "How did you know?"

"Leila," Jaelle said. "She's still tuned to this cottage, where Finn was. She told us you were here."

Kim nodded. "Anything else? Did she say anything else?"

"Not this morning. Did something happen?"

"Yes," Kim whispered. "Something happened. We've a lot to catch each other up on. Where's Jennifer?"

The other two women exchanged glances. It was Sharra who answered. "She went with Brendel to the Anor Lisen when the ship sailed."

Kim closed her eyes. So many dimensions to sorrow. Would there ever be an ending?

"Do you want to go into the cottage?" Jaelle asked.

She shook her head quickly. "No. Not inside. Let's stay out here." Jaelle gave her a searching look and then, without fuss, gathered her white robe and sat down on the stony beach. Kim and Sharra followed suit. A little distance away the men of Cathal and Brennin were watchfully arrayed. Tegid of Rhoden, prodigious in brown and gold, walked toward the three of them.

"My lady," he said, with a deep bow to Sharra, "how may I serve you on behalf of my Prince?"

"Food," she answered crisply. "A clean cloth, and a lunch to spread upon it."

"Instantly!" he exclaimed and bowed again, not entirely steady on the loose stones of the shoreline. He wheeled, and scrunched his way over the beach to find them provisions. Sharra looked sideways at Kim, who had an eyebrow raised in frank curiosity.

"A new conquest?" Kim asked with some of her old teasing, the tone she sometimes thought she'd lost forever.

Sharra, surprisingly, blushed. "Well, yes, I suppose. But not him. Um . . . Diarmuid proposed marriage to me before *Prydwen* sailed. Tegid is his Intercedent. He's looking after me, and so—"

She got no further, having been comprehensively enveloped in a second embrace. "Oh, Sharra!" Kim exclaimed. "That's the nicest news I've heard in I don't know how long!"

"I suppose," Jaelle murmured dryly. "But I thought we had more pressing matters to discuss than matrimonial tidings. And we still don't have any news of the ship."

"Yes, we do," said Kim quickly. "We know they got there, and we know they won a battle."

"Oh, Dana be praised!" Jaelle said, suddenly sounding very young, all cynicism stripped away. Sharra was speechless. "Tell us," the High Priestess said. "How do you know?"

Kim began the story with her capture in the mountains: with Ceriog and Faebur and Dalreidan and the death rain over Eridu. Then she told them of seeing that dread rain come to an end the morning before, of seeing sunshine to the east and so knowing that Metran on Cader Sedat had been stopped.

She paused a moment, for Tegid had returned with two soldiers in his wake, carrying armloads of food and drink. It took a few minutes for things to be arranged in a fashion that, to his critical eye, was worthy of the Princess of Cathal. When the three men had withdrawn, Kim took a deep breath and spoke of Khath Meigol, of Tabor and Imraith-Nimphais, of the rescue of the Paraiko and the last kanior, and then, at the end, very softly, of what she and her ring had done to the Giants.

When she finished it was quiet on the shore again. Neither of the other women spoke. They were both familiar with power, Kim knew, in a great many of its shadings, but what she had just told them, what she had done, had to be alien and almost impossible to grasp.

She felt very alone. Paul, she thought, might have understood, for his too was a lonely path. Then, almost as if reading her thoughts, Sharra reached out and squeezed her hand. Kim squeezed back and said, "Tabor told me that the Aven and all the Dalrei rode to Celidon three nights ago to meet an army of the Dark. I have no idea what happened. Neither did Tabor."

"We do," Jaelle said.

And in her turn she told of what had happened two evenings before, when Leila had screamed in anguish at the summoning of the Wild Hunt, and through her link every priestess in the sanctuary had heard Green Ceinwen's voice as she mastered Owein and drew him from his kill.

It was Kim's turn to be silent, absorbing this. There was still one thing left to be told, though, and so at length she said, "I'm afraid something else has happened."

"Who was here this morning?" Jaelle asked with unnerving anticipation.

It was beautiful where they were sitting. The summer air was mild and clean, the sky and lake were a brilliant blue. There were birds and flowers, and a soft breeze off the water. There was a glass of cool wine in her hand.

"Darien," she said. "I gave him the Circlet of Lisen. Ysanne had it hidden here. The light went out when he put it on, and he stole Colan's dagger, Lökdal, which she'd also had in the cottage. Then he left. He said he was going to his father."

It was unfair of her, she knew, to put it so baldly. Jaelle's face had gone bone white with the impact of what she'd just said, but Kim knew that it wouldn't have mattered how she'd told it. How could she cushion the impact of the morning's terror? What shelter could there be?

The breeze was still blowing. There were flowers, green grass, the lake, the summer sun. And fear, densely woven, at the very root of everything, threatening to take it all away: across a chasm, along a shadowed road, north to the heart of evil.

"Who," asked Sharra of Cathal, "is Darien? And who is his father?"

Amazingly, Kim had forgotten. Paul and Dave knew about Jennifer's child, and Jaelle and the Mormae of Gwen Ystrat. Vae, of course, and Finn, though he too was gone now. Leila, probably, who seemed to know everything connected in any way to Finn. No one else knew: not Loren or Aileron, Arthur or Ivor, or even Gereint.

She looked at Jaelle and received a look back, equally doubtful, equally anxious. Then she nodded, and after a moment the High Priestess did as well. And so they told Sharra the whole story, sitting on the shore of Eilathen's lake.

And when it was done, when Kim had spoken of the rape and the premature birth, of Vae and Finn, when Jaelle had told them both Paul's story of what had happened in the glade of the Summer Tree, and Kim had ended the telling with the red flash of Darien's eyes that morning and the effortless power that had knocked her sprawling, Sharra of Cathal rose to her feet. She walked a few quick steps away and stood a moment, gazing out over the water. Then she wheeled to face Kim and Jaelle again. Looking down on the two of them, at the bleak apprehension in their faces, Sharra, whose dreams since she was a girl had been of herself as a falcon flying alone, cried aloud, "But this is terrible! That poor child! No one else in any world can be so lonely."

It carried. Kim saw the soldiers glance over at them from farther along the shore. Jaelle made a queer sound, between a gasp and a breathless laugh. "Really," she began. "Poor child? I don't think you've quite understood—"

"No," Kim interrupted, laying an urgent hand on Jaelle's arm. "No, wait. She isn't wrong." Even as she spoke, she was reliving the scene under the cottage, scanning it again, trying to see past her terrified awareness of who this child's father was. And as she looked back, straining to remember, she heard again the sound that had escaped him when Lisen's Light had gone out.

And this time, removed from it, with Sharra's words to guide her, Kim heard clearly what she'd missed before: the loneliness, the terrible sense of rejection in that bewildered cry wrung from the soul of this boy—only a boy, they *had* to remember that —who had no one and nothing, and nowhere to turn. And from whom the very light had turned away, as if in denial and abhorrence.

He'd actually said that, she remembered now. He'd said as much to her, but in her fear she'd registered only the terrible threat that followed: he was going to his father bearing gifts. Gifts of entreaty, she now realized, of supplication, of longing for a place, from the most solitary soul there was.

From Darien, on the Darkest Road.

Kim stood up. Sharra's words had crystallized things for her, finally, and she had thought of the one tiny thing she could do. A desperate hope it was, but it was all they had. For although it might still be proven true that it was the armies and a battlefield that would end things one way or the other, Kim knew that there were too many other powers arrayed for that to be a certainty.

And she was one of the powers, and another was the boy she'd seen that morning. She glanced over at the soldiers, concerned for a moment, but only for a moment; it was too late for absolute secrecy, the game was too far along, and too much was riding on what would follow. So she stepped forward a little, off the stony shoreline onto the grass running up to the front door of the cottage.

Then she lifted her voice and cried, "Darien, I know you can hear me! Before you go where you said you would go, let me tell you this: your mother is standing now in a tower west of Pendaran Wood." That was all. It was all she had left: a scrap of information given to the wind.

After the shouting, a very great silence, made deeper, not broken, by the waves on the shore. She felt a little ridiculous, knowing how it must appear to the soldiers. But dignity meant less than nothing now; only the reaching out mattered, the casting of her voice with her heart behind it, with the one thing that might get through to him.

But there was only silence. From the trees east of the cottage a white owl, roused from daytime slumber, rose briefly at her cry, then settled again deeper in the woods. Still, she was fairly certain, and she trusted her instincts by now, having had so little else to guide her for so long; Darien was still there. He was drawn to this place, and held by it, and if he was nearby he could hear her. And if he heard?

She didn't know what he would do. She only knew that if anyone, anywhere, could hold him from that journey to his father, it was Jennifer in her Tower. With her burdens and her griefs, and her insistence, from the start, that her child was to be random. But he *couldn't* be left so any more, Kim told herself. Surely Jennifer would see that? He was on his way to Starkadh, comfortless and lonely. Surely his mother would forgive Kim this act of intervention?

Kim turned back to the others. Jaelle was on her feet as well, standing very tall, composed, very much aware of what had just been done. She said, "Should we warn her? What will she do if he goes to her?"

Kim felt suddenly weary and fragile. She said, "I don't know. I don't know if he'll go there. He might. I think Sharra's right, though, he's looking for a place. As to warning her—I have no idea how. I'm sorry."

Jaelle drew a careful breath. "I can take us there."

"How?" said Sharra. "How can you do that?"

"With the avarlith and blood," the High Priestess of Dana replied in a quieter, different tone of voice. "A great deal of each."

Kim looked at her searchingly. "Should you, though? Shouldn't you stay in the Temple?"

Jaelle shook her head. "I've been uneasy there these past few days, which has never happened before. I think the Goddess has been preparing me for this."

Kim looked down at the Baelrath on her finger, at its quiescent, powerless flickering. No help there. Sometimes she hated the ring with a frightening intensity. She looked up at the other women.

"She's right," Sharra said calmly. "Jennifer will need warning, if he is going to her."

"Or comfort, afterward, if nothing else," Jaelle said, surprisingly. "Seer, decide quickly! We will have to ride back to the Temple to do this, and time is the one thing we do not have."

"There are a lot of things we don't have," Kim amended, almost absently. But she was nodding her head, even as she spoke.

They had brought an extra horse for her. Later that afternoon, under the Dome of the Temple, before the altar with the axe, Jaelle spoke words of power and of invocation. She drew blood from herself—a great deal in fact, as she had warned—then she linked to the Mormae in Gwen Ystrat, and in concert the inner circle of the priestesses of Dana reached down into the earthroot for power of the Mother great enough to send three women a long way off, to a stony shore by an ocean, not a lake.

It didn't take very long by any measure of such things, but even so, by the time they arrived the gathering storm was very nearly upon them all, and the wind and the waves were wild.

Even in the owl shape the Circlet fitted about his head. He had to hold the dagger in his mouth, though, and that was tiring. He let it drop into the grass at the base of his tree. Nothing would come to take it. All the other animals in the copse of trees were afraid of him by now. He could kill with his eyes.

He had learned that just two nights before, when a field mouse he was hunting had been on the verge of escaping under the rotted wood of the barn. He had been hungry and enraged. His eyes had flashed—he always knew when they did, even though he couldn't entirely control them—and the mouse had sizzled and died.

He'd done it three times more that night, even though he was no longer hungry. There was some pleasure in the power, and a certain compulsion too. That part he didn't really understand. He supposed it came from his father.

Late the next night he'd been falling asleep in his own form, or the form he'd taken for himself a week ago, and as he drifted off a memory had come back, halfway to a dream.

He recalled the winter that had passed, and the voices in the storm that had called him every night. He'd felt the same compulsion then, he remembered. A desire to go outside in the cold and play with the wild voices amid the blowing snow.

He didn't hear the voices any more. They weren't calling him. He wondered—it was a difficult thought—if they had stopped calling because he had already come to them. As a boy, so little time ago, when the voices were calling he used to try to fight them. Finn had helped. He used to pad across the cold floor of the cottage and crawl into bed with Finn, and that had made everything right. There was no one to make anything right any more. He could kill with his eyes, and Finn was gone.

He had fallen asleep on that thought, in the cave high up in the hills north of the cottage. And in the morning he'd seen the white-haired woman walk down the path to stand by the lake. Then, when she'd gone back in, he'd followed her, and she'd called him, and he'd gone down the stairs he'd never known were there.

She'd been afraid of him too. Everyone was. He could kill with his eyes. But she'd spoken quietly to him and smiled, once. He hadn't had anyone smile at him for a long time. Not since he'd left the glade of the Summer Tree in this new, older shape he couldn't get used to.

And she knew his mother, his real mother. The one Finn had told him had been like a queen, and had loved him, even though she'd had to go away. She'd made him special, Finn had said, and he'd said something else . . . about having to be good, so Darien would deserve the being special. Something like that. It was becoming harder to remember. He wondered, though, why she had made him able to kill so easily, and to want to kill sometimes.

He'd thought about asking the white-haired woman about that, but he was uncomfortable now in the enclosed spaces of the cottage, and he was afraid to tell her about the killing. He was afraid she would hate him and go.

Then she'd showed him the Light and she'd said it was meant for him. Hardly daring to believe it, because it was so very beautiful, he'd let her put it on his brow. The Light against the Dark, she called it, and as she spoke Darien remembered another thing Finn had told him, about having to hate the Dark and the voices in the storm that came from the Dark. And now, astonishingly, it seemed that even though he was the son of Rakoth Maugrim he was being given a jewel of Light.

And then it went out.

Only Finn's going away had ever hurt as much. He felt the same emptiness, the same hollow sense of loss. And then, in the midst of it, because of it, he'd felt his eyes readying themselves to go red, and then they did. He didn't kill her. He could have, easily, but he only knocked her down and went to take the other shining thing he'd seen in that room. He didn't know why he took it or what it was. He just took it.

Only when he was turning to go and she tried to stop him did it come to him how he could hurt her as much as she'd hurt him, and so, in that moment, he'd decided he was going to take the dagger to his father. His voice had sounded cold and strong to his own ears, and he'd seen her face go white just before he left the room and went outside and made himself into an owl again.

Later in the day other people had come, and he'd watched them from his tree in the woods east of the cottage. He'd seen the three women talking by the lake, though he couldn't hear what they said, and he was too afraid, in the owl shape, to go nearer.

But then one of them, the one with dark hair, had stood up and had cried, loudly enough for him to hear, "That poor child! No one else in any world can be so lonely!" and he knew that she was speaking of him. He wanted to go down then, but he was still afraid. He was afraid that his eyes would want to turn red, and he wouldn't know how to stop them. Or to stop what he did when they were that way.

So he waited, and a moment later the one with white hair walked forward a little, toward him, and she called out to him by name.

The part of him that was an owl was so startled that he flew a few wingbeats, out of sheer reflex, before he was able to control himself again. And then he heard her tell him where his mother was.

That was all. A moment later they went away. He was

alone again. He stayed in the tree, in the owl form, trying to decide what to do.

She had been like a queen, Finn had said. She had loved him.

He flew down and took hold of the dagger again in his mouth, and then he started to fly. The part of him that was an owl didn't want to fly in the day, but he was more than an owl, much more. It was hard to carry the dagger, but he managed it.

He flew north, but only for a little way. West of Pendaran Wood, the white-haired one had said. He knew where that was, though he didn't know how he knew. Gradually he began to angle his flight northwest.

He went very fast. A storm was coming.

Chapter 5

In the place where they were going—all of them, the Wolflord running in his wolf shape, Darien flying as an owl with a blade in his mouth, the three women sent from the Temple by the power of Dana—Jennifer stood on Lisen's balcony gazing out to sea, her hair blown back by the freshening wind.

So still was she that save for the eyes restlessly scanning the white-capped waves, she might have been the figurehead at the prow of a ship and not a living woman waiting at the edge of land for that ship to come home. They were a long way north from Taerlindel, she knew, and a part of her wondered about that. But it was here that Lisen had waited for a ship to return from Cader Sedat, and deep within herself Jennifer felt an awareness, a certainty, that this was where she should be. And embedded within that certainty, as a weed in a garden, was a growing sense of foreboding.

The wind was southwest, and ever since the morning had turned to afternoon it had been getting stronger. Never taking her eyes from the sea, she moved back from the low parapet and sat down in the chair they had brought out for her. She ran her fingers along the polished wood. It had been made, Brendel had said, by craftsmen of the Brein Mark in Daniloth, long before even the Anor was built.

Brendel was here with her, and Flidais as well, familiar spirits never far from her side, never speaking unless she spoke to them. The part of her that was still Jennifer Lowell, and had taken pleasure in riding horses and teasing her roommate, and had loved Kevin Laine for his wit as well as his tenderness, rebelled against this weighty solemnity. But she had been kidnapped after riding a horse a year ago, and

Kim was white-haired now and a Seer with her own weight to carry, and Kevin was dead.

And she herself was Guinevere, and Arthur was here, drawn back again to war against the Dark, and he was everything he had ever been. He had broken through the walls she had raised about herself since Starkadh, and had set her free in the bright arc of an afternoon, and then had sailed away to a place of death.

She knew too much about his destiny and her own bitter role in that to ever truly be lighthearted again. She was the lady of the sorrows and the instrument of punishment, and there was little she could do, it seemed, about either of them. Her foreboding grew, and the silence began to oppress her. She turned to Flidais. As she did, her child was just then flying across the Wyth Llewen River in the heart of the Wood, coming to her.

"Will you tell me a story?" she asked. "While I watch?"

The one she'd known as Taliesin at Arthur's court, and who was now beside her in his truer, older shape, drew a curved pipe from his mouth, blew a circle of smoke along the wind, and smiled.

"What story?" he asked. "What would you hear, Lady?"

She shook her head. She didn't want to have to think. "Anything." She shrugged. Then, after a pause, "Tell me about the Hunt. Kim and Dave set them free, I know that much. How were they bound? Who were they, Flidais?"

Again he smiled, and there was more than a little pride in his voice, "I will tell you, all of what you ask. And I doubt there is a living creature in Fionavar, now that the Paraiko are dead and haunting Khath Meigol, who would know the story rightly."

She gave him an ironic, sidelong glance. "You did know all the stories, didn't you? All of them, vain child."

"I know the stories, and the answers to all the riddles in all the worlds save—" He broke off abruptly.

Brendel, watching with interest, saw the andain of the forest flush a deep, surprising red. When Flidais resumed it was in a different tone, and as he spoke Jennifer turned back to the waves, listening and watching, a figurehead again.

"I had this from Ceinwen and Cernan a very long time ago," Flidais said, his deep voice cutting through the sound of the wind. "Not even the andain were in Fionavar when this world was spun into time, first of the Weaver's worlds. The lios alfar were not yet on the Loom, nor the Dwarves, nor the tall men from oversea, nor those east of the mountains or in the sunburnt lands south of Cathal.

"The gods and the goddesses, given their names and powers by grace of the Weaver's hands, were here. There were animals in the woods, and the woods were vast then; there were fish in the lakes and rivers and the wide sea, and birds in the wider sky. And in the sky as well there flew the Wild Hunt, and in the forests and the valleys and across rivers and up the mountain slopes there walked the Paraiko in the young years of the world, naming what they saw.

"By day the Paraiko walked and the Hunt were at rest, but at night, when the moon rose, Owein and the seven kings and the child who rode Iselen, palest of the shadow horses, mounted up into the starry sky, and they hunted the beasts of woods and open spaces until dawn, filling the night with the wild terrible beauty of their cries and their hunting horns."

"Why?" Brendel could not forebear to ask. "Do you know why, forest one? Do you know why the Weaver spun their killing into the Tapestry?"

"Who shall know the design on the Loom?" Flidais said soberly. "But this much I had from Cernan of the Beasts: the Hunt was placed in the Tapestry to be wild in the truest sense, to lay down an uncontrolled thread for the freedom of the Children who came after. And so did the Weaver lay a constraint upon himself, that not even he, shuttling at the Loom of Worlds, may preordain and shape exactly what is to be. We who came after, the andain who are the children of gods, the lios alfar, the Dwarves, and all the races of men, we have such choices as we have, some freedom to shape our own destinies, because of that wild thread of Owein and the Hunt slipping across the Loom, warp and then weft, in turn and at times. They are there, Cernan told me one night long ago, precisely to be wild, to cut across the Weaver's measured will. To be random, and so enable us to be."

He stopped, because the green eyes of Guinevere had turned back to him from the sea, and there was that within them which stilled his tongue.

"Was that Cernan's word?" she asked. "Random?"

He thought back carefully, for the look on her face demanded care, and it had been a very long time ago. "It was," he said at length, understanding that it mattered, but not why. "He said it exactly so, Lady. The Weaver wove the Hunt and set them free on the Loom, that we, in our turn, might have a freedom of our own because of them. Good and evil, Light and Dark, they are in all the worlds of the Tapestry because Owein and the kings are here, following the child on Iselen, threading across the sky."

She had turned fully away from the sea to face him now. He could not read her eyes; he had never been able to read her eyes. She said, "And so, because of the Hunt, Rakoth was made possible."

It was not a question. She had seen through to the deepest, bitterest part of the story. He answered with what Cernan and Ceinwen had said to him, the only thing that could be said. "He is the price we pay."

After a pause, and a little more loudly because of the wind, he added, "He is not in the Tapestry. Because of the randomness of the Hunt, the Loom itself was no longer sacrosanct; it was no longer all. So Maugrim was able to come from outside of it, from outside of time and the walls of Night that bind all the rest of us, even the gods, and enter into Fionavar and so into all the worlds. He is here but he is not part of the Tapestry; he has never done anything that would bind him into it and so he cannot die, even if everything on the Loom should unravel and all our threads be lost."

This part Brendel had known, though never before how it had come to pass. Sick at heart, he looked at the woman sitting beside them, and as he gazed, he read a thought in her. He was not wiser than Flidais, nor had he even known her so long, but he had tuned his soul to her service since the night she'd been stolen from his care, and he said, "Jennifer, if all this is true, if the Weaver put a check on his own shaping of our destinies, it would follow—surely it would follow—that the Warrior's doom is not irrevocable."

It was her own burgeoning thought, a hint, a kernel of brightness in the darkness that surrounded her. She looked at him, not smiling, not venturing so much; but with a softening of the lines of her face and a catch in her voice that made him ache, she said, "I know. I have been thinking that. Oh, my friend, could it be? I felt a difference when I first saw him—I did! There was no one here who was Lancelot in the way that I was Guinevere, waiting to remember my story. I told him so. There are only the two of us this time."

He saw a brightness in her face, a hint of color absent since *Prydwen* had set sail, and it seemed to bring her back, in all her beauty, from the realm of statues and icons to that of living women who could love, and dared hope.

Better, far better, the lios alfar would think bitterly, later that night, unsleeping by the Anor, that she had never allowed herself that unsheathing of her heart.

"Shall I go on?" Flidais said, with a hint of the asperity proper to an upstaged storyteller.

"Please," she murmured kindly, turning back to him. But then, as he began the tale again, she fixed her gaze once more out to sea. Sitting so, she listened to him tell of how the Hunt had lost the young one, Iselen's rider, on the night they moved the moon. She tried to pay attention as his deep cadences rode over the wind to recount how Connla, mightiest of the Paraiko, had agreed to shape the spells that would lay the Hunt to rest until another one was born who could take the Longest Road with them—the Road that ran between the worlds and the stars.

However hard she tried, though, she could not entirely school her thoughts, for the andain's earlier explanation had reached into her heart, and not just in the way Brendel had discerned. The question of randomness, of the Weaver's gift of choice to his Children, touched Arthur's woven doom with a possibility of expiation she'd never really allowed herself to dream about before. But there was something else in what Flidais had said. Something that went beyond their own long tragedy in all its returnings, and this the lios alfar had not seen, and Flidais knew nothing at all of it.

Jennifer did, though, and she held it close to her rapidly beating heart. *Random*, Cernan of the Beasts had said of the Wild Hunt and the choice they embodied. It was her own word. Her own instinctive word for her response to

Maugrim. For her child, and his choice.

She looked out to sea, searching. The wind was very strong now, and there were storm clouds coming up fast. She forced herself to keep her features calm as she gazed, but inwardly she was as open, as exposed, as she had ever been.

And in that moment Darien landed near the river, at the edge of the trees, and took his human form again.

The sound of thunder was distant yet and the clouds were still far out at sea. But it was a southwest wind that was carrying the storm, and when the light began to change the weather-wise lios alfar grew uneasy. He took Jennifer's hand, and the three of them withdrew into the high chamber. Flidais rolled the curved glass windows shut along their tracks. They sealed tightly, and in the abrupt silence Brendel saw the andain suddenly tilt his head, as if hearing something.

He was. The howl of wind on the balcony had screened from him the alarms running through the Great Wood. There was an intruder. There were two: one was here, even now, and the other was coming and would arrive very soon.

The one who was coming he knew, and feared, for it was his own lord, lord of all the andain and mightiest of them, but the other one, the one standing below them at this moment, he knew not, nor did the powers of the Wood, and it frightened them. In their fear they grew enraged, and he could feel that rage now as a buffeting greater than the wind on the balcony.

Be calm, he sent inwardly, though he was anything but calm himself. *I will go down. I will deal with this.*

To the others, to the lios alfar and the woman he'd known as Guinevere, he said grimly, "Someone has come, and Galadan is on his way to this place even now."

He saw a look pass between the two of them, and he felt the tightening of tension in the room. He thought they were mirroring his own anxiety, knowing nothing of the memory they shared of the Wolflord in a wood east of Paras Derval a little more than a year ago.

"Are you expecting anyone?" he demanded. "Who would follow you here?"

"Who *could* follow us here?" Brendel replied quickly.

There was suddenly a new brightness to the lios, as if he had shed a cloak and his true nature was shining through. "No one has come by sea; we would have seen them—and how could anyone pass through the forest?"

"Someone stronger than the Wood," Flidais replied, vexed at the hint of apprehension that reached his voice.

Brendel was already by the stairwell. "Jennifer, wait here. We will go down and deal with this. Lock the door after us, and open only to one of our voices." He loosened his short sword in its scabbard as he spoke, then turned to Flidais, "How long before Galadan arrives?"

The andain sent the query out to the Wood and relayed the answer back, "Half an hour, perhaps less. He is running very fast, in his wolf shape."

"Will you help me?" Brendel asked him directly.

This was, of course, the question. The andain rarely cared for the affairs of mortals, and even more rarely intervened in them. But Flidais had a purpose here, his oldest, deepest purpose, and so he temporized. "I will go down with you. I told the forest I would see who this was."

Jennifer had gone very pale again, Brendel saw, but her hands were steady and her head very high, and once more he marveled at her sheer, unwavering courage as she said, "I will come down. Whoever is here has come because of me; it may be a friend."

"It may not be," Brendel replied gravely.

"Then I should be no safer in this room," she answered calmly, and paused at the head of the curving stairs waiting for him to lead her down. One more moment he hesitated, then his eyes went green, exactly the color of her own. He took her hand and brought it to his forehead and then his lips before turning to descend, sword drawn now, his tread quick and light on the stone stairs. She followed, and Flidais behind her, his mind racing with calculations, boiling over with considerations and possibilities and a frantically stifled excitement.

They saw Darien standing by the river as soon as they stepped out onto the beach.

The wind carried lashings of sea spray that stung when they struck, and the sky had grown darker even in the moments of their descent. It was purple now, shot through with streaks of red, and thunder was rolling out at sea beyond the rising waves.

But for Brendel of the lios alfar, who immediately recognized who had come, none of this even registered. Quickly he spun around, to fling some warning to Jennifer, to give her time to prepare herself. Then he saw from her expression that she didn't need his warning. She knew, already, who this boy standing before them was. He looked at her face, wet now with ocean spray, and stepped aside as she moved forward toward the river where Darien stood.

Flidais came up beside him, droplets of spray glittering on his bald head, an avid curiosity in his face. Brendel became aware of the sword he carried, and he sheathed it silently. Then he and the andain watched mother and child come together for the first time since the night Darien was born.

An overwhelming awareness filled Brendel's mind of how many things might lie in the balance here. He would never forget that afternoon by the Summer Tree, and the words of Cernan: *Why was he allowed to live?* He thought of that, he thought of Pwyll, far out at sea, and he was conscious every moment of Cernan's son, running toward them even now, as fast as the gathering storm and more dangerous.

He looked down at the andain beside him, not trusting the vivid, inquisitive brightness in Flidais' eyes. But what, after all, could he do? He could stand by, apprehensive and ready; he could die in Jennifer's defense, if it came to that; he could watch.

And, watching, he saw Darien step cautiously forward away from the riverbank. As the boy came nearer, Brendel saw some sort of circlet about his brow, with a dark gem enclosed within it, and deep in his mind a chime sounded, crystal on crystal, a warning from memories not his own. He reached back toward them, but even as he did he saw the boy hold out a sheathed dagger toward his mother, and as Darien spoke, Brendel's memories were wiped away by the urgent demands of the present.

"Will you . . . will you take a gift?" he heard. It seemed to him as if the boy were poised to take sudden flight at a breath, at the fall of a leaf. He held himself very still and, disbelieving, heard Jennifer's reply.

"Is it yours to give?" There was ice in her voice, and steel. Hard and cold and carrying, her tone knifed through the wind, sharp as the dagger her son was offering her.

Confused, unprepared, Darien stumbled back. The blade fell from his fingers. Aching for him, for both of them, Brendel kept silence though his whole being was crying out to Jennifer to be careful, to be gentle, to do whatever she had to do to hold the boy and claim him.

There was a sound from behind him. Quickly he glanced back, his hand gliding to his sword. The Seer of Brennin, her white hair whipping across her eyes, was standing at the edge of the forest east of the Anor. A moment later, his shocked eyes discerned the High Priestess, and then Sharra of Cathal's unmistakable beauty, and the mystery cleared and deepened, both. They must have come from the Temple, by using the earthroot and Jaelle's power. But why? What was happening?

Flidais, too, had heard them come, but not Jennifer or Darien, who were too intent on each other. Brendel turned back to them. He was behind Jennifer, could not see her face, but her back was straight and her head imperiously high as she faced her son.

Who said, small and seeming frail in the wild wind, "I thought it might . . . please you. I took it. I thought . . ."

Surely *now*, Brendel thought. Surely she would ease the path for him now?

"It does not," Jennifer replied. "Why should I welcome a blade that does not belong to you?"

Brendel clenched his hands. There seemed to be a fist squeezing his heart. *Oh, careful,* he thought. *Oh, please take care.*

"What," he heard Darien's mother say, "are you doing here?"

The boy's head jerked as if she'd struck him. "I—she told me. The one with white hair. She said you were . . ." His words failed him. Whatever else he said was lost in the tearing wind.

"She said I was here," his mother said coldly, very clearly. "Very well. She was right, of course. What of it? What do you want, Darien? You are no longer a baby—you arranged for that yourself. Would you have me treat you like one?"

Of course he would, Brendel wanted to say. Couldn't she see that? Was it so hard for her?

Darien straightened. His hands thrust forward, almost of themselves. He threw his head back, and Brendel thought he saw a flash. Then the boy cried, from the center of his heart, *"Don't you want me?"*

From his extended hands two bolts of power flew, to left and right of his mother. One hurtled into the bay, struck the small boat tied up to the dock, and blasted it into shards and fragments of wood. The other sizzled just past his mother's face and torched a tree at the edge of the Wood.

"Weaver at the Loom!" Brendel gasped. At his side, Flidais made a strangled sound and then ran, as fast as his short legs could carry him, to stand beneath the burning tree. The andain raised his arms toward the blaze, he spoke words too rapid and low to follow, and the fire went out.

A real fire this time, Brendel thought numbly. It had been only illusion the last time, by the Summer Tree. Weaver alone knew where this child's power ended or where it would go.

As if in answer to his thoughts, his unspoken fears, Darien spoke again, clearly this time, in a voice that mastered the wind and the thunder out at sea and the drumming, rising now from the forest floor.

"Shall I go to Starkadh?" he challenged his mother. "Shall I see if my father gives me a fairer welcome? I doubt Rakoth will scruple to take a stolen dagger! Do you leave me any choice—*Mother?*"

He's not a child, Brendel thought. It was not the words or the voice of a child.

Jennifer had not moved or flinched, even when the bolts of power flew by her. Only her fingers, spread-eagled at her sides, gave any hint of tension. And again, amid his doubt and fear and numbing imcomprehension, Brendel of the lios alfar was awed by what he saw in her.

She said, "Darien, I leave you the only choice there is. I will say this much and nothing more: you live, though your father wanted me dead so that you would never come into the Tapestry. I cannot hold you in my arms or seek shelter and love for you as I did in Vae's house when you were born.

We are past the time for that. There is a choice for you to make, and everything I know tells me that you must make it freely and unconstrained, or it will never have been made at all. If I bind you to me now, or even try, I strip you of what you are."

"What if I don't want to make that choice?"

Struggling to understand, Brendel heard Darien's voice suspended, halfway, it seemed, between the explosion of his power and the supplication of his longing.

His mother laughed, but not harshly. "Oh, my child," she said. "None of us want to make it, and all of us must. Yours is only the hardest, and the one that matters most."

The wind died a little, a lull, a hesitation. Darien said, "Finn told me . . . before . . . that my mother loved me and that she had made me special."

And now, as if involuntarily, Jennifer's hands did move, up from her sides, to clutch her elbows tightly in front of her.

"Acushla machree," she said—or so Brendel thought. She started to go on, then seemed to pull herself up short, as on a tight, harsh rein.

After a moment she added, in a different voice, "He was wrong . . . about making you special. You know that now. Your power comes from Rakoth when your eyes go red. What you have of me is only freedom and the right to choose, to make your own choice between Light and Dark. Nothing more than that."

"No, Jen!" the Seer of Brennin screamed, into the wind.

Too late. Darien's eyes changed again as the last words were spoken, and from the bitterness of his laughter Brendel knew they had lost him. The wind rose again, wilder than before; over it, over the deep drumming of Pendaran Wood, Darien cried, "Wrong, Mother! You have it all wrong. I am not here to choose *but to be chosen!"*

He gestured toward his forehead. "Do you not see what I wear on my brow? Do you not recognize it?" There was another peal of thunder, louder than any yet, and rain began to fall. Through it, over it, Darien's voice soared. "This is the Circlet of Lisen! The Light against the Dark—*and it went out when I put it on!"*

A sheet of lightning seared the sky west of them. Then thunder again. Then Darien: "Don't you see? The Light has turned away, and now you have as well. Choice? I have none! I am of the Dark that extinguishes the Light—and I know where to go!"

With those words he reclaimed the dagger from the strand before his feet; then he was running, heedless, contemptuous of the ominous drumming in the Wood, straight into Pendaran through the slashing, driving rain, leaving the six of them exposed on the shore to both the storm which had come and the rawness of their terror.

Jennifer turned. The rain was sheeting down; Brendel had no way to tell if there were tears or raindrops on her face.

"Come," he said, "we must go inside. It is dangerous out here in this!"

Jennifer ignored him. The other three women had come up. She turned to Kim, waiting, expecting something.

And it came. "What in the name of all that is holy have you done?" the Seer of Brennin screamed into the gale. It was hard to stand upright; they were all drenched to the bone. "I sent him here as a last chance to keep him from Starkadh, and you drove him straight there! All he wanted was comfort, Jen!"

But it was Guinevere who answered, colder, sterner than the elements. "Comfort? Have I comfort to give, Kimberly? Have you? Or any of us, today, now? You had no right to send him here, and you know it! I meant him to be random, free to choose, and I will not back away from that! Jaelle, what did you think you were doing? You were there in the music room at Paras Derval when I told that to Paul. I meant everything I said! If we bind him, or try, he is lost to us!"

There was another thing inside her, at the very deepest place in her heart, but she did not say it. It was her own, too naked for the telling: *He is my Wild Hunt*, she whispered over and over in her soul. *My Owein, my shadow kings, my child on Iselen. All of them.* She was not blind to the resonances. She knew that they killed, with joy and without discrimination. She knew what they were. She also knew, since Flidais' tale on the balcony, what they meant.

She glared at Kimberly through the slashing rain, daring her to speak again. But the Seer was silent, and in her eyes

Jennifer saw no more anger or fear, only sadness and wisdom and a love she remembered as never varying. There was a queer constriction in her throat.

"Excuse me." The women looked down at the one who had spoken. "Excuse me," Flidais repeated, fighting hard against the surging in his heart, straining to keep his voice calm. "I take it you are the Seer of Brennin?"

"I am," Kim said.

"I am Flidais," he said, unconscionably quick with even this casually chosen name. But he had no patience left; he was near now, so near. He was afraid he would go mad with excitement. "I should tell you that Galadan is very close to this place—minutes away, I think."

Jennifer brought her hands to her mouth. She had forgotten, in the total absorption of the last few minutes. But it all came back now: the night in the wood and the wolf who had taken her away for Maugrim and then had become a man who said, *She is still to go north. If it were not so, I might take her for myself.* Just before he gave her to the swan.

She shuddered. She could not help herself. She heard Flidais say, still for some reason addressing Kim, "I can be of aid, I believe. I think I could divert him from this place, if I go fast enough."

"Well then, go!" Kim exclaimed. "If he's only a few minutes—"

"Or," Flidais went on, unable now to keep the rising note from finally reaching his voice, "I could do nothing, as the andain usually do. Or, *if I choose, I could tell him exactly who just left the glade, and who is here.*"

"I would kill you first!" Brendel burst out, his eyes gleaming through the rain. A bolt of lightning knifed into the roiling sea. There came another peal of thunder.

"You could try," Flidais said, with equanimity. "You would fail. And then Galadan could come."

He paused, waiting, looking at Kim, who said, slowly, "All right. What is it you want?"

Amid the howling of the storm Flidais was conscious of a great, cresting illumination in his heart. Tenderly, with a delicate ineffable joy, he said, "Only one thing. A small thing. So small. Only a name. The summoning name of the Warrior." His soul was singing. He did a little dance on the wet strand; he couldn't help himself. It was here. It was in his hands.

"No," said Kimberly.

His jaw dropped into the soaked mat of his beard.

"No," she repeated. "I swore an oath when he came to me, and I will not break it."

"Seer—" Jaelle began.

"You must!" Flidais moaned. "You *must* tell me! It is the only riddle. The last one! I know all the other answers. I would never tell. Never! The Weaver and all the gods know I would never tell—but I must know it, Seer! It is the wish of my heart!"

Strange, fateful phrase crossing the worlds with her. Kim remembered those words from all the years that had gone by, remembered thinking of them again on the mountain plateau with Brock unconscious at her side. She looked down at the gnomelike andain, his hands writhing over and about each other in frantic, pleading desperation. She remembered Arthur, in the moment he had answered her summons on Glastonbury Tor, the bowed weight of his shoulders, the weariness, the stars falling and falling through his eyes. She looked at Jennifer, who was Guinevere.

And who said, softly, but near enough so as to be heard over the wind and rain, "Give it to him. Even so is the name handed down. It is part of the woven doom. Broken oaths and grief lie at the heart of it, Kim. I'm sorry, truly."

It was the apology at the end that reached through to her, as much as anything else. Wordlessly she turned and strode a little way apart. She looked back and nodded to the andain. Stumbling, almost falling in his eagerness and haste, he trotted to her side. She looked down on him, not bothering to mask her contempt. "You will go from here with this name, and I charge you with two things. To never repeat it to a soul in any world, and to deal with Galadan now, doing whatever must be done to keep him from this Tower, and to shield the knowledge of Darien from him. Will you do so?"

"By every power in Fionavar I swear it," he said. He could scarcely control his voice so as to speak. He rose up, on tiptoe so as to be nearer to her. Despite herself she was moved by the helpless longing, the yearning in his face.

"*Childslayer,*" she said, and broke her oath.

He closed his eyes. A radiant ecstasy suffused his face. "Ah!" he moaned, transfigured. "Ah!" He said no more, staying thus, eyes closed, head lifted to the falling rain as if to a benediction.

Then he opened his eyes and fixed her with a level gaze. With dignity she hadn't expected, so soon after his exaltation, he said, "You hate me now. And not without cause. But hear me, Seer: I shall do everything I swore to do, and more. You have freed me from desire. When the soul has what it needs it is without longing, and so it is with me now. From the darkness of what I have done to you there shall be light, or I shall die trying to make it so." He reached up and took her hand between both of his own. "Do not enter the Tower; he will know if there are people there. Endure the rain and wait for me. I shall not fail you."

Then was gone, running on stubby, bowed legs, but fleet and blurred as soon as he entered the forest, a power of Pendaran, moving into his element.

She turned back to the others, waiting west of her, farther down the strand. They stood gathered together under this fury of the elements. Something, an instinct, made her glance down at her hand. Not at the Baelrath, which was utterly subdued, but at the vellin stone about her wrist. And she saw it twisting slowly back and forth.

There was power here. Magic in the storm. She should have known it from the first rising of the wind. But there had been no time to absorb or think about anything but Darien from the moment Jaelle had brought them here. Now there was. Now there was a moment, a still space amid the wild fury of the elements. She lifted her eyes past the three other women and the lios alfar and, looking out to sea, she saw the ship running helplessly before the wind into the bay.

Chapter 6

For a long time Coll of Taerlindel at the helm of his ship had fought the wind. Tacking desperately and with a certain brilliance across the line of the southwesterly, he struggled through most of a darkening day to hold *Prydwen* to a course that would bring them back to the harbor from which they had set out. Bellowing commands, his voice riding over the gale, he kept the men of South Keep leaping from sail to sail, pulling them down, adjusting them, straining for every inch of eastward motion he could gain against the elements that were forcing him north.

It was an exercise in seamanship of the highest order, of calculations done by instinct and nerve on the deck of a wildly tossing ship, of raw strength and raw courage, as Coll fought with all the power of his corded arms to hold the tiller against the gale that was pulling the ship from his chosen path.

And this was only wind, only the first fine mist of rain. The true storm, massive and glowering to starboard and behind them, was yet to come. But it was coming, swallowing what was left of the sky. They heard thunder, saw sheets of lightning ignite in the west, felt the screaming wind grow wilder yet, were drenched by driving, blinding spray as they slid and slipped on the heaving deck, struggling to obey Coll's steadily shouted commands.

Calmly he called out his orders, angling his ship with consummate inbred artistry along the troughs and into the crests of the waves, gauging the seas on either side, casting a frequent eye above him to judge the filling of the sails and the speed of the oncoming storm. Calmly he did it all, though with fierce, passionate intensity and not a little pride. And calmly, when it was clear past doubt that he had no choice, Coll surrendered.

"Over to port!" he roared in the same voice he'd used throughout his pitched battle against the storm. "Northeast it is! I'm sorry, Diar, we'll have to run with it and take our chances at the other end!"

Diarmuid dan Ailell, heir to the High Kingdom of Brennin, was far too busy grappling with a sail rope in obedience to the command to do much in the way of dealing with the apology. Beside the Prince, soaked through and through, almost deafened by the scream of the gale, Paul struggled to be useful and to cope with what he knew.

With what he had known from the first rising of the wind two hours ago, and his first glimpse, far down on the southwest horizon of the black line that was a curtain now, an enveloping darkness blotting out the sky. From the pulsebeat of Mörnir within himself, the still place like a pool in his blood that marked the presence of the God, he knew that what was coming, what had come, was more than a storm.

He was Pwyll Twiceborn, marked on the Summer Tree for power, named to it, and he knew when power of this magnitude was present, manifesting itself. Mörnir had warned him but could do no more, Paul knew. This was not his storm despite the crashing thunder, nor was it Liranan's, the elusive god of the sea. It might have been Metran, with the Cauldron of Khath Meigol, but the renegade mage was dead and the Cauldron shattered into fragments. And this storm far out at sea was not Rakoth Maugrim's in Starkadh.

Which meant one thing and one thing only, and Coll of Taerlindel, for all his gallant skill, hadn't a chance. It was not a thing you tell a captain of a ship at sea, Paul was wise enough to know. You let him fight, and trusted him to know when he could not fight any longer. And after, if you survived, you could try to heal his pride with the knowledge of what had beaten him.

If you survived.

"By Lisen's blood!" Diarmuid cried. Paul looked up—in time to see the sky swallowed, quite utterly, and the dark green curling wave, twice the height of the ship, begin to fall.

"Hang on!" the Prince screamed again, and clutched Paul's

hastily donned jacket with an iron grip. Paul threw one arm around Diarmuid and looped the other through a rope lashed to the mast, gripping with all the strength he had. Then he closed his eyes.

The wave fell upon them with the weight of the sea and of doom. Of destiny not to be delayed or denied. Diarmuid held him, and Paul gripped the Prince, and they both clung to their handholds like children, which they were.

The Weaver's children. The Weaver at the Loom, whose storm this was.

When he could see again, and breathe, Paul looked up at the tiller through the sluicing rain and spray. Coll had help there now, badly needed help, in the muscle-tearing task of holding the ship to its new course, running now with the full speed of the storm, dangerously, shockingly fast in the raging sea, at a speed where the slightest turning of the rudder could heel them over like a toy into the waves. But Arthur Pendragon was with Coll now, balancing him, pulling shoulder to shoulder beside the mariner, salt spray drenching his greying beard, and Paul knew—though he could not actually see them from where he crouched in the shadow of the mainmast—that there would be stars falling and falling in the Warrior's eyes as he was carried toward his foretold fate again, by the hand of the Weaver who had woven his doom.

Children, Paul thought. Both the children they all were, helpless on this ship, and the children who had died when the Warrior was young, and so terribly afraid that his bright dream would be destroyed. The two images blurred in his mind, as the rain and the sea spray blurred together, driving them on.

Running before the wind, *Prydwen* tore through the seas at a speed no ship should have ever been asked to sustain, no sails to endure. But the timbers of that ship, screaming and creaking with strain, yet held, and the sails, woven with love and care and centuries of handed-down artistry in Taerlindel of the Mariners, caught that howling wind and filled with it and did not tear, though the black sky above might shred with lightning and the very sea rock with the thunder.

Riding the mad crest of that speed, the two men at the tiller fought to hold their course, their bodies taut with the brutal strain. And then, with no surprise at all, only a dulled, hurting sense of inevitability, Paul saw Lancelot du Lac grapple his way to their side. And so, at the last, it was the three of them: Coll conning his ship with Lancelot and Arthur at either side, their feet braced wide on the slippery deck, gripping the tiller together, in flawless, necessary harmony, guiding that small, gallant, much-enduring ship into the bay of the Anor Lisen.

And, helpless to do so much as veer a single point off the wind, onto the jagged teeth of the rocks that guarded the southern entrance to that bay.

Paul never knew, afterward, whether they had been meant to survive. Arthur and Lancelot had to, he knew, else there would have been no point to the storm that carried them here. But the rest of them were expendable, however bitter the thought might be, in the unfolding of this tale.

He never knew, either, exactly what it was that warned him. They were moving so fast, through the darkness and the pelting, blinding sheets of rain, that none of them had even seen the shore, let alone the rocks. Reaching back, trying to relive the moment afterward, he thought it might have been his ravens that spoke, but chaos reigned on *Prydwen* in that moment, and he could never be sure.

What he knew was that in the fraction of splintered time before *Prydwen* splintered forever into fragments and spars, he had risen to his feet, unnaturally surefooted in the unnatural storm, and had cried out in a voice that encompassed the thunder and contained it, that was of it and within it—exactly as he had been of and within the Summer Tree on the night he thought he'd died—and in that voice, the voice of Mörnir who had sent him back, he cried, "*Liranan!*" just as they struck.

The masts cracked with the sound of broken trees; the sides cracked, and the deck; the bottom of the ship was gouged mercilessly, utterly, and the dark sea blasted in. Paul was catapulted, a leaf, a twig, a meaningless thing, from the deck of the suddenly grounded ship. They all hurtled over the sides, every man of what had been, a moment before, Coll's grandfather's beloved *Prydwen*.

And as Paul flew, a split second in the air, another fraction of scintillated time, tasting his second death, knowing the rocks were there and the boiling, enraged, annihilating sea, even in that instant he heard a voice in his mind, clear and remembered.

And Liranan spoke to him and said, *I will pay for this, and pay, and be made to pay again, before the weaving of time is done. But I owe you, brother—the sea stars are shining in a certain place again because you bound me to your aid. This is not binding; this is a gift. Remember me!*

And then Paul cartwheeled helplessly into the waters of the bay.

The calm, unruffled, blue-green waters of the bay. Away from the jagged, killing rocks. Out of the murderous wind, and under a mild rain that fell gently down, bereft of the gale that had given it its cutting edge.

Just beyond the curve of the bay the storm raged yet, the lightning still slashed from the purpled clouds. Where he was, where all of them were, rain fell softly from an overcast summer sky as they swam, singly, in pairs, in clusters, to the strand of beach under the shadow of Lisen's Tower.

Where Guinevere stood.

It was a miracle, Kim realized. But she also realized too much more for her tears to be shed only for relief and joy. Too dense this weaving, too laden with shadings and textures and a myriad of intermingled threads, both warp and weft, for any emotion to be truly unmixed.

They had seen the ship cannon toward the rocks. Then, even in that moment of realization and terror, they had heard a single imperative crash of sound, halfway between thunder and a voice, and on the instant—absolutely on the instant—the wind had cut out completely and the waters of the bay had gone glassily calm. The men who manned *Prydwen* were spilled over the disintegrating sides of the ship into a bay that would have destroyed them not two seconds before.

A miracle. There might be time enough later to search for the source of it and give thanks. But not yet. Not now, in this tangled sorrow-strewn unfolding of a long destiny.

For there were three of them, after all, and Kim could do nothing, nothing at all to stop the hurting in her heart. A man stepped from the sea who had not been on *Prydwen* when she sailed. A man who was very tall, his hair dark, and his eyes as well. There was a long sword at his side, and beside him came Cavall, the grey dog, and in his arms, held carefully out before him, the man carried the body of Arthur Pendragon, and all five people on the beach, waiting, knew who this man was.

Four of them stayed a little way behind, though Kim knew how every instinct in Sharra's soul was driving her to the sea where Diarmuid was even now emerging, helping one of his men out of the water. She fought that instinct, though, and Kim honored her for it. Standing between Sharra and Jaelle, with Brendel a pace to the side and behind, she watched as Jennifer moved forward through the gentle rain to stand before the two men she had loved and been loved by through so many lives in so many worlds.

Guinevere was remembering a moment on the balcony of the Tower earlier that afternoon, when Flidais had spoken of randomness as the variable the Weaver had woven into his Tapestry for a limitation on himself. She was remembering, as if from a place infinitely far away, the explosion of hope in her mind, that this time might be different because of that. Because Lancelot was not here, no third angle of the triangle, and so the Weaver's design might yet be changed, because the Weaver himself had made a space in the Tapestry for change.

No one knew of that thought, and no one ever would. It was buried now, and smashed, and gone.

What was here, in its stead, was Lancelot du Lac, whose soul was the other half of her own. Whose eyes were as dark as they had been every single time before, as undemanding, as understanding, with the same pain buried in their depths that only she could comprehend, only she assuage. Whose hands . . . whose long, graceful fighter's hands were exactly as they had been the last time and the time before, every hurting time before, when she had loved them, and loved him as the mirror of herself.

Whose hands cradled now, gently, with infinite, unmistakable tenderness, the body of his liege lord, her husband. Whom she loved.

Whom she loved in the teeth of all the lies, all the crabbed, envious incomprehension, with a full and a shattering passion that had survived and would survive and would tear her asunder every time she woke again to who she had been and was fated to be. To the memory and the knowledge of betrayal like a stone at the center of everything. The grief at the heart of a dream, the reason why she was here, and Lancelot. The price, the curse, the punishment laid by the Weaver on the Warrior in the name of the children who had died.

She and Lancelot faced each other in silence on the strand, in a space that seemed to the watchers to have somehow been cut out from the ebb and flow of time: an island in the Tapestry. She stood before the two men she loved, bareheaded in the falling rain, and she had memories of so many things.

Her eyes went back again to his hands, and she remembered when he had gone mad—truly so, for a time—for desire of her and the denial within himself of that desire. How he had gone forth from Camelot into the woods and wandered there through the turning of the seasons, naked even in the wintertime, alone and wild, stripped to the very bone by longing. And she remembered those hands when he was finally brought back: the scars, cuts, scabs, the calluses, and broken nails, the frostbite from scrabbling in the snow for berries underneath.

Arthur had wept, she remembered. She had not. Not then, not until later, when she was alone. It had hurt so much. She had thought that death would be better than that sight. And as much as any other single thing, it had been those hands, the palpable evidence of what love of her was doing to him, that had opened her own barricades and let him in to the hearthside of her heart and the welcome so long denied. How could it be a betrayal, of anyone or anything, to offer shelter to such a one? And to let the mirror be made whole, that its reflection of the fire might show both of them beside it?

Still she was silent in the rain, and he, and nothing of this showed in her face. Even so, he knew her thoughts, and she knew that he did. Motionless, wordlessly, they touched after so long and yet did not touch. His hands, clean now, unscarred, slender and beautiful, held Arthur in a clasp of love that spoke so deeply to her that she heard it as a chorus in her heart, high voices in a vaulted place singing of joy and pain.

And in that moment she recalled something else, and this he could not know, though his dark eyes might darken further, looking into hers. She suddenly remembered the last time she had seen his face: not in Camelot, or any of the other lives, the other worlds where they had been brought back to the working of Arthur's doom, but in Starkadh, a little more than a year ago. When Rakoth Maugrim, breaking her for the pleasure it afforded him, had ransacked the effortlessly opened chambers of her memories and come out with an image she had not recognized, an image of the man who stood before her now. And now she understood. She saw again the moment when the dark god had taken this shape in mockery, in a defiling, an attempt to stain and soil her knowledge of love, to besmirch the memory, sear it from her with the blood that fell from the black stump of his lost hand, burning her.

And standing here by the Anor as the clouds began to break up in the west with the passing of the storm, as the first rays of the setting sun sliced through, low down over the sea, she knew that Rakoth had failed.

Better he had not failed, a part of her was thinking, ironic, detached. Better he had scorched this love from her, made a kind of good from the abyss of his evil, freed her from Lancelot, that the endless betrayal might have an end.

But he had not. She had only loved two men in all her life, the two most shining men in any world. And she loved them yet.

She was aware of the changing light: amber, shades of gold. Sunset after storm. The rain had ended. A square of sky appeared overhead, blue, toning downward toward the muted color of dusk. She heard the surge of the surf, and the withdrawal of it along the sand and stones. She held herself straight as she could, quite still; she had a sense that to move, just then, would be to break, and she could not break.

"He is all right," Lancelot said.

What is a voice? she thought. What is a voice that it can do this to us? Firelight. A mirror made whole. A dream shown broken in that mirror. The texture of a soul in four words. Four words not about her, or himself, not of greeting or desire. Four quiet words about the man he carried, and so about the man he was himself.

If she moved, it would be to break.

She said, "I know."

The Weaver had not brought him to this place, to her, to have him die in a storm at sea; too easy, that, by far.

"He stayed at the tiller too long," Lancelot said. "He cracked his head when we hit. Cavall led me to him in the water." As quietly as that, he said it. No bravado, no hint of drama or achievement. And then, after a pause, "Even in that storm, he was trying to steer for a gap in the rocks."

Over and over, she was thinking. How many ways were there for a story to circle back upon itself?

"He was always looking for gaps in the rocks," she murmured. She said nothing else. It was difficult to speak. She looked into his eyes and waited.

There was light now, clouds breaking apart, clear sky. And, suddenly, the track of the sunset along the sea, and then the setting sun below the western clouds. She waited, knowing what he would say, what she would say in response.

He said, "Shall I go away?"

"Yes," she said.

She did not move. A bird sang behind her, in the trees at the edge of the strand. Then another bird sang. The surf came in and withdrew, and then it came in again.

He said, "Where shall I go?"

And now she had to hurt him very badly, because he loved her and had not been here to save her when it happened.

She said, "You will know of Rakoth Maugrim; they will have told you on the ship. He took me a year ago. To the place of his power. He . . . did things to me."

She stopped: not for herself, it was an old pain now, and Arthur had taken much of it away. But she had to stop because of what was in his face. Then after a moment she went on, carefully, because she could not break, not now. She said, "I was to die, after. I was saved, though, and in time I bore his child."

Again she was forced to pause. She closed her eyes, so as not to see his face. No one else, she knew, and nothing else, did this to him. But she did it every time. She heard him kneel, not trusting his hands any longer, and lay Arthur gently down on the sand.

She said, eyes still closed, "I wanted to have the child. There are reasons words will not reach. His name is Darien, and he was here not long ago, and went away because I made him go away. They do not understand why I did this, why I did not try to bind him." She paused again and took a breath.

"I think I understand," said Lancelot. Only that. Which was so much.

She opened her eyes. He was on his knees before her, Arthur lying between the two of them, the sun and its track along the sea behind both men, red and gold and very beautiful. She did not move. She said, "He went into this wood. It is a place of ancient power and of hate, and before he went he burnt a tree with his own power, which comes from his father. I would . . ." She faltered. He had only just now come, and was here before her, and she faltered at the words that would send him away.

There was silence, but not for very long. Lancelot said, "I understand. I will guard him, and not bind him, and leave him to choose his road."

She swallowed and fought back her tears. What was a voice? A doorway, with nuances of light, intimations of shade: a doorway to a soul.

"It is a dark road," she said, speaking more truth than she knew.

He smiled, so unexpectedly that it stopped her heart for a beat. He smiled up at her, and then rose, and so smiled down upon her, tenderly, gravely, with a sure strength whose only place of vulnerability was herself, and he said, "All the roads are dark, Guinevere. Only at the end is there a hope of light." The smile faded. "Fare gently, love."

He turned with the last words, his hand moving automatically, unconsciously, to check the hang of the sword at his side. Panic rose within her, a blind surge.

"Lancelot!" she said.

She had not spoken his name before that. He stopped and turned, two separate actions, slowed by a weight of pain. He looked at her. Slowly, sharing the weight, with very great care, she held out one hand to him. And as slowly, his eyes on hers and naming her name over and over in their depths, he walked back, and took her hand, and brought it to his lips.

Then in her turn, not speaking, not daring to speak or able, she took the hand in which he held her own and laid the back of it against her cheek so that one tear fell upon it. Then she kissed that tear away and watched him go, past all the silent people who parted to make way for him, as he walked from her into Pendaran Wood.

Once, a long time ago, he had met Green Ceinwen by chance in a glade of the Wood by moonlight. Cautiously, for it always paid to be cautious with the Huntress, Flidais had entered the glade and saluted her. She had been sitting on the trunk of a fallen tree, her long legs outstretched, her bow laid down, a dead boar lying beside her with an arrow in its throat. There was a small pool in the glade, and from it the moonlight was reflected back into her face. The stories of her cruelty and capriciousness were legion, and he knew all of them and had started many of the tales himself, so it was with extreme diffidence that he approached, grateful that she had not been bathing in the pool, knowing he would very likely have died had he seen her so.

She had been in a mood of catlike languor that night, though, having just killed, and she greeted him with amusement, stretching her supple body, making room for him beside her on the fallen trunk.

They had spoken for a time, softly, as befitted the place and the moonlight, and it had pleasured her to tease him with stirred desire, though it was gently done, and not with malice that night.

Then, as the moon made ready to pass over into the trees west of them and so be lost to that glade, Green Ceinwen had said, lazily but with a different, more meaningful tone than hitherto, "Flidais, little forest one, do you not ever wonder what will happen to you if you ever do learn the name you seek?"

"How so, goddess?" he remembered asking, his nerves bared suddenly by this merest, most idle mention of his long desire.

"Will your soul not lie bereft and purposeless should that day come? What will you do, having gained the last and only thing you covet? With your thirst slaked will you not be stripped of all joy in life, all reason to live? Consider it, little one. Give it thought."

The moon had gone then. And the goddess too, though not before stroking his face and body with her long fingers, leaving him rampant with desire by the dark pool.

She was capricious and cruel, elusive and very dangerous, but she was also a goddess and not the least wise of them. He sat in the grove a long time, thinking about what she said, and he had thought about it often in the years that followed.

And only now, now that it had happened, could he draw breath after breath that tasted of joy and realize that she had been wrong. It might have been otherwise, he knew: gaining his heart's desire might indeed have been a blight, not this transcendent brightness in his life. But it had fallen out differently; his dream had been made real, the gapped worlds made whole, and along with joy Flidais of the andain now finally knew peace.

It had come at the price of a broken oath, he knew. He had some fleeting, distant sense of regret that this had been demanded, but it scarcely even ruffled the deep waters of his contentment. And, in any case, he had balanced those scales with an oath of his own to the Seer, one that he would keep. She would see. However bitter her contempt for him now, she would have cause to change before the story spun to its close. For the first time, one of the andain would lend himself freely to the cause of the mortals and their war.

Starting now, he thought, with the one who was his lord.

He is here, the lone deiena in the tree above him whispered urgently, and Flidais barely had time to register the sudden easing of the rain and the passing of the thunder, and to fling the swift mental call he'd decided upon, before there came a sound of something crashing through the trees and the wolf had come.

And then, a moment later, Galadan was there instead. Flidais felt light; he had an illusion that he could fly if he wanted to, that he was only tied to the forest floor by the thinnest threads of constraint. But he had cause to know how dangerous the figure standing before him was, and he had a task to perform now, a deception to perpetrate on one who had been known for a long time as the subtlest mind in Fionavar. And who was also the lieutenant of Rakoth Maugrim.

So Flidais schooled his features as best he could, and he bowed, gravely and low, to the one who had only once been challenged in his claim of lordship over the elusive, estranged, arrogant family of the andain. Only once—and Flidais remembered, very well, how Liranan's son and Macha's daughter had both died, not far from here, by the Cliffs of Rhudh.

What are you doing here? said Galadan in his mind. Straightening, Flidais saw that the Wolflord looked lean and deadly, his features tight with anger and unease.

Flidais clasped his hands loosely together in front of his rounded belly. "I am always here," he said mildly, speaking aloud.

He winced, as a sudden knife of pain slashed into his mind. Before speaking again he put up his mental barricades, not displeased, for Galadan had just given him an excuse.

"Why did you do that?" he asked plaintively.

He felt the quick probe bounce away from his barriers. Galadan could kill him, with disturbing ease, but the Wolflord could not see into his mind unless Flidais chose to let him in, and that, at the moment, was what mattered.

Do not be too clever, forest one. Not with me. Why are you speaking aloud, and who was in the Anor? Answer quickly. I have little time and less patience. The mind voice was cold and arrogantly confident, but Flidais had knowledge of his own, and memories. He knew that the Wolflord was feeling the strain of being near to the Tower—which made him more, not less, of a danger, if it came to that.

Half an hour ago he would never have done it, never have dreamt of doing it, but everything had changed since he had learned the name, and so Flidais said, still carefully aloud, "How dare you probe me, Galadan? I care nothing for your war, but a great deal for my own secrets, and will certainly not open my mind to you when you come to me—in Pendaran, if you please—in this fashion, and with such a tone. Will you kill me for my riddles, Wolflord? You *hurt* me just now!" He thought he had the tone right, grievance and pride in equal measure, but it was hard to tell, very hard, given the one with whom he was dealing.

Then he drew a quiet, satisfied breath, for when the Wolflord addressed him again it was aloud and with the courtly grace that had always been a part of him. "Forgive me," he murmured, and bowed in his turn with unconscious elegance. "I have been two days running to get here and am not myself." His scarred features relaxed into a smile. "Whoever that is. I sensed someone in the Anor, and . . . wanted to know who."

There was some hesitation at the end, and this, too, Flidais understood. In the cold, rational, utterly clinical soul that was Galadan's, the blinding passion that still assailed him in connection with Lisen was brutally anomalous. And the memory of his rejection in favor of Amairgen would be a wound scraped raw every time he neared this place. From the new harbor of peace where his soul was moored, Flidais looked at the other figure and pitied him. He kept that out of his eyes, though, having no pressing desire to be slain.

He also had an oath to keep. So he said, reaching for the right tone of casual appeasement, "I'm sorry, I should have known you would sense it. I would have tried to send word. I was in the Anor myself, Galadan. I am just now leaving it."

"*You*? Why?"

Flidais shrugged expressively. "Symmetry. My own sense of time. Patterns on the Loom. You know they sailed from Taerlindel some days ago, for Cader Sedat. I thought someone should be in the Anor, in case they returned this way."

The rain had stopped, though the leaves overhead were still dripping. The trees grew too thickly to show much of the clearing sky. Flidais waited to see if his bait would be taken, and he guarded his mind.

"I did *not* know that," Galadan admitted, a furrow creasing his brow. "It is news and it matters. I think I will have to take it north. I thank you," he said, with much of the old calculation in his voice again. Careful, very careful, not to smile, Flidais nodded. "Who sailed?" the Wolflord asked.

Flidais made his expression as stern as he could. "You should not have hurt me," he said, "if you were going to ask questions."

Galadan laughed aloud. The sound rang through the Great Wood. "Ah, Flidais, is there anyone like you?" he queried rhetorically, still chuckling.

"There is no one with the headache I have!" Flidais replied, not smiling.

"I apologized," Galadan said, sobering quickly, his voice suddenly silken and low. "I will not do so twice." He let the silence hold for a moment, then repeated, "Who sailed, forest one?"

After a brief pause, to show a necessary flicker of independence, Flidais said, "The mage and the Dwarf. The Prince of Brennin. The one called Pwyll, from the Tree." An expression he could not read flashed briefly across Galadan's aristocratic face. "And the Warrior," he concluded.

Galadan was silent a moment, deep in thought. "Interesting," he said at length. "I am suddenly glad I came, forest one. All of this matters. I wonder if they killed Metran? What," he asked swiftly, "do you think of the storm that just passed?"

Off balance, Flidais nonetheless managed to smile. "Exactly what you think," he murmured. "And if a storm has driven the Warrior to land somewhere, I, for one, am going to look for him."

Again Galadan laughed, more softly than before. "Of course," he said. "Of course. The name. Do you expect him to tell you himself?"

Flidais could feel a bright color suffuse his face, which was all right; let the Wolflord think he was embarrassed. "Stranger things have happened," he said stoutly. "Have I your leave to go?"

"Not yet. What did you do in the Anor?"

A flicker of unease rippled through the forest andain. It was all very well to have successfully dissembled with Galadan so far, but one didn't want to push one's fortune by lingering too long. "I cleaned it," he said, with an edgy impatience he did not have to feign. "The glass and the floors. I rolled back the windows to let air in. And I watched for two days, to see if the ship would come. Then, with the storm, I knew it had been driven to land, and since it was not here . . ."

Galadan's eyes were cold and grey and fixed downward on his own. "Were there not flowers?" he whispered, and menace was suddenly a vivid, rustling presence where they stood.

Feigning nothing at all, his heart racing, mouth suddenly dry, Flidais said, "There were, my lord. They . . . crumbled from age when I was dusting the room. I can get more for you. Would you desire me to—"

He got no further. Faster than eye could follow or most cunning mind anticipate, the figure in front of him melted away and in its stead a wolf was there, a wolf that leaped, even in the instant it appeared. With one swift, precisely calculated motion, a huge paw raked the forest andain's head.

Flidais never even moved. He was cunning and wise and surprisingly swift within his Wood, but Galadan was what he was. And so, an instant later, the little bearded andain lay, writhing in genuine agony on the sodden forest floor, holding both hands to the bloodied place where his right ear had been ripped away.

"Live a while longer, forest one," he heard, through the miasma of pain flowing over him. "And name me merciful in your innermost heart. You touched the flowers I laid in that place for her," the voice said, benign, reflective, elegant. "Could you really expect to have been allowed to live?"

Fighting to hold consciousness, Flidais heard, within his reeling mind, another voice then, that sounded near and very far away, at one and the same time. And the voice said, *Oh, my son, what have you become?*

Wiping away blood, Flidais managed to open his eyes. The forest rocked wildly in his vision, then righted itself, and through the curtain of blood and pain he saw the tall, naked, commanding figure and the great horns of Cernan of the Beasts. Whom he had called to this place just before Galadan came.

With a snarl of rage mingled with another thing, the

Wolflord turned to his father. A moment later, Galadan was in his human shape again, elegant as ever. "You lost the right to ask me that a long time ago," he said.

He spoke aloud to his father, a part of Flidais noted, even as he himself had spoken aloud to Galadan, to deny him access to his thoughts.

Magestic and terrible in his nakedness and power, the god of the forests came forward. Speaking aloud, his voice reverberating, Cernan said, "Because I would not kill the mage for you? I will not make answer to that again, my son. But will ask you once more, in this Wood where I fathered you, how have you so lost yourself that you can do this thing to your own brother?"

Flidais closed his eyes. He felt consciousness slipping away, ripple by ripple, like a withdrawing sea. But before he went out with the tide he heard Galadan laugh again, in mockery, and say to his father, to their father, "Why should it signify anything to me that this fat drudge of the forest is another byblow of your profligate seed? Sons and their fathers," he snarled, halfway to the wolf he could so easily become. "Why should any of that matter now?"

Oh, but it does, Flidais thought, with his last shred of consciousness. *Oh, but it matters so much. If only you knew, brother!* He sent it out to neither of the others, that thought. Closely to himself he clutched his memory of the torched tree, and Darien with the Circlet of Lisen on his brow. Then Flidais, having kept his oath, having found his heart's desire, was hit by another surge of pain and knew nothing more at all of what his father said to his brother in the Wood.

Chapter 7

To the east, at Celidon, the sun was low in a sky unmarred by clouds or the hint of any storm as the army of Brennin came at last to the mid-Plain. Galloping beside Niavin, Duke of Seresh, at the front of the host, Teyrnon the mage, weary to the bone after three days of riding, nonetheless managed to pull his chunky body erect in the saddle at his first glimpse of the standing stones.

Beside him, his source chuckled softly and murmured, "I was about to suggest you do that."

Teyrnon glanced over, amused, at Barak, the tall, handsome boyhood friend who was the source of his power, and his good-natured face slipped easily into a self-deprecating grin. "I've lost more weight on this ride than I care to think about," the mage said, slapping his still-comfortable girth.

"Do you good," said Niavin of Seresh, on the other side.

"How," Teyrnon replied indignantly, over Barak's laughter, "can a complete scrambling of my bones possibly do me good? I'm afraid if I try to scratch my nose I'll end up rubbing my knee instead, if you know what I mean."

Niavin snorted, then gave way to laughter of his own. It was hard to stay grim and warlike in the company of the genial, unprepossessing mage. On the other hand, he had known Teyrnon and Barak since they were children in Seresh, in the early days of Ailell's reign, when Niavin's own father was the newly appointed Duke of Seresh, and he had little concern about their capabilities. They would be very serious indeed when the time called for it.

And the time, it seemed, was upon them now. Riding toward them from between the massive stones were three figures. Niavin raised a hand, unnecessarily, to point for the mage's benefit.

"I see them," said Teyrnon quietly. Niavin glanced over sharply, but the other man's face had lost its open ingenuousness and was unreadable.

It was probably just as well that Niavin could not discern the mage's thoughts. They would have worried him deeply, as deeply as Teyrnon himself was troubled, by self-doubts and diffidence and by one other thing.

Formally the two of them greeted Aileron the High King, and formally they returned to him the command of his army, in the presence of his two companions, Ra-Tenniel of the lios alfar, and the Aven of the Plain, who had ridden out to greet the host of Brennin. As formally, Aileron returned their salutations. Then, with the brusque efficiency of the war king he was, he asked Teyrnon, "Have you been contacted, mage?"

Slowly Teyrnon shook his round head. He had expected the question. "I have reached out, my lord High King. Nothing from Loren at all. There is something else, though." He hesitated, then went on. "A storm, Aileron. Out at sea. We found it while we were reaching. A southwest gale, bringing a storm."

"That should not happen," Ra-Tenniel said quickly.

Aileron nodded, not speaking, his bearded features grim.

"Southwest will not be Maugrim," Ivor murmured. "You have seen nothing of the ship?" he asked Teyrnon.

"I am not a Seer," the mage explained patiently. "I can sense, to some degree, an assertion of magic such as this storm, and I can reach out to another mage across a fair distance. If the ship had returned I would have found or been reached by Loren before now."

"And so," Aileron said heavily, "it has not returned, or else Silvercloak has not returned with it." His dark eyes met those of Teyrnon for a long moment, as a late-afternoon breeze stirred the grasses of the Plain all around them.

No one else spoke; they waited for the High King. Still looking at Teyrnon, Aileron said, "We cannot wait. We will push north toward Gwynir now, not in the morning as planned. We have at least three hours of light by which to ride."

Swiftly he explained to Niavin and the mage what had happened in the battle two nights before. "We have been handed an advantage," he said grimly, "one not of our own doing, but by virtue of Owein's sword and Ceinwen's intercession. We must turn that advantage to good effect, while the army of Maugrim is disorganized and fearful. Weaver knows what I would give to have Loren and the Seer with us now, but we cannot wait. Teyrnon of Seresh, will you act as my First Mage in the battles that lie before us?"

He had never been so ambitious, never aimed half so high. It had been derided as a flaw when he was younger, then gradually accepted and indulged as the years passed: Teyrnon was what he was, everyone said, and smiled as they said it. He was clever and reliable; very often he had useful insights into matters of concern. But the paunchy, easy-smiling mage had never been seen—or seen himself, for that matter—as being of real importance in any scheme of things, even in time of peace. Metran and Loren were the mages who mattered.

He'd been content to let that be the case. He'd had his books and his studies, which mattered a great deal. He'd had the comfort of the mages' quarters in the capital: servants, good food and drink, companionship. He'd enjoyed the privileges of rank, the satisfactions of his power, and, indeed, the prestige that went with both. Not a few ladies of Ailell's court had found their way to his bedroom or invited him to their own scented chambers, when they would have scorned to look twice at a chubby scholar from Seresh. He'd taken his duties as a mage seriously, for all his genial good nature. He and Barak had performed their peacetime tasks quietly and without fuss and had served unobtrusively as buffers between the other two members of the Council of the Mages. He hadn't begrudged that either. Had he been asked, in the last years of Ailell's reign, before the drought had come, he would have numbered his own thread on the Loom as one of those that shone most brightly with the glow of the Weaver's benevolence.

But the drought *had* come, and Rangat had flamed, and Metran, who'd had wisdom once, as well as cleverness, had proven himself a traitor. So now they found themselves at war against the unleashed power of Rakoth Maugrim, and suddenly he, Teyrnon, was acting First Mage to the High King of Brennin.

He was also, or so the nagging, unspoken premonition at the remotest turning of his mind had been telling him since yesterday morning, the only mage in Fionavar.

Since yesterday morning, when the Cauldron of Khath Meigol had been destroyed. He knew nothing specific about that, nothing about any of the consequences of that destruction, only this distant premonition, so vague and terrifying he refused to speak of it or give it a tangible name in his mind.

What he felt, though, was lonely.

The sun had gone down. The rain had stopped, and the clouds were scudding away to the north and east. The sky in the west still held to its last hues of sunset shading. But on the beach by the Anor Lisen it was growing dark, as Loren Silvercloak finished telling the truth that had to be told.

When he was done, when his quiet, sorrowful voice had come to an end, those gathered on the beach listened as Brendel of the lios alfar wept for the souls of his people slain as they sailed to their song. Sitting on the sand with Arthur's head cradled in her lap, Jennifer saw Diarmuid, his expressive features twisted with pain, turn away from the kneeling figure of the lios and enfold Sharra of Cathal in his arms, not with passion or desire but in an unexpectedly vulnerable seeking of comfort.

There were tears on her own cheeks; they kept falling, even as she wiped them away, grieving for her friend and his people. Then, looking down, she saw that Arthur was awake and was gazing back at her, and suddenly she saw herself reflected in his eyes. A single star, very bright, fell across her reflection as she watched.

Slowly he raised a hand and touched the cheek where Lancelot's hand had lain.

"Welcome home, my love," she said, listening to the brokenhearted grief of the lios alfar who had guided her to this place, hearing all the while, within her mind, the patient, inexorable shuttling of the Loom. "I have sent him away," she said, feeling the words as warp to the weft of the storm that had passed. The story playing itself out again. Crossings and recrossings.

Arthur closed his eyes. "Why?" he asked, only shaping the word, not quite a sound.

"For the same reason you brought him back," she answered. And then, as he looked up at her again, she hurt him, as she had hurt Lancelot: to do it and have it over and done, because he too had a right to know.

So Guinevere, who had been childless in Camelot, told Arthur about Darien, as the western sky gave up its light and the first stars came out overhead. When she was done, Brendel's quiet weeping came also to an end.

There was a star in the west, low down over the sea, brighter than all the others in the sky, and the company on the beach watched as the lios alfar rose to his feet and faced that star. For a long time he stood silent; then he raised both hands and spread them wide, before lifting his voice in the invocation of song.

Rough at first with the burden of his grief, but growing more crystalline with each word, each offering, Na-Brendel of the Kestrel Mark of Daniloth took the leaden weight of his sorrow and alchemized it into the achingly beautiful, timeless notes of Ra-Termaine's Lament for the Lost, sung as it had never been sung in a thousand years, not even by the one who had created it. And so on that strand at the edge of the sea, under all the shining stars, he made a silver shining thing of his own out of what evil had done to the Children of Light.

Alone of those on the beach below the Anor, Kimberly took no comfort, no easing of pain, from the clear distillation of the lament that Brendel sang. She heard the beauty of it, understood, and was humbled by the grandeur of what the lios alfar was doing, and she knew the power such music had to heal—she could see it working in the faces of those beside her. Even in Jennifer, in Arthur, in stern cold Jaelle, as they listened to Brendel's soul in his voice, lifted to the watching, wheeling stars, to the dark forest and the wide sea.

But she was too far gone in guilt and self-laceration for any of that easing to reach through to her. Was everything she touched, every single thing that came within the glowering ambit of the ring she bore, to be twisted and torn by her presence? She was a healer herself, in her own world! Was she to carry nothing at all but pain to those she loved? To those who needed her?

Nothing but sorrow. From the summoning of Tabor and the corruption of the Paraiko last night to her brutal mishandling of Darien, this morning and then again this evening—when she hadn't even arrived in time to warn Jennifer of what was coming. And then, most bitterly of all, the breaking of the oath she had sworn on Glastonbury Tor. Was the Warrior's portion of grief not great enough, she asked herself savagely, that she'd had to add to it by bandying about the terrible name he was cursed to answer to?

No matter, she swore, lashing herself, that Guinevere had said what she had said, giving dispensation. No matter how desperately they'd needed Flidais to aid them, to hold the secret of Darien. They would not have needed that aid, or anything at all from him, had she not presumed to send Darien to this place. She pushed her wet hair back from her eyes. She looked, she knew, like a half-drowned water rat. She could feel the single vertical crease in her forehead. It might, she thought derisively, fool someone into thinking she was wise and experienced: that, and her white hair. Well, she decided, trembling, if anyone was still fooled after tonight, it was their own lookout!

A last long wavering note rose up and then faded away as Brendel's song came to an end. He lowered his arms and stood silent on the strand. Kim looked over at Jennifer, sitting on the wet sand with Arthur's head cradled in her lap, and saw her friend, who was so much more than that, motion for her to come over.

She took an unsteady breath and walked across the sand to kneel beside them. "How is he?" she asked quietly.

"He is fine," Arthur replied himself, fixing her with that gaze that seemed to have no ending and to be filled, so much of the time, with stars. "I have just paid a fairly mild price for being a too-stubborn helmsman."

He smiled at her, and she had to smile back.

"Guinevere has told me what you had to do. She says she

gave you leave, and explained why, but that you will still be hating yourself. Is this true?"

Kim shifted her glance and saw the ghost of a smile tracing the edges of Jennifer's mouth. She swallowed. "She knows me pretty well," she said ruefully.

"And me," he answered calmly. "She knows me very well, and the dispensation she gave you was also mine. The one you know as Flidais was Taliesin once—we both knew him a very long time ago. He is clearly part of the story, though I am not certain how. Seer, do not despair of brightness flowing from what you had to do."

There was so much comfort in his voice, in the calm, accepting eyes. In the face of this it would be hubris, mere vanity, to hold to her self-condemnation. She said, diffidently, "He said it was his heart's desire. The last riddle he did not know. He said . . . he said he would make light from the darkness of what he had done or die trying to do so."

There was a little silence, as the other two absorbed this. Kim listened to the surf coming in, so gentle now after the wildness of the storm. Then they sensed rather than heard someone approaching, and the three of them glanced up at Brendel.

He seemed more ethereal than ever in the starlight, less tied to the earth, to the pull of gravity. In the dark they could not see the color of his eyes, but they were not shining. He said, in a voice like the whisper of the breeze, "My lady Guinevere, with your permission, I must leave you now for a time. It is . . . it is now my task, over and above all else I am afraid, to carry the tidings I have just heard to my King in Daniloth."

Jennifer opened her mouth to reply, but another voice made answer to the lios alfar.

"He is not there," said Jaelle, from behind them. Her hard voice, usually so imperious, was muted now, more mild than Kim had thought it could be. "There was a battle two nights ago by the banks of the Adein, near Celidon. The Dalrei and the men of Rhoden met an army of the Dark, and Ra-Tenniel led the lios alfar out of the Shadowland, Na-Brendel. He led them to war on the Plain."

"And?" It was Loren Silvercloak.

Kimberly listened as Jaelle, stripped of her usual arrogance, told the tale of how Leila had heard the blowing of Owein's Horn, and seen the battlefield through Finn's presence there, and then how all of them in the Temple had heard Ceinwen intercede. "The High King rode north in response to the summonglass the night *Prydwen* set sail," she concluded. "They will all be on the Plain by now, though what they will do I know not. Perhaps Loren can reach for Teyrnon and answer that for us."

It was the first time Kim could remember that High Priestess speaking so to the mage.

Then, a moment later, she learned that Loren wasn't a mage any longer. And even as the tale was being told the ring on her finger began to glow with returning life. She looked down upon it, fighting hard against the now-instinctive aversion she felt, and within her mind, as Loren and then Diarmuid spoke of Cader Sedat, an image began to coalesce.

It was an image she remembered, the first vision she'd ever had in Fionavar, on the path to Ysanne's Lake: a vision of another lake, high among mountains, with eagles flying over it.

Loren said quietly, "The circles, it seems, have been made complete. It is now my task to go with Matt to Banir Lök, to help him regain the Crown that he never truly lost, so that the Dwarves may be brought back from the edge of the Dark."

"We have a long way to go," Matt Sören said, "and not a great deal of time. We will have to set out tonight." He sounded exactly as he always had. Kim had a sense that nothing, absolutely nothing, would ever make him other than he was: the rock upon which all of them, it seemed, had rested at one time or another.

She looked at Jen and saw the same thought in her face. Then she looked down at the Baelrath again and said, "*You will not get there in time.*"

Even now, even after so much had happened, it was with a deep humility that she registered the instant silence that descended over those gathered there when the Seer within her spoke. When she looked up, it was to meet the single eye of Matt Sören.

"I must try," he said simply.

"I know," she replied. "And Loren is right as well, I think. It does matter, somehow, that you try. But I can tell you you will not get there in time from this place."

"What are you saying?" It was Diarmuid who asked, his voice stripped of nuance as Jaelle's had been, pared clean to the simple question.

Kim held up her hand, so they could all see the flame. "I'm saying I'll have to go there too. That the Baelrath will have to take us there. And I think all of us know by now that the Warstone is a mixed blessing, at the very best." She tried hard to keep the bitterness from her voice.

She almost succeeded, too. But in the stillness that followed, someone asked, "Kim, what happened in the mountains?"

She turned to Paul Schafer, who had asked the question, who always seemed to ask the questions that went below the surface. She looked at him, and then at Loren, beside Paul, gazing at her with the mix of gentleness and strength that she remembered from the beginning, and then, most vividly, from the night they'd shared in the Temple, before Kevin had died. Before she went to Khath Meigol.

So it was to the two of them, so different yet so much alike in some inexplicable way, that she told the story of the rescue of the Paraiko and what had followed. Everyone heard, everyone had to know, but it was to Loren and Paul that she spoke. And it was to Matt that she turned, at the end, to repeat, "And so you see what I mean: whatever blessing I carry will not be unmixed."

For a moment he looked at her, as if considering the point. Then his expression changed; she saw his mouth move in the grimace that she knew to be his smile and heard him say wryly, "No blade I have ever known to be worth anything at all has had only a single edge."

That was all, but she knew those quiet words were all the reassurance she had any right to seek.

Inclination matched training in the High Priestess of Dana. And so Jaelle, cold in the falling rain, chilled by what had happened with Darien and what was happening now, since the shipwreck, showed nothing at all of her apprehension to anyone on the strand.

She knew, being what she was, that it had been the voice of Mörnir that had thundered to still the waves, and so her gaze was on Pwyll first, of all of them, when he came ashore. She remembered him standing on another beach, far to the south, speaking with Liranan in a perilous light that came not from the moon. He was alive, though, and had come back. She supposed she was pleased about that.

They had all come back, it seemed, and there was someone new with them, and it was not hard to tell, from Jennifer's face, who this was.

She had made herself cold and hard, but she was not stone, however she might try to be. Pity and wonder had moved her equally to see Guinevere and Lancelot stand together in the rain, as the setting sun slanted through disappearing clouds low in the west.

She had not heard what they said to each other, but the language of gesture was plain, and, at the end, when the man walked away alone into the Wood, Jaelle found herself unexpectedly grieved. She watched him go, knowing the history, not finding it hard at all to guess what distancing quest Guinevere had now imposed upon her second love. What was hard was to preserve her own necessary image of detachment—in the presence of so many men, and in the turbulent wake of what had happened in the Temple before she had taken Kim and Sharra away, with blood and the earthroot tapped.

She had needed the Mormae in Gwen Ystrat to wield such a potent magic, and that meant dealing with Audiart, which was never pleasant. Most of the time she could manage it without real trouble, but that afternoon's exchange was different.

She had been on dubious ground, and she'd known it, and so had Audiart. It was beyond the irregular, bordering on a real transgression for the High Priestess to be leaving the Temple—and the Kingdom—even at a time like this. It was her sacred duty, Audiart reminded her, along the mindlink the Mormae shared, to remain in the sanctuary, ready and able to deal with the needs of the Mother. Furthermore, her second-in-command did not scruple to point out, had not the High King charged her to remain in Paras Derval and govern the country with the Chancellor? Was it not her further duty to exploit this unexpected opportunity as best she could in the service of their unwavering quest for Dana's return to primacy in the High Kingdom?

All of this, unfortunately, was true.

In response, all she could really do was pull rank, and not for the first time. Not actually dissembling, she had drawn upon the unease and restlessness she'd been feeling in the Temple and told the Mormae, without amplification, that it was her judgment, as High Priestess, that for her to leave at this time was according to the will of Dana—superseding any traditions or opportunities for gain.

There was also, she had sent along the mindlink, a very real urgency—which was true, as she had seen from Kim's white face and clenched hands as she waited tensely with Sharra under the dome, oblivious to the closed exchange of the priestesses.

She had made that sending white-hot with her anger, and she was, still, stronger than any of the others. *Very well,* Audiart had replied. *If you must do this, you must. I will leave for Paras Derval immediately to act as best I can in your absence.*

This was when the real clash had come, making what had gone before seem like a minor skirmish in a children's game.

No, she'd sent back, absolute firmness masking her inner anxiety. *It is my command, and so Dana's, that you stay where you are. It is only a week since the sacrifice of Liadon, and the rites of response are not complete.*

Are you mad? Audiart had replied, more nakedly rebellious than ever before. *Which of those chattering idiots, those insipid nonentities, do you propose to have act in your stead in a time of war?*

A mistake. Audiart always let her contempt and ambition show through too clearly. Sensing the response of the Mormae, Jaelle drew a breath of relief. She was going to get away with it. Every established pattern of precedent would have demanded that the Second of the Mother come to Paras Derval to take charge in her absence. Had Audiart said so quietly, with even the most cursorily assumed humility, Jaelle might have lost this battle. As it was, she sprang to the attack.

Would you like to be cursed and cast out, Second of Dana?

she sent, with the silken clarity she alone could command over the mindlink. She felt the Mormae's collectively in-drawn breath at the unveiled threat. *Dare you speak so to your High Priestess? Dare you so denigrate your sisters? Have a care, Audiart, lest you lose everything your scheming has won you thus far!*

Strong words, almost too strong, but she'd needed to throw them all off balance for what she had to say next.

I have chosen my surrogate, and the Chancellor has been informed on behalf of the High King. I have this afternoon named the newest member of the Mormae, and she stands beside me, robed in red and opened now to the mindlink.

Greetings, sisters of the Mother, Leila sent, on cue.

And even Jaelle, half prepared for it, had been stunned by the vividness of her words.

On the strand beneath the Anor Lisen, as the rain slowly came to an end and the sunset tinted the western sky, Jaelle was remembering that vividness. It offered a confirmation of sorts for her own instinctive actions and had served to still, quite effectively, whatever opposition to her peremptory behavior might have been mounted in Gwen Ystrat. Even so, there was something profoundly unsettling about the mixture of child and woman in Leila, and her link to the Wild Hunt. Dana had not yet chosen to reveal to her High Priestess any indication of what all this might mean.

The voice of Loren Silvercloak, the mage she had hated and feared all her life, brought her fully back to the strand. She heard him reveal what had happened to him, and the triumph she might once have felt at such a revelation of weakness was quite lost in a wave of fear. They had need of Silvercloak's power, and they were not going to have it.

She'd hoped he might be able to send her home. So far from the Temple she had no magic of her own, no way to get back by herself—and, it now appeared, no one to help her. She saw the Baelrath come to life on the Seer's hand; then she heard where Kim was going with that power.

She listened to Pwyll's question—his first words spoken since *Prydwen* had run aground and they'd come ashore. She wondered about him, how one who could speak with the thundered voice of the God could be so quiet and self-contained and then surface, when his presence had almost been forgotten, with words that cut through to the heart of what was happening. She was, she realized, a little afraid of him, and her attempts to channel that fear into hatred or contempt were not really working.

Once more she forced her mind back to the beach. It was growing darker by the minute. In the shadows Diarmuid's fair hair was still bright, catching the last color of the western sky. It was the Prince who spoke now.

"Very well," he said. "It seems that what we have been told is all we are going to learn. Let us be grateful to our charming Priestess for such information as we do have. Now, Loren can't reach Teyrnon any more. Kim, I gather, has had a vision of Calor Diman but nothing of the armies. And Jaelle has exhausted her store of useful tidings." The gibe seemed reflexive, halfhearted; she didn't bother to respond. Diarmuid didn't wait. "Which leaves us dependent," he murmured, with what seemed to be a genuinely rueful shake of his head, "upon my own less than exhaustive store of knowledge about what my beloved brother is likely to do."

In some inexplicable way, the glib flow of words had a calming effect. Once more, Jaelle realized, the one she used to dismiss as the "princeling" knew exactly what he was doing. He had already decided, and now he was making the decision sound effortless and of little consequence. Jaelle looked at Sharra, standing beside the Prince. She wasn't sure whether or not to pity her, which was another change: once she would have had no trouble doing so.

"At a time like this," Diarmuid continued, "I can do no better than go back to my precocious childhood memories. Some of you may have known patient, supportive older brothers. I have been blighted sadly by the lack of such a one. Loren will remember. From the time I was able to take my first stumbling steps in my brother's wake, one thing was manifestly clear: *Aileron never, ever, waited for me.*"

He paused and glanced at Loren, as if seeking his confirmation, but then continued in a voice from which the flippancy was suddenly gone. "He will not wait now, nor could he, given where we went. If he is on the Plain with the army and the lios with him, Aileron will push for battle; I would stake my life on that. In fact, with your leave, I *will* stake my life on it, and all of yours. Aileron will take the fight to Starkadh as swiftly as he can, which to my mind means one thing only."

"Andarien," said Loren Silvercloak, who, Jaelle suddenly recalled, had taught both Diarmuid and his brother.

"Andarien," the Prince echoed quietly. "He will go through Gwynir to Andarien."

There was a silence. Jaelle was aware of the sea, and of the forest to the east, and, acutely now, of the dark shape of Lisen's Tower looming above them in the darkness.

"I suggest," Diarmuid went on, "that we skirt the western edge of Pendaran, going north from here, angle up through Sennett across the River Celyn to meet, if childhood memories have any merit at all, with the army of Brennin and Daniloth and the Dalrei on the borders of Andarien. If I am wrong," he concluded, with a generous smile at her, "then at least we will have Jaelle with us, to terrify whatever the fifty of us find there."

She favored him with nothing more than a wintry glance. His smile grew broader, as if her expression had only confirmed his statement, but then, in one of his mercurial changes of mood, he turned and looked at Arthur, who had risen to stand.

"My lord," said the Prince, with no levity at all, "such is my counsel at this time. I will attend to any suggestion you might make, but I know the geography here, and I think I know my brother. Unless there is something you know or sense, Andarien is where I think we must go."

Slowly the Warrior shook his head. "I have never been in this world before," Arthur said in his deep, carrying voice, "and I never had a brother in any world. These are your men, Prince Diarmuid. Number me as one of them and lead us to war."

"We will have to take the women," Diarmuid murmured.

She was about to make a stinging retort, but in that moment something very bright caught her eye, and she turned to see the Baelrath on Kim's finger burst into even more imperative flame.

She looked at the Seer as if seeing her for the first time: the small slim figure with tangled hair, so improbably white, the sudden appearance of the vertical crease on her forehead.

Again she had a sense that there seemed to be burdens here greater than her own.

She remembered the moment she had shared with Kim in Gwen Ystrat, and she wished, a little surprised at herself, that there were something she could do, some comfort she might offer that was more than merely words. But Jennifer has been right in what she'd said when Darien had gone: none of them had any real shelter to offer each other.

She watched as Kim walked over to Pwyll and put her arms around him, gripping him very hard; Jaelle saw her kiss him on the mouth. He stroked her hair.

"Till next," the Seer said, an echo, clearly, of the world the two of them had left behind. "Try hard to be careful, Paul."

"And you," was all he said.

The Priestess saw her walk over to Jennifer then, and saw the two women speak, though she could not hear what they said. Then the Seer turned. She seemed to Jaelle to grow more remote, even as she watched. Kim gestured Loren and Matt to either side of her. She bade them join hands, and she laid her own left hand over both of theirs. Then she lifted her other hand high in the darkness and closed her eyes. In that instant, as if a connection had been made, the Warstone blazed so brightly it could not be looked upon, and when the blinding light was gone, so were the three of them.

When he woke it was quite dark in the Wood. Putting a hand to his head, Flidais could feel that his wound had healed. The pain seemed to be gone. So too, however, was his right ear. He sat up slowly and looked around. His father was there.

Cernan had crouched down on his haunches, not very far away, and was regarding him gravely, the horned head held motionless. Flidais met the gaze for a long moment in silence.

"Thank you," he said at length, speaking aloud.

The antlers dipped briefly in acknowledgment. Then Cernan said, also aloud, "He was not trying to kill you."

Nothing has changed, Flidais thought. *Nothing at all.* It was too old a pattern, laid down far too long ago, when both he and Galadan were young, for the anger or the hurt to be strong. He said mildly, "He wasn't trying not to, either."

Cernan said nothing. It was dark in the forest, the moon not yet high enough to lend silver to the place where they were. Both of them, though, could see very well in the dark, and Flidais, looking at his father, read sorrow and guilt, both, in the eyes of the god. It was the latter that disarmed him; it always had.

He said, with a shrug, "It could have been worse, I suppose."

The antlers moved again. "I healed the wound," his father said defensively.

"I know." He felt the ragged edge of tissue where his ear had been. "Tell me," he asked, "am I very ugly?"

Cernan tilted his magnificent head in appraisal. "No more than before," he said judiciously.

Flidais laughed. And so too, after a moment, did the god—a deep, rumbling, sensuous sound that reverberated through the Wood.

When the laughter subsided, it seemed very quiet among the trees, but only for those not tuned to Pendaran as were both of these, the forest god and his son. Even with only one ear, Flidais could hear the whispering of the Wood, the messages running back and forth like fire. It was why they were talking out loud: there was too much happening on the silent link. And there were other powers in Pendaran that night.

He was suddenly reminded of something. Of fire, to be precise. He said, "It really could have gone worse for me. I lied to him."

His father's eyes narrowed. "How so?"

"He wanted to know who had been in the Anor. He was aware that someone had. You know why. I said: only myself. Which was not true." He paused, then said softly, "Guinevere was, as well."

Cernan of the Beasts rose to his feet with a swift animal-lithe motion. "That," he said, "explains something."

"What?"

In response, Flidais was offered an image. It was his father who was offering, and Cernan had never done him actual harm, although, until just now, little good either. And so, in uncharacteristic trust, he opened his mind and received the image: a man walking swiftly through the forest with an utterly distinctive grace, not stumbling, even with the darkness and the entangling roots.

It was not the one he'd expected to see. But he knew, quite well, who this was, and so he knew what must have happened while he lay unconscious on the forest floor.

"Lancelot," he breathed, an unexpected note, most of the way to awe, in his voice. His mind raced. "He will have been in Cader Sedat. Of course. The Warrior will have awakened him. And she has sent him away again."

He had been in Camelot. Had seen those three in their first life, and seen them again, without their knowing him, in many of the returnings they had been forced to make. He knew the story. He was a part of it.

And now, he remembered with a flash of joy, like light in the darkness of the Wood, he knew the summoning name. That, however, brought back the memory of his oath. He said, "The child is in the Wood as well . . . Guinevere's child." And, urgently, "Where is my brother now?"

"He is running north," Cernan replied. For an instant he hesitated. "he passed by the child, not a hundred yards away . . . some time ago, while you slept. He did not see or sense him. You have friends in the Wood angry for your shed blood: he was offered no messages. No one is speaking to him."

Flidais closed his eyes and drew a ragged breath. So close. He had a vision of the wolf and the boy passing by each other in the blackness of the Wood in the hour before moonrise, passing by so near and not knowing, not ever to know. *Or did they?* he wondered. Was there a part of the soul that reached out, somehow, toward possibilities barely missed, futures that would never be, because of such a little distance in a forest at night? He felt a stir of air just then. Wind, with a hint—only imagined, perhaps—of something more.

He opened his eyes. He felt alert, sharpened, exalted still, by what had come to pass. There was no pain. He said, "I need you to do one thing for me. To help me keep an oath."

The dark eyes of Cernan flashed with anger. "You too?" he said softly, like a hunting cat. "I have done what I will. I have healed the damage my son did. How many of the Weaver's bonds would you have me break?"

"I too am your son," Flidais said, greatly daring, for he could feel the wrath of the god.

"I have not forgotten. I have done what I will do."

Flidais stood up. "I cannot bind the forest in a matter such as this. I am not strong enough. But I do not want the child killed, even though he burned the tree. I swore an oath. You are god of the Wood as well as the Beasts. I need your help."

Slowly, Cernan's anger seemed to fade away. Flidais had to look up a long way to see his father's face. "You are wrong. You do not need my help in this," the god said, from the majesty of his great height. "You have forgotten something, wise child. For reasons I will never accept, Rakoth's son has been given the Circlet of Lisen. The powers and spirits of the Wood will not harm him directly, not while he wears it. They will do something else, and you should know what that is, littlest one."

He did know. "The grove," he whispered. "He is being guided to the sacred grove."

"And against what will meet him there," said Cernan, "what will meet him and kill him, I have no power at all. Nor would I desire such power. Even could I do so, I would not intervene. He should never have been allowed to live. It is time for him to die, before he reaches his father and all hope ends."

He was turning to go, having said all he intended to say, having done the one thing he felt bound to do, when his son replied, in a voice deep as tree roots, "Perhaps, but I think not. I think there is more to this weaving. You too have forgotten something."

Cernan looked back. There was a first hint of silver in the space where they stood. It touched and molded his naked form. He had a place where he wanted to be when the moon rose, and the very thought of what would be waiting for him there stirred his desire. He stayed, though, for one more moment, waiting.

"*Lancelot,*" said Flidais.

And turned, himself, to run with that always unexpected speed toward the grove where Lisen had been born so long ago in the presence of all the goddesses and gods.

In his anger and confusion, the bitterness of rejection, Darien had run a long way into the forest before realizing that it was not the wisest thing to have done.

He hadn't intended to burn the tree, but events, the flow of what happened, never seemed to go the way he expected them to, they never seemed to go right. And when that happened, something else took place inside of him, and his power, the change in his eyes, came back and trees burned.

Even then, he'd only wanted the illusion—the same illusion of fire he'd shaped in the glade of the Summer Tree—but he'd been stronger this time, and uneasy in the presence of so many people, and his mother had been beautiful and cold and had sent him away. He hadn't been able to control what he did, and so the fire had been real.

And he'd run into the shadows of the Wood from what seemed to be the colder, more hurtful shadows on the beach.

It was quite dark by now, the moon had not yet risen, and gradually, as his rage receded, Darien became increasingly aware that he was in danger. He knew nothing of the history of the Great Wood, but he was of the andain himself and so could half understand the messages running through Pendaran, messages about him, and what he had done, and what he wore about his brow.

As the sense of danger increased, so too grew his awareness that he was being forced in a particular direction. He thought about taking his owl shape to fly over and out of the forest, but with the thought he became overwhelmingly conscious of weariness. He had flown a long way very fast in that form, and he didn't know if he could sustain it again. He was strong, but not infinitely so, and he usually needed a cresting tide of emotion to source his power: fear, hunger, longing, rage. Now he had none of them. He was aware of danger but couldn't summon any response to it.

Numbed, indifferent, alone, he stayed in his own shape, wearing the clothes Finn had worn, and followed, unresisting, the subtly shifting paths of Pendaran Wood, letting the powers of the forest guide him where they would, to whatever was waiting for him there. He heard their anger, and the anticipation of revenge, but he offered no response to it. He walked, not really caring about anything, thinking about his mother's imperious, cold face, her words: *What are you doing here? What do you want, Darien?*

What did he want? What could he be allowed to want, to hope for, dream of, desire? He had only been *born* less than a year ago. How could he know what he wanted? He knew only that his eyes could turn red like his father's, and when they did trees burned and everyone turned away from him. Even the Light turned away. It had been beautiful and serene and sorrowful, and the Seer had put it on his brow, and it had gone out as soon as it was clasped to him.

He walked, did not weep. His eyes were blue. The half-moon was rising; soon it would shine down through spaces in the trees. The Wood whispered triumphantly, malice in the leaves. He was guided, unresisting, the Circlet of Lisen on his brow, into the sacred grove of Pendaran Wood to be slain.

Numberless were the years that grove had lain steeped in its power. Nor was there any place in any world with roots so deeply woven into the Tapestry. Against the antiquity of this place even Mörnir's claiming of the Summer Tree in the Godwood of the High Kingdom had been but a blink of time ago—in the days when Iorweth had been summoned to Brennin from over the wide sea.

For thousands upon thousands of years before that day, Pendaran Wood had seen summers and winters in Fionavar, and through all the turnings and returnings of the seasons this grove and the glade within it had been the heart of the Wood. There was magic here. Ancient powers slumbered beneath the forest floor.

Here, more than a thousand years ago (a blink of time, no more), Lisen had been born in the rapt, silent presence of all the powers of the Wood and the shining company of the goddesses whose beauty had been hers from the beginning of her days. Here too had come Amairgen Whitebranch, first mortal, first child of the Weaver not born of the Wood, to dare a night in that grove, seeking a power for men that did not find its source in the blood magic of the priestesses. And here had he found that power, and more, as Lisen, wild and glorious, had returned to the violated glade of her birth to slay him in the morning and had fallen in love instead, and so left the Wood.

After that a great deal had changed. For the powers of the grove, for all of Pendaran, time ran up to the moment she had died, leaping from the balcony of the Anor, and then it moved forward more slowly, as if weighted down, from that day.

Since then, since those war-shattered days of the first coming of Rakoth Maugrim, only one other mortal had ever come into this place, and he too was a mage, a follower of Amairgen, and he was a thief. With guile and a cunning use of lore, Raederth the mage had known exactly when it might be safe to enter Pendaran in search of the thing he sought.

There was one day and one day only in every year when the Wood was vulnerable, when it grieved and could not guard itself. When the seasons came around to the day of Lisen's leap, the river running past the Anor ran red into the killing sea with the memory of her blood, and all the spirits of the forest that could do so gathered at the foot of the Tower to mourn, and all those that could not travel projected their awareness toward that place, to see the river and the Anor through the eyes of those assembled there.

And one year on the morning of that day Raederth came. Without his source, casting no aura of power, he had entered the sacred grove and knelt in the glade by the birthing place, and he had taken the Circlet of Lisen that lay shining on the grass.

By the time the sun went down and the river ran clear again into the sea, he had been running himself, for a whole day without pause, and was very near to the eastern fringes of the forest.

Pendaran had become aware of him then, and of what he had done, but all the mightiest powers of the Wood were gathered by the sea and there was agonizingly little they could do. They made the forest paths change for him, the trees shift and close menacingly about the fleeing man, but he was too near the Plain, he could see the tall grass in the light of the setting sun, and his will and courage were very strong, greater than those of any ordinary thief, and he made his way—though they hurt him, they hurt him badly—out of the forest and away south again with a shining thing held in his hands that only Lisen had ever worn.

So now it was with exultation, with a fierce collective joy, that Pendaran became aware that the Circlet had come home. Home and in pain, the spirits whispered to each other. It had to be in agony, with its light extinguished on the brow of one who had torched a tree. He would go mad and be flayed, mind and body both, before they released him to death. So they vowed, one to another: the deiena to the leaves of the sentient trees; the leaves to the silent powers and the singing ones; the dark, shapeless things of dread to the old, unmoving, deep-rooted forces that had once been trees and were now something more and intimately versed in hate.

For a moment the whispering stopped. In that instant they heard Cernan, their lord. They heard him say aloud that it was past time for this one to die, and they gloried in what he said. There would be no staying them, no god's voice to cry them off the kill.

The sacrifice was led to the grove: delicately he was guided, the forest paths made smooth and even for his tread; and as he walked his doom was decreed, and it was decided who would effect it. All the powers of the Wood were agreed: however bitter his sacrilege, however sharp the desire to kill lay upon them, they would not themselves act against one who wore Lisen's Circlet about his head.

There was another power, though, the mightiest of all. A power of earth, not of forest, not bound by the griefs and constraints of the Wood. Even as Darien was being guided, unresisting, to the sacred grove, the spirits of Pendaran sent down their summons to the guardian who slept below that place. They woke the Oldest One.

It was very dark in the forest, but even when he wasn't in his owl shape he could see very well at night. In some ways, in fact, the darkness was easier, which was another source of unease. It reminded him, this affinity, of the night voices calling from the winter of his boyhood and of how he had been drawn to them.

And *that* reminded him of Finn, who had held him back, and told him he had to hate the Dark, and then had left him alone. He remembered the day, he would always remember: the day of his first betrayal. He had made a flower in the snow and colored it with the power of his eyes.

It was quiet in the grove. Now that he was here, the whisper of the leaves had died down to a gentle rustle in the night. There was a scent in the air he did not recognize. The grass of the glade was even and smooth and soft under his feet. He could not see the moon. Overhead, the stars shone down from the narrow circle of sky framed by the looming trees.

They hated him. Trees, leaves, the soft grass, the spirits present behind the trunks of trees, the deiena peeking through the leaves—all of them hated him, he knew. He should be terrified, a part of him acknowledged. He should be wielding his own power to break free of this place, to make them all pay in flame and smoke for their hate.

He couldn't seem to do it. He was tired and alone, and he hurt in ways he could never have expressed. He was ready for an ending.

Near the northern edge of the glade there was a mound, grass-covered, and upon it there were night flowers open in the darkness. He walked over. The flowers were very beautiful; the scent of the grove came from them. Carefully, so as to give no further injury or offense, Darien sat down on the grass of the mound between two clusters of dark flowers.

Immediately there came a surging, thrashing sound of fury from the Wood. He leaped to his feet, an involuntary cry of protest escaping his throat. He'd been careful! He'd harmed nothing! He'd only wanted to sit awhile in the starlit silence before he died. His arms went out, openhanded, in a hopeless gesture of appeasement.

Gradually the sound faded, though there remained, after it was gone, a kind of drumming, a rumbling, scarcely audible, beneath the grass of the grove. Darien drew a breath and looked around again.

Nothing moved, save the leaves rustling slightly in the

breeze. On the lowest branch of one of the trees of the grove a small geiala perched, its soft furry tail held inquisitively high. It regarded him with a preternatural gravity. Had he been in his owl shape, Darien knew, the geiala would have fled frantically at first sight of him. But he appeared harmless now, he supposed. A curiosity. Only a boy at the mercy of the Wood—which was merciless.

It was all right, he decided, with a kind of desperate acceptance. It was even easier this way. Everyone, from the time of his first memories, had spoken to him of choice. Of Light and Dark, and choosing between the two. But they hadn't even been able to choose or decide about him among themselves: Pwyll, who'd taken him to the Summer Tree, had wanted Dari to be older, to come into this shape so he could come to greater knowledge. Cernan of the Beasts had wanted to know why he'd even been allowed to live. The white-haired Seer, fear in her eyes, had given him a shining object of Light and had watched with him as it went out. Then she'd sent him to his mother, who'd driven him away. Finn, even Finn, who'd told him to love the Light, had gone away without a farewell to find a kind of darkness of his own, in the wide spaces between the stars.

They spoke of choice, of his being balanced between his mother and his father. He was *too* finely balanced, he decided. It was too hard for all of them and, at the last, for him. It was easier this way, easier to surrender that need to decide, to give himself over to the Wood in this place of ancient power. To accept his dying, which would make things better for everyone. Dead, you couldn't be lonely, Darien thought. You couldn't be this hurt. They were all afraid of him, afraid of what he might do with the freedom to choose, of what he might become. They wouldn't have to be afraid any more.

He remembered the face of the lios alfar that last cold morning of winter by the Summer Tree—how beautiful and shining he had been. And how afraid. He remembered the Seer with her white hair. She'd given him a gift, which no stranger had ever done, but he'd seen her eyes, the doubt and apprehension, even before the Light went out. It was true: they were all afraid of what he would choose.

Except his mother.

The thought found him totally unprepared. It hit with the force of revelation. *She* wasn't afraid of what he might do. She was the only one who hadn't tried to lure him, like the storm voices, or persuade him like the Seer. She had not tried to bind him to her, or even suggest a path to him. She had sent him away because the choice was his own, and she was the only one willing to allow that to be so. Maybe, he thought suddenly, maybe she trusted him.

In the grove, in the darkness, he saw the flowers on the mound where Lisen had been born, and he saw them clearly with the night vision of his father, thinking of his mother as he did.

For some reason, then, he remembered Vae and Shahar, the first mother and father he'd known. He thought about his two fathers: the one, a helpless minor soldier in the army of Brennin, obedient to the impersonal orders of the High King, unable to stay by his wife and sons in the winter cold, unable to keep them warm; the other, a god and the strongest god, shaper of winter and war. Feared, as he, Darien, was feared for being his son.

He was supposed to choose between them.

Looked at one way, there was no choice at all to be made. His sight in the darkness, the fear he aroused, the dying of the Light on his brow, all spoke to that. It was as if the choice had already been made. On the other hand—

He never finished the thought.

"It would please me if you pleaded for your life."

If the rocks of the earth's crust could speak, they would have sounded like that. The words were a rumbling, a sliding, as of gigantic stones lurching into motion, a prelude to avalanche and earthquake.

Darien wheeled. There was a shape darker than darkness in the glade, and there was a huge hole in the ground, jagged and irregular, beside the creature that had spoken with the voice of the earth. Fear leaped in Darien, primeval, instinctive, despite all his resignation of the moments before. He felt his eyes explode to red; he lifted his hands, fingers spread, pointing—

And nothing happened.

There came a laugh, deep and low, like a shifting of boulders long at rest. "Not here," said the shape. "Not in this grove, and not untutored as you are. I have your name, and your father's. It is clear what you might become; enough, even, to test me somewhat had we met long after this. But tonight you are nothing in this place. You do not go nearly deep enough. It would please me," it said again, "to hear you plead."

Darien lowered his arms. He felt his eyes return to the blue he had from neither father nor mother, the blue that was his own; perhaps the only thing that was. He was silent, and in that silence he regarded what had come under the half-moon that rose at last above the eastern trees to shine palely down.

It held to no fixed shape or hue. Even as he watched, the creature oscillated ceaselessly through amorphous forms. It had four arms, then three, then none. Its head was a man's, then a hideous mutant shape covered with slugs and maggots, then a boulder, featureless, as the maggots fell back into the grass and the gaping hole beside it. It was grey, and mottled brown, and black; it was huge. In all the blurred shiftings of its shape it had two legs, always, and one of them, Darien saw, was deformed. In one hand it carried a hammer that was the grey-black color of wet clay and was almost as large as Darien himself.

Again it spoke, amid the suddenly absolute, fearful silence of the forest, and again it said, "Will you not plead, Circlet-bearer? Give me a voice to carry back to my sleep under stone. They have asked me to leave you alive, tree-burner. They want your flesh and your mind to flay when the Circlet is gone from your brow. I will offer you an easier, quicker release, if you but ask for it. Ask, grove-defiler. Only ask; there is nothing else you can do."

The face was almost human now, but huge and grey, and there were worms crawling over it, in and out of the nose and mouth. The voice was the thickened voice of earth and stone. It said, "It is night in the sacred grove, son of Maugrim. You are nothing beside me, and less than that. You do not go nearly deep enough even to make me swing my hammer."

"*I do,*" said another voice, and Lancelot du Lac entered the moonlit grove.

They were sleeping on the beach just south of the Anor. Brendel had disobeyed Flidais' instructions to the extent of going inside alone and bringing out blankets and bedding from the lower rooms where Lisen's guards had slept. He did not go upstairs again, for fear of once more stirring Galadan's awareness of that place.

On a pallet beside Arthur, a little apart from the others, Jennifer lay in the motionless sleep of utter exhaustion. Her head was on his shoulder, one hand rested on his broad chest, and her golden hair was loose on the pillow they shared. Wide awake, the Warrior listened to her breathing and felt the beat of the heart he loved.

Then the heartbeat changed. She hurtled bolt upright, instantly awake, her gaze riveted on the high, watching moon. Her face was so white it made her hair look dark. He saw her draw a shuddering, afflicted breath. He felt it as a pain within himself.

He said, "He is in danger, Guinevere?"

She said nothing at all, her gaze never leaving the face of the moon. One hand was over her mouth. He took the other, as gently as he could. It trembled like an aspen leaf in an autumn wind. It was colder than it should ever have been in the mild midsummer night.

He said, "What do you see? Is he in danger, Guinevere?"

"They both are," she whispered, eyes on the moon. "They both are, my love. And I sent them both away."

He was silent. He looked up at the moon, and he thought of Lancelot. He held one of Guinevere's hands clasped between both of his own broad, square ones, and he wished her peace and heart's ease with longing fiercer and more passionate than any he had ever felt for his own release from doom.

"I go as deep as you," said the tall man quietly as he entered the glade. He had a drawn sword in his hand; it shimmered faintly, catching the silver of the moon. "I know who you are," he went on, speaking softly and without haste. "I know you Curdardh, and whence you come. I am here as champion of this child. If you wish his death, you will have first to accomplish my own."

"Who are you?" the demon rumbled. The trees were loud again all around them, Darien realized. He looked at the man who had come and he wondered.

"I am Lancelot," he heard. A memory stirred at the back of his mind, a memory of games-playing with Finn in the winter snow. A game of the Warrior, with his King Spear and his friend, his *tanist,* Finn had said. First of the Warrior's company, whose name was Lancelot. Who had loved the Warrior's Queen, whose name, whose name . . .

The demon, Curdardh, shifted position, with a sound of granite dragging over grass. It hefted its hammer and said, "I had not thought to see you here, but I am not surprised." It laughed softly, gravel rolling down a slope. It shifted shape again. It had two heads now, and both were demon heads. It said, "I will claim no quarrel with you, Lancelot, and Pendaran knows that you lived a winter in a forest and did no evil there. You will come to no harm if you leave here now, but I must kill you if you stay."

With an absolutely focused inner quietude, Lancelot said, "You must try to kill me. It is not an easy task, Curdardh, even for you."

"I am deep as the earth's core, swordsman. My hammer was forged in a pit so deep the fire burns downward." It was said as a fact, without bravado. "I have been here since Pendaran was here," said Curdardh, the Oldest One. "For all that time I held this grove sacrosanct, waking only when it was violated. You have a blade and unmatched skill with it. It will not be enough. I am not without mercy. *Leave!*"

With the last rumbled command, the trees at the edge of the grove shook and the earth rocked. Darien fought to keep his balance. Then, as the tremor came to an end, Lancelot said, with a courtesy strangely, eerily befitting to the place, "I have more than you think, though I thank you for the kindness of your praise. You should know, before we begin, for we are going to do battle here, Curdardh, that I have lain dead in Caer Sidi, which is Cader Sedat, which is the Corona Borealis of the Kings among the stars. You will know that that castle lies at the axle-tree of all the worlds, with the sea pounding at its walls and all the stars of heaven turning about it."

Darien's heart was racing, though he understood only a fragment of what he had heard. He had remembered something else: Finn, who in those days had seemed to know everything there was in the world to know, had told him that his mother had been a Queen. The knowledge made everything even more confusing than it had been already. He swallowed. He felt like a child.

"Even so," Curdardh was saying to Lancelot. "Even with where you have lain, you are mortal, swordsman. Would you die for the son of Rakoth Maugrim?"

"I am here," said Lancelot simply, and the battle began.

Chapter 8

His secretary, Shalhassan of Cathal decided, at about the same moment, had not been born for the military life. Raziel on horseback was just a pale shadow—almost literally, in fact—of his usual efficient self. Already the Supreme Lord had been forced to pause twice in his dictation while Raziel rummaged frantically in his saddlebag to replace a broken stylus. Waiting, Shalhassan ran his fingers through his long pleated beard and scanned the moonlit road in front of his racing chariot.

They were in Brennin, on the road from Seresh to the capital, riding by moonlight and at speed because war demanded such things of men. It was a mild summer night, though the tail end of a major storm had whipped through Seresh late in the day, when he and his reinforcements from Cathal had crossed the river.

Raziel retrieved a stylus and promptly dropped it, as he attempted to shift his grip on the reins of his horse. Shalhassan betrayed not a flicker of response. With his feet firmly on the ground, Raziel was quite good at what he did; Shalhassan was willing, marginally, to allow him this deviation from absolute competence. With a wave of his hand he dismissed his secretary to fall back into the ranks. The dictation could wait until they reached Paras Derval.

They were not far away. Shalhassan had a sudden vivid recollection of the last time he'd taken this road eastward at the head of an army. It had been a winter's day, diamond-bright, and he'd been met in the road by a Prince in a white fur cloak and a white hat, with a red djena feather, brilliant against the snow, for ornament.

And now, not two weeks later, the snow was utterly gone and the glittering Prince was betrothed to Shalhassan's daughter. He was also away at sea; there had been no word in Seresh as to the fate of the ship that had sailed for Spiral Castle.

There *had* been word of the High King: he had ridden north at the head of the army of Brennin and those of Cathal who were already there, in response to a summonglass calling from Daniloth, the same night *Prydwen* had set sail. Shalhassan nodded tersely to his charioteer and gripped the front rail more firmly as they picked up speed. It was probably unnecessary, he knew. The odds were that he and this second contingent were too late to constitute anything but a rear guard at this stage, but he wanted to see Gorlaes, the Chancellor, to confirm that, and he also wanted to see his daughter.

They went very fast in the moonlight. A short time later he was in Paras Derval, and then he was being ushered, travel-stained, allowing himself no luxury of time to change his clothing, into the torchlit Great Hall of the palace where Gorlaes stood, one dutiful step below the level of the empty throne. The Chancellor bowed to him, the triple obeisance, which was unexpected and gratifying. Beside Gorlaes, and a farther step below him, stood someone else who also bowed, as deferentially though rather less ornately, which was understandable, given who it was.

Then Tegid of Rhoden, Intercedent for Prince Diarmuid, told the Supreme Lord of Cathal that Sharra had gone away, and stood flinching in anticipation of the explosion that had to come.

Inwardly, it did. Fear and a towering rage exploded in Shalhassan's breast, but neither found expression in his face or bearing. There was ice in his voice, though, as he asked where and with whom.

It was Gorlaes who answered. "She went with the Seer and the High Priestess, my lord. They did not tell us where. If I may say so, there is wisdom in both . . . in all three of them. I do not think—"

He stopped short at a keen glance from Shalhassan, whose gaze had quelled more formidable speakers than this one. At the same time, Shalhassan was aware that his rage had already sluiced away, leaving only the fear. He himself had never been able to keep his daughter under control. How could he expect this fat man and the overextended Chancellor to do better?

He also remembered the Seer very well, and his respect for her went deep. For what she had done one night in the Temple at Gwen Ystrat—knifing her way alone into the darkness of Rakoth's designs to show them the source of winter—he would always honor her. If she had gone away it was to a purpose, and the same applied to the High Priestess, who was equally formidable in her own way.

However formidable they both were, though, he doubted they would have been able to stop his daughter from joining them, if she'd decided that was what she wanted to do. *Oh, Sharra,* he thought. For the ten-thousandth time he wondered if he had been wise not to remarry when his wife died. The girl had needed *some* sort of guidance, that much was more and more evident.

He looked up. Above and behind the Oak Throne of Brennin, set high in the walls of the Great Hall were the stained-glass windows of Delevan. The one behind the throne showed Conary and Colan riding north to war. The light of the half-moon, shining outside, silvered their yellow hair. Well, Shalhassan thought, it would be up to their successor, the young High King, Aileron, to wage whatever war the northlands would see now. The instructions were as he'd expected—as, indeed, they had to be. He would have done exactly the same thing. The men of the second contingent of Cathal, under the leadership of their Supreme Lord, were to remain in Brennin, distributed as Shalhassan and Gorlaes deemed wisest, to guard the High Kingdom and Cathal beyond, as best they could.

He drew his gaze slowly down from the glory of the window. Looking at Tegid—a contrast worthy of an aphorism—he said kindly, "Do not reproach yourself. The Chancellor is right—the three of them will know what they are doing. You may join me, if you like, in sympathizing with your Prince, who will have to deal with her from henceforth. If we survive."

He turned to the Chancellor. "I would appreciate food, my lord Gorlaes, and instruction to my captains for the quartering of my men. After that, if you are not weary, I wonder if we might share some wine and a game of ta'bael? That may be the closest we two get to war, it seems, and I find it soothes me to play at night."

The Chancellor smiled. "Ailell used to say the same thing, my lord. I will be glad to play with you, though I must warn that I am an indifferent player at best."

"Might I come watch?" the fat man asked diffidently.

Shalhassan scrutinized him. "Do you play ta'bael?" he asked dubiously.

"A little," said Tegid.

The Supreme Lord of Cathal pulled his sole remaining Rider backward, interposing it in defense of his Queen. He favored his opponent with a glance that had made more than one man contemplate a ritual suicide.

"I think," he said, more to himself than to either of the other two men, "that I have just been set up quite royally."

Gorlaes, watching, grunted in commiseration. Tegid of Rhoden picked off the intervening Rider with his Castle.

"Prince Diarmuid insists," he murmured, putting the captured piece beside the board, "that every member of his band know how to play ta'bael properly. None of us have ever beaten him, though." He smiled and leaned back in his chair, patting his unmatched girth complacently.

Studying the board intently, searching for a defense to the two-pronged attack that would be unleashed as soon as Tegid moved the Castle again, Shalhassan decided to divert some of his earlier sympathy to his daughter, who was going to have to live with this Prince.

"Tell me," he asked, "does Aileron also play?"

"Ailell taught both his sons when they were children," Gorlaes murmured, filling Shalhassan's wine flask from a beaker of South Keep vintage.

"And does the High King also play now at some rarified level of excellence?" Shalhassan noted the hint of exasperation in his voice. The two sons of Ailell seemed to elicit that in him.

"I have no idea," Gorlaes replied. "I've never seen him play as an adult. He was very good, when he was a boy. He used to play with his father all the time."

"He doesn't play ta'bael any more," said Tegid. "Don't you know the story? Aileron hasn't touched a piece since the first time Diarmuid beat him when they were boys. He's like that, you know."

Absorbing this, considering it, Shalhassan moved his Mage threateningly along the diagonal. It was a trap, of course, the last one he had. To help it along, he distracted the fat man with a question. "I don't know. Like what?"

Pushing hard on the arms of his chair, Tegid levered himself forward to see the board more clearly. Ignoring the trap and the question, both, he slid his Castle laterally, exposing Shalhassan's Queen once more to attack and simultaneously threatening the Cathalian Lord's own King. It was quite decisive.

"He doesn't like to lose at anything," Tegid explained. "He doesn't do things when he thinks he might lose."

"Doesn't that limit his activities somewhat?" Shalhassan said testily. He didn't much like losing, himself. Nor was he accustomed to it.

"Not really," said Tegid, a little reluctantly. "He's extremely good at almost everything. Both of them are," he added loyally.

With such grace as he could muster, Shalhassan tipped his King sideways in surrender and raised his glass to the victor.

"A good game," said Tegid genially. "Tell me," he added, turning to Gorlaes, "have you any decent ale here? Wine is all very well, but I'm grievously thirsty tonight, if you want to know the truth."

"A pitcher of ale, Vierre," the Chancellor advised the page standing silently in the doorway.

"Two!" Shalhassan said, surprising himself. "Set up the pieces for another game!"

He lost that one, too, but won the third decisively, with immense evening-redeeming satisfaction. Then both he and Tegid made cursory work of Gorlaes in two other games. It was all unexpectedly congenial. And then, quite late at night, he and the Chancellor further surprised themselves by accepting a highly unorthodox suggestion from the sole member of Prince Diarmuid's band remaining in Paras Derval.

What was even more surprising to Shalhassan, ultimately,

was how entertaining he found the music and the ambience and the undeniably pert serving women in the huge downstairs room of the Black Boar tavern and in a smaller, darker room upstairs.

It was a late night.

If he did nothing further, Paul thought, nothing at all from now until whatever ending lay waiting for them, no one could tax him with not having done his share.

He was lying on the strand near the river, a little apart, as usual, from all the others. He had lain awake for hours, watching the wheeling stars, listening to the sea. The moon had climbed as high as it could go and was westering now. It was very late.

He lay by himself and thought about the night he had ended the drought and then about the predawn hour when he had seen the Soulmonger and summoned Liranan, with Gereint's aid, to battle Rakoth's monster in the sea. And then he let his mind come forward to the moment, earlier this evening, when he had spoken with the voice of Mörnir, and the sea god had answered again and stilled the waves to let the mariners of *Prydwen* survive the Weaver's storm.

He had also, he knew, done something else almost a year ago: his had been the crossing between the worlds that had saved Jennifer from Galadan and allowed Darien to be born.

He wondered if those who came after would curse his name for that. He wondered if there would be anyone to come after.

He had done his part in this war. No one could question that. Furthermore, he knew, no one but himself would even think to raise the issue. The reproaches here, the sleeplessness, the striving, always, for something *more*—all of it was internal, a part of the pattern of his life.

The pattern that seemed woven into what he was, even in Fionavar. It lay at the heart of why Rachel had left him, it encompassed the solitariness Kevin Laine had tried so hard to break through—and had, in some way Paul still hadn't found time to assimilate.

But solitude appeared, truly, to be bound into the tangled roots of what he was. Alone on the Summer Tree he'd come into his power, and it seemed that even in the midst of a great many people, he still came into it alone. His gift seemed profoundly secret, even from himself. It was cryptic and self-contained, shaped of hidden lore, and solitary stubborn resistance to the Dark. He could speak with gods and hear them but never move among them, and every such exchange drew him farther away from everyone he knew, as if he'd needed something to do that. Not feeling the cold of the winter or the lash of the rain that had passed. Sent back by the God. He was the arrow of Mörnir, and arrows flew alone.

He was, he realized, hopelessly far from falling asleep. He looked at the half-moon, out over the sea. It seemed to be calling him.

He rose, with the sound of the surf loud in his ears. North, toward the Anor, he could see the shadows that were the sleeping men of South Keep. Behind him the river ran west toward the sea. He followed it. As he walked, the sand became pebbles and then boulders. He climbed up on one of them by the water's edge and saw, by moonlight, that he was not the only sleepless person on the beach that night.

He almost turned back. But something—a memory of another beach the night before *Prydwen* had sailed—made him hesitate, and then speak to the figure sitting on the dark rock nearest to the lapping waves.

"We seem to be reversing roles. Shall I give you a cloak?" It came out more sardonically than he'd intended. But it didn't seem to matter. Her icy self-possession was unsettlingly complete.

Without turning or startling, her gaze still on the water, Jaelle murmured, "I'm not cold. You were, that night. Does it bother you so much?"

Immediately he was sorry he'd spoken. This always seemed to happen when they met: this polarity of Dana and Mörnir. He half turned to climb back down and away but then stopped, held by stubbornness more than anything else.

He drew a breath and, carefully keeping any inflection

from his voice, said, "It really doesn't, Jaelle. I spoke by way of greeting, nothing more. Not everything anyone says to you has to be taken as a challenge."

This time she did turn. Her hair was held back by the silver circlet, but the ends still lifted and blew in the sea breeze. He could not make out her eyes; the moonlight was behind her, shining on his own face. For a long moment they were both silent; then Jaelle said, "You have an unusual way of greeting people, Twiceborn."

He let out his breath. "I know," he conceded. "Especially you." He took a step, and a short jump down, and sat on the boulder nearest to hers. The water slapped below them; he could taste salt in the spray.

Not answering, Jaelle turned back to look out to sea. After a moment, Paul did the same. They sat like that for a long time; then something occurred to him. He said, "You're a long way from the Temple. How were you planning to return?"

She pushed a loop of hair back with an impatient hand. "Kimberly. The mage. I didn't really think about it. She needed to come here quickly, and I was the only way."

He smiled, then suppressed it, lest she think he was mocking her. "At the risk of being cursed or some such thing, may I say that that sounds uncharacteristically unselfish?"

She turned sharply, glaring at him. Her mouth opened and then closed, and even by moonlight he could see her flush.

"I didn't mean that to sting," he added quickly. "Truly, Jaelle. I have some idea of what it meant for you to do this."

Her color slowly faded. Where the moon touched it her hair gleamed with a strange, unearthly shading of red. Her circlet shone. She said simply, "I don't think you do. Not even you, Pwyll."

"Then tell me," he said. "Tell someone something, Jaelle." He was surprised at the intensity in his voice.

"Are you one to talk?" she shot back reflexively. But then, as he kept silent, she added, more slowly and in a different voice, "I named someone to act in my stead, but I broke the patterns of succession when I did so."

"Do I know her?"

She smiled wryly. "Actually, you do. The one who spied on us last year."

He felt the edge of a shadow pass over him. He looked up quickly. No clouds across the moon; it was in his mind.

"Leila? Is it a presumption to ask why? Is she not very young?"

"You know she is," Jaelle said sharply. Then, again as if fighting her own impulses, she went on. "As to why: I am not certain. An instinct, a premonition. As I told you all earlier this evening, she is still tuned to Finn, and so to the Wild Hunt. I am not easy with it, though. I don't know what it means. Do you always know why you do what you do, Pwyll?"

He laughed bitterly, touched on the raw nerve that had kept him awake. "I used to think I did. Not any more. Since the Tree I'm afraid I don't know why I do *any* of what I do. I'm going by instinct too, Jaelle, and I'm not used to it. I don't seem to have any control at all. Do you want to know the truth?" The words tumbled out of him, low and impassioned. "I almost envy you and Kim—you both seem so sure of your places in this war."

Her face grave, she considered that. Then she said, "Don't envy the Seer, Pwyll. Not her. And as for me . . ." She turned away toward the water again. "As for me, I have been feeling uneasy in my own sanctuary, which has never happened before. I don't think I need be an object of anyone's envy."

"I'm sorry," he said, risking it.

And seemed to fail, as her glance flashed swiftly back to him.

"That is presumption," she said coldly, "and unasked for." He held her gaze, refusing to yield to it but reaching, nonetheless, for something to say. Even as he did, her expression changed and she added, "In any case, such sorrow as you might feel would be balanced—overbalanced, in truth—by Audiart's pleasure, did she learn of this. She would sing for joy, and, Dana knows, she cannot sing."

Paul let his mouth drop open. "Jaelle," he whispered, "did you just make a joke?"

She gestured in exasperation. "What do you think we are in the Temple?" she snapped. "Do you think we stalk around intoning chants and curses day and night, and gathering blood for amusement?"

He left a little silence before answering, over the sound of the waves. "That sounds about right," he said gently. "You haven't been at pains to suggest otherwise."

"There are reasons for that," Jaelle shot back, quite unfazed. "You are sufficiently acquainted with power by now, surely, to be able to guess why. But the truth is that the Temples have been my only home for a long time now, and there was laughter there, and music, and quiet pleasures to be found, until the drought came, and then the war."

The problem with Jaelle, or one of the problems, he decided wryly, was that she was right too much of the time. He nodded. "Fair enough. But if I was wrong you must concede that it was because you wanted me to be wrong. You can't tax me with that misunderstanding now. That's one blade that shouldn't cut both ways."

"They all cut both ways," she said quietly. He had known she would say that. In many ways she was still very young, though it seldom showed.

"How old were you when you entered the Temple?" he asked.

"Fifteen," she answered, after a pause. "And seventeen when I was named to the Mormae."

He shook his head. "That is very—"

"Leila was fourteen. She is only fifteen now," she cut in, anticipating him. "And because of what I did this morning, she is of the Mormae now herself, and even more than that."

"What do you mean?"

She fixed him with a careful regard. "I have your silence on this?"

"You know you do."

Jaelle said, "Because I named her to act for me while I was away and in a time of war, it will follow, by the patterns of Dana, that if I do not return to Paras Derval, Leila is High Priestess. At fifteen."

Despite himself, he felt another chill, though the night was mild and the skies fair. "You knew this. You knew this when you named her, didn't you?" he managed to ask.

"Of course," she said, with more than a trace of her effortless scorn. "What do you think I am?"

"I don't really know," he said honestly. "Why did you do it, then?"

The question was direct enough to give her pause. At length, she answered, "I told you a few moments ago: instinct, intuition. I have little more than those, much of the time, which is something for you to consider. You were lamenting your lack of control just now. Power such as ours is not so easy to manipulate, nor, in truth, should it be. I do not command Dana, I speak for her. And so, it seems to me, do you speak for the God, when he chooses to speak. You might give thought, Twiceborn of Mörnir, as to whether control matters too much to you."

And with the words, he was suddenly on a highway in the rain again, hearing the woman he loved tax him with the same cold flaw, hearing her announce that she was leaving because of it, unable to find a place in him where need of her found a true voice.

He seemed to be on his feet, standing above the Priestess by the sea. He wasn't sure how that had happened. He looked down and saw his hands clenched at his sides. And then he turned and was walking away, not from the truth, for that came with him under the stars, but from the icy green eyes and the voice that had spoken that truth here.

She watched him go, and suprised herself with regret. She had not meant to wound. Dana knew, she'd intended to hurt with so many things she'd said to him at one time or another, but not with that last. It had been kindly meant, as much so as lay within her nature, and instead she'd found a place where he was raw and vulnerable.

She should, she knew, keep that knowledge in readiness for encounters to come. But sitting on the rock, thinking back over what they each had said, it was hard to hold to such cold, controlling thoughts. She smiled a little to herself at the irony and turned back toward the sea—to see a ghost ship passing between herself and the setting moon.

"*Pwyll!*" She cried the name almost without thought. She was on her feet, her heart pounding with terror and awe.

She could not take her eyes from the ship. Slowly it moved from north to south across her line of sight, though the wind was from the west. Its sails were tattered and ragged, and the low moon shone through them easily. It lit the broken masts, the shattered figurehead, the smashed upheaval of the deck where the tiller was. Low down by the waterline she thought she could see a dark hole in the side of the ship where the sea must have rushed in.

There was no way that ship could remain afloat.

She heard Pwyll's quick, running footsteps, and then he was beside her again. She did not turn or speak. She registered the sharp intake of his breath and voiced an inward prayer of relief: he, too, saw the ship. It was not a phantom of her own mind, not a prelude to madness.

Suddenly he extended one hand, pointing in silence. She followed the line of his finger.

There was a man, a solitary mariner, standing near the front of the ship by the railing nearest to them, and the moon was shining through him as well.

He was lifting something in his hands, holding it out over the side of the ship toward the two of them, and Jaëlle saw, with a second surge of awe, that it was a spear.

"I would be grateful for your prayers," said Pwyll.

She heard a beat of unseen wings. She looked up and then quickly back to him. She saw him step down off the rock where they stood.

And begin to walk across the waves toward the ship.

The provinces of Dana ended at the sea. Nevertheless, thought Jaëlle, the High Priestess. Nevertheless. She closed her eyes for the first step, knowing she was going to sink, and set out after him.

She did not sink. The waves barely wet the sandals she wore. She opened her eyes, saw Pwyll striding purposefully in front of her, and quickened her pace to catch up.

She received a startled glance as she came abreast. "You may need more than prayers," she said shortly. "And invocations of Dana hold no sway at sea; I told you that once before."

"I remember," he said, stepping a little upward to clear an advancing wave. "Which makes you either very brave or very foolish indeed. Shall we call it both?"

"If you like," she said, masking an unexpected rush of pleasure. "And accept that I am sorry if what I said before caused you pain. For once, I hadn't meant it."

"For once," he repeated dryly, but she was finally beginning to catch the shifting tones in his voice, and this was mild irony and nothing more. "I know you didn't mean it," he said, negotiating a trough between waves. "I did that one to myself. I'll try to explain someday, if you like."

She said nothing, concentrating on moving over the water. The sensation was uncanny. Jaelle felt perfectly, flawlessly balanced. She had to watch where they were going, and what the sea was doing in front of them, but having done so, it was no trouble to skim along the surface. The hem of her robe was wet; nothing more. If they hadn't been walking toward a ship that had been destroyed a thousand years ago, she might even have found it pleasurable.

As it was, though, the closer they came, the more eerily translucent loomed that hollow craft. As they came alongside, Jaelle could clearly see the gaping holes torn in it at the waterline, and in the exposed hold of Amairgen's ship, the sea sparkled with moonlight.

For such, of course, it was. There was nothing else it could be, not in the bay of the Anor Lisen. She had absolutely no idea what power kept it in the visible world, let alone afloat. But she did know, beyond doubt, who the one mariner high above them had to be. For a moment, when they stopped, standing upon the waves just below that tall, ghostly figure, Jaelle thought about the power of love, and she did pray then, briefly, for Lisen's peace at the Weaver's side.

Then Amairgen spoke, or what was left of him spoke, after so long a death, with the moonlight shining through. He said, in a voice like a deep-toned reed played by the wind, "Why have you come?"

Jaelle felt herself rocked, her balance slipped. She had expected—though she couldn't think why—a welcome. Not this cold, flat query. Suddenly the sea seemed terrifyingly dark and deep, the land a long way off. She felt an impersonal hand on her elbow steadying her. Pwyll waited until he saw her nod, before turning his attention back to the one who had spoken from the deck above their heads.

She saw him look up at the mage slain by the Soulmonger. Pale at the best of times, Pwyll was white and ghostly himself in the long moonlight. There was no flicker of doubt in his eyes, though, no hesitation in his voice as he made reply.

"We have come for the spear, unquiet one. And to bring you the tidings you have sought this many a year."

"Someone was in the Tower," the ghost cried. It seemed to Jaelle as if the wind lifted with the pain in the words, the long burden of loss. "Someone was in the Tower, and so I am come again, where I never came as living man, to the place where she died. Who stood in that room to draw me back?"

"Guinevere," said Pwyll, and waited.

Amairgen was silent. Jaelle was aware of the rocking of the sea beneath her. She glanced down a moment and then quickly back up: it had seemed to her, dizzyingly, that she'd seen stars below her feet.

Amairgen leaned forward over the railing. She was the High Priestess of Dana, and standing above her was the ghost of the one who had broken the power of Dana in Fionavar. She should curse him, a part of her was saying, curse him as the priestesses of the Goddess did at the turning of every month. She should let her blood fall in the sea below where she stood as she spoke the most bitter invocation of the Mother. It was, as much as anything had ever been, her duty. But she could not do it. Such hatred for his ancient deed was not within her tonight, nor would it ever be again, she somehow knew. There was too much pain, too pure a sorrow here. All the stories seemed to be merging into each other. She gazed up at him and at what he held and kept silent, watching.

He was foreshortened by the angle, but she could descry his chiseled, translucent features, the long pale locks of his hair, and the mighty gleaming spear he cradled in both his hands. He wore a ring on one finger; she thought she knew what it was.

"Is the Warrior here, then?" Amairgen asked, a breath on a moonlit reed.

"He is," said Pwyll. And added, after a moment, "So too is Lancelot."

"What!"

Even in darkness and from where she stood, Jaelle saw his eyes suddenly gleam like sapphires in the night. His hands shifted along the spear. Pwyll waited, unhurried, for the figure above them to absorb the implications of that.

Then, both of them standing on the tossing waves beside the ship heard Amairgen say, very formally now, "What tidings have you for me after so long?"

Jaelle, surprised, saw tears on Pwyll's face. He said, very gently, "Tidings of rest, unquiet one. You are avenged, your staff has been redeemed. The Soulmonger of Maugrim is dead. Go home, first of the mages, beloved of Lisen. Sail home between the stars to the Weaver's side and be granted peace after all these years. We have gone to Cader Sedat and destroyed the evil there with the power of your staff held by one who followed you: by Loren Silvercloak, First Mage of Brennin. What I tell you tonight is true. I am the Twiceborn of Mörnir, Lord of the Summer Tree."

There came a sound then that Jaelle never forgot for what was left of her days. It came not from Amairgen but, rather, seemed to rise from the ship itself, though no one at all was to be seen: a high keening sound, twinned somehow to the slanting moon in the west, balanced achingly between ecstasy and pain. She realized, suddenly, that there *were* other ghosts here, though they could not be seen. Others manned that doomed ship.

Then Amairgen spoke, over the sound of his mariners, and he said to Pwyll, "If this is so, if it has come to pass, then in the name of Mörnir I release the Spear into your trust. But there is one thing I will ask of you, one thing further that is needed before I can rest. There is one more death."

For the first time she saw Pwyll hesitate. She didn't know why, but she did know something else, and she said, "Galadan?"

She heard Pwyll draw a breath, even as she felt the sapphire eyes of the one who had found the skylore fix themselves on her own. She willed herself not to flinch.

She heard him say, "You are a long way from your Temples and your thirsty axe, Priestess. Do you not fear the killing sea?"

"I fear the Unraveller more," she said, pleased to hear her voice strong and unwavering. *The killing sea,* she registered, sorrowing: *Lisen.* "And I hate the Dark more than I ever hated you, or any of the mages who followed you. I am saving my curses for Maugrim, and"—she swallowed—"and I will pray, after tonight, to Dana, for your peace and Lisen's." She ended, ritually, as Pwyll had done, "What I tell you tonight is true. I am the High Priestess of the Goddess in Fionavar."

What have I said? she thought in bemused wonder. But she kept that, she hoped, from her eyes. Gravely, he looked down upon her from the ruined ship, and she could see, for the first time, something in him that went beyond power and pain. He had been loved, she remembered. And had loved so much that it had bound him in grief, beyond death through all the years, to this bay where Lisen had died.

Over the sounds that came from the torn hulk of his ship, Amairgen said, "I will be grateful for your prayers."

Pwyll's words earlier, she thought, exactly his words. It seemed to her that this had become a night outside of time, where everything signified, in some way or another.

"Galadan," Amairgen repeated. The wailing from the dark ship was louder now. Joy and pain, she heard them both. She saw the moon shine through the sundered hulk. It was dissolving, even as she watched. "Galadan," Amairgen cried, one last time, looking down at the Twiceborn as he spoke.

"I have sworn it," said Pwyll, and Jaelle heard, for the first time, a doubt in his voice. She saw him draw a breath and lift his head higher. "I have sworn that he is mine," he said, and this time it carried.

"Be it so," said Amairgen's ghost. "May your thread never be lost." He was starting to fade; she could see a star shine through him. He raised the spear, preparing to drop it over the side to them.

The provinces of Dana ended at the sea; she had no power here. But she was still what she was, and a thought came to Jaelle then, as she stood on the dark waves.

"*Wait!*" she cried, sharp and clear in the starry night. "Amairgen, hold!"

She thought it was too late, he was already so translucent,

the ship so ephemeral they could see the low moon through its timbers. The wailing of the invisible mariners seemed to be coming from very far away.

He came back, though. He did not let loose the spear, and slowly, as they watched, he took again a more substantial form. The ship had gone silent, bobbing on the gentle swells of the bay.

Beside her, Pwyll said nothing, waiting. There was nothing, she knew, he could say. He had done what he could: had recognized this ship for what it was, had known the spear and ventured forth out over the waves to claim it and set the mage free of his long, tormented sailing. He had brought tidings of revenge, and so of release.

The other thing, what might happen now, was hers, for he could not know what she knew.

The mage's cold, spectral gaze was fixed upon her. He said, "Speak, Priestess. Why should I hold for you?"

"Because I have a question to ask, speaking not only for Dana but in the name of Light." Suddenly she was afraid of her own thought, of what she wanted from him.

"Ask it then,"Amairgen said, high above.

She had been High Priestess for too long to be so direct, even now. She said, "You were about to let go of the spear. Did you think thus to be so easily quit of your task in carrying it?"

"I did," he replied. "By giving it into your custody with the Warrior in Fionavar."

Summoning all her courage, Jaelle said coldly, "Not so, mage. Should I tell you why?"

There was ice in his eyes, they were colder than her own could go, and with her words there came a low, ominous sound from the ship again. Pwyll said nothing. He listened, balanced on the waves beside her.

"Tell me why," Amairgen said.

"Because you were to give the spear to the Warrior for use against the Dark, not to carry far off from the fields of war."

From the moonlit winter of his death, the mage's expression seemed acidly sardonic. "You argue like a Priestess," he murmured. "It is clear that nothing has changed in Gwen Ystrat, for all the years that have run by."

"*Not so,*" said Pwyll quietly, surprising both her and the mage. "She offered to pray for you, Amairgen. And if you are able to see us clearly, you will know that she was crying for you as she spoke. You will also know, better than I, what a change that marks."

She swallowed, wondering if she had really wanted him to see that. No time to think about it.

Instead, she lifted her voice again. "Hear me, Amairgen Whitebranch, long said to have hated Rakoth Maugrim and the legions of the Dark more than any man who ever lived. The High King of Brennin is riding from Celidon even now—so we believe. He is taking war to Maugrim in Andarien again, as the High King did in your own day. We have as far to go as the army does, and we are on foot. Neither the Warrior with his spear nor any of us here by the Anor will be there in time. We have three days' walking through Sennett, perhaps a fourth, before we cross Celyn into Andarien."

It was true. She had known it, and Diarmuid and Brendel too. They'd had no other choices, though, once agreeing that Aileron would be riding north from the battle he'd missed by Celidon. They would simply have to walk, as fast and as far as they could. And pray.

Now they might have a choice. A terrible one, but the times were terrible and it seemed as if she might be charged with this part of their remedy.

"If what you tell me is true," the ghost said, "then, indeed, you have cause to fear. You had a question, though. I have stayed for it. Speak, for courtesy will not hold me any longer in this hour of our release."

And so she asked it: "Will your ship carry mortal men, Amairgen?"

Pwyll drew a sharp breath.

"Do you know what you are asking?" Amairgen said, very softly.

It was cold now among the waves, in the lee of that pale ship. She said, "I think I do."

"Do you know that we are released now? That tidings of the Soulmonger's death mark our release from bondage in the sea? And you would bind us longer yet?"

It had all become very hard. She said, "There is no binding I have, mage. I have no power here, no hold upon you. I have asked a question, nothing more." She realized that she was trembling.

For what seemed an interminable time, the ghost of Conary's mage was silent. Then, in a voice like a stir of wind, he said, "Would you sail with the dead?"

The killing sea, she thought for the second time. There was a marrow-deep fear within her, so far from the Temples she knew. She masked it, though, and then beat it back.

"*Can* we do so?" she asked. "There are some fifty of us, and we must be at the mouth of the Celyn two mornings hence."

In front of them the timbers of the ship showed black and splintered. There were broken shards at the waterline and one vast, gaping hole where the sea was flowing in.

Amairgen looked down, his pale hair ruffled by the night breeze. He said, "We will do this thing. For a night and a day and a night we will carry you past the Cliffs of Rhudh into Sennett Strand and then down again to where Celyn finds the sea. I will earn the prayers you offered, High Priestess of Dana. And the salt of your tears."

It was hard to tell in the thin moonlight, and she was a long way below him, but it seemed to her there was some kindness in his smile.

"We can carry you," he said. "Though you will see none of the mariners, and myself only when the stars are overhead. There is a ladder aft of where you stand. You may both come aboard, and we will moor the ship by the jetty at the foot of the Anor for your companions."

"It is very shallow," said Pwyll. "Can you go so close?"

At that, Amairgen suddenly threw back his head and laughed, harsh and cold in the darkness above the sea.

"Twiceborn of Mörnir," he said, "be very clear what you are about to do. There are no seas too shallow for this ship. *We are not here*. Nor will you be, when once you stand upon this deck. I ask you again—would you sail with the dead?"

"I would," said Pwyll calmly, "if that is what we must do."

Together the two of them walked along the sea to where a rope ladder hung over the almost translucent side of the rotting ship. They looked at each other, saying nothing. Pwyll went first, entrusting his weight to the ladder. It held, and slowly he went up, to stand at length upon the deck. Jaelle followed. It seemed a long way to climb, upon nothing, to reach nothingness. She tried not to let herself think about it. Pwyll reached out a hand for her. She took it, and let him help her onto the deck. It held her weight, though looking down she could see right through the planks. There were waves washing through the hold below. Quickly she looked up again.

There seemed to be no wind suddenly, but the stars were brighter where they stood, and the moon also. Amairgen did not approach. He walked to the tiller and, with no one visible to aid him, began bringing the ship in toward the dock.

No one visible, but all around her Jaelle now heard footsteps, and then the creaking of the tattered sails as they suddenly flapped full, though still she could feel no breath of wind.

There were faint voices, a thread of what might have been laughter; then they were sailing toward the Anor. Looking to the land, she saw that all the others had awakened by now and were waiting there in silence. She wondered if they could see her and what she and Pwyll must look like, standing here; if they had become as ghosts themselves. And what they would be when they stepped down off this ship, if ever they did.

It did not seem that words were necessary. Diarmuid, unsettlingly quick as he always seemed to be, had already grasped what was happening. Amairgen gentled his ship to the foot of Lisen's Tower, a thing, Jaelle knew, that he had never done as living man. She looked over at him but could read nothing at all in his face. She wondered if she had imagined the smile she thought she'd seen from below.

There was no more time for wondering. The first of the men from the jetty were coming over the rail, wonder in their eyes and apprehension in various measures. She and Pwyll moved to help them. Last of all were Sharra, then Guinevere and Arthur; finally, Diarmuid dan Ailell came aboard.

He looked at Pwyll, and then his blue eyes swung to Jaelle

to hold her with a long glance. "Not much of a ship," he murmured at length, "but I'll concede it was fairly short notice."

She was too strained to even try to think of a response. He didn't give her a chance, in any case. Bending swiftly, he kissed her cheek—which was not, by any measure, something to be permitted—and said, "Very brightly woven, First of Dana. Both of you." And he moved over and kissed Pwyll, as well.

"I didn't know," said Pwyll dryly, "that you found this sort of thing so stimulating."

And that, Jaelle decided gratefully, would do for her response as well.

They were all on board now, all silent among the tread of the invisible mariners, and the filling of sails that should have been too tattered to fill, in a wind that none of them felt.

Jaelle turned to see Amairgen walking slowly toward Arthur, the spear cradled in his hands. There was one more thing to be done, she realized.

"Be welcome," the dead mage said to the Warrior. "Insofar as the living can be welcome here."

"Insofar as I am living," Arthur replied quietly.

Amairgen looked at him a moment, then sank down on one knee. "I have had charge, in this world, of a thing that belongs to you, my lord. Will you accept the King Spear from my hands?"

They were moving out to sea, rounding the curve of the bay, swinging north under the stars.

They heard Arthur say, simply, in the deep voice that carried the shadings of centuries and of so many wars, "I will accept it."

Amairgen lifted the spear. Arthur took it, and as he did, the head of the King Spear blazed blue-white for a dazzling instant. And in that moment the moon set.

Guinevere wheeled abruptly as if she'd heard a sound. In silence she looked back at the strand, and at the forest beyond. Then, "Oh, my love," she whispered. "Oh, my dear love."

Chapter 9

The battle had been going on for a long time when Flidais finally reached the sacred grove. He was the last to arrive, he realized. All the moving spirits of the Wood were here, ringing the circle of the glade, watching, and those who could not travel were present as well, having projected their awareness to this place, to see through the eyes of those assembled here.

They made way for him as he approached, though some more readily than others, and he registered that. He was the son of Cernan, though. They made room for him to pass.

And passing through that shadowy company he came to the very edge of the glade and, looking within, saw Lancelot battling desperately by starlight for his life, and Darien's.

Flidais had lived a very long time, but he had only seen the Oldest One once before, on the night the whole of Pendaran had gathered, as it had now, to watch Curdardh rise up from the riven earth in order to slay Amairgen of Brennin, who had dared to pass a night in the glade. Flidais had been young then, but he was always a wise, watchful child, and the memory was clear: the demon, disdaining its mighty hammer, had sought to smash and overwhelm the mind of the arrogant intruder who was mortal, and nothing more, and could never resist. And yet, Flidais remembered, Amairgen had resisted. With an iron will and courage that Cernan's younger son had never yet, in all the years that had spun between, seen surpassed, he had battled back against the Oldest One and prevailed.

But only because he had help.

Flidais would never forget the shocked thrill he'd felt (like the taste of forbidden wine in Macha's cloud palace, or his first and only glimpse of Ceinwen rising naked from her pool in Faelinn Grove) at his sudden realization that Mörnir was intervening in the battle. At the end, after Amairgen had driven back Curdardh, in the grey hour before dawn, the God—asserting after, with the daunting authority of his thunder voice, that he had been summoned and bound by Amairgen's victory—sent down a visitation of his own to the mortal, and so granted him the runes of the skylore.

Afterward, Mörnir had had to deal with Dana—which had occasioned a chaos among the goddesses and gods that, Flidais thought, back in the glade again a thousand years later, had nothing and everything to do with what was happening now. But two clear truths manifested themselves to the diminutive andain as he watched the figures battling here under the stars.

The first was that, for whatever unknown reason—and Flidais was ignorant, as yet, of Lancelot's sojourn among the dead in Cader Sedat—the demon was using his hammer and his terrifying physical presence as well as the power of his mind in this battle. The second was that Lancelot was fighting alone, with nothing but his sword and his skill, without aid from any power at all.

Which meant, the watching andain realized, that he could not win, despite what he was and had always been: matchless among all mortals in any and all of the Weaver's worlds.

Flidais, remembering with brilliant clarity when he had been Taliesin in Camelot and had first seen this man fight, felt an ache in his throat, a tightness building in his broad chest, to see the hopeless, dazzling courage being wasted here. He surprised himself: the andain were not supposed to care what happened to mortals, even to this one, and beyond that he was a guardian of the Wood himself and the sacred grove was being violated by this man. His own duty and allegiance should have been as clear as the circle of sky above the glade.

A day ago, and with anyone else perhaps, they would have been. But not any more, and not with Lancelot. Flidais watched, keen-eyed by starlight, and betrayed his long trust by grieving for what he saw.

Curdardh was shifting shape constantly, his amorphous, fluid physicality finding new and deadly guises as he fought. He grew an extra limb, even as Flidais watched, and fashioned a stone sword at the end of it, a sword made from his own body. He challenged Lancelot, backed him up to the trees at the eastern side of the glade with that sword, and then, with effortless, primeval strength, brought his mighty hammer swinging across in an obliterating blow.

Which was eluded, desperately, by the man. Lancelot hurled himself down and to one side, in a roll that took him under the crushing hammer and *over* the simultaneously slashing sword, and then, even as he landed, he was somehow on his knees and lashing out backhanded with his own blade—to completely sever Curdardh's newest arm at the shoulder. The stone sword fell harmlessly on the grass.

Flidais caught his breath in wonder and awe. Then, after a moment of wild, irrational hope, he exhaled again, a long sigh of sorrow. For the demon only laughed—unwearied, unhurt—and shaped another limb from its slate-grey torso. Another limb with another sword, exactly as before.

And it was attacking again, without slackening, without respite. Once more Lancelot dodged the deep-forged hammer, once more he parried a thrust of the stone sword, and this time, with a motion too swift to clearly follow, he knifed in, himself, and stabbed upward at the earth demon's dark maggot-encrusted head.

That *had* to cause it pain, Flidais thought, astonished, still, to find how much he cared. And he seemed to be right, for Curdardh hesitated, rumbling wordlessly, before sinuously beginning to change again: shaping this time into a living creature of featureless stone, invulnerable, impervious to blade, wherever forged, however wielded. And it began to track the man about the small ambit of the glade, to cut him off and crush the life out of him.

Flidais realized then that he had been right from the first. Every time Lancelot did damage, any kind of injury, the demon could withdraw into a shape that was impregnable. It could heal itself of any sword-delivered wound while still forcing the tiring man to elude its dangerous pursuit. Even with the crippled leg, Flidais saw—ritually maimed millennia ago to signify the tethering of the demon to guardianship of this place—Curdardh was agile and deadly, and the glade was small, and the trees of the grove around and the spirits watching there would not allow the man any escape, however momentary, from the sacrosanct place he had violated. And where he was to die.

He, and someone else. Tearing his eyes away from the grueling hurtful combat, Flidais looked over to his right. The boy, his face bone white, was watching with an expression absolutely unreadable. As he looked at Rakoth's son, Flidais felt the same instinctive withdrawal he had known on the beach by the Anor, and he was honest enough to name it fear. Then he thought about who the mother was, and he looked back again at Lancelot battling silently in darkness for this child's life, and he mastered his own doubts and walked over the grass at the edge of the glade to Darien.

"I am Flidais," he said, thereby breaking his own oldest rule for such things. What were rules, though, he was thinking, on a night such as this, talking to such a one as this child was?

Darien moved sideways a couple of steps, shying away from closer proximity. His eyes never left the two figures fighting in front of them.

"I am a friend to your mother," Flidais said, struggling uncharacteristically for the right words. "I ask you to believe that I mean you no malice."

For the first time the boy turned to him. "It doesn't really matter," he said, scarcely above a whisper. "You can't make any difference, can you? The choice is being taken away."

Chilled, Flidais seemed to see him clearly for the first time, suddenly aware in that moment of how young Darien was, and how fair, and, for his vision was keen in the darkness, of how blue the boy's eyes were.

He couldn't, though, however hard he tried, escape the image of their crimson flashing on the beach and the blaze of the burning tree.

There was a sudden loud rumble of sound from the glade, and Flidais pressed quickly back against the trunk of one of the trees. Not six feet away, Lancelot was retreating toward them, pursued, with a sound like dragging scree, by the demon in its impervious rock shape.

As Lancelot drew near, Flidais saw that his whole body was laced with a network of cuts and purpling bruises. Blood flowed freely from his left shoulder and his right side. His clothing hung in tattered, bloodstained ribbons from his body, and his thick black hair lay plastered to his head. Rivulets of perspiration ran continuously down his face. Every few moments, it seemed, he had to lift his free hand, ignoring the wound, and claw sweat free from his eyes so he could see.

Insofar as he could see at all. For he was only mortal, and unaided, and even the half-moon had long since passed out of sight to the west, hidden by the towering trees that ringed the glade. Only a handful of stars looked down from above on this act of courage by the tormented, scintillant soul of Lancelot du Lac—the single most gallant, impossible act of courage ever woven into the Tapestry.

Bound by his own duty to the Wood and by the power of that place, Flidais watched helplessly as the two of them drew closer yet. He saw Lancelot, lithe and neat-footed, mastering pain and weariness, drop to one knee, just out of reach of the advancing demon and, lunging forward and down, level a scything blow of his sword at the demon's leg, the only part of the slate-grey rock shape that was not impervious to iron.

But nimbly, for all its grotesque, worm-infested ugliness, the demon of the grove spun away from the thrust. With terrifying speed, he shaped a new sword arm and, even as the weapon coalesced, launched a savage blow downward against the sprawling man. Who rolled, in a racking, contorted movement, and thrust up his own bright blade to meet the overpowering descent of Curdardh's stone sword.

The blades met with a crash that shook the glade. Flidais clenched his fists, his heart hammering, and then he saw that even against this, even against the full brutal strength of the demon's arm, Lancelot had held firm. His blade did not break, nor his muscled arm give way. The swords met and it was the stone that shattered, as Lancelot rolled again, away from the edge of the glade, and scrambled, chest heaving convulsively, to his feet.

With, Flidais saw, another wound. A jagged fragment of the broken sword of the demon had cut him anew. His shirt shredded to confining strips, Lancelot tore it off and stood bare-chested in the middle of the glade, dark blood welling from a wound over his heart. He balanced on the balls of his feet, his unflinching eyes on his adversary, his sword held out once more, as he waited for Curdardh to come at him again.

And Curdardh, with the primeval, pitiless, unwearied power of earth, came. Once more shifting shape, away from the awkward though invulnerable guise of rock, once more it gave itself a head—almost human it was, though with only a single monstrous eye in the center from which black grubs and beetles fell like tears—and once more, most terribly, it brought forth the colossal hammer from some place within itself. Taking hold of it with an arm so brawny it seemed as thick around as Lancelot was at the chest, the demon surged forward, seeming to cover the space of the glade with one huge stride, and, roaring like an avalanche, brought the hammer crashing down on the waiting man.

Who dodged yet again, though narrowly, for the demon was brutally swift. Flidais felt the ground shake again with the impact of the blow, and when Curdardh moved on, pursuing, always pursuing, the watching andain saw a smoking hole in the scorched grass of the glade where the hammer had fallen like doom.

On it went, on and on, till Flidais, driving his nails unconsciously into the palms of his hands, thought that his own heart would shatter from strain and weariness. Again and again Lancelot eluded the ruinous hammer and the slashing swords the demon shaped from its own body. Twice more the man succeeded in severing the arms that swung the stone blades, and twice more he was able to leap in, with a shining grace worthy of the watching stars, and wound Curdardh, once in the eye and then in the neck, forcing it each time into the protective, recuperative shape of rock.

This gave some respite to the man, but only a little, for even in that form the demon could attack, striving to corner Lancelot against the impervious wall of the trees ringing the glade and crush his life away against the dark, mottled mass of its body.

Once more an attack brought demon and man near to where Flidais stood beside Darien. And once more Lancelot managed to fling himself away. But this time his shoulder landed in one of the smoking holes the hammer had gouged, and Flidais heard him grunt involuntarily with pain, and saw him scramble, with an awkward desperation this time, away from the renewed assault. He was burnt now, the andain realized, horror and pity consuming his own soul.

He heard a strangled sound from beside him and realized that Darien, too, had registered what had happened. He looked over, briefly, at the boy, and his heart stopped, literally, for a moment. Over and over in his hands Darien was twisting a bright dagger blade, seeming almost oblivious to the fact that he was doing so. Flidais had glimpsed a telling flash of blue, and so he knew what that blade was.

"Be careful!" he whispered urgently. He coughed; his throat was dry. "What are you thinking of doing?"

For only the second time Darien looked directly at him. "I don't know," the boy said, painfully young. "I made my eyes red before you came . . . that is how I have my power." Flidais fought, successfully this time, to conceal his fear. He nodded. Darien went on, "But nothing happened. The rock thing said it was because I did not go deep enough to master it. That I had no power here. So I . . ." He paused and looked down at the knife. "I thought I might . . ."

Through the black night, and through the blackness of what was happening and the pity and horror he felt, Flidais of Pendaran seemed to see, within his mind, a faint, almost illusionary light gleaming in a far, far distance. A little light like the small cast glow of a candle in a cottage window at night, seen by a traveler in a storm far from home.

He said, in his rich, deep voice, "It is a good thought, Darien. It is worthy of you, and worthy of the one who is doing this for you. But do not do it now, and not with that blade."

"Why?" Darien asked, in a small voice.

"Once shall I tell you, and for your ears only, and once is enough for those who are wise," Flidais intoned, reverting, if briefly, to his cryptic elusiveness. He felt a familiar rush of pleasure, even here, even with what was happening, that he *knew* this. And that reminded him—past pleasure, reaching joy—of what else, now, he knew. And remembering that, he remembered also that he had sworn an oath earlier that night, to try to shape a light from the darkness all around. He looked at Darien, hesitating, then said, quite directly, "What you are holding is named Lökdal. It is the enchanted dagger of the Dwarves, give to Colan dan Conary a long time ago."

He closed his eyes for a moment, to summon up the exact phrasing, given him by a wine-drowsy mage one spring night seven hundred years ago beside an evening fire on the edge of the Llychlyn Marsh. "*Who strikes with this blade without love in his heart,*" said Flidais, as the words came back, "*shall surely die.*" And then he told the rest of it: "*Who kills with love may make of his soul a gift to the one marked with the pattern on the dagger's haft.*" Potent words, and a deep-delved, intricate magic.

Darien was looking down, gazing at the traced pattern on the hilt of the blade. He glanced up again and said, so quietly Flidais had to strain to hear him, "I wouldn't wish my soul on anything alive." And then, after a pause, the andain heard him say, "My gift was to be the dagger itself, before I was brought to this place."

"A gift to whom?" Flidais asked, though within himself he knew.

"To my father, of course," said Darien. "That I might find a welcome somewhere in the worlds."

There had to be something to say to that, Flidais was thinking. There *had* to be an adequate response, so much depended on it. But he couldn't think, for once. He couldn't find words, and then, suddenly, he didn't have time for them either.

There came a rumbling crash from the glade, louder than any before, and this time there was a resonance of triumph within it. Flidais turned back just in time to see Lancelot hurtle through the air, clipped by the very end of a hammer swing he'd not quite dodged. It would have smashed the life from him had it hit more squarely. As it was, the merest glancing blow had knocked him flying halfway across the glade, to a bruising, crumpled landing beside Darien.

Curdardh, tireless, sensing an ending at last, was advancing toward him again. Dripping blood, desperately weary, his left arm now hanging uselessly at his side, Lancelot somehow, by an effort of will Flidais could not even comprehend, dragged himself to his feet.

In the instant before the demon was upon him he turned to Darien. Flidais saw their eyes lock and hold. Then he heard Lancelot say quickly, in a voice drained of all inflection, "One final cast, in memory of Gawain. I have nothing left. *Count ten for me, then scream. And then pray to whatever you like.*"

He had time for no more. Sidestepping with a half-spin, he launched himself in another rolling dive away from the murderous hammer. It smote the ground where he had stood, and Flidais flinched back from the thunder of that stroke and the heat that roared up from the riven ground.

Curdardh wheeled. Lancelot was on his feet again, swaying a little. The demon made a loose, spilling sound and slowly advanced.

Flidais felt as if his heart was going to tear apart in his chest even as he stood there. The ticking seconds were the longest he had ever known in a long life. He was a guardian of the Wood, of this grove, as much as was Curdardh. These two had defiled the glade! *Three*. He couldn't look at Darien. The demon slashed with his sword. Lancelot parried, stumbling. *Five*. Again Curdardh thrust with the stone blade, the gigantic hammer held high, in readiness. Again the man defended himself. He almost fell. Flidais suddenly heard a rustling of anticipation in the leaves of the watching trees. *Seven*. Chained to silence, forced to bear witness, the andain tasted blood in his mouth: he had bitten his tongue. Curdardh, fluid, sinuous, utterly unwearied, moved forward, feinting with the sword. Flidais saw the hammer rise higher. He lifted his hands in a useless, pitiful gesture of denial.

And in that instant a sound such as Flidais had never heard in all his years exploded from Darien.

It was a scream of anguish and rage, of terror and blinding agony, torn whole and bleeding from a tortured soul. It was monstrous, insupportable, overwhelming. Flidais, battered to his knees by the pain of it, saw Curdardh quickly glance backward.

And Lancelot made his move. With two quick strides and

a straining upward leap he slashed his bright blade downward with stupefying strength and completely severed the arm that he'd never been able to reach until now.

The arm that held the monstrous hammer.

The demon roared with shock and pain, but even as it did, it was already causing itself to flow back over the amputated limb, growing it again. Flidais saw that out of the corner of one eye.

But he was watching Lancelot who had landed neatly from his unbelievable blow, who had hurled his sword away from him, toward Darien and Flidais, and who was bending now, breathing harshly, over the hammer of Curdardh.

His left arm was useless. He wrapped his right hand about the shaft and, groaning with the effort, fought to lift it. And failed. The hammer was vast, unimaginably heavy. It was the weapon of a demon, of the Oldest One. It had been forged in fires deeper than the chasms of Dana. And Lancelot du Lac was only a man.

Flidais saw the demon shape two new swords from its body. He saw it advance again, with a wet, gurgling sound of rage and pain. Lancelot glanced up. And Flidais, on his knees, unable to move, unable to so much as breathe, was given a new measure, in that moment, of the magnitude of mortal man. He saw Lancelot *will* himself—there was no other word—to raise the black hammer with one hand.

And it moved.

The handle came off the ground, and then, beyond comprehension, so did the monstrous head. The demon stopped, with a grinding sound, as Lancelot, his mouth wide open in a soundless scream of uttermost endeavoring, used the initial momentum of that lifting to wheel himself through a full circle, his arm extended flat out, the muscles ridged, corded, glistening, the hammer inexorably rising with the speed of his motion.

Then he let it fly. And that mighty hammer, forged in downward-burning fires, thrown with all the passion of an unmatched soul, smashed into the chest of Curdardh, the Oldest One, with a sound like the earth's crust cracking, and it shattered the demon of the grove into fragments and pieces and shards, killing it utterly.

* * *

Flidais felt the silence as a weight upon his life. He had never known Pendaran to be so still. Not a leaf rustled, not a spirit whispered; the powers of the Wood lay as if enchanted in an awed stupefaction. Flidais had a sense, absurdly, that even the stars above the glade had ceased to move, the Loom itself lying silent and still, the Weaver's hands at rest.

He looked down on his own trembling hands, and then, slowly, he stood up, feeling the motion like a returning into time from another world entirely. He walked over, amid the silence, to stand by the man in the center of the grove.

Lancelot had pulled himself to a sitting position, his knees bent, his head lowered between them. His left arm hung uselessly at his side. There was dark blood on the grass, and it was welling still from half a dozen wounds. There was an ugly burn on his shoulder, raw and blistered, where he had rolled in the scorching pit of hammer blow. Then Flidais, coming nearer, saw the other burn, and his breath lodged painfully in his chest.

Where the man's hand—once so beautiful—had gripped the hammer of Curdardh, the skin of his palm was blackened and peeled away in thick strips of violated flesh.

"Oh, Lancelot," the andain murmured. It came out as a croak, almost inaudible.

Slowly the man lifted his head. His eyes, clouded with pain, met those of Flidais, and then, unbelievably, the thinnest trace of a smile lifted the corners of his mouth.

"Taliesin," he whispered. "I thought I saw you. I am sorry—" He gasped and looked down at the seared flesh of his palm. Then he looked away and continued. "I am sorry I could not greet you properly, before."

Flidais shook his head mutely. He opened his mouth, but no words came. He cleared his throat and tried again, formally. "It has been told for centuries that you were never matched in your day of earthly knight's hand. What you battled tonight was not mortal and should never have been defeated. I have never seen a thing to match it and I never will. What may I offer you, my lord Lancelot?"

The mortal eyes, holding his own, seemed to grow clearer. "Your silence, Taliesin. I need your silence about what happened here, lest all the worlds learn of my shame."

"*Shame?*" Flidais felt his voice crack.

Lancelot lifted his head to gaze at the high stars overhead. "This was single combat," he said quietly. "And I sought aid from the boy. It will be a mark against my name for so long as time shall run."

"In the name of the Loom!" Flidais snapped. "What idiocy is this? What about the trees, and the powers of the Wood that aided Curdardh and hemmed you in? What about this battleground where the demon's power was greater than anywhere else? What about the darkness, where it could see and you could not? What about—"

"Even so," murmured Lancelot, and the little andain's sharp voice was stilled. "Even so, I besought aid in single combat."

"Is that so terrible?" said a new voice.

Flidais turned. Darien had come forward from the edge of the glade. His expression was calm now, but Flidais could still see the shadow of its contorted anguish when the boy had screamed.

"We both would have died," Darien went on. "Why is it so terrible to have asked that one small thing?"

Lancelot swung to look at him. There was a moment's stillness; then he said, "Save in one thing only, a love for which I will make eternal redress, I have served the Light in everything I have ever done. In that service, a victory won with a tool of the Dark is no victory at all."

Darien took a step backward. "Do you mean me?" he asked. "A tool of the —"

"No," Lancelot murmured quietly. Flidais felt his cold fear coming back, as he looked at the boy. "No. I mean the thing I did."

"You saved my life," Darien said. It sounded like an accusation. He did not step forward again.

"And you, mine." Quietly, still.

"Why?" Darien shouted suddenly. "Why did you do it?"

The man closed his eyes for a moment, then opened them. "Because your mother asked me to," he said simply.

With the words Flidais heard a rustling in the leaves again. There was an ache in his heart.

Darien stood as if poised for flight, but he had not yet moved. "She knew I was going to my father," he said, less loudly. "Did she tell you? Do you know that you have saved me to do that?"

Lancelot shook his head. He lifted his voice, though clearly it took an effort. "I have saved you to follow your road."

Darien laughed. The sound knifed into Flidais. "And if it leads north?" the boy asked coldly, in a voice that sounded older suddenly. "Due north to the Dark? To Rakoth Maugrim?"

Lancelot's eyes were undisturbed, his voice utterly calm. "Then it leads there by your choice, Darien. Only thus are we not slaves: if we can choose where we would walk. Failing that, all is mockery."

There was a silence, broken, to Flidais' horror, by the sound of Darien laughing again, bitter, lonely, lost. "It is, though," said the boy. "It *is* all mockery. The light went out when I put it on. Don't you know that? And why, why should I choose to *walk* in any case?"

There was an instant of silence.

"No!" Flidais cried, reaching out to the child.

Too late. Perhaps it had always been too late: from birth, from conception amid the unlight of Starkadh, from the time the worlds first were spun, Flidais thought, heartsick.

The eyes blazed savagely red. There came a roaring sound from the powers of the Wood, a blurring of shapes in the grove, and suddenly Darien was not there any more.

Instead, an owl, gleaming white in the darkness, darted swiftly down into the grass, seized a fallen dagger in its mouth, and was aloft and away, wheeling out of sight to the north.

To the north. Flidais gazed at the circle of night sky framed by the towering trees, and with all his soul he tried to will a shape to be there. The shape of a white owl returning, flying back to land beside them and turn into a child again, a fair child, with mild blue eyes, who had chosen the Light and been chosen by it to be a bright blade in the looming dark.

He swallowed. He looked away from the empty sky. He turned back to Lancelot—who was on his feet, bleeding, burnt, swaying with fatigue.

"What are you doing?" Flidais cried.

Lancelot looked down on him. "I am following," he said calmly, as if it were the most obvious thing imaginable. "Will you help me with my sword?" He held up his mangled palm; his left arm hung at his side.

"Are you mad?" the andain spluttered.

Lancelot made a sound that managed to be a laugh. "I have been mad," he admitted. "A long time ago. But not now, little one. What would you have me do? Lie here and lick my wounds in a time of war?"

Flidais did a little dance of sheer exasperation. "What role can you play if you kill yourself?"

"I am aware that I'm not good for much, right now," Lancelot said gravely, "but I don't think these wounds are going to—"

"You're going to *follow*?" the andain interrupted, as the full import of Lancelot's words struck him. "Lancelot, he's an owl now, he's *flying*! By the time you even get out of Pendaran he will be—"

He stopped abruptly, in mid-sentence.

"What is it? What have you thought of, wise child?"

He hadn't been a child for a very long time. But he had, indeed, thought of something. He looked up at the man, saw the blood on his bare chest. "He was going to fly due north. That will take him over the western edge of Daniloth."

"And?"

"And he may not get through. Time is very strange in the Shadowland."

"My sword," said Lancelot crisply. "Please."

Somehow Flidais found himself collecting the discarded blade and then the scabbard. He came back to Lancelot and, as gently as he could, buckled the sword about the man's waist.

"Will the spirits of the Wood let me pass?" Lancelot asked quietly.

Flidais paused to listen to the messages passing around them and beneath their feet.

"They will," he said at length, not a little surprised. "For Guinevere, and for your blood spilled tonight. They do you honor, Lancelot."

"More than I merit," the man said. He drew a deep breath, as if gathering reserves of endurance, from where, Flidais knew not.

He scowled upward at Lancelot. "You will go easier with a guide. I will take you to the borders of Daniloth, but I have a condition."

"Which is?" Always, the mild courtesy.

"One of my homes lies on our way. You will have to let me dress your wounds when we come there."

"I will be grateful for it," said Lancelot.

The andain opened his mouth, a cutting retort readied. He never said it. Instead, he turned and stomped from the grove, walking north. When he had gone a short way he stopped and looked back, to see a thing of wonder.

Lancelot was following, slowly, on the dark and narrow path. All about him and from high above, the mighty trees of Pendaran Wood were letting fall their green leaves, gently, on a night in the midst of summer, to honor the passage of the man.

PART III

Calor Diman

Chapter 10

She had flamed red to travel once before, in her own world, not this one: from Stonehenge to Glastonbury Tor. It was not like the crossings. Passing between the worlds was a coldness and a dark, a time without time, deeply unsettling. This was different. When the Baelrath blazed to let her travel, Kim felt as if she truly touched the immensity of its power. Of her own power. She could blink distance to nothingness. She was wilder than any other magic known, more akin to Macha and Red Nemain in those hurtling seconds than to any mortal woman ever born.

With one difference: an awareness harbored deep within her heart that they were goddesses, those two, profoundly in control of what they were. And she? She *was* a mortal woman, only that, and as much borne by the Baelrath as bearing it.

And thinking so, carrying her ring, carried by it, she found herself coming down with Loren and Matt—three mortals riding the currents of time and twilit space—onto a cleared threshold high up in sharp mountain air. Before them, two mighty bronze doors towered in majesty, worked with intricate designs in blue thieren and shining gold.

Kim turned to the south and saw the wild dark hills of Eridu rolling away into shadow. Land where the death rain had fallen. Above her, some night bird of the high places lifted a long lonely cry. She listened to its echoes fading, thinking of the Paraiko moving, even now, among those desolate tarns and the high-walled, plague-ravaged cities beyond, gathering the raindead, cleansing Eridu.

She turned north. A gleam of light from high above drew her eyes. She looked up, far up, beyond the grandeur of the twinned doors of the Kingdom of the Dwarves, to see the peaks of Banir Lök and Banir Tal as they caught the last light of the setting sun. The bird called again, one long, quavering, descending note. Far off, there was another gleam, as if in answer to the day's-end shining of the twin peaks overhead. To the north and west, higher by far than anything else, Rangat claimed the last of the light for its own.

None of them had spoken. Kim looked over at Matt Sören, and her hands closed involuntarily at her side. *Forty years*, she thought, gazing at her friend who had once been—who yet was—the true King of the realm beyond these doors. His arms were spread wide, hands open, in a gesture of propitiation and utmost vulnerability. In his face she read, clear as calligraphy, the marks of longing, of bitterness, and bitterest pain.

She turned away, to meet the eyes of Loren Silvercloak. In them she saw the burden of his own difficult, complex grief and guilt. She remembered—knew that Loren had never forgotten—Matt's telling them all in Paras Derval about the tide of Calor Diman in his heart, the tide he had fought ceaselessly for the forty years he'd served as source to the one-time mage.

She turned back to the doors. Even in the dusk she could make out the exquisite tracery of gold and thieren. It was very quiet. She heard the thin sound of a pebble, dislodged somewhere and falling. The twin peaks were dark now, overhead, and dark, too, she knew, would be Calor Diman, the Crystal Lake, high and hidden in its meadow bowl between the mountains.

The first stars appeared delicately in the clear sky. Kim looked down at her hand: the ring flickered quietly, its surge of power spent. She tried to think of something to say, of words to ease the sorrows of this threshold, but she feared there might be danger in sound. Beyond that, there was a texture, a woven weight to this silence that, she sensed, was not hers to shoulder or to shoulder aside. It encompassed the spun threads of the lives of the two men here with her, and more—the long, many-stranded destiny of an ancient people, of the Dwarves of Banir Lök and Banir Tal.

It went back too far beyond her, even with her own twinned soul. So she kept her peace, heard another pebble dislodged, another bird cry, farther away, and then listened as Matt Sören finally spoke, very softly, never looking around. "Loren, hear me. I regret nothing: not a breath, not a moment, not the shadow of a moment. This is truth, my friend, and I swear it to be such in the name of the crystal I fashioned long ago, the crystal I threw in the Lake on the night the full moon made me King. There is no weaving the Loom could have held to my name that I can imagine to be richer than the one I have known."

He lowered his hands slowly, still facing the awesome grandeur of the doors. When he spoke again, his voice was rougher and even lower than before. "I am . . . glad, though, that the threads of my days have brought me to this place again, before the end."

Loving him, loving them both, Kim wanted to weep. *Forty years*, she thought again. Something shone in the depths of Loren's eyes, shone as the twin peaks had with the last of the sun. She felt a swirl of mountain winds on the high threshold, heard a sound behind her of gravel sliding.

Was turning to see, when the blow fell on the base of her skull and knocked her sprawling to the ground.

She felt consciousness sliding away. Tried desperately to cling to it, as if it were a physical thing that could be held, that *had* to be held. But, despairing, she knew she was going to fail. It was going, sliding. Pain exploding in her head. Blackness coming down. There were sounds. She could not see. She was lying on the stony plateau before the doors, and the last thought she had was of brutal self-mockery. Akin to the goddesses of war, she had imagined herself, only moments ago. Yet, for all the arrogance of that, and for all the gifts of the Seers that Ysanne had lavished upon her, she'd not been able to sense a simple ambush.

That was her last thought. The very last thing she felt, with a helpless terror that went beyond thought, was someone taking the Baelrath from her hand. She tried to cry out, to resist, to flame, but then it seemed as if a slow wide river had come and it carried her away into the dark.

She opened her eyes. The room rocked and spun, both. The floor dropped sickeningly away, then rushed precipitously back toward her. She had a stupefying headache and, even without moving a hand to feel it, knew she had to have an egg-sized lump on the back of her head. Lying carefully motionless, she waited for things to settle. It took a while.

Eventually she sat up. She was in a windowless chamber by herself. There was a pearly light, mercifully gentle, in the room, though she couldn't see where it was coming from: the stone walls themselves, it seemed, and the ceiling. There was no door either, or none that she could see. A chair and a footstool stood in one corner. On a low table beside them rested a basin of water—which reminded her of how thirsty she was. The table seemed a long way off, though; she decided to wait a few moments before chancing that journey.

She was sitting—had been lying—on a small bed at least a foot too short for her. Which reminded her of where she was. She remembered something else and looked down.

The ring was gone. She had not imagined that last, terrible sensation. She thought she was going to be sick. She thought of Kaen, who was leader here, though not King. Kaen and his brother, Blöd, who had broken the wardstone of Eridu, who had found the Cauldron of Khath Meigol and given it to Maugrim. And now they had the Baelrath.

Kim felt naked without it, though she still wore the belted gown she'd been wearing all day, from the time she'd risen in the cottage and seen Darien. All day? She didn't even know what day it was. She had no idea of the time, but the diffused light emanating from the stone had the hue of dawn to it. She wondered about that, and about the absence of any door. The Dwarves, she knew, could do marvelous things with stone under their mountains.

They could also, under Kaen and Blöd, be servants of the Dark such as Maugrim had never had before. She thought about Lökdal and then, of course, about Darien: the constant fear at the bedrock of everything. Apprehension mastered sickness and pain, driving her to her feet. She had to get out! Too much was happening. Too much depended on her!

The surge of panic faded, leaving her with the sudden grim awareness that without the Baelrath not much, in fact, really did depend on her any more. She tried to take heart from the simple fact that she was still alive. They had not killed her, and there was water here, and a clean towel. She tried to draw strength from the presence of such things: tried and failed. The ring was gone.

Eventually she did walk over to the low table. She drank deeply of the water—some property of the stone basin had kept it chilled—and washed herself, jolted breathlessly awake by the cold. She probed her wound: a bruise, large, very tender, but there was no laceration. For small favors she gave thanks.

Things do happen, she remembered her grandfather saying, in the days after her gran had died. *We got to soldier on*, he had said. She set her jaw. A certain resolution came back into her grey eyes. She sat down in the chair, put her feet up on the stool, and composed herself to wait, grim and ready, as the color of the light all around gradually grew brighter, and then brighter still, through the hours of what had to be morning outside, echoed, by craft or magic or some fusion of both, in the glowing of the stones within the mountain.

A door opened. Or, rather, a door *appeared* in the wall opposite Kim and then swung soundlessly outward. Kim was on her feet, her heart racing, and then she was suddenly very confused.

She could never have explained rationally why the presence of a Dwarf woman should surprise her so much, why she'd assumed, without ever giving it a moment's thought, that the females among the Dwarves should look like . . . oh, beardless, stocky equivalents of fighting men like Matt and Brock. After all, she herself didn't much resemble Coll of Taerlindel or Dave Martyniuk. At least on a good day she didn't!

Neither did the woman who had come for her. A couple of inches shorter than Matt Sören, she was slim and graceful, with wide-set dark eyes and straight black hair hanging down her back. For all the delicate beauty of the woman, Kim nonetheless sensed in her the same resilience and fortitude she'd come to know in Brock and Matt. Formidable, deeply valued allies the Dwarves would be, and very dangerous enemies.

With everything she knew, with the pain in her head and the Baelrath gone, with the memory of what Blöd had done to Jennifer in Starkadh and the brutal awareness of the death rain unleashed by the Cauldron, it was still, somehow, hard to confront this woman as an avowed foe. A weakness? A mistake? Kim wondered, but nevertheless she managed a half smile.

"I was wondering when someone would come," she said. "I'm Kimberly."

"I know," the other woman said, not returning the smile. "We have been told who you are, and what. I am sent to bring you to Seithr's Hall. The Dwarfmoot is gathering. The King has returned."

"I know," said Kim dryly, trying to keep the irony out of her tone, and the quick surge of hope. "What is happening?"

"A challenge before the Elders of the Moot. A word-striving, the first in forty years. Between Kaen and Matt Sören. No more questions; we have little time!"

Kim wasn't good with orders. "Wait!" she said. "Tell me, who . . . who do you support?"

The other woman looked up at her with eyes dark and unrevealing. "No more questions, I said." She turned and went out.

Pushing her hair back with one hand, Kim hastened to follow. They turned left out the door and made their way along a series of ascending, high-ceilinged corridors lit by the same diffused natural-seeming light that had brightened her room. There were beautifully sculpted torch brackets along the walls, but they were not in use. It was daytime, Kim concluded; the torches would be lit at night. There were no decorations on the walls, but at intervals—random, or regulated by some pattern she had no chance to discern—Kim saw a number of low plinths or pillars, and resting on top of each of them were crystalline works of art, exquisite and strange. Most were abstract shapes that caught and reflected the light of the corridors, but some were not: she saw a spear, embedded in a mountain of glass; a crystal eagle, with a wingspan fully five feet across; and, at a junction of many hallways, a dragon looked down from the highest pedestal of all.

She had no time to admire or even think about any of this. Or about the fact that the hallways of this kingdom under the two mountains were so empty. Despite the width of the corridors—clearly built to allow the passage of great numbers—she and the Dwarf woman passed only a few other people, men and women of the Dwarves, all of whom stopped in their tracks to gaze up at Kimberly with cold, repressive stares.

She began to be afraid again. The art and mastery of the crystal sculptures, the casual power inherent in the vanishing doorways and the corridor lighting, the very fact of a race of people dwelling for so very long under the mountains . . . Kim found herself feeling more alien here than she had anywhere else in Fionavar. And her own wild power was gone. It had been entrusted to her, dreamt by a Seer on her hand, and she had lost it. They had left her the vellin bracelet, though, her screen and protection from magic. She wondered why. Were vellin stones so commonplace here as to be not worth taking?

She had no time to think this through either, no time, just then, for anything but awe. For her guide turned a last corridor, and Kim, following her, did the same and stood within one of the vast, arched entranceways to the hall named for Seithr, King during the Bael Rangat.

Even the Paraiko, she thought, let alone mortal men or the lios alfar, would be made to feel small in this place. And thinking so, she came most of the way to an awareness of why the Dwarves had built their Moot Hall on this scale.

On the level she and her guide were on, there were eight other arched entrances to the circular chamber, each of them as lofty and imposing as the one wherein she stood. Looking up, dumbfounded, Kim saw that there were two other levels of access to the chamber, and on each of these, as well, nine arches allowed entry into the prodigious hall. Dwarves were filtering through all the arches, on all three levels. A cluster of Dwarf women walked past, just then, pausing to fix Kim with a collective regard, stern and unrevealing. Then they went in.

Seithr's Hall was laid out in the manner of an amphitheater. The ceiling of the chamber was so high, and the light all around so convincingly natural, that it seemed to Kim as if they might, indeed, be outside, in the clear cold air of the mountains.

Caught in that illusion, still gazing upward, she saw that there seemed to be birds of infinite variety wheeling and circling in the huge bright spaces high above the hall. Light flashed, many-colored, from their shapes, and she realized that these too were creations of the Dwarves, held aloft and in apparent freedom of flight by a craft or art beyond her comprehension.

A dazzle of light from the stage below drew her eye, and she looked down. After a moment she recognized what she was looking at, and as soon as she did, her gaze whipped back, incredulous, to the circling birds overhead, from which the reflection of color and light was exactly the same as it was from the two objects below.

Which meant that the birds, even the spectacular eagles, were made not of crystal, as were the sculptures she had seen in the corridors as they approached, but of diamond.

For resting on deep red cushions on a stone table in the middle of the stage were the Diamond Crown and Scepter of the Dwarves.

Kim felt a childish desire to rub her eyes in disbelief, to discover if, when she took her hands away, she would still see what she was seeing now. There were diamond eagles overhead!

How could the people who were able to place them there, who *wanted* them there, be allies of the Dark? And yet . . .

And yet from the real sky outside these mountain halls a death rain had fallen on Eridu for three full nights and days. And it had fallen because of what the Dwarves had done.

For the first time she became aware that her guide was watching her with a cool curiosity, to gauge her response to the splendor of the Hall, perhaps to glory in it. She was awed and humbled. She had never seen anything like it, not even in her Seer's dreams. And yet . . .

She put her hands in the pockets of her gown. "Very pretty," she said casually. "I like the eagles. How many of the real ones died in the rain?"

And was rewarded—if it really was a reward—to see the Dwarf woman go pale as the stone walls of Kim's room had been when she awoke at dawn. She felt a quick surge of pity but fiercely suppressed it, looking away. They had freed Rakoth. They had taken her ring. And this woman had been sufficiently trusted by Kaen to be sent to bring Kim to this place.

"Not all the birds died," her guide said, very low, so as

not to be overheard, it seemed. "I went up by the Lake yesterday morning. There were some eagles there."

Kim clenched her fists. "Isn't that just wonderful," she said, as coldly as she could. "For how much longer, do you think, if Rakoth Maugrim defeats us?"

The Dwarf woman's glance fell away before the stony rage in Kim's eyes. "Kaen says there have been promises," she whispered. "He says—" She stopped. After a long moment she looked Kim squarely in the face again, with the hardihood of her race. "Do we really have any choice? Now?" she asked bitterly.

Looking at her, her anger sluicing away, Kim felt as if she finally understood what had happened, what was still happening within these halls. She opened her mouth to speak, but in the moment there came a loud murmur from within Seithr's Hall, and she quickly glanced over at the stage.

Loren Silvercloak, limping slightly, leaning on Amairgen's white staff, was making his way behind another Dwarf woman to a seat near the stage.

Kim felt an overwhelming relief: only momentarily, though—for as Loren came to his seat she saw armed guards move to take up positions on either side of him.

"Come," her own guide said, her cool detachment completely restored by the pause. "I am to lead you to that place as well."

And so, pushing back that one aggravating strand of hair yet again, walking as regally and as tall as she could, Kim followed her into the Moot Hall. Ignoring the renewed rustle of sound that greeted her appearance, she descended the long, wide aisle between the seats on either side, never turning her head, and, pausing before Loren, chanced and succeeded in the first curtsy of her life.

In the same grave spirit he bowed to her and, bringing one of her hands to his lips, kissed it. She thought of Diarmuid and Jen, the first night they had come to Fionavar. Most of a long lifetime ago, it seemed. She gave Loren's hand a squeeze and then, ignoring the guards, let her glance—imperious, she devoutly hoped—sweep over the assembled Dwarves.

Doing so, she noticed something. She turned back to Loren and said, softly, "Almost all women. Why?"

"Women and older men. And the members of the Moot

who will be coming out soon. Oh, Kim, my dear, why do you think?" His eyes—so kind, she remembered them being—seemed to hold a crushing weight of trouble within their depths.

"Silence!" one of the guards snapped. Not harshly, but his tone meant business.

It didn't matter. Loren's expression had told her what she had to know. She felt the weight of knowledge that he carried come into her as well.

Women, and the old, and the councillors of the Moot. The men in their prime, the warriors, away. *Away, of course, at war.*

She didn't need to be told which side they would be fighting on, if Kaen had sent them forth.

And in that moment Kaen himself came forth from the far wing of the stage, and so for the first time she saw the one who had unchained blackest evil in their time. Quietly, without any evident pride or arrogance, he strode to stand at one side of the stone table. His thick hair was raven black, his beard closely trimmed. He was slighter than Matt or Brock, not as powerful, except for one thing: his hands were those of a sculptor, large, capable, very strong. He rested one of them on the table, although, carefully, he did not touch the Crown. He was clad unpretentiously in simple brown, and his eyes betrayed no hint of madness or delusions. They were meditative, tranquil, almost sorrowful.

There was another footfall on the stage. Kim tore her eyes away from Kaen to watch Matt Sören step forward from the near wing. She expected a babble of noise, a murmur, some level of response. But the Dwarf she knew and loved—unchanged, she saw, always unchanged, no matter what might come to pass—moved to stand at the other side of the table from Kaen, and as he came there was not a single thread of sound in all the vastness of Seithr's Hall.

In the well of that silence Matt waited, scanning the Dwarves assembled there with his one dark eye. She heard the guards shift restively behind her. Then, without any fuss at all, Matt took the Diamond Crown and placed it upon his head.

It was as if a tree in a dry forest had been struck by lightning, so explosive was the response. Her heart leaping,

Kim heard a shocked roar of sound ignite the hall. In the thunder of it she felt anger and confusion, strove to detect a hint of joy, and thought that she did. But her gaze had gone instinctively to Kaen, as soon as Matt claimed the Crown.

Kaen's mouth was crooked in a wry, caustic smile, unruffled, even amused. But his eyes had given him away, for in them Kim had seen, if only for an instant, a bleak, vicious malevolence. She read murder there, and it knifed into her heart.

Powerless, a prisoner, fear within her like a living, sharp-clawed creature, Kim turned back to Matt and felt her racing heartbeat slow. Even with a Crown of a thousand diamonds dazzling upon his head, the aura of him, the essence, was still a quiet, reassuring certitude, an everlasting calm.

He raised one hand and waited patiently for silence. When he had it, nearly, he said, "Calor Diman never surrenders her Kings."

Nothing more, and he did not say it loudly, but the acoustics of that chamber carried his words to the farthest corners of Seithr's Hall. When their resonance had died away, the silence once more was complete.

Into it, emerging from either wing of the stage, there came some fifteen or twenty Dwarves. They were all clad in black, and Kim saw that each of them wore, upon the third finger of his right hand, a diamond ring gleaming like white fire. None of them were young, but the one who came first was the eldest by far. White-bearded and leaning for support upon a staff, he paused to let the others file past him to stone seats placed on one side of the stage.

"The Dwarfmoot," Loren whispered softly. "They will judge between Kaen and Matt. The one with the staff is Miach, First of the Moot."

"Judge what?" Kim whispered back apprehensively.

"The word-striving," Loren murmured, not very helpfully. "Of the same kind as the one Matt lost forty years ago, when the Moot judged in favor of Kaen and voted to continue the search for the Cauldron—"

"Silence!" hissed the same guard as before. He emphasized the command by striking Loren on the arm with his hand, not gently.

Silvercloak turned swiftly and fixed the guard with a gaze

that made the Dwarf stumble quickly backward, blanching.

"I am . . . I am ordered to keep you quiet," he stammered.

"I do not intend to say overmuch," Loren said. "But if you touch me again I will turn you into a geiala and roast you for lunch. Once warned is all you will be!"

He turned back to the stage, his face impassive. It was a bluff, nothing more, Kim knew, but she also realized that none of the Dwarves, not even Kaen, could know what had happened to the mage's powers in Cader Sedat.

Miach had moved forward, the click of his staff on the stone sounding loud in the silence. He took a position in front of Kaen and Matt, a little to one side. After bowing with equal gravity to each of them, he turned and addressed the assembled Dwarves.

"Daughters and sons of Calor Diman, you will have heard why we are summoned to Seithr's Hall. Matt, who was King once here under Banir Lök, has returned and has satisfied the Moot that he is who he claims to be. This is so, despite the passage of forty years. He carries a second name now—Sören—to mark the loss of an eye in a war far from our mountains. A war," Miach added quietly, "in which the Dwarves had no proper role to play."

Kim winced. Out of the corner of her eye she saw Loren bite his lower lip in consternation.

Miach continued in the same judicious tones. "Be that as it may, Matt Sören it is who is here again, and last night before the convened Moot he issued challenge to Kaen, who has ruled us these forty years—ruled, but only by the support and sufferance of the Dwarfmoot, not as a true King, for he has never shaped a crystal for the Lake nor spent a night beside her shores under the full moon."

There was a tiny ripple of sound at that. It was Kaen's turn to react. His expression of attentive deference did not change, but Kim, watching closely, saw his hand on the table close into a fist. A moment later, he seemed to become aware of this, and the fist opened again.

"Be that as it may," Miach said a second time, "you are summoned to hear and the Moot to judge a word-striving after the old kind, such as we have not seen in forty years—

since last these two stood before us. I have lived long enough, by grace of the Weaver's hand upon my thread, to say that a pattern is unfolding here, with a symmetry that bears witness to interwoven destinies."

He paused. Then, looking directly at Kim, to her great surprise, he said, "There are two here not of our people. Tidings are slow to come across the mountains, and slower still to come within them, but the Dwarves know well of Loren Silvercloak the mage, whose source was once our King. And Matt Sören has named the woman here as Seer to the High King of Brennin. He has also undertaken to stand surety with his life that both of them will respect our laws here by the Crystal Lake, that they will not wield the magics we know they carry, and will accept whatever judgment the Dwarfmoot makes of this striving. Matt Sören has said this. I now ask that they acknowledge, by whatever oath they deem most binding, that this is true. In return, I offer the assurance of the Dwarfmoot, to which Kaen has acceded—indeed, it was his suggestion—that they will be conducted safely from our realm if such need be after the striving is judged."

Lying snake, Kim thought furiously, looking at Kaen's bland, earnest expression. She schooled her features, though, placed her ringless hand in the pocket of her gown, and listened as Loren rose from his seat to say, "In the name of Seithr, greatest of the Dwarf Kings, who died in the cause of Light, battling Rakoth Maugrim and the legions of the Dark, I swear that I will abide by the words you have spoken." He sat down.

Another rustle, quiet but unmistakable, went through the Hall. *Take that!* Kim thought as, in her turn, she rose. She felt Ysanne within her then, twin soul under the twin mountains, and when she spoke, it was with a Seer's voice that rang out sternly in the huge spaces.

"In the name of the Paraiko of Khath Meigol, gentlest of the Weaver's children, the Giants who are not ghosts, who live and even now are cleansing Eridu, gathering the innocent dead of the Cauldron's killing rain, I swear that I will abide by the words you have spoken."

More than a murmur now, an urgent cascade of sound.

"That is a lie!" an old Dwarf shouted from high up in the Hall. His voice cracked. "The Cauldron we found brought life, not death!"

Kim saw Matt looking at her. He shook his head, very slightly, and she kept quiet.

Miach gestured for silence again. "Truth or lies will be for the Dwarfmoot to decree," he said. "It is time for the challenge to begin. Those of you gathered here will know the laws of the word-striving. Kaen, who governs now, will speak first, as Matt did forty years ago, when governance was his. They will speak to you, not to the Moot. You who are gathered here are to be as a wall of stone off which their words will come to us. Silence is law for you, and from the weight of it, the shape, the woven texture, will the Dwarfmoot seek guidance for the judgment we are to make between these two."

"He paused. "I have one thing, only, left to ask. Though no one else has known a full moon night by Calor Diman, at issue today is Matt Sören's continued right to wear the Diamond Crown. In fairness, then, I would ask him to remove it for the striving."

He turned, and Kim's eyes went, with those of everyone else in the Hall to Matt, to discover that, having made his initial point, he had already placed it again on the stone table between himself and Kaen. *Oh, clever,* Kim thought, fighting to suppress a grin. Oh, clever, my dear friend. Matt nodded gravely to Miach, who bowed in response.

Turning to Kaen, Miach said simply, "You may begin."

He shuffled over, leaning upon his staff, to take his seat among the others of the Dwarfmoot. Kaen's hand, Kim saw, had closed into a fist again, at Matt's smooth anticipation of Miach's request.

He's rattled, she thought. Matt has him way off balance. She felt a quick rush of hope and confidence.

Then Kaen, who had not said a single word until that moment, began the word-striving, and as he did, all Kim's hopes were blown away, as if they were wispy clouds torn by mountain winds.

She had thought that Gorlaes, the Chancellor of Brennin, was a deep-voiced, mellifluous speaker; she had even feared his persuasiveness in the early days. She had heard Diarmuid dan Ailell in the Great Hall of Paras Derval and remembered the power of his light, sardonic, riveting words. She had heard Na-Brendel of the lios alfar take speech to the edge of music and beyond. And within herself, engraved on her heart and mind, she held close the sound of Arthur Pendragon speaking to command or to reassure—with him, somehow, the two became as one.

But in Seithr's Hall within Banir Lök that day she learned how words could be claimed and mastered, brought to a scintillant, glorious apex—turned into diamonds, truly—and all in the service of evil, of the Dark.

Kaen spoke, and she heard his voice rise majestically with the passion of a denunciation; she heard it swoop downward like a bird of prey to whisper an innuendo or offer a half-truth that sounded—even, for a moment, to her—like a revelation from the warp and weft of the Loom itself; she heard it soar with confident assertions of the future and then shape itself into a cutting blade to slash to ribbons the honor of the Dwarf who stood beside him. Who had *dared* to return and strive a second time with Kaen.

Her mouth dry with apprehension, Kim saw Kaen's hands—his large, beautiful, artisan's hands—rise and fall gracefully as he spoke. She saw his arms spread suddenly wide in a gesture of entreaty, of transparent honesty. She saw a hand stab savagely upward to punctuate a question and then fall away, open, as he spoke what he deemed to be—what he made them believe to be—the only possible response. She saw him point a long shaking finger of undisguised, overwhelming rage at the one who had returned, and it seemed to her, as to all the others in Seithr's Hall, that the denouncing hand was that of a god, and it became a source of wonder that Matt Sören had the temerity still to be standing upright before it, instead of crawling on his knees to beg for the merciful death he did not deserve.

From the weight of the silence, Miach had said, from the shape and texture of it, the Dwarfmoot would seek guidance. As Kaen spoke, the stillness in Seithr's Hall was a palpable thing. It *did* have shape, and weight, and a discernible texture. Even Kim, utterly unversed in reading such a subtle message, could feel the silent Dwarves responding to Kaen, giving him back his words: thousands of voiceless auditors for chorus.

There was awe in that response, and guilt, that Kaen, who had labored so long in the service of his people, should be forced yet again to defend himself and his actions. Beyond these two things—beyond awe and guilt—there was also a humbled, grateful acquiesence in the rightness and clarity of everything Kaen said.

He came one step forward from where he had been standing, seeming with that small motion to have come among them, to be one with all of them, to be speaking directly, intimately, to every single listener in the Hall. He said: "It may be thought that the Dwarf beside me now will see farther with his one eye than anyone else in this Hall. Let me remind you of something, something I *must* say before I end, for it cries out within me for utterance. Forty years ago Matt, the sister-son of March, King of the Dwarves, shaped a crystal for Calor Diman on a new moon night: an act of courage, for which I honored him. On the next night of the full moon, he slept by the shore of the Lake, as all who would be King must do: an act of courage, for which I honored him."

Kaen paused. "I honor him no more," he said into the silence. "I have not honored him since another thing he did forty years ago—an act of cowardice that wiped away all memory of courage. Let me remind you, people of the twin mountains. Let me remind you of the day when he took the Scepter lying here beside us and threw it down upon these stones. The Diamond Scepter, treated like a stick of wood! Let me remind you of when he discarded the Crown he so arrogantly claimed just now—after forty years!—discarded it like a trinket that no longer gave him pleasure. And let me remind you"—the voice dipped down, laden with marrow-deep sorrow—"that after doing these things, Matt, King under Banir Lök, abandoned us."

Kaen let the grim stillness linger, let it gather full weight of condemnation. Said gently, "The word-striving forty years ago was his own choice. The submission of the matter of the Cauldron of Khath Meigol to the Dwarfmoot was his own decision. No one forced his hand, no one could. He was

King under the mountains. He ruled not as I have striven to do, by consensus and counsel, but absolutely, wearing the Crown, wedded to the Crystal Lake. And in pique, in spite, in petulance, when the Dwarfmoot honored me by agreeing that the Cauldron I sought was a worthy quest for the Dwarves, King Matt abandoned us."

There was grief in his voice, the pain of one bereft, in those long-ago days, of sorely needed guidance and support. "He left us to manage as best we could without him. Without the King's bond to the Lake that has always been the heartbeat of the Dwarves. For forty years I have been here, with Blöd, my brother, beside me, managing, with the Dwarfmoot's counsel, as best I could. For forty years Matt has been far away, seeking fame and his own desires in the wide world across the mountains. And now, now he would come back after so long. Now, because it suits him—his vanity, his pride—he would come back and reclaim the Scepter and Crown he so contemptuously threw away."

One more step forward. From his mouth to the ear of their hearts. "Do not let him, Children of Calor Diman! Forty years ago you decided that the search for the Cauldron—the Cauldron of Life—was worthy of us in our time. In your service, following the decision the Dwarfmoot made that day, I have labored all these years here among you. Do not turn away from me now!"

Slowly, the extended arms came down and Kaen was done.

Overhead, high above the rigid, absolute silence, the birds fashioned from diamonds circled and shone.

Her chest tight with strain and apprehension, Kim's glance went, with that of everyone else in Seithr's Hall, to Matt Sören, to the friend whose words, ever since she'd met him, had been parceled out in careful, plain measures. Whose strengths were fortitude and watchfulness and an unvoiced depth of caring. Words had never been Matt's tools: not now, not forty years ago when he had lost, bitterly, his last striving with Kaen, and, losing, had surrendered his Crown.

She had an image of how it must have been that day: the young proud King, newly wedded to the Crystal Lake, afire with its visions of Light, hating the Dark then as he did now.

With her inner Seer's eye she could picture it: the rage, the anguished sense of rejection that Kaen's victory had created in him. She could see him hurling away the Crown. And she knew he had been wrong to do so.

In that moment she thought of Arthur Pendragon, another young king, new to his crown and his dreams, learning of the child—incestuous seed of his loins—who was destined to destroy everything Arthur shaped. And so, in a vain attempt to forstall that, he'd ordered so many infants slain.

For the sins of good men she grieved.

For the sins, and the way the shuttling of the Loom brought them back. Back, as Matt had come back again after so long to his mountains. To Seithr's Hall, to stand beside Kaen before the Dwarfmoot.

Praying for him, for all the living in search of Light, knowing how much lay in the balance here, Kim felt the cast spell of Kaen's last plea still lingering in the Hall, and she wondered where Matt would ever find anything to match what Kaen had done.

Then she learned. All of them did.

"We have heard nothing," said Matt Sören, "nothing at all of Rakoth Maugrim. Nothing of war. Of evil. Of friends betrayed into the Dark. We have heard nothing from Kaen of the broken wardstone of Eridu. Of the Cauldron surrendered to Maugrim. *Seithr would weep, and curse us through his tears!*"

Blunt words, sharp, prosaic, unadorned. Cold and stern, they slashed into the Hall like a wind, blowing away the mists of Kaen's eloquent imagery. Hands on his hips, his legs spread wide, seemingly anchored in the stone, Matt did not even try to lure or seduce his listeners. He challenged them. And they listened.

"Forty years ago I made a mistake I will not cease to regret for the rest of my days. Newly crowned, unproven, unknown, I sought approval for what I knew to be right in a striving before the Dwarfmoot in this Hall. I was wrong to do so. A King, when he sees his way clear, must act, that his people may follow. My way should have been clear, and it would have been, had I been strong enough. Kaen and Blöd, who had defied my orders, should have been taken to Traitor's Crag upon Banir Tal and hurled to their deaths. I was wrong. I was not strong enough. I accept, as a King must accept, my share of the burden for the evils since done.

"The very great evils," he said, his voice uncompromising in its message. "Who among you, if not bewitched or terrified, can accept what we have done? How far the Dwarves have fallen! Who among you can accept the wardstone broken? Rakoth freed? The Cauldron of the Paraiko given over unto him? And now I must speak of the Cauldron."

The transition was clumsy, awkward; Matt seemed not to care. He said, "Before this striving began, the Seer of Brennin spoke of the Cauldron as a thing of death, and one of you—and I remember you, Edrig; you were wise already when I was King in these halls, and I never knew any evil to rest in your heart—Edrig named the Seer a liar and said that the Cauldron was a thing of life."

He crossed his arms on his broad chest. "It is not so. Once, maybe, when first forged in Khath Meigol, but not now, not in the hands of the Unraveller. He used the Cauldron the Dwarves gave him to shape the winter just now past, and then—grief to my tongue to tell—to cause the death rain to fall on Eridu."

"That is a lie," said Kaen flatly. There was a shocked whisper of sound. Kaen ignored it. "You are not to tell a pure untruth in word-striving. This you know. I claim this contest by virtue of a breaching of the rules. The Cauldron revives the dead. It does not kill. Every one of us here knows this to be true."

"*Do we so?*" Matt Sören snarled, wheeling on Kaen with such ferocity that the other recoiled. "Dare you speak to say I lie? Then hear me! Every one of you hear me! Did not a mage of Brennin come, with perverted wisdom and forbidden lore? Did Metran of the Garantae not enter these halls to give aid and counsel to Kaen and Blöd?"

Silence was his answer. The silence of the word-striving. Intense, rapt, shaping itself to surround his questions. "Know you that when the Cauldron was found and given over to Maugrim, it was placed in the care of that mage. And he bore it away to Cader Sedat, that island not found on any map, which Maugrim had made a place of unlife even in the days of the Bael Rangat. In that unholy place Metran used the Cauldron to shape the winter and then the rain. He drew his unnatural mage-strength to do these terrible things from a host of svart alfar. He killed them, draining their life force with the power he took, and then used the Cauldron to bring them back to life, over and over again. This is what he did. And this, Children of Calor Diman, descendants of Seithr, this, my beloved people, is what we did!"

"A lie!" said Kaen again, a little desperately. "How would you know this if he truly took it to that place? How would the rain have stopped if this were so?"

This time there was no murmuring, and this time Matt did not wheel in rage upon the other Dwarf. Very slowly he turned and looked at Kaen.

"You would like to know, wouldn't you?" he asked softly. The acoustics carried the question; all of them heard. "You would like to know what went wrong. We were there, Kaen. With Arthur Pendragon, and Diarmuid of Brennin, and Pwyll Twiceborn, Lord of the Summer Tree, we went to Cader Sedat and we killed Metran and we broke the Cauldron. Loren and I did it, Kaen. For the evil done by a mage and the evil done by the Dwarves we made what recompense we could in that place."

Kaen's mouth opened and then closed again.

"You do not believe me," Matt went on, inexorably, mercilessly. "You want not to believe, so your hopes and plans will not have gone so terribly awry. Do not believe me, then! Believe, instead, the witness of your eyes!"

And thrusting a hand into the pocket of the vest he wore, he drew from it a black shard that he threw down on the stone table between the Scepter and the Crown. Kaen leaned forward to look, and an involuntary sound escaped him.

"Well may you wail!" Matt intoned, his voice like that of a final judgment. "Though even now you are grieving for yourself and not for your people to see a fragment of the broken Cauldron return to these mountains."

He turned back to face the high-vaulted Hall, under the ceaseless circling of the diamond birds.

Again the shift in his speech was awkward, rough. Again he seemed oblivous to that. "Dwarves," Matt cried, "I claim no blamelessness before you now. I have done wrong, but have made redress as best I might. And I will continue to do so, now and forward from this day until I die. I will bear the burdens of my own transgressions and take upon myself as many of your own burdens as I can. For so must a King do, and I am your King. I have returned to lead you back among the armies of the Light where the Dwarves belong. Where we have always belonged. Will you have me?"

Silence. Of course.

Scarcely breathing, Kim strove with all her untutored instincts to take its measure.

The shape of the silence was sharp; it was heavy with unnamed fears, inchoate apprehensions; it was densely, intricately threaded with numberless questions and doubts. There was more, she knew there was more, but she was not equal to discerning any of it clearly.

And then, in any case, the silence was broken.

"*Hold!*" Kaen cried, and even Kim knew how flagrant a transgression of the laws of the word-striving this had to be.

Kaen drew three quick sharp breaths to calm and control himself. Then, coming forward again, he said, "This is more than a striving now, and so I must deviate from the course of a true challenging. Matt Sören seeks not only to reclaim a Crown he tossed away, when he elected to be a servant in Brennin rather than to rule in Banir Lök, but now he also invites the Moot—commands it, if his tone be heard, and not only his words—to adopt a new course of action without a moment's thought!"

With every word he seemd to be growing in confidence again, weaving his own thick tapestry of persuasive sound. "I did not raise this matter when I spoke because I did not dream—in my own innocence—that Matt would so presume. But he has done so, and so I must speak again, and beg your forgiveness for that mild transgression. Matt Sören comes here in the last days of war to order us to bring our army over to the King of Brennin. He uses other words, but that is what he means. He forgets one thing. He chooses to forget it, I think, but we who will pay the price of his omission must not be so careless."

Kaen paused and scanned the Hall for a long moment, to be sure he had them all with him.

Then, grimly, he said, "*The army of the Dwarves is not here!* My brother has led it from these halls and over the mountains to war. We promised aid to the Lord of Starkadh in exchange for the aid we asked of him in the search for the Cauldron—aid freely given, and accepted by us. I will not shame you or the memory of our fathers by speaking overmuch of the honor of the Dwarves. Of what it might mean to have asked assistance from him and to now refuse the help we promised in return. I will not speak of that. I will say only the clearest, most obvious thing—a thing Matt Sören has chosen not to see. The army is gone. We have chosen a course. I chose, and the Dwarfmoot chose with me. Honor and necessity, both, compel us to stay on the path we are set upon. We could not reach Blöd and the army in time to call them back, even if we wanted to!"

"*Yes we could!*" Kim Ford lied, shouting it.

She was on her feet. The nearest guard shifted forward, but quailed at a paralyzing glare from Loren. "I brought your true King here from the edge of the sea last night, by the power I carry. I can take him to your army as easily, should the Dwarfmoot ask me to."

Lies, lies. The Baelrath was gone. She kept both hands in her pockets all the time she spoke. It was no more than a bluff, as Loren's words to the guard had been. So much was at stake, though, and she really wasn't good at this sort of thing, she knew she wasn't. Nonetheless she held her gaze fixed on Kaen's and did not flinch: if he wanted to expose her, to show the Baelrath that had been stolen from her, then let him! He would have to explain to the Dwarfmoot how he got it—and then where would his talk of honor be?

Kaen did not speak or move. But from the side of the stage there came suddenly three loud, echoing thumps of a staff on the stone floor.

Miach moved forward, slowly and carefully as before, but his anger was palpable, and when he spoke he had to struggle to master his voice.

"Bravely done!" he said with bitter sarcasm. "A striving to remember! Never have I seen the rules so flouted in a challenge. Matt Sören, not even forty years away can justify the ignorance involved in your bringing an *object* into a striving! You knew the rules governing such things before you had seen ten summers. And you, Kaen! A 'minor transgression'? How *dare* you speak a second time in a word-striving! What have we become that not even the oldest rules of our people are remembered and observed? Even to the extent"—he swung around to glare at Kimberly—"of having a *guest* speak in Seithr's Hall during a challenge."

This, she decided, was too much! Feeling her own pent-up fury rising, she began a stinging retort and felt Loren's punishing grip on her arm. She closed her mouth without saying a word, though her hands inside the pockets of her gown clenched into white fists.

Then she relaxed them, for Miach's rage seemed to have spent itself with that brief, impassioned flurry. He seemed to shrink back again, no longer an infuriated patriarch but only an old man in troubled times, faced now with a very great responsibility.

He said, in a quieter, almost an apologetic voice, "It may be that the rules that were clear and important enough for all our Kings, from before Seithr down to March himself, are no longer paramount. It may be that none of the Dwarves have had to live through times so cloudy and confused as these. That a longing for clarity is only an old man's wistfulness."

Kim saw Matt shaking his head in denial. Miach did not notice. He was looking up at the lofty half-filled Hall. "It may be," he repeated vaguely. "But even if it is, this striving is ended, and it is now for the Moot to judge. We will withdraw. You will all remain here"—the voice grew stronger again, with words of ritual—"until we have returned to declare the will of the Dwarfmoot. We give thanks for the counsel of your silence. It was heard and shall be given voice."

He turned, and the others of the black-garbed Moot rose, and together they all withdrew from the stage, leaving Matt and Kaen standing there on either side of a table which held a shining Crown, and a shining Scepter, and a black sharp-edged fragment of the Cauldron of Khath Meigol.

Kim became aware that Loren's hand was still sqeezing her arm, very hard. He seemed to realize it in the same moment.

"I'm sorry," he murmured, easing but not releasing his grasp.

She shook her head. "I was about to say something stupid."

This time the guards were careful not to test Loren's

patience by intervening again. Indeed, all about the Hall there was a rising swell of sound as the Dwarves, released from the bond of silence that had held them during the striving, began animatedly to discuss what had taken place. Only Matt and Kaen, motionless on the stage, not looking at each other, remained silent.

"Not stupid at all," said Loren quietly. "You took a chance by speaking, but they needed to hear what you could do."

Kim looked over at him with sudden dismay. His eyes narrowed at the sight of her consternation.

"What is it?" he whispered, careful not to be overheard.

Kim said nothing. Only withdrew her right hand slowly from its pocket, so that he could see what, clearly, he hadn't seen before—the terrible absence of fire, the Baelrath gone.

He looked, and then he closed his eyes. She put her hand back in her pocket.

"When?" Loren asked, his voice thin and stretched.

"When we were ambushed. I felt it being taken. I woke this morning without it."

Loren opened his eyes and looked at the stage, at Kaen. "I wonder," he murmured. "I wonder how he knew."

Kim shrugged. It hardly seemed to matter at this point. What mattered was that, as things stood, Kaen had been quite accurate in what he'd told the Dwarves. If the army was west of the mountains, there was nothing they could do to stop them now from fighting among the legions of the Dark.

Loren seemed to read her thoughts, or else they were his own as well. He said, "It is not over yet. In part, because of what you did. That was brightly woven, Kimberly—you blunted a thrust of Kaen's, and you may have bought us time to do something." He paused. His expression changed, became diffident and strained.

"Actually," he amended, "you may have bought Matt time, and perhaps yourself. There isn't much of anything I can do any more."

"That isn't true," Kim said, with all the conviction she could muster. "Wisdom carries its own strength."

He smiled faintly at the platitude and even nodded his head. "I know. I know it does. Only it is a hard thing, Kim, it is a very hard thing to have known power for forty years and to have none of it now, when it matters so much."

To this, Kim, who had carried her own power for only a little over a year and had fought it for much of that time, could find nothing to say.

There was no time for her to reply, in any case. The rustle of sound in the Hall rose swiftly higher and then, as swiftly, subsided into a stiff, tense silence.

In that silence the Dwarfmoot filed soberly back to their stone seats on the stage. For the third time Miach came forward to stand beside Kaen and Matt, facing the multitude in the seats above.

Kim glanced at Loren, rigid beside her. She followed the tall man's gaze to his friend of forty years. She saw Matt's mouth move silently. *Weaver at the Loom,* she thought, echoing the prayer she read on the Dwarf's lips.

Then, wasting no time, Miach spoke. "We have listened to the speech of the word-striving and to the silence of the Dwarves. Hear now the rendering of the Dwarfmoot of Banir Lök. Forty years ago in this Hall, Matt, now also called Sören, threw down the symbols of his Kingship. There was no equivocation in what he did, no mistaking his intention to relinquish the Crown."

Kim would have sold her soul, both her souls, for a glass of water. Her throat was so dry it hurt to swallow.

Miach went on, soberly, "At that same time did Kaen assume governance here under the mountains, nor was he challenged in this, nor has he been until this day. Even so, despite the urging of the Moot, Kaen chose not to make a crystal for the Lake or to pass a full moon night beside her shores. He never became our King.

"There is then, over and above all else, the Moot has decided, one question that must be answered in this striving. It has long been said in these mountain halls—so long it is now a catchphrase for us—that Calor Diman never surrenders her Kings. It was said today by Matt Sören, and the Moot heard him say it before we came forth for the judging. That, we have now decided, is not the question at issue here."

Kim, desperately struggling to understand, to anticipate, saw Kaen's eyes flash with a swiftly veiled triumph. Her heart was a drum, and fear beat the rhythm of it.

"The question at issue," said Miach softly, "is whether the King can surrender the Lake."

The silence was absolute. Into it, he said, "It has never happened before in all the long history of our people that a King in these halls should do what Matt did long ago, or seek to do what he strives for now. There are no precedents, and the Dwarfmoot has decreed that it would be presumption for us to decide. All other questions—the disposition of our armies, everything we shall do henceforth—are contained in this one issue: who, truly, is our leader now? The one who has governed us forty years with the Dwarfmoot at his side, or the one who slept by Calor Diman and then walked away?

"It is, the Dwarfmoot decrees, a matter for the powers of Calor Diman to decide. Here then is our judgment. There are now six hours left before sunset. Each of you, Matt and Kaen, will be guided to a chamber with all the tools of the crystal maker's craft. You will each shape whatsoever image you please, with such artistry as you may command. Tonight, when darkness falls, you shall ascend the nine and ninety steps to the meadow door that leads from Banir Tal to Calor Diman, and you shall cast your artifices into the Crystal Lake. I will be there, and Ingen, also, from the Moot. You may each name two to come with you to bear witness on your behalf. The moon is not full. This is not properly a night for the naming of a King, but neither has anything such as this ever confronted us before. We will leave it to the Lake."

A place more fair than any in all the worlds, Matt Sören had named Calor Diman long ago, before the first crossing. They had been still in the Park Plaza Hotel: five people from Toronto, en route to another world for two weeks of partying at a High King's celebrations.

A place more fair . . .

A place of judgment. Of what might be final judgment.

Chapter 11

That same day, as the Dwarves of the twin mountains prepared for the judgment of their Lake, Gereint the shaman, cross-legged on the mat in his dark house, cast the net of his awareness out over Fionavar and vibrated like a harp with what he sensed.

It was coming to a head, all of it, and very soon.

From that remote elbow of land east of the Latham he reached out, an old brown spider at the center of his web, and saw many things with the power of his blinding.

But not what he was looking for. He wanted the Seer. Feeling helplessly removed from what was happening, he sought the bright aura of Kimberly's presence, groping for a clue to what was shuttling on the loom of war. Tabor had told him the morning before that he had flown the Seer to a cottage by a lake near Paras Derval, and Gereint had known Ysanne for much of his life and so knew where this cottage was.

But when he reached to that place he found only the ancient green power that dwelt beneath the water, and no sign of Kim at all. He did not know—he had no way of knowing—that since Tabor had set her down beside that shore, she had already gone, by the tapped power of the avarlith, to Lisen's Tower, and from there that same night, with the red flaming of her own wild magic, over the mountains to Banir Lök.

And over the mountains he could not go, unless he sent his soul traveling, and he was too recently returned from journeying out over the waves to do that again so soon.

So she was lost to him. He felt the presence of other powers, though, lights on a map in the darkness of his mind. The other shamans were all around him, in their houses much like his own, here beside the Latham. Their auras were like the trace flickerings of lienae at night, erratic and insubstantial. There would be no aid or comfort there. He was preeminent among the shamans of the Plain, and had been since his blinding. If any of them were to have a role yet to play in what was to come, it would have to be him, for all his years.

There came a tapping on his door. He had already heard footsteps approaching from outside. He quelled a quick surge of anger at the intrusion, for he recognized both the tread and the rhythm of the knocking.

"Come in," he said. "What can I do for you, wife of the Aven?"

"Liane and I have brought you a lunch," Leith replied in her brisk tones.

"Good," he said energetically, though for once he wasn't hungry. He was also discomfited: it seemed that his hearing was finally starting to go. He'd only heard one set of footsteps. Both women entered, and Liane, approaching, brushed his cheek with her lips.

"Is that the best you can do?" he mock-growled. She squeezed his hand, and he squeezed back. He would have ferociously denied it, if pressed, but in his heart Gereint had long acknowledged that Ivor's daughter was his favorite child of the tribe. Of the Plain. Of all the worlds, if it came to that.

It was to her mother that he turned, though, to where he heard her kneel in front of him, and a little to the side. "Strength of the Plain," he said respectfully, "may I touch your thoughts?"

She leaned forward, and he raised his hands to run them along the bones of her face. The touch let him into her mind, where he saw anxiety, a weight of cares, the burdens of sleeplessness, but—and he marveled, even as he touched her face—not even a shadow of fear.

His touch became, briefly, a caress. "Ivor is lucky in you, bright soul. We all are. Luckier than we deserve."

He had known Leith since her birth, had watched her grow into womanhood, and had feasted at her wedding to Ivor dan Banor. In those far-off days he had first seen a certain kind of brightness shining within her. It had been there ever since, growing even stronger as her children were born, and Gereint knew it for what it was: a deep, luminous love that was rarely allowed to shine forth. She was a profoundly private person, Leith, never given to open demonstration, not trusting it in others. She had been called cold and unyielding all her life. Gereint knew better.

He drew his hands away reluctantly, and as he did he felt the reverberations of war sweep over him again.

Diffidently, Leith asked, "Have you seen anything, shaman? Is there something you can tell me?"

"I am looking now," he said quietly. "Sit, both of you, and I will tell you what I can."

He reached out again, seeking interstices of power along the webs of time and space. He was a long way off, though, no longer young and but recently returned from the worst journeying of his days. Nothing was clear, except for the reverberations: the sense of a climax coming. An end to war, or an ending to everything.

He did not tell them that; it would be needlessly cruel. Instead, he ate the lunch they had brought for him—it seemed he was hungry, after all—and listened to the dispositions Leith had made of resources within the crowded camp of women and children and the old. And eight blind, useless shamans.

All through that day and the next, as premonitions gathered more closely about him, Gereint sat on the mat in his dark house and strove, whenever his waning strength allowed, to see something clearly, to find a role to play.

Both days would pass, though, before he felt the touch of the god, of Cernan's offered gift of foreknowledge. And with that voice, that vision, there would come a fear such as he'd never known, not even out over the waves. This would be something new, something terrible. The more so because it was not directed at him, with all his years, with his long, full life behind him. It was not his price to pay, and there was not a single thing he could do about it. With sorrow in his heart, two mornings hence, Gereint would lift his voice in summons.

And call for Tabor to come to him.

Over the Plain the army of Light was riding to war. North of Celidon, of the Adein, of the green mound Ceinwen had raised for the dead, they rode and the white magnificence of Rangat towered ahead of them, filling the blue, cloud-scattered summer sky.

Every one of them was on horseback save for a number of the Cathalians, racing in their scythe-wheeled war chariots at the outer rim of the army. When the summonglass had flamed in Brennin, Aileron had had too much need of speed to allow the presence of foot soldiers. By the same token, throughout the long, unnatural winter, he'd been laying his plans against such a time as this: the horses had been ready, and every man in the army of Brennin could ride. So, too, could the men and women of the lios alfar from Daniloth. And of the Dalrei there was not and never had been any question.

Under the benevolent, miraculous sun of summer returned they rode amid the smell of fresh grass and vibrant splashes of wildflowers. The Plain rolled away in every direction as far as the eye could follow. Twice they passed great swifts of eltor, and the heart of every one of them had lifted to see the beasts of the Plain, released from the killing bondage of snow, run free again over the tall grass.

For how long? Amid all the beauty that surrounded them, that remained the question. They were not a company of friends out for a gallop under summer skies. They were an army, advancing, very fast, to the door of the Dark, and they would be there soon.

They *were* going fast, Dave realized. It was not the headlong pace of the Dalrei's wild ride to Celidon, but Aileron was pushing them hard, and Dave was grateful for the brief rest period they were granted midway through the afternoon.

He swung down off his horse, muscles protesting, and he flexed and limbered them as best he could before stretching out on his back on the soft grass. As Torc dropped down beside him, a question occurred to Dave.

"Why *are* we hurrying?" he asked. "I mean, we're missing Diarmuid and Arthur, and Kim and Paul . . . what advantage does Aileron see in pushing on?"

"We'll know when Levon gets back from the conference up front," Torc answered. "My guess is that it's geography as much as anything else. He wants to get close to Gwynir this evening, so we can go through the woods in the morning. If we do that, we should be able to be north of Celyn Lake in Andarien before dark tomorrow. That would make sense, especially if Maugrim's army is waiting for us there."

The calmness of Torc's voice was unsettling. *Maugrim's army:* svart alfar, urgach upon slaug, Galadan's wolves, the swans of Avaia's brood, and Weaver alone knew what else. Only Owein's Horn had saved them last time, and Dave knew he didn't dare blow it again.

The larger picture was too daunting. He focused on immediate goals. "Will we make the forest, then? Gwynir? Can we get there by dark?"

He saw Torc's eyes flick beyond him and then the dark man said, "If we were Dalrei alone, we could, of course. But I'm not sure, with all this excess weight of Brennin we're carrying."

Dave heard a loud snort of indignation and turned to see Mabon of Rhoden subside comfortably down beside him. "I didn't notice any of us falling behind on the way to Celidon," the Duke said. He took a pull of water from his flask and offered it to Dave, who drank as well. It was icy cool; he didn't know how.

Mabon's presence was a surprise of sorts, though a happy one. The wound he'd taken by the Adein had been healed last night by Teyrnon and Barak, after Aileron had finally let them make camp. Mabon had flatly refused to be left behind.

Since the journey from Paras Derval to the Latham where Ivor and the Dalrei had been waiting, the Duke seemed to favor the company of Levon and Torc and Dave. Dave wasn't displeased. Among other things, Mabon had saved his life, when Avaia had exploded out of a clear sky on that ride. Beyond that, the Duke, though no longer young, was an experienced campaigner, and good company too. He had already established a relationship with Torc that had the otherwise grim Dalrei joking back and forth with him.

Now Mabon tipped Dave a surreptitious wink and continued. "In any case, this isn't a sprint, my young hero. This is a long haul, and for that you need Rhoden staying power. None of your Dalrei brashness that fades as the hours roll by."

Torc didn't bother to reply. Instead he tore up a handful of long grass and threw it at Mabon's recumbent figure. The wind was against him, though, and most of it landed on Dave.

"I wish I knew," said Levon, walking up, "why I continue to spend my time with such irresponsible people."

The tone was jocular, but his eyes were sober. All three of them sat up and looked at him gravely.

Levon crouched down on his heels and played idly with a handful of grass stems as he spoke. "Aileron does want to make Gwynir by tonight. I have never been this far north, but my father has, and he says we should be able to do it. There is a problem, though."

"Which is?" Mabon was grimly attentive.

"Teyrnon and Barak have been mind-scanning forward all day to see if they can sense the presence of evil. Gwynir would be an obvious place to ambush us. The horses, and especially the chariots, are going to be awkward, even if we keep to the edges of the forest."

"Have they seen anything?" Mabon was asking the questions; Dave and Torc listened and waited.

"After a fashion, which is the problem. Teyrnon says he finds only the tracest flicker of evil in Gwynir, but he has a feeling of danger nonetheless. He cannot understand it. He *does* sense the army of the Dark ahead of us, but far beyond Gwynir. They are in Andarien already, we think, gathering there."

"So what is in the forest?" Mabon queried, his brow furrowed with thought.

"No one knows. Teyrnon's guess is that the evil he apprehends is the lingering trace of the army's passage, or else a handful of spies they have left behind. The danger may be inherent in the forest, he thinks. There were powers of darkness in Gwynir at the time of the Bael Rangat."

"So what do we do?" Dave asked. "Do we have a choice?"

"Not really," Levon replied. "They talked about going through Daniloth, but Ra-Tenniel said that even with the lios alfar to guide us, we are too many for the lios to guarantee that a great many of us would not be lost in the Shadowland. And Aileron will not ask him to let down the woven mist with the army of the Dark in Andarien. They would move south the moment that happened, and we would be fighting in Daniloth. The High King said he will not permit that."

"So we take our chances in the forest," Mabon summarized.

"So it seems," Levon agreed. "But Teyrnon keeps saying that he doesn't really see evil there, so I don't know how much of a chance we're taking. We're doing it, in any case. In the morning. No one is to enter the forest at night."

"Was that a direct order?" Torc asked quietly.

Levon turned to him. "Not actually. Why?"

Torc's voice was carefully neutral. "I was thinking that a group of people, a very small group, might be able to scout ahead tonight and see what there is to see."

There was a little silence.

"A group, say, of four people?" Mabon of Rhoden murmured, in a tone of purely academic interest.

"That would be a reasonable number, I would guess," Torc replied, after judicious reflection.

Looking at the other three, his heartbeat suddenly quickening, Dave saw a quiet resolution in each of them. Nothing more was said. The rest period was almost over. They rose, prepared to mount up again.

Something was happening, though. A commotion was stirring the southeastern fringes of the army. Dave turned with the others, in time to see three strange riders being escorted past them to where the High King was, and the Aven, and Ra-Tenniel of Daniloth.

The three were travel-stained, and each of them slumped in his saddle with weariness written deep into his features. One was a Dalrei, an older man, his face obscured by mud and grime. The second was a younger man, tall, fair-haired, with a pattern of green tattoo markings on his face.

The third was a Dwarf, and it was Brock of Banir Tal.

Brock. Whom Dave had last seen in Gwen Ystrat, preparing to ride east into the mountains with Kim.

"I think I want to see this," said Levon quickly. He started forward to follow the three newcomers, and Dave was right beside him, with Mabon and Torc in stride.

By virtue of Levon's rank, and the Duke's, they passed through into the presence of the Kings. Dave stood there, half a head taller than anyone else, and watched, standing just behind Torc, as the three newcomers knelt before the High King.

"Be welcome, Brock," Aileron said, with genuine warmth. "Bright the hour of your return. Will you name your companions to me and give me what tidings you can?"

Brock rose, and for all his fatigue his voice was clear.

"Greetings, High King," said the Dwarf. "I would wish you to extend your welcome to these two who have come with me, riding without stop through two nights and most of two days to serve in your ranks. Beside me is Faebur of Larak, in Eridu, and beyond him is one who styles himself Dalreidan, and I can tell you that he saved my life and that of the Seer of Brennin, when otherwise we would surely have died."

Dave blinked at the Dalrei's name. He caught a glance from Levon, who whispered, "Rider's Son? An exile. I wonder who it is."

"I bid you both welcome," Aileron said. And then, with a tightening in his voice, "What tidings beyond the mountains?"

"Grievous, my lord," Brock said. "One more grief to lay at the door of the Dwarves. A death rain fell for three days in Eridu. The Cauldron shaped it from Cader Sedat, and—bitter to my tongue the telling—I do not think there is a man or woman left alive in that land."

The stillness that followed was of devastation beyond the compassing of words. Faebur, Dave saw, stood straight as a spear, his face set in a mask of stone.

"Is it falling still?" Ra-Tenniel asked, very softly.

Brock shook his head. "I would have thought you knew. Are there no tidings from them? The rain stopped two days ago. The Seer told us that the Cauldron had been smashed in Cader Sedat."

After pain, after grief, hope beyond expectation. A murmur of sound suddenly rose, sweeping back through the ranks of the army.

"Weaver be praised!" Aileron exclaimed. And then: "What of the Seer, Brock?"

Brock said, "She was alive and well, though I know not where she is now. We were guided to Khath Meigol by the two men here with me. She freed the Paraiko there, with the aid of Tabor dan Ivor and his flying creature, and they bore her west two nights ago. Where, I know not."

Dave looked at Ivor.

The Aven said, "What was he doing there? I left him with orders to guard the camps."

"He was." The one called Dalreidan spoke for the first time. "He was guarding them, and was going back to do so again. He was summoned by the Seer, Ivor . . . Aven. She knew the name of his creature, and he had no choice. Nor did she—she could not have done what she had to do with only the three of us. Be not angry with him. I think he is suffering enough."

Levon's face had gone white. Ivor opened his mouth and then closed it again.

"What is it you fear, Aven of the Plain?" It was Ra-Tenniel.

Again, Ivor hesitated. Then, as if drawing the thought up from the wellspring of his heart, he said, "He goes farther away every time he flies. I am afraid he will soon be like . . . like Owein and the Wild Hunt. A thing of smoke and death, utterly cut off from the world of men."

Silence once more, a different kind, shaped of awe as much as fear. It was broken by Aileron in a deliberately crisp voice that brought them all back to the Plain and the day moving inexorably toward dusk.

"We've a long way to go," the High King said. "The three of you are welcome among us. Can you ride?"

Brock nodded.

"It is why I am here," said Faebur. A young voice, trying hard to be stern. "To ride with you, and do what I can when battle comes."

Aileron looked over at the older man who called himself Dalreidan. Dave saw that Ivor was looking at him too, and that Dalreidan was gazing back, not at the High King but at the Aven.

"I can ride," Dalreidan said, very softly. "Have I leave?"

Abruptly, Dave realized that something else was happening here.

Ivor looked at Dalreidan for a long time without answering. Then: "No Chieftain can reclaim an exile within the Law. But nothing I know in the parchments at Celidon speaks to what the Aven may do in such a case. We are at war, and you have done service already in our cause. You have leave to return. As Aven I say so now."

He stopped. Then, in a different voice, Ivor said, "You have leave to return to the Plain and to your tribe, though not under the name you have taken now. Be welcome back under the name you bore before the accident that thrust you forth into the mountains. This is a brighter thread in darkness than I ever thought to see, a promise of return. I cannot say how glad I am to see you here again."

He smiled. "Turn now, for there is another here who will be as glad. Sorcha of the third tribe, turn and greet your son!"

In front of Dave, Torc went rigid, as Levon let out a whoop of delight. Sorcha turned. He looked at his son, and Dave, still standing behind Torc, saw the old Dalrei's begrimed face light up with an unlooked-for joy.

One moment the tableau held; then Torc stumbled forward with unwonted awkwardness, and he and his father met in an embrace so fierce it seemed as if they meant to squeeze away all the dark years that had lain between.

Dave, who had given Torc the push that sent him forward, was smiling through tears. He looked at Levon and then at Ivor. He thought of his own father, so far away—so far away, it seemed, all his life. He looked over and up at Rangat and remembered the hand of fire.

"Do you think," Mabon of Rhoden murmured, "that that

small expedition we were planning might just as easily be done with seven?"

Dave wiped his eyes. He nodded. Then, still unable to speak, he nodded again.

Levon signaled them forward. Careful of the axe he carried, moving as silently as he could, Dave crawled up beside his friend. The others did the same. Lying prone on a hillock—scant shelter on the open Plain—the seven of them gazed north toward the darkness of Gwynir.

Overhead, clouds scudded eastward, now revealing, now obscuring the waning moon. Sighing through the tall grass, the breeze carried for the first time the scent of the evergreen forest. Far beyond the trees Rangat reared up, dominating the northern sky. When the moon was clear of the clouds the mountain glowed with a strange, spectral light. Dave looked away to the west and saw that the world ended there.

Or seemed to. They were on the very edge of Daniloth: the Shadowland, where time changed. Where men could wander lost in Ra-Lathen's mist until the end of all the worlds. Dave peered into the moonlit shadows, the drifting fog, and it seemed to him that he saw blurred figures moving there, some riding ghostly horses, others on foot, all silent in the mist.

They had left the camp at moonrise, with less difficulty than expected. Levon had led them to the guard post manned by Cechtar of the third tribe, who was not about to betray or impede the designs of the Aven's son. Indeed, his only objection had been in not being allowed to accompany them.

"You can't," Levon had murmured very calmly, in control. "If we aren't back before sunrise, we will be captured or dead, and someone will have to warn the High King. The someone is you, Cechtar. I'm sorry. A thankless task. If the gods love us, it is a message you'll not have to carry."

After that, there had been no more words for a long time. Only the whisper of the night breeze across the Plain, the hoot of a hunting owl, the soft tread of their own footsteps as they walked away from the fires of the camp into the dark. Then the rustling sound of grasses parting as they dropped down and crawled the last part of the way toward the low tummock Levon had pointed out, just east of Daniloth, just south of Gwynir.

Crawling along beside Mabon of Rhoden, behind Torc and Sorcha, who seemed unwilling to allow more than a few inches of space between them now, Dave found himself thinking about how much a part of his reality death had been since he came to Fionavar.

Since he had crashed through the space between worlds here on the Plain and Torc had almost killed him with a dagger. There *had* been a killing that first night: he and the dark Dalrei he called a brother now had slain an urgach together in Faelinn Grove, first death among so many. There had been a battle by Llewenmere, and then among the snows of the Latham. A wolf hunt in Gwen Ystrat, and then, only three nights ago, the carnage along the banks of the Adein.

He had been lucky, he realized, moving more cautiously forward as the moon came out from between two banks of cloud. He could have died a dozen times over. Died a long way from home. The moon slid back behind the clouds. The breeze was cool. Another owl hooted. There were scattered stars overhead, where the cloud cover broke.

He thought of his father for the second time that day. It wasn't hard, even for Dave, to figure out why. He looked at Sorcha, just ahead, moving effortlessly over the shadowed ground. Almost against his will, a trick of distance and shadows and of long sorrow, he pictured his father here with them, an eighth figure on the dark Plain. Josef Martyniuk had fought among the Ukrainian partisans for three years. More than forty years ago, but even so. Even so, a lifetime of physical labor had kept his big body hard, and Dave had grown up fearing the power of his father's brawny arm. Josef could have swung a killing axe, and his icy blue eyes might have glinted just a little—too much to ask?—to see how easily his son handled one, how honored Dave was among people of rank and wisdom.

He could have kept up, too, Dave thought, going with the fantasy a little way. At least as well as Mabon, surely. And he wouldn't have had any doubts, any hesitations about the rightness of doing this, of going to war in this cause. There had been stories in Dave's childhood about his father's deeds in his own war.

None from Josef, though. Whatever fragments Dave had heard had come from friends of his parents, middle-aged men pouring a third glass of iced vodka for themselves, telling the awkward, oversized younger son stories about his father long ago. Or beginning the stories. Before Josef, overhearing, would silence them with a harsh storm of words in the old tongue.

Dave could still remember the first time he had beaten up his older brother. When Vincent, late one night in the room they shared, had let slip a casual reference to a railway bombing their father had organized.

"How do you know about that?" Dave, perhaps ten, had demanded. He could still remember the way his heart had lurched.

"Dad told me," Vincent had answered calmly. "He's told me lots of those stories."

Perhaps even now, fifteen years after, Vincent still didn't know why his younger brother had so ferociously attacked him. For the first time ever, and the only time. Leaping upon his smaller, frailer older brother and punching him about. Crying that Vincent was lying.

Vincent's own cries had brought Josef storming into the room, to block the light from the hallway with his size, to seize his younger son in one hand and hold him in the air as he cuffed him about with an open, meaty palm.

"He is smaller than you!" Josef had roared. "You are never to hit him!"

And Dave, crying, suspended helplessly in the air, unable to dodge the slaps raining down on him, had screamed, almost incoherently, "But I'm smaller than you!"

And Josef had stopped.

Had set his gangly, clumsy son down to weep on his bed. And had said, in a strained, unsettling voice, "This is true. This is correct."

And had gone out, closing the bedroom door on the light.

Dave hadn't understood any of it then, and, to be honest, he grasped only a part of what had happened that night, even now. He didn't have that kind of introspection. Perhaps by choice.

He did remember Vincent, the next night offering to tell his younger brother the story of the train bombing. And himself, inarticulate but defiant, telling Vince to just shut up.

He was sorry about that now. Sorry about a lot of things. Distance, he supposed, did that to you.

And thinking so, he crawled up beside Levon on the hillock and looked upon the darkness of Gwynir.

"This isn't," Levon murmured, "the most intelligent thing I've ever done." The words were rueful, but the tone was not.

Dave heard the barely suppressed excitement in the voice of Ivor's son and, within himself, rising over his fears, he felt an unexpected rush of joy. He was among friends, men he liked and deeply respected, and he was sharing danger with them in a cause worthy of that sharing. His nerves seemed sharp, honed; he felt intensely alive.

The moon slipped behind another thick bank of clouds. The outline of the forest became blurred and indistinct. Levon said, "Very well. I will lead. Follow in pairs behind me. I do not think they are watching for us—if, indeed, there is anything there beyond bears and hunting cats. I will make for the depression a little east of north. Follow quietly. If the moon comes out, hold where you are until it is gone again."

Levon slipped over the ridge and, working along on his belly, began sliding over the open space toward the forest. He moved so neatly the grasses scarcely seemed to move to mark his passage.

Dave waited a moment, then, with Mabon beside him, began propelling himself forward. It wasn't easy going with the axe, but he hadn't come here to share in something easy. He found a rhythm of elbows and knees, forced himself to breathe evenly and slowly, and kept his head low to the ground. Twice he glanced up, to make sure of his orientation, and once the thinning moon did slide out, briefly, pinning them down among the silvered grasses. When it disappeared again, they went on.

They found the downward slope, just where the trees began to thicken. Levon was waiting, crouched low, a finger to his lips. Dave rested on one knee, balancing his axe, breathing carefully. And listening.

Silence, save for night birds, wind in the trees, the quick scurrying of some small animal. Then a barely audible rustle of grass, and Torc and Sorcha were beside him, followed, a moment later, as silently, by Brock and Faebur. The young Eridun's face was set in a grim mask. With the dark tattoos he looked like some primitive, implacable god of war.

Levon motioned them close. In the faintest thread of a whisper he said, "If there is an ambush of any kind, it will not be far from here. They will expect us to skirt as close to Daniloth as we can. Any attack would pin us against the Shadowland, with the horses useless among these trees. I want to check due north from here and then loop back along a line farther east. If we find nothing, we can return to camp and play at dice with Cechtar. He's a bad gambler with a belt I like."

Levon's teeth flashed white in the blackness. Dave grinned back at him. Moments like this, he decided, were what you lived for.

Then the armed guard stepped into their hollow from the north.

Had he given the alarm, had he had time to do so, all of them would probably have died.

He did not. He had no time.

Of the seven men he stumbled upon, every one was terribly dangerous in his own fashion, and very quick. The guard saw them, opened his mouth to scream a warning—and died with the quickest blade of them all in his throat.

Two arrows struck him, and a second knife before he hit the ground, but all seven of them knew whose blade had killed, whose had been first.

They looked at Brock of Banir Tal, and then at the Dwarf he had slain, and they were silent.

Brock walked forward and stood looking down at his victim for a long time. Then he stooped and withdrew his knife, and Sorcha's as well, from the Dwarf's heart. He walked back to the six of them, and his eyes, even in the night shadows, bore witness to a great pain.

"I knew him," he whispered. "His name was Vojna. He was very young. I knew his parents too. He never did an evil thing in all his days. *What has happened to us?*"

It was Mabon's deep voice that slipped quietly into the

silence. "To some of you," he amended gently. "But I think we have an answer now to Teyrnon's riddle. There is danger here, but not true evil, only a thread of it. The Dwarves are sent to ambush us, but they are not truly of the Dark."

"Does it matter?" Brock whispered bitterly.

"I think so," Levon replied gravely. "I think it might. Enough words, though: there will be other guards. I want to find out how many of them there are, and exactly where. I also need two of you to carry word back to the camp, right now." He hesitated. "Torc. Sorcha."

"Levon, no!" Torc hissed. "You cannot—"

Levon's jaw tightened and his eyes blazed. Torc stopped abruptly. The dark Dalrei swallowed, nodded once, jerkily, and then, with his father beside him, turned and left the forest, heading back south. The night took them, as if they'd never been there.

Dave found Levon looking at him. He returned the gaze. "I couldn't," Levon whispered. "Not so soon after they'd found each other!"

Words were useless sometimes, they were stupid. Dave reached forward and squeezed Levon's shoulder. None of the others spoke either. Levon turned and started ahead. With Mabon beside him again, and Brock and Faebur following, Dave set out after him, his axe held ready, into the blackness of the forest.

The guard had come from the northeast, and Levon led them the same way. His heart racing now, Dave walked, crouched low among the scented outlines of the evergreens, his eyes straining for shapes in the night. There was death here, and treachery, and for all his fear and anger, there was room within him to pity Brock and grieve for him—and he knew he would never have felt either a year and a half ago.

Levon stopped and held up one hand. Dave froze.

A moment later he heard it too: the sounds of a great many men, too many to maintain an absolute silence.

Carefully he sank to one knee and, bending low, caught a glimpse of firelight in the space between two trees. He tapped Levon's leg, and the fair-haired Dalrei dropped down as well and his gaze followed Dave's pointing finger.

Levon looked for a long time; then he turned back, and his eyes met Brock's. He nodded, and the Dwarf silently moved past Levon to lead them toward the camp of his people. Levon fell back beside Faebur, who had drawn his bow. Dave looped his hand tightly through the thong at the end of his axe handle; he saw that Brock had done the same. Mabon drew his sword.

They went forward, crawling again, careful of their weapons, desperately careful of twigs and leaves on the forest floor. With excruciating slowness Brock guided them toward the glow of light Dave had seen.

Then suddenly he stopped.

Dave held himself rigidly still, save for his own warning hand raised for Levon and Faebur behind him. Holding motionless, hardly breathing, he heard the crunching footsteps of another guard approach on the right, and then he saw a Dwarf walk past, not five feet away, returning to the camp. Dave wiped perspiration from his brow and drew a long, quiet breath.

Brock was slipping forward again, even more slowly than before, and Dave, sharing a quick glance with Mabon, followed. He found himself thinking, absurdly, about Cechtar's belt, the one Levon had wanted to gamble for. It seemed farther away than anything had any right to be. He crawled, moving each hand and knee with infinite deliberation. He hardly dared lift his head to look up, so fearful was he of making a sound on the forest floor. It seemed to go on forever, this last stage of the journey. Then, out of the corner of his eye, Dave saw that Brock had stopped. Glancing up, he saw that they were within sight of the fires.

Dave looked, and his heart sank.

There was a huge clearing in Gwynir; it seemed unnatural, man-made. He wondered, briefly, how it had come to be there. But there were more pressing concerns than that. This was no raiding party waiting for them, no delaying contingent readying a skirmish. There were a great many watch fires in the clearing, the flames kept low to avoid discovery, and around them, mostly sleeping, was the entire army of the Dwarves of Banir Lök and Banir Tal.

Dave had a horrifying premonition of the kind of havoc these fighters could wreak among Aileron's horsemen. He pictured the horses screaming, hampered and dangerous in the congested woods. He saw the Dwarves, small, quick, deadly, far more courageous than the svart alfar, slashing horseflesh and men amid the encircling trees.

He looked over at Brock, and his heart ached for the transparent anguish he saw in the other's face. Then, even as he watched, Brock's expression changed, and a cold hatred invested the Dwarf's normally kind features. Brock touched Levon on the arm and pointed.

Dave followed his finger and saw a Dwarf beside the nearest of the fires, talking softly to three others, who then ran off to the east, obviously carrying orders. The one who had spoken remained, and Dave saw that he was bearded and dark, as were Brock and Matt, and that his eyes were deep-set and hidden under an overhanging brow. He was too far away, though, to make out anything else. Dave turned to Brock, his eyebrows raised in a question.

Blöd, Brock mouthed, not making a sound.

And then Dave knew. This was the one they'd spoken of before, the one who'd given the Cauldron to Maugrim and had been in Starkadh when Jennifer was taken there. He felt his own hatred rising, his own eyes going flinty and cold, as he looked back at the Dwarf by the fire. He tightened his grip on the axe.

But this was a reconnaissance, not a raid. Even as he stared at Blöd, hungering for his death, he heard Levon's soft whisper commanding them to turn back.

They never had a chance, though.

There came a sound to their right, a loud crashing at the edge of the clearing, and then sudden hoarse shouts of alarm very near them.

"*Someone's here!*" a Dwarf guard screamed. Another one echoed the alarm.

Dave Martyniuk thought of his father blowing up bridges in darkest night in a darkest time.

He saw Brock rise, and Levon, weapons out.

He rose, hefting his axe. Saw Faebur's strung bow, and Mabon's long sword glint in the red light of the fire. For a moment he looked up. The moon was hidden, but there were stars up there between the banks of clouds, high above the trees, the fires, high above everything.

He stepped forward into the open, to have room to swing the axe. Levon was beside him. He exchanged one glance with the man he called his brother; there was time for nothing more. Then Dave turned toward the roused army of the Dwarves and prepared to send as many of them as he could into night before he died.

It was still dark when Sharra woke on the deck of Amairgen's ship. A heavy fog lay over the sea, shrouding the stars. The moon had long since set.

She pulled Diarmuid's cloak more tightly about herself; the wind was cold. She closed her eyes, not really wanting to be awake yet, to become fully aware of where she was. She knew, though. The creaking of the masts and the flap of the torn sails told her. And every few moments she would hear the sound of invisible footsteps passing: mariners dead a thousand years.

On either side of her Jaelle and Jennifer still slept. She wondered what time it was; the fog made it impossible to tell. She wished that Diarmuid were beside her, warming her with his nearness. She only had his cloak, though, damp with the mist. He'd been too scrupulous of her honor to lie anywhere near her, either on the ship or, before they'd boarded, on the beach below the Anor.

They had found a moment together, though, after Lancelot had gone into the woods alone, in the deceptively tranquil hour between twilight and full dark.

All tranquility was deceptive now, Sharra decided, huddling under the cloak and the blankets they'd given her. There were too many dimensions of danger and grief all around. And she'd learned new ones with the tale Diarmuid had unfolded as they walked along the northwest curving of the strand past the Anor, and saw—first time for both of them—the sheer Cliffs of Rhudh gleam blood-red in the last of the light.

He had told her of the voyage in a voice stripped of all its customary irony, of any inflections of mockery and irreverence. He spoke of the Soulmonger, and she held his hand in her own and seemed to hear, as backdrop to the musing fall of his voice, the sound of Brendel singing his lament again.

Then he told her of the moment in the Chamber of the

Dead under Cader Sedat, the moment when, amid the ceaseless pounding of all the seas of all the worlds, Arthur Pendragon had wakened Lancelot from his death on the bed of stone.

Sharra lay on the boat, eyes closed, listening to wind and sea, remembering what he'd said. "Do you know," he'd murmured, watching the Cliffs shade to a darker red, "that if you loved someone else, as well as me, I do not think I could have done that, to bring him back to you. I really don't think I'm man enough to have done what Arthur did."

She was wise enough to know that it was a hard admission for him to make. She'd said, "He is something more than a mortal, now. The threads of their three names on the Loom go back so far, intertwined in so many ways. Do not reproach yourself, Diar. Or, if you must"—she smiled—"do so for thinking I could ever love another as I do you."

He had stopped at that, brow furrowed, and turned to make some serious reply. She wondered, now, what it was he'd been meaning to say. Because she hadn't let him speak. She had risen up, instead, on tiptoe and, putting her hands behind his head, had pulled his mouth down so she could reach it with her own. To stop him from talking. To finally, properly, begin to welcome him home from the sea.

After which, they *had* greeted each other properly, lying upon his cloak on that strand north of Lisen's Tower, slipping out of their clothes under the first of the stars. He'd made love to her with an aching tenderness, holding her, moving upon her with the gentle rhythm of the quiet sea. When she cried out, at length, it was softly—a sound, to her own ears, like the sighing of a wave, a deep surging on the sand.

And so it was all right, after a fashion, that he did not lie with her when they came back to the Anor. Brendel brought a pallet out from the Tower for her, and blankets woven in Daniloth for Lisen, and Diarmuid left her the cloak, so she might have at least that much of him next to her, as she fell asleep.

To awaken, not long after, along with every one else on the beach, to see a ghostly ship sailing toward them, with Jaelle aboard, and Pwyll, and a pale proud figure beside them both who was, they gave her to understand, the ghost of Amairgen Whitebranch, beloved of Lisen, dead these long, long years.

They had boarded that spectral ship by starlight, by the cast glimmer of the setting moon, and unseen sailors had brought it about, and they had begun moving north as a mist descended over the sea to hide the stars.

Footsteps passed again, though there was no one to be seen. It had to be close to morning now, but there was no real way to tell. Try as she might, Sharra could not sleep. Too many thoughts chased each other around and around in her mind. Amid fear and sorrow, perhaps because of them, she felt a new keenness to all of her memories and perceptions, as if the context of war had given an added intensity to everything, an intensity that Sharra recognized as the awareness of possible loss. She thought about Diar, and about herself—a solitary falcon no more—and found herself yearning, more than she ever had before, for peace. For an end to the terrors of this time, that she might lie in his arms every night without fearing what the mists of morning might bring.

She rose, careful not to wake the others sleeping beside her, and wrapping the cloak about herself she walked to the leeward rail of the ship, peering out into the darkness and the fog. There were voices farther along the deck. Others, it seemed were awake as well. Then she recognized Diarmuid's light inflections and, a moment later, the cold clear tones of Amairgen.

"Nearly morning," the mage was saying. "I will be fading any moment. Only at night can I be seen in your time."

"And during the day?" Diarmuid asked. "Is there anything we must do?"

"Nothing," the ghost replied. "We will be here, though you will not know it. One thing: do not, for fear of your lives, leave the ship in daylight."

Sharra glanced over. Arthur Pendragon stood there as well, beside Diarmuid and Amairgen. In the greyness and the mist, all three of them looked like ghosts to her. She made a sudden gesture rooted in old, foolish superstitions, to unsay the thought. She saw Cavall then, a grey shadow upon shadow, and in the fog he too seemed to belong to some realm of the supernatural, terribly far from her own.

From sunlight on the waterfalls and flowers of Larai Rigal.

The sea slapped against the hull with a cold, relentless sound, magnified in the fog. She looked over the rail but couldn't even see the waterline. It was probably just as well; one glimpse, on first boarding, of water foaming through the shattered timbers of the ship had been enough.

She looked back at the three men, then caught her breath and looked more closely yet. There were only two of them.

Arthur and Diar stood together, with the dog beside them, but the ghost of the mage was gone. And in that moment Sharra became aware that the eastern darkness was beginning to lift.

Peering through the grey, thinning mist, she could now make out a long, low, rolling tongue of land. This had to be Sennett Strand, of the legends. They had passed the Cliffs of Rhudh in the night, and if her geography master in Larai Rigal had told true, and she remembered rightly, before the day was out they would come to the mouth of Linden Bay and see the fjords of ice and the vast glaciers looming in the north.

And Starkadh: the seat of Rakoth Maugrim, set like a black claw in the heart of a world of whitest light. She honestly didn't know how she was going to deal with looking upon it. It had as much to do with the ice as with anything else, she realized, with how far north they were, in a world so alien to one raised amid the gentle seasons of Cathal and the shelter of its gardens.

Sternly she reminded herself that they were not sailing to Starkadh or anywhere near it. Their journey would take them back south down Linden Bay to the mouth of the Celyn River. There, Diarmuid had explained, Amairgen would set them down, if all went well, in the darkness before dawn tomorrow, bringing an end to this strangest of voyages. It would have to be in darkness, she now realized, given what Amairgen had just said: *Do not, for fear of your lives, leave the ship in daylight.*

The mist was still rising, quickly now. She saw a small patch of blue overhead, then another, and then, gloriously, the sun burst into the sky over Sennett and the lands beyond.

And in that moment Sharra, looking toward the morning, was the first to notice something about the strand.

"Diar!" she called, hoping she'd kept the fear out of her voice.

He was still speaking to Arthur, just along the rail, standing quite deliberately on a part of the deck where the timbers had been completely torn away. He seemed to be suspended in air. And she knew that below him, if she looked, she would see seawater rushing in to swirl through the dark hold of Amairgen's ship.

He broke off the conversation and came over, quickly. Arthur followed.

"What is it?"

She pointed. By now the mist was entirely gone from off the water and there was a great deal of light. Morning in summer, bright and fair. She heard a babble of sound along the deck. Others had seen as well. The men of South Keep were crowding to the rail, and other hands were pointing to the same thing she was.

They were sailing along a green and fertile coast. Sennett Strand had always been known (if she remembered her lessons rightly) for the richness of its soil, though the growing season was short this far north.

But Sennett had been ruined, as Andarien beyond the bay had been, in the time of the Bael Rangat, despoiled by a killing rain and then ravaged by Rakoth's armies in the late days of the war before Conary came north with the armies of Brennin and Cathal. Ruined and emptied, both of those once-fair lands.

How then could they be seeing what now they saw? A quilting of fields laid out under the blue summer sky, farmhouses of stone and wood scattered across the strand, the smoke of cooking fires rising from chimneys, crops flourishing in rich shades of brown and gold and in the reddish hues of tall solais growing in row upon row.

Nearer to the ship, at the water's edge, as they continued north and the light grew clearer yet, Sharra saw a harbor indenting the long coastline, and within that harbor were a score or more of many-colored ships, some tall-masted with deep holds for grain and timber, others little more than fishing boats to chance the ocean waters west of the strand.

With a catch in her heart, as the cries of wonder grew louder all about her, Sharra saw that the very tallest of the ships carried proudly upon its mainmast a green flag with a curved sword and a red leaf: the flag of Raith, westernmost of the provinces of Cathal.

Next to it she saw another tall ship, this one flying the crescent moon and oak flag of Brennin. And the mariners of both ships were waving to them! Clearly, from over the sparkling water, came the sound of their greetings and laughter.

Beyond the ships the quayside bustled with early-morning life. One ship was off-loading, and a number of others were taking on cargo. Dogs and little boys careened about, getting in everyone's way.

Beyond the docks the town stretched, along the bay in both directions and back up from the sea. She saw brightly painted houses under slanting shingled roofs. Wide laneways ran up from the waterside, and following the widest with her gaze Sharra saw a tall manor house to the north and east with a high stone wall around it.

She could see it all, as they sailed past the mouth of the harbor and she knew this town had to be Guiraut upon Iorweth's Bay.

But Iorweth's Bay had been reclaimed by the rising land hundreds and hundreds of years ago, and Guiraut Town had been burnt and utterly razed to the ground by Rakoth Maugrim in the Bael Rangat.

It was so full of life, so beautiful; she suddenly realized that if she wasn't careful she would weep.

"Diar, how has this happened?" she asked, turning to him. "Where are we?"

"A long way off," he said. "We're sailing through the seas this ship knew before she was destroyed. In the days after Rakoth had come to Fionavar, but before the Bael Rangat." His voice was husky.

She turned back to look at the harbor, trying very hard to deal with that.

Diarmuid touched her hand. "I don't think there is anything that endangers us directly," he said. "So long as we stay on the ship. We will return to our own seas, our own time, after the sun has set."

She nodded, never taking her eyes from the brilliant colors of the harbor. She said, wonderingly, "Do you see that ship from Raith? And the smaller one—over there—with the flag of Cynan? Diar, my country doesn't even exist yet! Those are ships of the principalities. They only became a country after Angirad returned from the Bael Rangat."

"I know that," he said gently. "We're looking at a world that was destroyed."

From over the water now she recognized the sound of a t'rena, played high and sweet on the deck of the ship from Cynan. She knew that music; she had grown up with it.

A thought came to her, born of the ache lodged in her heart. "Can't we warn them? Can't we do something?"

Diarmuid shook his head. "They can't see us or hear us."

"What do you mean? Can't you hear the music? And look—they're waving to us!"

His hands were loosely clasped together as he leaned on the rail, but the strain in his voice gave the lie to that casualness. "Not to us, my dear. They aren't waving to us. What they see isn't this broken hulk. They see a beautiful ship passing, with a picked crew from Brennin. They see Amairgen's mariners, Sharra, and his ship as it was before it sailed for Cader Sedat. We're invisible, I'm afraid."

So, finally, she understood. They sailed north along the line of the coast, and Guiraut Town disappeared from sight, soon to disappear forever from the world of men, its brightness remembered only in song. Soon, and yet long ago. Both. Loops in the weaving of time.

The sound of the t'rena followed them a long way, even after the town was lost behind the curve of the bay. They left it, because they had no choice, to the fires of its future and their past.

After that the mood of the ship turned grim, not with apprehension, but with a newer, sterner resolution, a deeper awareness of what evil was, and meant. There was a harder tone to the speech of the men on the deck, a crispness to the movements with which they cleaned and polished their weapons, that boded ill for those who would seek to oppose them in what was to come. And it was coming, Sharra knew that now, and she too was ready for it. Some of that same resolution had hardened in her own heart.

They sailed north up the seaward coast of Sennett Strand, and late in the afternoon, with the sun well out over the sea, they came to the northernmost tip of Sennett and rounded that cape, swinging east, and they saw the glaciers and the fjords, and the blackness of Starkadh beyond.

Sharra gazed upon it and did not flinch or close her eyes. She looked upon the heart of evil, and she willed herself not to look away.

She could not, of course, see herself in that moment, but others could, and there was a murmuring along the ship at how fierce and cold the beauty of the Dark Rose of Cathal had suddenly become. An Ice Queen from the Garden Country, a rival to the Queen of Rük herself, as stern and as unyielding.

And even here, on this doorstep of the Dark, there was a thing of beauty to be found. High above and far beyond Starkadh, Rangat reared up, snow-crowned, cloud-shouldered, mastering the northlands with its glory.

Sharra understood suddenly, for the first time, why the conflict of a thousand years ago had come to be called the Bael Rangat even though not one of the major battles had taken place by the mountain. The truth was that Rangat loomed so imperiously high, this far north, there was no place in these lands that could not be said to lie under the sovereignty of the mountain.

Unless and until Rakoth defeated them.

They sailed down the bay of a thousand years ago under the westering sun. To the east they could see the golden beaches of Andarien and, beyond them, a hint of a green fair land, rising in gentle slopes toward the north. It would be dotted with strands of tall trees, Sharra knew, and there would be deep blue lakes, sparkling in the sun, with fish leaping from them in curved homage to the light.

All gone, she knew, all gone to dust and barrenness, to bleak highlands where the north wind whistled down over nothingness. The forests were leveled, the lakes dry, the thin grasses scattered and brown. Ruined Andarien, where the war had been fought.

And would be again, if Diarmuid was right. If even now, Aileron the High King was leading his armies from the Plain toward Gwynir, to come on the morrow through the evergreens to Andarien. They too would be there, those on this ship, if Amairgen's promise held.

It did. They sailed southeast down Linden Bay, through the growing shadows of that afternoon and the long summer twilight, watching the golden sands where Andarien met the bay gradually grow dark. Looking back to the west, over Sennett Strand again, Sharra saw the evening star—Lauriel's—and then, a moment later, the sun set.

And Amairgen was among them again, shadowy and insubstantial, but growing clearer as the night deepened. There was a cold arrogance to him and she wondered for a moment that Lisen had loved this man. Then she thought about how long ago she had died, and how long he had wandered, a ghost, loveless and unrevenged, through lonely, endless seas. He would have been different, she guessed, when he was a living man, and young, and loved by the fairest child of all the Weaver's worlds.

A pity she could never have expressed rose in her as she looked upon the proud figure of the first mage. Later it grew too dark, and she could no longer see him clearly under the starlight. The moon, thinning toward new, rose very late.

Sharra slept for a time; most of them did, knowing how little rest might lie in the days ahead—or how much rest, an eternity of it. She woke long before dawn. The moon was over the Strand, west of them. They carried no lights on that ship. Andarien was a dark blur to the east.

She heard low voices speaking again—Amairgen, Diar, and Arthur Pendragon. Then the voices were gradually stilled. Sharra rose, Diarmuid's cloak about her in the chill. Jaelle, the High Priestess, came to stand beside her, and the two of them watched as the Warrior walked to the prow of the ship. He stood there—Cavall beside him, as ever—and in the darkness of that night he suddenly thrust high his spear, and the head of the King Spear blazed, blue-white and dazzling.

And by that light Amairgen Whitebranch guided his ship to land by the mouth of the River Celyn where it ran into Linden Bay.

They disembarked in the shallows by that sweetest of rivers, which flowed from Celyn Lake along the enchanted borders of Daniloth. Last of all to leave the ship, Sharra saw, was the one they called Pwyll Twiceborn. He stood on the deck above the swaying ladder and said something to Amairgen, and the mage made reply. She couldn't hear what they said, but she felt a shiver raise the hairs of her neck to look upon the two of them.

Then Pwyll came down the rope ladder, and they were all gathered on land again. Amairgen stood above them, proud and austere in what was left of the moonlight.

He said, "High Priestess of Dana, I have done as you bade me. Have I still the prayers you promised?"

Gravely, Jaelle replied, "You would have had them even had you not carried us. Go to your rest, unquiet ghost. All of you. The Soulmonger is dead. You are released. May there be Light for you at the Weaver's side."

"And for you," Amairgen said. "And for all of you."

He turned to Pwyll again and seemed about to speak once more. He did not. Instead, he slowly lifted high both his hands, and then, amid the sudden enraptured crying of his unseen mariners, he faded from sight in the darkness. And his ship faded away with him, and the crying of the mariners fell slowly away on the breeze, leaving only the sound of the surf to carry its echo awhile from so far back in time.

In that place where the river met the bay they turned and, led by Brendel of the lios alfar, who knew every slope and shadow of this country so near his home, they began walking east, toward where the sun would rise.

Chapter 12

"I will not go within," Flidais said, turning way from the mist. He looked up at the man standing beside him. "Not even the andain are proof against wandering lost in Ra-Lathen's woven shadows. Had I any words left that might prevail upon you, I would urge you again not to go there."

Lancelot listened with that always grave courtesy that was so much a part of him, the patience that seemed virtually inexhaustible. He made one ashamed, Flidais thought, to be importunate or demanding, to fall too far short of the mark set by that gentleness.

And yet he was not without humor. Even now there was a glint of amusement in his eyes as he looked down on the diminutive andain.

"I was wondering," he said mildly, "if it were actually possible that you might run out of words. I was beginning to doubt it, Taliesin."

Flidais felt himself beginning to flush, but there was no malice in Lancelot's teasing, only a laughter they could share. And a moment later they did.

"I am bereft neither of words nor yet of arguments of dappled, confusing inconsequentiality," Flidais protested. "Only of time am I now run short, given where we stand. I am not about to try to restrain you physically here on the borders of Daniloth. I am somewhat wiser than that, at least."

"At least," Lancelot agreed. Then, after a pause, "Would you really want to restrain me now, even if you could? Knowing what you know?"

An unfairly difficult question. But Flidais, who had been the wisest, most precocious child of all in his day, was a child no longer. Not without sorrow, he said, "I would not. Knowing the three of you, I would not constrain you from doing a thing she asked. I fear the child though, Lancelot. I fear him deeply." And to this the man made no reply.

The first hint of grey appeared in the sky, overture to morning and all that the day might bring. To the west, Amairgen's ghostly ship was just then sailing north along Sennett Strand, its passengers looking out upon a town given to the fire long ago, long since turned to ashes and to shards of pottery.

A bird lifted its voice in song behind them from some hidden place among the trees of the dark forest. They stood between wood and mist and looked at each other for what, Flidais knew, might be the last time.

"I am grateful for your guidance to this place," said Lancelot. "And for the tending of my wounds."

Flidais snorted brusquely and turned away. "Couldn't have done the one without the other," he growled. "Couldn't have guided you anywhere, let alone through the whole of a night, unless I'd first done something about those wounds."

Lancelot smiled. "Should I unsay my thanks, then? Or is this some of your dappled inconsequentiality?"

He was, Flidais decided, altogether too clever, always had been. It was the key to his mastery in battle: Lancelot had always been more intelligent than anyone he fought. The andain found himself smiling back and nodding a reluctant agreement.

"How is your hand?" he asked. It had been by far the worst of the wounds: the palm savagely scored by the burning of Curdardh's hammer.

Lancelot didn't even spare it a glance. "It will do. I shall make it do, I suppose." He looked north toward the mists of Daniloth looming in front of them. Something changed in his eyes. It was almost as if he heard a horn, or a call of another kind. "I must go, I think, or there will have been no point in our having come so far. I hope we meet again, old friend, in a time of greater light."

Flidais found himself blinking rapidly. He managed a shrug. "It is in the Weaver's hands," he said. He hoped it sounded casual.

Lancelot said gravely, "Half a truth, little one. It is in our own hands as well, however maimed they are. Our own choices matter, or I would not be here. She would not have asked me to follow the child. Fare kindly, Taliesin. Flidais. I hope you find what you want."

He touched the andain lightly on the shoulder, and then he turned and after a dozen strides was swallowed up by the mists of the Shadowland.

But I have, Flidais was thinking. *I have found what I want!* The summoning name was singing in his head, reverberating in the chambers of his heart. He had sought it so long, and now it was his. He had what he wanted.

Which did not do anything to explain why he stood rooted to that spot for so long afterward, gazing north into the dense, impenetrable shadows.

It was only afterward, thinking about it, that she consciously understood that this was something of which she must have always been inwardly aware: the terrible danger that lay in wait for her if she ever fell in love.

How else explain why Leyse of the Swan Mark, fairest and most desired of all the women in Daniloth—long sought by Ra-Tenniel himself, in vain—had chosen to abjure each and every such overture, however sweetly sung, these long, long years?

How else indeed?

The Swan Mark, alone of the lios alfar, had not gone to war. Dedicated in memory of Lauriel, for whom they were named, to serenity and peace, they lingered, few in number, in the Shadowland, wandering alone and in pairs through the days and nights since Ra-Tenniel had led the brothers and sisters of the other two Marks to war on the Plain.

Leyse was one of those who wandered alone. She had come, early of this mild summer's dawning, to glimpse the muted light of sunrise—all light was muted here—through the waters of the upward-rushing waterfall of Fiathal, her favorite place within the Shadowland.

Though truly her favorite place of all lay beyond the borders, north, on the banks of Celyn Lake, where the sylvain could be gathered in spring by one who was careful not to be seen. That place was closed to her now. It was a time of war outside the protection of the mist and what it did to time.

So she had come south instead, to the waterfall, and she was waiting for the sunrise, sitting quietly, clad as ever in white, beside the rushing waters.

And so it was that she saw, just before the sun came up, a mortal man walk into Daniloth.

She had a momentary spasm of fear—this had not happened for a very long time—but then she relaxed, knowing the mists would take him, momentarily, and leave him lost to time, no threat to anyone.

She had an instant to look at him. The graceful, slightly stiff gait, the high carriage of his head, dark hair. His clothes were nondescript. There was blood on them. He carried a sword, buckled about his waist. He saw her, from across the green, green glade.

That did not matter. The mist would have him, long before he could cross to where she sat.

It did not. She raised a hand almost without thought. She spoke the words of warding to shield him, to leave him safe in time. And, speaking them, she shaped her own doom, the doom her inward self had tried to avoid, all these long years, and had instead prepared, as a feast upon the grass.

The sun came up. Light sparkled gently, mildly, in the splash of the upward-running falls. It was very beautiful. It always was.

She hardly saw. He walked toward her over the carpet of the grass, and she rose, so as to be standing, drops of water in her hair, on her face, when he came to where she was. Her eyes, she knew, had come to crystal. His were dark.

She thought, afterward, that she might have known who he was before he even spoke his name. It was possible. The mind had as many loops as did time itself, even here in Daniloth. She forgot who had told her that.

The tall man came up to her. He stopped. He said, with deepest, gravest courtesy, "Good morning, my lady. I am come in peace and trespass only by reason of utmost need. I must ask of you your aid. My name is Lancelot."

She had already given her aid, she might have said, else he would not have walked this far, not be seeing her now. He would be locked in a soundless, sightless world of his own. Forever. Until the Loom was stilled.

She might have said that, were her eyes not crystal—past that, even—brighter, clearer than she had thought they could go. She might have, had her heart not already been given and lost even before she heard the name, before she knew who he was.

There were droplets of water in her hair. The grass was very green. The sun shone down gently through the shadows, as it always did. She looked into his eyes, knowing who he was, and already, even in that first moment, she sensed what her own destiny was now to be.

She heard it: the first high, distant, impossibly beautiful notes.

She said, "I am Leyse of the Swan Mark. Be welcome to Daniloth."

She could see him drinking in her beauty, the delicate music of her voice. She let her eyes slide into a shade of green and then return to crystal again. She offered a hand and let him take it and bring it to his lips.

Ra-Tenniel would have passed a sleepless night, walking through fields of flowers, shaping another song, had she done as much for him.

She looked into Lancelot's eyes. So dark. She saw kindness there, and admiration. Gratitude. But behind everything else, and above it all, shaping the worlds he knew and woven through them all, over and over, endlessly, she saw Guinevere. And the irrevocable finality, the fact of his absolute love.

What she was spared—a dimension of his kindness—was seeing in his calm gaze even a hint of how many, many times this meeting had come to pass. In how many forests, meadows, worlds; beside how many liquescent waterfalls, making sweet summer music for a maiden's heartbreak.

She was shielded by him, even as she shaped her own warding, from knowing how much a part of the long threefold doom this was. How easily and entirely her sudden transfigured blazing could be gathered within the telling, one more note of an oft-repeated theme, a thread of a color already in the Tapestry.

Her beauty deserved more, the incandescent, crystalline flourishing of it. So, also, did the centuries-long simplicity of her waiting. That too, by any measure, deserved more.

And he knew this, knew it as intimately as he knew his name, as deeply as he named his own transgression within his heart. He stood in that place of sheerest beauty within the Shadowland and he shouldered her sorrow, as he had done so many others, and took the guilt and the burden of it for his own.

And all this happened in the space of time it might take a man to cross a grassy sward and stand before a lady in the morning light.

It was by an act of will, of consummate nobility, that Leyse kept the shading of her eyes as bright as before. She held them to crystal—fragile, breakable crystal, she was thinking—and she said, with music in her voice, "How may I be of aid to thee?"

Only the last word betrayed her. He gave no hint that he had heard the caress in it, the longing she let slip into that one word. He said formally, "I am on a quest set me by my lady. There will have been another who came within the borders of your land last night, flying in the shape of an owl, though not truly so. He is on a journey of his own, a very dark road, and I fear he may have been caught within the shadows over Daniloth, unknowing in the night. It is my charge to keep him safe to take that road."

There was nothing she wanted more than to lie down again beside the rising, rushing waters of the falls of Fiathal with this man beside her until the sun had gone and the stars and the Loom had spun its course.

"Come, then," was all she said, and led him from that place of gentlest beauty and enchantment, in search of Darien.

Along the southern margins of Daniloth they walked side by side, a little distance between, but not a great deal, for he was deeply aware of what had happened to her. They did not speak. All around them the muted, serene spaces of grass and hillocks stretched. There were flowing rivers, and flowers in pale, delicate hues growing along their banks. Once he knelt, to drink from a stream, but she shook her head quickly, and he did not.

She had seen his palm, though, as he cupped it to drink, and when he stood she took it between both her own and looked upon his wound. He felt the pain of it then, seeing it in her eyes, more keenly than he had when he'd lifted the black hammer in the sacred grove.

She did not ask. Slowly she released his hand—did so as if surrendering it to everything in the world that was not her touch—and they went on. It was very quiet. They passed no one else walking as the went.

Once, only, they came upon a man clad in armor, carrying a sword, his face contorted with rage and fear. He seemed to Lancelot to be frozen in place, motionless, his foot thrust forward in a long stride he would never complete.

Lancelot looked at Leyse, clad in white beside him, but he said nothing.

Another time it seemed to him that he heard the sound of horses rushing toward them, very near. He spun, shielding her reflexively, but he saw no one at all riding past, whether friend or foe. He could tell though, from the turning of her gaze, that she *did* see a company riding there, riding right through the two of them perhaps, lost as well, in a different way, amid the mists of Daniloth.

He released his grip on her arm. He apologized. She shook her head, with a sadness that went into him like a blade.

She said, "This land was always dangerous to anyone other than our kind, even before Lathen Mistweaver's time, when these shadows came down. Those men were horsemen from before the Bael Rangat, and they are lost. There is nothing we can do for them. They are in no time we know, to be spoken to or saved. Had we space for the telling, I might spin you the tale of Revor, who risked that fate in the service of Light a thousand years ago."

"Had we space for the telling," he said, "I would take pleasure in that."

She seemed about to say something more, but then her eyes—they were a pale, quiet blue now, much like the last of the flowers they had passed—looked beyond his face, and he turned.

West of them lay a thicket of trees. The leaves of the trees were of many colors even in midsummer, and the woods were very beautiful, offering a promise of peace, of quiet shade, of a place where the sunlight might slant down through the leaves, with a brook murmuring not far away.

Above the southernmost of the trees of that small wood, at the very edge of Daniloth, an owl hung suspended, wings spread wide and motionless in the clear morning air.

Lancelot looked, and he saw the sheath of a dagger held in the owl's mouth glint with a streak of blue in the mild light. He turned back to the woman beside him. Her eyes had changed color. They were dark, looking upon the owl that hung in the air before them.

"Not this one," she said, before he could speak. He heard the fear, the denial in her voice, "Oh, my lord, surely not this one?"

He said, "This is the child I have been sent to follow and to guard."

"Can you not see the evil within him?" Leyse cried. Her voice was loud in the quiet of that place. There was music in it still, but strained now, and overlaid by many things.

"I know it is there," he said. "I know also that there is a yearning after light. Both are part of his road."

"Then let the road end here," she said. It was a plea. She turned to him. "My lord, there is too much darkness in this one. I can feel it even from where we stand."

She was a Child of Light, and she stood in Daniloth. Her certainty planted a momentary doubt in his own heart. It never took root; he had his own certainties.

He said, "There is darkness everywhere now. We cannot avoid it; only break through, and not easily. In the danger of this might lie our hope of passage."

She looked at him for a long moment. "Who is he?" she asked finally.

He had been hoping she would not ask, for many reasons. But when the question came, he did not turn away. "Guinevere's child," he said levelly, though it cost him something. "And Rakoth Maugrim's. He took her by force in Starkadh. And therein lies the evil you see, and the hope of light beyond."

There was pain now, overlying the fear in her eyes. And under both of those things, at bedrock, was love. He had seen it before, too many times.

She said, "And you think she will prove stronger?" Music in her voice again, distant but very clear.

"It is a hope," he replied, gravely honest. "No more than that."

"And you would act and have me act upon that hope?" Music still.

"She has asked me to guard him," he said quietly. "To see him through to the choice he has to make. I can do no more than ask you. I have only the request."

She shook her head. "You have more than that," she said.

And with the words she turned away from him, leaving her heart. She looked at the motionless bird, child of Dark and Light. Then she gestured with her long graceful hands and sang a word of power to shape a space through which he could fly over the Shadowland. She made a corridor for Darien, a rift in the mists of time that coiled through Daniloth, and she watched with an inner, brilliant sight, as he flew north along that corridor, over the mound of Atronel and beyond, coming out at length above the River Celyn, where she lost him.

It took a long time. Lancelot waited beside her, silent all the while. He had seen Darien's flight begin, but when the owl had gone some distance north over the many-colored leaves of the forest, it was lost to his mortal sight. He continued to wait, knowing, among many other things, that this was as far as he would be able to follow Guinevere's child, the last service he could offer. It was a sorrow.

He was conscious, as he stood beside Leyse and the pale sun climbed higher in the sky, of a great weariness and not a little pain. There was a fragrance in the meadow, and birdsong in the woods nearby. He could hear the sound of water. Without actually being aware of having done so, he found himself sitting upon the grass at the woman's feet. And then, in a trance half shaped by Daniloth and half by marrow-deep exhaustion, he lay down and fell asleep.

When the owl had passed beyond the northernmost borders of her land and she had lost him beyond the mist, Leyse let her mind come back to where she stood. It was early in the afternoon, and the light was as bright as it ever became. Even so, she too was very tired. What she had done was not an easy thing, made harder for one of the Swan Mark by the inescapable resonance of evil she had sensed.

She looked down upon the man, fast asleep beside her. There was a quiet now in her heart, an acceptance of what had come to her beside the waters of Fiathal. She knew he would not stay unless she bound him by magic to this place, and she would not do that.

One thing, only, she would allow herself. She looked at his sleeping face for a very long time, committing it to the memory of her soul. Then she lay down beside him on the soft, scented grass and slipped her hand into his wounded one. No more than that, for in her pride she would go no further. And linked in that fashion for a too-brief summer's afternoon, joined only by their interwoven fingers, she fell asleep for one time and the only time beside Lancelot, whom she loved.

Through the afternoon they slept, and in the quiet peace of Daniloth nothing came, not so much as a dream, to cause either of them to stir. Far to the east, across the looming barrier of the mountains, the Dwarves of Banir Lök and Banir Tal waited for sunset and the judgment of their Crystal Lake. Nearer, on the wide Plain, a Dwarf and an Eridun and an exile of the Dalrei reached the camp of the High King and were made welcome there, before the army set out for the last hours of the ride to Gwynir and the eastern borders of this Shadowland.

And north of them, as they slept, Darien was flying to his father.

They woke at the same time, as the sun went down. In the twilight Lancelot gazed at her, and he saw her hair and eyes gleam in the dusk beside him, beautiful and strange. He looked down at her long fingers, laced through his own. He closed his eyes for a moment and let the last of that deep peace wash over him like a tide. A withdrawing tide.

Very gently, then, he disengaged his hand. Neither of them spoke. He rose. There was a faint phosphorescence to the grass and to the leaves of the wood nearby, as if the growing things of Daniloth were reluctant to yield the light. It was the same gleaming he saw in her eyes and in the halo of her hair. There were echoes of many things in his mind, memories. He was careful not to let her see.

He helped her rise. Slowly the glow of light faded—from the leaves and the grass and then, last of all, from Leyse. She turned to the west and pointed. He followed the line of her arm and saw a star.

"Lauriel's," she said. "We have named the evening star for her." And then she sang. He listened, and partway through he wept, for many reasons.

When her song was done she turned and saw his tears. She said nothing more, nor did he speak. She led him north through Daniloth, sheltered from the mist and the loops of time by her presence. All the night they walked. She led him up the mound of Atronel, past the Crystal Throne, and then down the other side, and Lancelot du Lac was the first mortal man ever to ascend that place.

In time they came to the southern bay of Celyn Lake, the arm that dipped down into Daniloth, and they went along its banks to the north, not because it was quickest or easiest but because she loved this place and wanted him to see. There were night flowers in bloom along the shore, giving off their scent, and out over the water he saw strange, elusive figures dancing on the waves and he heard music all the while.

At length they came to the edge of a river, where it left the waters of the lake, and they turned to the west as the first hint of dawn touched the sky behind them. And a very little while later Leyse stopped, and turned to Lancelot.

"The river is quiet here," she said, "and there are stepping stones along which you may cross. I can go no farther. On the other side of Celyn you will be in Andarien."

He looked upon the beauty of her for a long time in silence. When he opened his mouth to speak he was stopped, for she placed her fingers over his lips.

"Say nothing," she whispered. "There is nothing you can say."

It was true. A moment longer he stood there; then very slowly she drew her hand away from his mouth, and he turned and crossed the river over the smooth round stones and so left Daniloth.

He didn't go far. Whether it was an instinct of war, or of love, or of the two bound into each other, he went only as far as a small copse of trees on the banks of the river near the lake. There were willows growing in the Celyn, and beautiful flowers, silver and red. He didn't know their name. He sat down in that place of beauty as the dawn broke—dazzling after the muted light of the Shadowland—and he gazed out upon the ruined desolation of Andarien. He looped his hands over his knees, placed his sword where he could reach it, and composed himself to wait, facing west toward the sea.

She waited as well, though she had told herself all through the long night's silent walking that she would not linger. She had not expected him to stay so near, though, and her resolution faltered as soon as he was not there.

She saw him walk toward the aum trees and then sit down amid the sylvain she loved in her most cherished place of any in this one world she knew. She knew he could not see her standing here, and it was not easy for her to see clearly either, beyond the encircling billows of the mist.

She waited, nonetheless, and toward the middle of the afternoon a company of some fifty people approached from the west, along the riverbank.

She saw him rise. She saw the company stop not far away from him. Leading them was Brendel of the Kestrel Mark, and she knew that if he looked to the south he would see her. He did not.

He remained with the others and watched with the others as a woman, fair-haired, very tall, walked toward Lancelot. It seemed to Leyse that the mists parted a little for her then—a blessing or a curse, she could not say—and she saw Lancelot's face clearly as Guinevere came up to him.

She saw him kneel, and take her hand in his good one, and bring it to his lips, the same as he had done with hers when he had first approached her over the grass by Fiathal.

Yet not the same. Not the same.

And it came to pass that in that moment Leyse of the Swan Mark heard her song.

She went away from that place, walking alone, hidden by the screening of the shadows, and within her a song was building all the time, a last song.

Along the riverbank farther west she found, amid the

willows and corandiel, a small craft of aum wood with a single sail white as her own white robe. She had walked past this place a thousand times before and never seen that boat. It had not been there, she realized. The music of her song had called it forth. She'd always thought that she would have to build her boat, when the time came, and had wondered how she would.

Now she knew. The song was within her, rising all the while, shaping a sweeter and sweeter sadness and a promise of peace to come beyond the waves.

She stepped down into the boat and pushed off from the restraining shallows and the willows. As she drifted close to the northern bank of the Celyn she plucked one red flower of sylvain and one of silver to carry with her, as the music carried her and the river carried her to the sea.

She did not know, and it was a granting of grace that she was spared the knowing, how very much an echo this too was of the story she had been brought into, how deeply woven it was into that saddest story of all the long tales told. She drifted with the current with her flowers in her hand, and at length she reached the sea.

And that craft, shaped by magic, brought into being by a longing that was of the very essence of the lios alfar, did not founder among the waves of the wide sea. Westward it went, and farther westward still, and farther yet, until at length it had gone far enough and had reached the place where everything changed, including the world.

And in this fashion did Leyse of the Swan Mark sail past the waters where the Soulmonger had lain in wait, and so became the first of her people for past a thousand years to reach the world the Weaver had shaped for the Children of Light alone.

Chapter 13

The sun had set and so the glow of the walls had faded. Torches flickered in the brackets now. They burned without smoke; Kim didn't know how. She stood with the others at the foot of the ninety-nine stairs that led to the Crystal Lake, and a feeling of dread was in her heart.

There were eight of them there. Kaen had brought two Dwarves she didn't know; she and Loren had come with Matt; and Miach and Ingen were present for the Dwarfmoot, to bear witness to the judgment of Calor Diman. Loren carried an object wrapped in a heavy cloth, and so did one of Kaen's companions. The crystals—fruits of an afternoon's crafting. Gifts for the Lake.

Kaen had donned a heavy black cloak clasped at the throat with a single brooch worked in gold, with a vein of blue thieren that flashed in the torchlight. Matt was dressed as he always was, in brown with a wide leather belt, and boots, and no adornment at all. Kim looked at his face. It was expressionless, but he seemed strangely vivid, flushed, almost as if he were glowing. No one spoke. At a gesture from Miach, they began to climb.

The stairs were very old, the stone crumbling in places, worn smooth and slippery in others, an inescapable contrast to the polished, highly worked architecture everywhere else. The walls were rough, unfinished, with sharp edges that might cut if not avoided. It was hard to see clearly. The torches cast shadows as much as light.

The primitive stairway seemed to Kim to be carrying her back in time more than anything else. She was profoundly aware of being within a mountain. There was a growing consciousness of raw power massed all about her, a power of rock and stone, of earth upthrust to challenge sky. An image came into her mind: titanic forces battling, with mountains for boulders to hurl at each other. She felt the absence of the Baelrath with an intensity that bordered on despair.

They came to the door at the top of the stairs.

It was not like the ones she had seen—entranceways of consummate artistry that could slide into and out of the surrounding walls, or high carved arches with their perfectly measured proportions. She had known, halfway up, that this door wouldn't be like any of the others.

It was of stone, not particularly large, with a heavy, blackened iron lock. They waited on the threshold as Miach walked up to it, leaning upon his staff. He drew an iron key from within his robe and turned it slowly, with some effort, in the lock. Then he grasped the handle and pulled. The door swung open, revealing the dark night sky beyond, with a handful of stars framed in the opening.

They walked out in silence to the meadow of Calor Diman.

She had seen it before, in a vision on the road to Ysanne's lake. She'd thought that might have prepared her. It had not. There was no preparing for this place. The blue-green meadow lay in the bowl of the mountains like a hidden, fragile thing of infinite worth. And cradled within the meadow, as the meadow lay within the circle of the peaks, were the motionless waters of the Crystal Lake.

The water was dark, almost black. Kim had a swift apprehension of how deep and cold it would be. Here and there, though, along the silent surface of the water she could see a gleam of light, as the Lake gave back the light of the early stars. The thinning moon had not yet risen; she knew Calor Diman would shine when the moon came up over Banir Lök.

And she suddenly had a sense—only a sense, but that was a good deal more than enough—of how utterly alien, how terrifying this place would be when a full moon shone down on it, and Calor Diman shone back upon the sky, casting an inhuman light over the meadow and the mountainsides. This would be no place for mortals on such a night. Madness would lie in the sky and in the deep waters, in every gleaming blade of grass, in the ancient, watchful, shining crags.

Even now, by starlight, it was not easy to bear. She had never realized how sharp a danger lay in beauty. And there was something more as well, something deeper and colder, as the Lake itself was deep and cold. Each passing second, while the night gathered and the stars grew brighter, made her more and more conscious of magic here, waiting to be unleashed. She was grateful beyond words for the green shielding of the vellin stone: Matt's gift, she remembered.

She looked at him, who *had* been here on a night of the full moon, and had survived and been made King by that. She looked, with a newer, deeper understanding, and saw that he was gazing back at her, his face still vivid with that strange, glowing intensity. He had come home, she realized. The tide of the Lake in his heart had drawn him back. There was no longer any need to fight its pull.

No need to fight. Only judgment to be endured. With so very much at risk here in this mountain bowl, most of the way, it seemed, to the stars. She thought of the army of the Dwarves across the dividing range of the mountains. She had no idea of what to do, none at all.

Matt came over to her. With a gesture of his head, not speaking, he motioned her to walk a little way apart. She went with him from the others. She put up the hood of her robe and plunged her hands in the pockets. It was very cold. She looked down at Matt and said nothing, waiting.

He said, very softly, "I asked you, a long time ago, to save some of your words of praise for Ysanne's lake against the time when you might see this place."

"It is past beauty," she replied. "Beyond any words I might offer. But I am very much afraid, Matt."

"I know. I am, as well. If I do not show it, it is because I have made my peace with whatever judgment is to come. What I did forty years ago I did in the name of Light. It may still have been an act of evil. Such things have happened before and will happen again. I will abide the judging."

She had never seen him like this. She felt humbled in his presence. Behind Matt, Miach was whispering something to Ingen, and then he motioned Loren to approach, and Kaen's companion, carrying their crystals wrapped in cloth.

Matt said, "It is time now, I think. And it may be an ending to my time. I have something for you, first."

He lowered his head and brought a hand up to the patch over his lost eye. She saw him lift the patch and, for the first time, she caught a glimpse of the ruined socket behind. Then something white fell out, and he caught it in the palm of his hand. It was a tiny square of soft cloth. Matt opened it—to show her the Baelrath gleaming softly in his hand.

Kim let out a wordless cry.

"I am sorry," Matt said. "I know you will have been tormented by fear of who had it, but I have had no chance to speak with you. I took it from your hand when we were first attacked by the doorway to Banir Lök. I thought it would be best if I . . . kept an eye on it until we knew what was happening. Forgive me."

She swallowed, took the Warstone, put it on. It flared on her finger, then subsided again. She said, reaching for the tone that used to come so easily to her, "I will forgive you anything and everything from now until the Loom's last thread is woven, except that wretched pun."

His mouth crooked sideways. She wanted to say more, but there really wasn't time. It seemed that there had never been enough time. Miach was calling to them. Kim sank to her knees in the deep, cold grass and Matt embraced her with infinite gentleness. Then he kissed her once, on the lips, and turned away.

She followed him back to where the others stood. There was power on her hand now, and she could feel it responding to the magic of this place. Slowly, gradually, but there was no mistaking it. And suddenly, now that it was hers again, she remembered some of the things the Baelrath had caused her to do. There was a price to power. She had been paying it all along, and others had been paying it with her: Arthur, Finn, Ruana and the Paraiko. Tabor.

Not a new grief but sterner, now, and sharper. She had no chance to think about it. She came up to stand beside Loren, in time to hear Miach speak, with a hushed gravity.

"You will not need to be told that there is no history for this. We are living through days that have no patterns to draw upon. Even so, the Dwarfmoot has taken counsel, and this is what shall be done, with six of us to witness a judgment between two."

He paused to draw breath. There was no stir of wind in

the mountain bowl. The cold night air was still, as if waiting, and still, too, were the starry waters of the Lake.

Miach said, "You will each unveil your crystal fashionings that we may take note of them and what they might mean, and then you will cast them together into the waters and we will wait for a sign from the Lake. If there is fault found with this, speak to it now." He looked at Kaen.

Who shook his head. "No fault," he said, in the resonant, beautiful voice. "Let he who turned away from his people and from Calor Diman seek to avoid this hour." He looked handsome and proud in his black cloak, with the golden and blue brooch holding it about him.

Miach looked to Matt.

"No fault," said Matt Sören.

Nothing more. When, Kim thought, a lump in her throat, had he ever wasted a word in all the time she'd known him? Legs spread wide, hands on his hips, he seemed to be as one with the rocks all around them, as enduring and as steadfast.

And yet he had left these mountains. She thought of Arthur in that moment, and the children slain. She grieved in her heart for the sins of good men, caught in a dark world, longing for light.

The question at issue, Miach had said in Seithr's Hall, *is whether the King can surrender the Lake.*

She didn't know. None of them did. They were here to find out.

Miach turned back to Kaen and nodded. Kaen walked over to his companion, who held up his hands, the covered crystal within them, and with a sweeping, graceful motion Kaen drew the cloth away.

Kim felt as if she'd been punched in the chest. Tears sprang to her eyes. Her breath was torn away and she had to fight for some time before it came back. And all the while she was inwardly cursing the terrible unfairness, the coruscating, ultimate irony of this—that someone so twisted with evil, with deeds so very black laid down at the door of his heart, should have so much beauty at his command.

He had shaped, out of crystal, in miniature, the Cauldron of Khath Meigol.

It was exactly as she had seen it, in her long, dark mind journey from the Temple in Gwen Ystrat. When she had ventured so far into the blackness of Rakoth's designs that she could never have come back without Ruana's chanting to shield her and give her a reason to return.

It was exactly the same, but with everything reversed, somehow. The black Cauldron she had seen, the source of the killing winter in midsummer and then the death rain that had unpeopled Eridu, was now a glittering, delicate, ineffable glorious thing of crystalline light, even to the runic lettering around the rim and the symmetrical design at the base. Kaen had taken the image of that dark, shattered Cauldron and made of it a thing that caught the starlight as brightly as did the Lake.

It was a thing to be longed for, to be heartachingly desired by every single one of the Weaver's mortal children in all the worlds of time. Both for itself, and for what it symbolized: the return from death, from beyond the walls of Night, the passionate yearning of all those fated to die that there might be a coming back or a going on. That the ending not be an ending.

Kim looked at the Dwarf who had done this, saw him gaze at his own creation, and understood in that moment how he could have come to release Maugrim and surrender the Cauldron into his hand. Kaen's, she realized, was the soul of an artist carried too far. The search, the yearning for knowledge and creation taken to the point where madness began.

Using the Cauldron would have meant nothing to such a one: it was the *finding* that mattered, the knowledge of where it was. It was all abstract, internalized, and so all-consuming that nothing could be allowed to stand between the searcher and his long desire. Not a thousand deaths or tens of thousands, not a world given over to the Dark or all the worlds given over.

He was a genius, and mad. He was self-absorbed to the point where that could no longer be separated from evil, and yet he held this beauty within himself, pitched to a level Kim had never thought to see or ever imagined could be seen.

She didn't know how long they stood transfixed by that shining thing. At length Miach gave a small, almost an apologetic cough. He said, "Kaen's gift has been considered." His voice was husky, diffident. Kim couldn't even blame him. Had she been able to speak, that, too, would have been her tone, even with all she knew.

"Matt Sören?" Miach said.

Matt walked over to Loren. For a moment he paused before the man for whom he had forsaken these mountains and this Lake. A look passed between the two of them that made Kimberly turn away for a moment, it was so deeply private, speaking to so many things that no one else had a right to share. Then Matt quietly drew the cloth from his own fashioning.

Loren was holding a dragon in his hands.

It bore the same relationship to Kaen's dazzling artistry that the stone door at the top of the stairs did to the magnificent archways that led into Seithr's Hall. It was roughly worked, all planes and sharp angles, not polished. Where Kaen's cauldron glittered brilliantly in the starlight, Matt's crafted dragon seemed dull beside it. It had two great, gouged eyes, and its head was turned upward at an awkward, straining angle.

And yet Kim couldn't take her eyes off it. Nor, she was aware, had any of the others there, not even Kaen, whose quick chuckle of derision had given way to silence.

Looking more closely, Kim saw that the roughness was entirely deliberate, a matter of decision, not inability or haste. The line of the dragon's shoulder, she saw, would have been a matter of moments to smooth down, and the same was true of the sharp edge of the averted neck. Matt had wanted it this way.

And slowly she began to understand. She shivered then, uncontrollably, for there was power in this beyond words, rising from the soul and the heart, from an awareness not sourced in the conscious mind. For whereas Kaen had sought—and found—a form to give expression to the beauty of this place, to catch and transmute the stars, Matt had reached for something else.

He had shaped an approach—no more than that—to the ancient, primitive power Kim had sensed as they mounted the stairs and had been overwhelmingly conscious of from the moment they had come into the meadow.

Calor Diman was infinitely more than a place of glory,

however much it was that. It was hearthstone, bedrock, root. It encompassed the roughness of rock and the age of earth and the cold depths of mountain waters. It was very dangerous. It was the heart of the Dwarves, and the power of them, and Matt Sören, who had been made King by a night in this high meadow, knew that better than anyone alive, and his crafting for the Lake bore witness to it.

None of them there could know it, and the one man who might have told them had died in Gwen Ystrat to end the winter, but there was a cracked stone bowl of enormous antiquity lying, even then, beside a chasm in Dana's cave at Dun Maura. And that bowl embodied the same unthinking awareness of the nature of ancient power that Matt Sören's dragon did.

"You did this before," said Miach quietly. "Forty years ago."

"You remember?" Matt asked.

"I do. It was not the same."

"I was young then. I thought I might strive to equal in crystal the truth of what I was shaping. I am older now, and some few things I have learned. I am glad of a chance to set matters right before the end."

There was a grudging respect in Miach's eyes, and in Ingen's as well, Kim saw. In Loren's face was something else: an expression that combined somehow a father's pride, and a brother's, and a son's.

"Very well," Miach said, straightening as much as his bent years would allow. "We have considered both of your craftings. Take them and cast them forth, and may the Queen of Waters grant her guidance to us now."

Matt Sören took his dragon then, and Kaen his shining crystal cauldron, and the two of them went, side by side, away from the six who would watch. And they came, in the silence of that night, under the stars but not yet the late-rising moon, to the shore of Calor Diman, and there they stopped.

There were stars mirrored in the Lake, and high overhead, and then a moment later there were two more shining things above the water, as both Dwarves who had come to be judged threw their crystal gifts in arcs out over the Lake.

And they fell, both of them, with splashes that echoed in the brooding stillness, and disappeared in the depths of Calor Diman.

There were, Kim saw with a shiver, no ripples at all to ruffle the water and so mark the place where they fell.

Then came a time of waiting, a time outside of time, so charged with the resonances of that place it seemed to go on forever, to have been going on since first Fionavar was spun onto the Loom. Kimberly, for all her dreaming, all her Seer's gifts, had no hint of what they were waiting to see, what form the Lake's answer was to take. Never taking her eyes from the two Dwarves by the water, she reached within and found her own twin soul, searching for a reply to the question she could not answer. But neither, it seemed, could the part of her that was Ysanne. Not even the old Seer's dreams or her own vast store of knowledge were equal to this: the Dwarves had guarded their secret far too well.

And then, even as Kim was thinking this, she saw that Calor Diman was moving.

Whitecaps began to take shape in the center of the Lake, and with them there suddenly came a sound, high and shrill, a wailing, haunted cry unlike anything she'd ever heard. Loren, beside her, murmured something that must have been a prayer. The whitecaps became waves and the wailing sound grew higher and higher, and then so too did the waves, and suddenly they were rushing hugely from the agitated heart of the dark water toward the shore, as if Calor Diman were emptying her center.

Or rising from it.

And in that moment the Crystal Dragon came.

Understanding burst in Kimberly then, and with it a sense, after the fact, as so many times before, that it should have been obvious all along. She had seen the enormous sculpture of a dragon dominating the entrance to Seithr's Hall. She had seen Matt's crafting and heard what he and Miach had said to each other. She had known there was more than beauty in this place. She had been aware of magic, ancient and deep.

This was it. This crystalline, shimmering Dragon of the Lake was the power of Calor Diman. It was the heart of the Dwarves, their soul and their secret, which she and Loren had now been allowed to see. A fact, she was grimly aware, that made their deaths doubly certain if Kaen should prevail in what was coming.

She forced her mind from that thought. All around her everyone else, including Loren, had knelt. She did not. Not clearly understanding the impulse that kept her on her feet—pride, but more than that—she met the shining eyes of the Crystal Dragon as they fell upon her, and she met them with respect but as an equal.

It was hard, though. The Dragon was unimaginably beautiful. Creature of mountain meadow and the icy depths of mountain waters, it glittered, almost translucent in the starlight, rising from the agitated waves high above the kneeling figures of the two Dwarves on the banks of Calor Diman.

Then it spread its wings, and Kimberly cried aloud in wonder and awe, for the wings of the Dragon dazzled and shone with a myriad of colors like gems in infinite variety, a play of light in the meadow bowl of night. She almost did sink to her knees then, but again something kept her on her feet, watching, her heart aching.

The Dragon did not fly. It held itself suspended, half within the water, half rising from it. Then it opened its mouth, and flame burst forth, flame without smoke, like the torches on the walls within the mountain; blue-white flame, through which the stars could still be seen.

The fire died. The Dragon's wings were still. A silence, cold and absolute, like the silence that might have lain at the very beginning of time, wrapped the meadow. Kim saw one of the Dragon's claws slowly emerge, glittering, from the water. There was something clutched in its grasp. Something the Crystal Dragon suddenly tossed, with what seemed to her to be contemptuous disdain, on the grass by the Lake.

She saw what it was.

"*No,*" she breathed, the sound torn from her like flesh from a wound. Discarded on the grass, glinting, lay a miniature crafting of a crystal dragon.

"Wait!" Loren whispered sharply, rising to his feet. He touched her hand. "Look."

Even as she watched, she saw the Dragon of Calor Diman raise a second claw, holding a second object. And this was a cauldron, of shining, scintillant beauty, and this object too the Dragon threw away, to lie sparkling on the blue-green grass.

She didn't understand. She looked at Loren. There was a curious light in his eyes.

He said, "Look again, Kim. Look closely."

She turned back. Saw Matt and Kaen kneeling by the Lake. Saw the Dragon shining above them. Saw stars, subsiding waves, dark mountain crags. Saw a crystal cauldron tumbled on the grass and a small crafted dragon lying beside it.

Saw that the dragon discarded there was not the one Matt had just offered to the Lake.

And in that moment, as hope blazed in her like the Dragon's blue-white fire, Kim saw something else come up from Calor Diman. A tiny creature exploded from the water, furiously beating wings holding it aloft. A creature that now shone more brilliantly than it ever had before, with eyes that dazzled in the night, no longer dark and lifeless.

It was the heart's crafting Matt had offered, given life by the Lake. Which had accepted his gift.

There was a flurry of motion. Kaen scrambled forward on his knees. He reclaimed his cauldron. Rose to his feet, holding it outstretched beseechingly. "No!" he pleaded. "Wait!"

He had time for nothing more. Time ended for him. In that high place of beauty which was so much more than that, power suddenly made manifest its presence for a moment only, but a moment was enough. The Dragon of the Lake, the guardian of the Dwarves, opened its mouth, and flame roared forth a second time.

Not up into the mountain air, not for warning or display. The Dragonfire struck Kaen of Banir Lök where he stood, arms extended, offering his rejected gift again, and it incinerated him, consumed him utterly. For one horrifying instant Kim saw his body writhing within the translucent flame, and then he was gone. There was nothing left at all, not even the cauldron he had made. The blue-white fire died, and when it did Matt Sören was kneeling alone, in the stunned silence of aftermath, by the shore of the Lake.

She saw him reach out and pick up the sculpted dragon lying beside him, the one, Kim now realized—seeing what

Loren had grasped from the first—that he had shaped forty years ago, when the Lake had made him King. Slowly Matt rose to stand facing the Dragon of Calor Diman. It seemed to Kim that there was a tinted brightness to the air.

Then the Dragon spoke. "You should not have gone away," it said with an ancient sorrow.

So deep a sadness after so wild a blaze of power. Matt lowered his head.

"I accepted your gift that night," the Dragon said, in a voice like a mountain wind, cold and clear and lonely. "I accepted it, because of the courage that lay beneath the pride of what you offered me. I made you King under Banir Lök. You should not have gone away."

Matt looked up, accepting the weight of the Dragon's crystal gaze. Still he said nothing. Beside her, Kim became aware that Loren was weeping quietly.

"Nevertheless," said the Dragon of the Lake, and there was a new timbre in its voice, "nevertheless, you have changed since you went from here, Matt Sören. You have lost an eye in wars not properly those of your people, but you have shown tonight, with this second gift, that with one eye only you still see more deeply into my waters than any of the Kings of the Dwarves have ever done before."

Kimberly bit her lip. She slipped her hand into Loren's. There was a brightness in her heart.

"You should not have gone away," she heard the Dragon say to Matt, "but from what you have done tonight, I will accept that a part of you never did. Be welcome back, Matt Sören, and hear me as I name you now truest of all Kings ever to reign under Banir Lök and Banir Tal."

There was light, there seemed to be so much light: a tinted, rosy hue of fiercest illumination.

"*Oh, Kim, no!*" Loren suddenly cried in a choked, desperate voice. "*Not this. Oh, surely not this!*"

Light burned to ash in the wake of knowledge, of bitter, bitterest, recurring understanding. Of *course* there was light in the meadow, of course there was. *She* was here.

With the Baelrath blazing in wildest summons on her hand.

Matt had wheeled at Loren's cry. Kim saw him look at the ring he had only just returned to her, and she read the brutal anguish in his face as this moment of heart-deep triumph, the moment of his return, was transformed into something terrible beyond words.

She wanted desperately not to be here, not to understand what this imperative blazing meant. She *was* here, though, and she did know. And she had not knelt to the Dragon because, somehow, a part of her must have been aware of what was to come.

What had come now. She carried the Warstone again, the summons to war. And it was on fire to summon. To compel the Crystal Dragon from its mountain bowl. Kim had no illusions, none at all—and the sight of Matt's stricken face would have stripped them away from her, if she'd had any.

The Dragon could not leave the Lake, not if it was to be what it had always been: ancient guardian, key to the soul, heart-deep symbol of what the Dwarves were. What she was about to do would shatter the people of the twin mountains as much and more as she had smashed the Paraiko in Khath Meigol.

This crystal power of Calor Diman, which had endured the death rain of Maugrim, would not be able to resist the fire she carried. Nothing could.

Matt turned away. Loren released her hand.

I don't have a choice! she cried. Within her heart, not aloud. She knew why the stone was burning. There was tremendous power here in this creature of the Lake, and its very shining made it a part of the army of Light. They were at war with the Dark, with the unnumbered legions of Rakoth. She had carried the ring here for a reason, and this was it.

She stepped forward, toward the now-still waters of Calor Diman. She looked up and saw the clear eyes of the Dragon resting upon her, accepting and unafraid, though infinitely sorrowful. As deeply rooted in power as anything in Fionavar and knowing that Kim's was a force that would bind it and change it forever.

On her hand the Baelrath was pulsing now so wildly that the whole of the meadow and all the mountain crags were lit by its glow. Kim lifted her hand. She thought of Macha and Nemain, the goddesses of war. She thought of Ruana and the Paraiko, remembered the kanior: the last kanior. Because of her. She thought of Arthur, and of Matt Sören, who stood, not far away, not looking at her, lest his expression plead.

She thought upon the evil that good men had done in the name of Light, remembered Jennifer in Starkadh. War was upon them, it was all around them, threatening those living now, and all who might come after, with the terrible dominion of the Dark.

"No," said Kimberly Ford quietly, with absolute finality. "I have come this far and have done this much. I will go no farther on this path. There is a point beyond which the quest for Light becomes a serving of the Dark."

"Kim—" Matt began. His face was working strangely.

"Be silent!" she said, stern because she would break if she heard him speak. She knew him, and knew what he would say. "Come here beside me! Loren! And Miach too, I'll need you!" Her mind was racing as fast as it ever had.

They moved toward her, drawn by the power in her voice—her Seer's voice—as much as by the burning on her hand. She knew exactly what she was doing and what it might mean, knew the implications as deeply as she had ever known anything at all. And she would shoulder them. If it made her name a curse from now to the end of time, then so be it. She would not destroy what she had seen tonight.

There was understanding in the Dragon's crystal eyes. Slowly it spread its wings, like a curtain of benison, many-colored, glittering with light. Kim had no illusions about that, none at all.

The two Dwarves and the man were beside her now. The flame on her hand was still driving her to summon. It was *demanding* that she do so. There was war. There was need! She met the eyes of the Dragon for the very last time.

"No," she said again with all the conviction of her soul—both her souls.

And then she used the incandescent, overwhelming blazing of the ring, not to bind the Dragon of the Dwarves but to take herself away across the mountains, herself and three others with her, far from that hidden place of starlight and enchantment, though not so far as she had gone in coming there.

The Baelrath's power was rampant within her, flaming with the fire of war. She entered into it, saw where it was she had to go, gathered and channeled what she carried, and took them there.

They came down, in what seemed to all of them to be a corona of crimson light. They were in a clearing. A clearing in the forest of Gwynir, not far from Daniloth.

"*Someone's here!*" a voice screamed in strident warning. Another echoed it: voices of Dwarves from the army Blöd commanded. They had come in time!

Kim was driven to her knees by the impact of landing. She looked quickly around. And saw Dave Martyniuk standing not ten feet away from her with an axe in his hand. Behind him she recognized, with an incredulity that bordered on stupefaction, Faebur and Brock, swords drawn. There was no time to think.

"Miach!" she screamed. "Stop them!"

And the aged leader of the Dwarfmoot did not fail her. Moving more swiftly than she had ever thought he could, he stepped between Dave and the trio of Dwarves menacing him, and he cried, "*Hold arrows and blades, people of the mountains!* Miach of the Moot commands you, in the name of the King of the Dwarves!"

There was thunder in him for that one moment, a ringing peal of command. The Dwarves froze. Slowly Dave lowered his axe, Faebur his bow.

In the brittle silence of the forest clearing, Miach said, very clearly, "Hear me. There has been judgment tonight by the shores of Calor Diman. Matt Sören returned to our mountains yesterday, and it was the decision of the Moot, after a word-striving in Seithr's Hall between him and Kaen, that their dispute be left to the Lake. So did it come to pass tonight. I must tell you that Kaen is dead, destroyed by the fire of the Lake. The spirit of Calor Diman came forth tonight, and I saw it with my eyes and heard it name Matt Sören to be our King again, and more: I heard it name him as truest of all Kings ever to reign under the mountains."

"You are lying!" A harsh voice intruded. "None of this is true. Rinn, Nemed—*seize him!*" Blöd pointed a shaking finger at Miach.

No one moved.

"I am First of the Moot," Miach said calmly. "I cannot lie. You know this is true."

"I know you are an old fool," Blöd snarled in response. "Why should we let ourselves be deceived by that children's fable? You can lie as well as any of us, Miach! Better than any of—"

"Blöd," said the King of the Dwarves, "have done. It is over."

Matt stepped forward from the darkness of the trees. He said nothing more, and his voice had not been loud, but the tone of command was complete and not to be mistaken.

Blöd's face worked spasmodically, but he did not speak. Behind him a swelling murmur of sound rushed backward through the army to the ends of the clearing and beyond, where Dwarves had been sleeping among the evergreens. They were sleeping no longer.

"Oh my King!" a voice cried. Brock of Banir Tal stumbled forward, throwing down his axe, to kneel at Matt's feet.

"Bright the hour of our meeting," Matt said to him formally. He laid a hand on Brock's shoulder. "But stand back now, old friend, there is a thing yet to be done." There was something in his voice that evoked an abrupt image, for Kim, of the iron lock on the door to the meadow of Calor Diman.

Brock withdrew. Gradually the murmur and the cries of the army subsided. A watchful silence descended. Occasionally someone coughed or a twig crackled underfoot.

In that stillness, Matt Sören confronted the Dwarf who had served in Starkadh, who had done what he had done to Jennifer, who had been leading the Dwarves even now in the army of the Dark. Blöd's eyes darted back and forth, but he did not try to run or plead. Kim had thought he would be a coward, but she was wrong. None of the Dwarves lacked courage, it seemed, even those who had surrendered themselves to evil.

"Blöd of Banir Lök," Matt said, "your brother has died tonight, and your Dragon waits for you now as well in judgment, astride the wall of Night. In the presence of our people I will grant you what you do not deserve: a right to combat, and life in exile if you survive. As atonement for my own wrongs, which are many, I will fight you in this wood until one of us is dead."

"Matt, no!" Loren exclaimed.

Matt held up one hand. He did not turn around. "First, though," he said, "I would ask leave of those assembled here, to take this battle upon myself. There are a very great many here who have a claim upon your death."

He did turn, then, and of all of them it was to Faebur that he looked first. "I see one here whose face marks him as an Eridun. Have I leave to take this death for you and in the name of your people, stranger of Eridu?"

Kim saw the young man step forward a single pace. "I am Faebur, once of Larak," he said. "King of the Dwarves, you have leave to do this for me and for all the raindead of Eridu. And in the name of a girl called Arrian, whom I loved, and who is gone. The Weaver guide your hand." He withdrew, with a dignity that belied his years.

Again Matt turned. "Dave Martyniuk, you too have a claim to this, for the sufferings of a woman of your own world, and the death of a man. Will you surrender that claim to me?"

"I will surrender it," Dave said solemnly.

"Mabon of Rhoden?" Matt asked.

And Mabon said gravely, "In the name of the High King of Brennin, I ask you to act for the army of Brennin and Cathal."

"Levon dan Ivor?"

"This hour knows his name," Levon said. "Strike for the Dalrei, Matt Sören, for the living and the dead."

"Miach?"

"Strike for the Dwarves, King of the Dwarves."

Only then did Matt draw forth his axe from where it hung by his side and turn again, his face grim as mountain stone, to Blöd, who was waiting contemptuously.

"Have I your word," Blöd asked now, in the sharp, edgy voice so unlike his brother's, "that I will walk safely from this place if I leave you dead?"

"You have," said Matt clearly, "and I declare this in the presence of the First of the Dwarfmoot and—"

Blöd had not waited. Even as Matt was speaking, the other Dwarf had thrown himself sideways into the shadows and hurled a cunning dagger straight at Matt's heart.

Matt did not even bother to dodge. With an unhurried movement, as if he had all the time in the world, he blocked the flung blade with the head of his axe. It fell harmlessly to the grass. Blöd swore and scrambled to his feet, reaching for his own weapon.

He never touched it.

Matt Sören's axe, thrown then with all the strength of his arm and all the passion of his heart, flew through the firelit clearing like an instrument of the watching gods, a power of ultimate justice never to be denied, and it smote Blöd between the eyes and buried itself in his brain, killing him where he stood.

There were no shouts, no cheering. A collective sigh seemed to rise and fall, within the clearing and beyond it, to where Dwarves stood watching among the trees. Kim had a sudden image in that moment of a spirit, bat-winged, malevolent, rising to fly away. There was a Dragon waiting for him, Matt had said. Let it be so, she thought. She looked at the body of the Dwarf who had savaged Jennifer, and it seemed to her that vengeance should mean more, somehow. It should be more of a reply, something beyond this bloodied, torchlit body in Gwynir.

Oh, Jen, she thought. *He's dead now. I'll be able to tell you that he's dead.* It didn't mean as much as she'd once thought it would. It was only a step, a stage in this terrible journey. There was too far yet to go.

She had no more time for thoughts, which was a blessing and not a small one. Brock came rushing up to her, and Faebur, and she was embracing them both with joy. Amid the steadily growing noise all around, there was time for a quick question and answer about Dalreidan, and for delighted wonder as she learned who he really was.

Then, finally, she was standing in front of Dave, who had, of course, been hanging back, letting the others approach her first. Pushing her hair from her eyes, she looked up at him. "Well—" she began.

And got no further.

She was gathered in an embrace that lifted her completely off the ground and threatened to squeeze every trace of air out of her lungs. "I have never," he said, holding her close, his mouth to her ear, "been so happy to see anyone in all my life!"

He let her go. She dropped to the ground and stumbled,

gasping frantically for breath. She heard Mabon of Rhoden chuckle. She was grinning like an idiot, she knew.

"Me neither," she said, aware, abruptly, of how true that was. "Me neither!"

"Ahem!" said Levon dan Ivor, with the broadest stage cough she'd ever heard. They turned, to find him grinning as much as they were. "I hate to intrude with petty matters of concern," the Aven's son said, striving to sound sardonic, "but we do have a report to make to the High King on tonight's events, and if we're to get back before Torc and Sorcha raise a false alarm, we'd best get moving."

Aileron. She'd be seeing Aileron again too. So much was happening so fast. She drew a breath and turned, to see that Matt had come over to her.

Her smile faded. In her mind, even as she stood among the evergreens of Gwynir, she was seeing a Crystal Lake and a Dragon rising from it, glittering wings spread wide. A place where she would never walk again, under stars or sun or moon. She was a Seer; she knew that this was so. She and Matt looked at each other for a long time.

At length, he said, "The ring is dark."

"It is," she said. She didn't even have to look. She knew. She knew something else, too, but that was her own burden, not his. She said nothing about it.

"Seer," Matt began. He stopped. "Kim. You were supposed to bind it, weren't you? To bring it to war?" Only Loren and Miach, standing behind Matt, would know what he was talking about.

Picking her words carefully, she said, "We have a choice, Matt. We are not slaves, even to our gifts. I chose to use the ring another way." She said nothing more. She was thinking about Darien, even as she spoke about choices, remembering him running into Pendaran, past a burning tree.

Matt drew a breath, and then he nodded slowly. "May I thank you?" he asked.

This was hard. Everything was hard, now. "Not yet," she said. "Wait and see. You may not want to. I don't think we'll have long to wait."

And that last thing was said in her Seer's voice, and so she knew it was true.

"Very well," Matt said. He turned to Levon. "You say

you must carry word to the High King. We will join you tomorrow. The Dwarves have gone through a time worse than any in all our days. We shall remain by ourselves in these woods tonight and try to deal with what has happened to us. Tell Aileron we will meet him here when he comes, and that Matt Sören, King of the Dwarves, will bring his people into the army of the Light at that time."

"I will tell him," said Levon simply. "Come, Davor. Mabon. Faebur." He glanced at Kim, and she nodded. With Loren and Dave on either side, she began to follow Levon south, out of the clearing.

"*Wait!*" Matt cried suddenly. To her astonishment, Kim heard real fear in his voice. "Loren, where are you going?"

Loren turned, an awkward expression investing his lined face. "You asked us to leave," he protested. "To leave the Dwarves alone for tonight."

Matt's grim face seemed to change in the firelight. "Not you," he whispered softly. "Never you, my friend. Surely you will not leave me now?"

The two of them looked at each other in that way they had of seeming to be alone in the midst of a great many people. And then, very slowly, Loren smiled.

As they followed Levon out of the clearing into the darkness of the evergreens, Kim and Dave paused for a moment to look back. They saw Matt Sören standing with Brock on one side and Loren Silvercloak on the other. Matt had placed his fingertips together in front of his chest, with his palms held a little way apart—as if to form a mountain peak with his hands. And one by one the Dwarves of the twin mountains were filing up to him, and kneeling, and placing their own hands between his, inside the sheltering mountain the Dwarf King formed.

PART IV

Andarien

Chapter 14

In one way, Leila thought, listening to the last notes of the morning's Lament for Liadon, it had been easier than she'd had any right to expect. She stood alone behind the altar, looking out upon all the others, closest to the axe but careful not to touch it, for that the High Priestess alone could do.

She stood closest, though. She was fifteen years old, only newly clad in the grey of the priestesses, yet Jaelle had named her to act in her stead while the High Priestess was away from Paras Derval. Dun to grey to red. She was of the Mormae now. Jaelle had warned her that there might be difficulties here in the Temple.

The fact that there hadn't been, so far, had a great deal to do with fear.

They were all a little afraid of her, ever since the evening when, only four nights ago, she had seen Owein and the Wild Hunt arrive at the battle by Celidon and had served as a conduit for Ceinwen's voice to resound in the sanctuary, so far from the river where the goddess was. In the supercharged atmosphere of war, that manifestation of her own unsettling powers was still reverberating in the Temple.

Unfortunately it didn't help much with Gwen Ystrat. Audiart was another matter entirely. Three separate times in the day and a half following Jaelle's departure, the Second of the Goddess had reached for Leila through the gathered Mormae in Morvran. And three times Audiart had graciously offered to make her way to Paras Derval to assist the poor beleaguered child, so unfairly taxed with such a heavy burden in such a terrible time.

It had taken all the clarity and firmness Leila could muster to hold her back. She knew the issues at stake as well as any of them: if Jaelle did not return, then Leila, named in a time of war to act as High Priestess, would *become* the High Priestess, notwithstanding all the normal peacetime rituals of succession. She also knew that Jaelle had been explicit about this one thing: Audiart was *not* to be allowed to come to the Temple.

During the last mindlink, the evening before, diplomacy hadn't worked at all. Jaelle had warned her it might not and had told her what to do, but that didn't make the doing any easier for a fifteen-year-old, confronting the most formidable figure of the Mormae.

Nonetheless, she had done it. Aided by the astonishing clarity—she even surprised herself with it—of her own mind voice during the linkings and speaking as acting High Priestess, invoking the Goddess by the nine names in sequence, she had formally ordered Audiart to remain precisely where she was, in Gwen Ystrat, and to initiate no further mindlinks. She, Leila, had far too much to do to tolerate any more of these avarlith-draining communications.

And then she had broken the link.

That had been last night. She hadn't slept very well afterward, troubled by dreams. One was of Audiart, mounted on some terrible six-legged steed, thundering over the roads from Morvran to seize and bind her with cold curses from millennia ago.

There had been other dreams, having nothing to do with the Mormae. Leila didn't understand the way her own mind worked, where her swirling premonitions came from, but they had been with her all night long.

And most of them were about Finn, which, since she knew where he really was and with whom he rode, became the most unsettling thing of all.

Darien never even knew he'd been frozen in time over Daniloth. As far as he was concerned, he'd been flying north, the dagger in his mouth, all the while. It was evening and not morning when he left the Shadowland and came out over Andarien, but he didn't know the geography here, so that didn't concern him.

In any case, it was hard to think clearly in the owl shape, and he was very tired by now. He had flown from Brennin to the Anor Lisen, and then walked to the sacred grove, and flown again from there through an unsleeping night to Daniloth, and then through the whole of yet another day to where he now was, heading north to his father.

Through the growing darkness he flew, and his keen night sight registered the presence of an unimaginably vast army gathering beneath him on the barren desolation of this land. He knew who they were, but he didn't descend or slow to take a closer look. He had a long way to go.

Below him, a lean scarred figure lifted his head suddenly to cast a keen glance at the darkening sky. There was nothing there, only a single owl, its plumage still white despite the changed season. Galadan watched it flying north. There was an old superstition about owls: they were good luck or bad, depending on which way they curved overhead.

This one did not swerve, arrowing straight north over the massing army of the Dark. The Wolflord watched it, troubled by a nameless disquiet, until it disappeared. It was the color, he decided, the strange whiteness at sunset over this barren desolation. He put it out of his mind. With the snow gone, white was a vulnerable color, and more of the swans were due to be coming back down from the north tonight. The owl was unlikely to survive.

It almost didn't.

A few hours later Darien was even more tired than before, and fatigue made him careless. He became aware of danger only an instant before the unnatural claws of one of Avaia's brood reached his flesh. He screeched, almost dropping the dagger, and veered sharply downward and to his left. Even so, one claw claimed a half dozen feathers from his side.

Another black swan swooped hugely toward him, wings lashing the air. Darien wheeled desperately back to his right and forced his tired wings into a steep climb—straight toward the last of the three black swans, which had been waiting patiently behind the other two for precisly this move. Owls, for all their vaunted intelligence, were fairly predictable in combat. With a carnivorous grin the third swan waited for the little white owl, keen to slake its continuous hunger for blood.

In Darien's breast fear beat back tiredness, and following upon terror came a red surge of rage. He did not even try to dodge this last pursuing swan. Straight at it he flew, and an instant before they collided—a collision that would surely have killed him—he let his eyes burn as red as they could go. With the same blast of fire he had used to torch the tree, he incinerated the swan.

It didn't even have time to scream. Darien wheeled again, fury pulsing within him, and he raked the other two swans with the same red fire and they died.

He watched them fall to the dark earth below. All around him the air was full of the smell of singed feathers and charred flesh. He felt dizzy, suddenly, and overwhelmingly weak. He let himself descend, in a slow, shallow glide, looking for a tree of any kind. There were none. This was Andarien, and nothing so tall as a tree grew here, not for a thousand years.

He came to rest, for want of a better place, on the slope of a low hill littered with boulders and sharp-edged stones. It was cold. The wind blew from the north and made a keening sound as it passed between the rocks. There were stars overhead; low in the east, the waning moon had just risen. It offered no comfort, casting only a chill, faint illumination over the stony landscape, the stunted grass.

Darien took his own shape again. He looked around. Nothing moved, as far as he could see in the wide night. He was completely alone. In a gesture that had become a reflex in the past two days, though he was unaware of that, he reached up to touch the stone set in the Circlet of Lisen. It was as cool and dark and distant as it had been from the moment he'd put it on. He remembered the way it had shone in the Seer's hands. The memory was like a blade, or the wound made by a blade. Either, or both.

He lowered his hand and looked around again. About him, in every direction, stretched the desolation of Andarien. He was so far to the north that Rangat was almost east of him. It towered over the whole of the northlands, dominant and magnificent. He didn't look at the Mountain for long.

Instead he turned his gaze due north. And because he was much more than mortal and his eyes were very good, he could discern, far off through the moonlit shadows, where the stony highlands reached the mountains and the ice, a cold greenish glow. And he knew that this was Starkadh, beyond the Valgrind Bridge, and that he could fly there by tomorrow.

He decided that he would not fly, though. Something about the owl shape felt wrong. He wanted to hold to his own form, he realized: to be Darien, whatever and whoever that might be, to regain the clarity of thought that came in his human shape, though at the price of loneliness. Even so, he would do it this way. He would not fly. He would go on foot over the stones and the barren soil, over the ruin of this wasteland. He would go, with an extinguished light upon his brow, bearing a blade in his hand as a gift for the Dark.

Not tonight, though. He was much too tired, and there was a pain in his side where the swan's claw had caught him. He was probably bleeding but was too weary to even check. He lay down on the south side of the largest of the boulders—for such scant shelter as it might offer from the wind—and in time he did fall asleep, despite his fears and cares. He was young yet, and had come a long distance to a lonely place, and his soul was as much overtaxed as his body was.

As he passed over into the far countries of sleep, his mother was sailing in a ghostly ship down Linden Bay, just beyond the moonlit western ridges of the land, toward the river mouth of the Celyn.

He dreamt of Finn all night, just as Leila did in the Temple, a long way south. His dream was of the last afternoon, when he had still been small, playing in the yard behind the cottage with his brother, and they had seen riders passing on the snow-clad slopes east of them. He had waved a mittened hand, because Finn had told him to. And then Finn had gone away after the riders, and then much farther than they had gone, farther than anyone else, even Darien, even in dream, could go.

He did not know, huddled in the shadow of a leaning boulder on the cold ground of Andarien, that he was crying in his sleep. Nor did he know that all night long his hand kept returning to the lifeless gem bound about his brow, reaching, reaching out for something, finding no response.

"Do you know," said Diarmuid, gazing east with an enigmatic expression, "this is almost enough to make one believe in fraternal instincts, after all."

Beside him on the banks of the River Celyn, Paul remained silent. Across the northwestern spur of the lake the army was coming. They were too far off yet for him to make out individual details, but that didn't matter. What mattered was that Diarmuid, for all the reflexive irony of his words, had indeed been right.

Aileron had not waited, for them or for anyone. He had carried this war to Maugrim. The army of the High King was in Andarien again, a thousand years after it had last swept through these wild, desolate highlands. And waiting for them in the late-afternoon light was his brother, with Arthur and Lancelot and Guinevere, with Sharra of Cathal, and Jaelle, the High Priestess, with the men of South Keep who had manned *Prydwen*, and with Pwyll Twiceborn, Lord of the Summer Tree.

For what, Paul thought, that last was worth. It didn't, at the moment, feel like much. He should be used to this by now, he knew: this sense of latency without control. Of holding power without harnessing it. He remembered Jaelle's words on the rocks, and he was acutely aware that she was right—aware of how much his difficulties were caused by his own overdeveloped need for controlling things. Particularly himself. All of this was true; it made sense; he even understood it. It didn't make him feel any better, though. Not now, not so near to whatever ending lay in wait, whatever future toward which they were toiling.

"He has the Dwarves with him!" keen-eyed Brendel suddenly cried.

"Now that," said Diarmuid sharply, "is news!"

It was. "Matt succeeded, then!" Paul exclaimed. "Do you see him, Brendel?"

The silver-haired lios alfar scanned the distant army. "Not yet," he murmured, "but . . . yes. It has to be her! The Seer is with the High King. No one else has her white hair."

Paul looked quickly over at Jennifer. She returned his glance and smiled. It was strange, he thought, in some ways it was the strangest thing of all, how she could be at once so different, so remote, so much Guinevere of Camelot,

Arthur's Queen, Lancelot's love, and then, a moment later, with the quickness of a smile, be Jennifer Lowell again, sharing his own flash of joy at Kimberly's return.

"Should we walk around the lake to meet them?" Arthur asked.

Diarmuid shook his head with exaggerated decisiveness. "They have horses," he said pointedly, "and we have been walking all day. If Brendel can see them, then the lios alfar in the army can see us. There are limits, I'm afraid, to how far I will stumble over those rocks in order to meet a brother who didn't bother to wait for me!"

Lancelot laughed. Glancing over at him, Paul was hit with a renewed sense of awe and, predictably, by another wave of his own frustrated impotence.

Lancelot had been waiting for them here, sitting patiently under the trees, as they had walked up along the river two hours ago. In the gentle restraint of his greeting of Guinevere, and then of Arthur, Paul had glimpsed again the depths of the grief that bound these three. It was not an easy thing to watch.

And then Lancelot had told, sparely, without inflection, the tale of his night battle with the demon in the sacred grove for the life of Darien. He made it sound prosaic, almost a negligible event. But every man and the three women there could see the wounds and burns of that battle, the price he had paid.

For what? Paul didn't know. None of them did, not even Jennifer. And there had been nothing at all to be read in her eyes as Lancelot told of freeing the owl in Daniloth and watching it fly north: the random thread in this weaving of war.

A war that seemed to be upon them now. The army had come closer; it was rounding the tip of Celyn Lake. Beneath Diarmuid's acerbic flippancy Paul could read a febrile tension building: the reunion with his brother, the nearness of battle. They could make out figures now. Paul saw Aileron under the banner of the High Kingdom, and then he realized that the banner had changed: the tree was still there, the Summer Tree for which he himself was named, but the moon above it was no longer the silver crescent of before.

Instead, the moon above the tree was the red full moon

Dana had caused to shine on a new moon night—the Goddess's challenge to Maugrim and the challenge Aileron was carrying now, at the head of the army of Light.

And so that army rode up around the lake, and it came to pass that the sons of Ailell met again on the borders of Daniloth, north of the River Celyn among the broad-leafed aum trees and the silver and red flowers of sylvain on the riverbank.

Diarmuid, with Sharra holding him by the hand, walked a little forward from the others, and Aileron, too, stepped apart from the army he led. Paul saw Ivor watching, and a lios alfar who had to be Ra-Tenniel, and Matt was there, with Loren beside him. Kim was smiling at him, and next to her was Dave, a crooked, awkward grin on his face. They were all here, it seemed, here on the edge of Andarien for the beginning of the end. All of them. Or, not quite all. One was missing. One would always be missing.

Diarmuid was bowing formally to the High King. "What kept you so long?" he said brightly.

Aileron did not smile. "It took some doing to maneuver the chariots through the forest."

"I see," said Diarmuid, nodding gravely.

Aileron, his eyes unrevealing as ever, looked his brother carefully up and down, then said expressionlessly, "Your boots seem seriously in need of repair."

It was Kim who laughed, letting all of them know that they could. Amid the release of tension, Diarmuid swore impressively, his color suddenly high.

Aileron finally smiled. "Loren and Matt have told us what you did, on the island and at sea. I have seen Amairgen's staff. You will know without my telling you how brightly woven a journey that was."

"You might tell me anyhow," Diarmuid murmured.

Aileron ignored that. "There is a man among you I would greet," he said. They watched as Lancelot stepped quietly forward, limping very slightly.

Dave Martyniuk was remembering something: a wolf hunt in Leinanwood, where the High King had slain the last seven wolves himself. And Arthur Pendragon had said, a strangeness in his voice, *Only one man I ever saw could do what you just did.*

Now the one man was here, and kneeling before Aileron. And the High King bade him rise and, gently, with care for the other's wounds, he clasped him about the shoulders as he had not clasped his brother. Who stood a little way behind, a slight smile on his face, holding the Princess of Cathal by the hand.

"My lord High King," said Mabon of Rhoden, stepping forward from the ranks of the army, "the daylight wanes, and it has been a long day's riding to this place. Would you make camp here? Shall I give the orders to do so?"

"I would not advise it," said Ra-Tenniel of Daniloth quickly, turning from conversation with Brendel.

Aileron was already shaking his head. "Not here," he said. "Not with the Shadowland so near. If the army of the Dark were to advance overnight we would have the worst possible ground for battle, with the river behind us, and no retreat beyond it into the mist. No, we will move on. It will not be dark for a few hours yet."

Mabon nodded agreement and withdrew to alert the captains of the army. Ivor, Paul noted, already had the Dalrei mounted up again, waiting for the signal to ride.

Diarmuid coughed loudly. "May I," he said plaintively, as his brother turned to him, "be so bold as to entreat the loan of horses for my company? Or did you want me to trundle along in your wake?"

"That," Aileron said, laughing for the first time, "has more appeal than you know." He turned to walk back to the army but over his shoulder, as if offhandedly, added, "We brought your own horse, Diar. I thought you would find a way to get back in time."

They mounted up. Behind them, as they left the river for Andarien's stony ground, a boat was drifting gently down the current of the Celyn. Within that craft Leyse of the Swan Mark was listening to the music of her song, even as she came out upon the waves, to follow the setting sun across the wideness of the sea.

Kim looked over at Dave for encouragement. She didn't really have a right to any support, but the big man gave her an unexpectedly shrewd glance, and when she began picking her way forward and to the left, to where Jennifer was riding, he detached himself from Ivor's side and followed her.

There was something she had to tell Jennifer, and she wasn't happy about it at all. Especially not when she thought about the disastrous results of her sending Darien to the Anor two days ago. Still, there was really no avoiding this, and she wasn't about to try.

"Hi," she said brightly to her closest friend. "Are you still speaking to me?"

Jennifer smiled wearily and leaned across in her saddle to kiss Kim on the cheek. "Don't be silly," she said.

"It's not that silly. You were pretty angry."

Jennifer lowered her gaze. "I know. I'm sorry." She paused. "I wish I could explain better why I'm doing what I'm doing."

"You wanted him to be left alone. It isn't that complicated."

Jennifer looked up again. "We *have* to leave him alone," she said quietly. "If I'd tried to bind him we'd never have known what he really was. He might have changed at any time. We'd never have been sure what he might do."

"We aren't very sure now," Kim said, rather more sharply than she'd intended.

"I know that," Jennifer replied. "But at least he'll do it freely, whatever he does. By his own choice. I think that's the whole point, Kim. I think it has to be."

"Would it have been so terrible," Kim asked, not wisely, but she couldn't hold the question back, "if you had just told him you loved him?"

Jennifer didn't flinch, nor did she flare into anger again. "I did," she said mildly, a hint of surprise in her voice. "I did let him know. Surely you can see that. I left him free to make his choice. I . . . trusted him."

"Fair enough," said Paul Schafer. They hadn't heard him ride up. "You were the only one of us who did," he added. "Everyone else has been busy trying to cajole him or make him into something. Including me, I suppose, when I took him to the Godwood."

"Do you know," Jennifer asked Paul suddenly, "why the Weaver made the Wild Hunt? Do you know what Owein *means*?"

Paul shook his head.

"Remind me to tell you, if we ever have the time," she said. "You, too," she added, turning to Kim. "I think it might help you understand."

Kim was silent. She really didn't know how to respond. It was too hard, this whole question of Darien, and since what she'd done, or refused to do, last night by Calor Diman, she no longer trusted her own instincts about anything. Besides, this confrontation wasn't why she'd come over.

She sighed. "You may hate me after all," she said. "I interfered again, I'm afraid."

Jen's green eyes were calm, though. She said, "I can guess. You told Aileron and the others about Darien."

Kim blinked. She must have looked comical, because Dave grinned suddenly, and Jennifer leaned across again to pat her hand.

"I thought you might have," Jen explained. "And I can't say you were wrong. By now he has to know. Arthur told me that on the ship last night. I would have talked to him myself if you hadn't. It may affect his planning, though I can't see how." She paused and then, in a different voice, added, "Don't you see? The secret doesn't matter now, Kim. None of them can stop him from whatever he's going to do—Lancelot freed him from Daniloth yesterday morning. He's a long way north of us now."

Involuntarily, Kim's gaze went out over the land that stretched in front of them. She saw Dave Martyniuk do the same. Wild and empty in the late-afternoon light, Andarien rolled away, all stony hills and barren hollows, and she knew it was like this all the way to the Ungarch River. To the Valgrind Bridge across that river, to Starkadh on the other side.

As it happened, they did not have nearly so far to go, themselves.

They were very close to the front of the army, only a few paces behind Aileron and Ra-Tenniel, ascending a wide, lightly sloping ridge with yet another bleak depression beyond. The reddened sun was well over to the west and a breeze had come up, overture to twilight.

Then they saw the front-riding auberei suddenly reappear on the crest of the ridge. The High King reached the summit. He reined in his own black charger and froze, utterly still. They topped the rise themselves, the four of them riding together for the first and only time, and looked down onto a vast, stony plain and saw the army of the Dark.

The plain was huge, easily the largest expanse of level ground they'd yet reached in Andarien, and Paul knew this was no accident of chance. He also guessed, as he tried to control his accelerating heartbeat, that this would be the broadest such expanse in all the land between here and the Ice. It had to be. With subtleties of contour and land formation stripped away, less of Aileron's training in war, little of his life's studies, could be drawn into play. The ridge upon which they now were, looking down the gentle slope, was the only distinguishing feature in all the level land to east or west. This would be a battle of force on force, with nowhere to hide or seek advantage, where sheer numbers would tell the tale.

Between them and whatever lands lay beyond was an army so huge it numbed the mind. It could scarcely be registered. That was another reason why this plain had been chosen: nowhere else could such obliterating numbers have been assembled to move freely without hindering each other. Paul looked up and saw hundreds of swans, all black, circling ominously in the sky over Rakoth's army.

"Well done, Teyrnon," the High King said calmly. Paul realized with a shock that Aileron, as always, seemed to have been prepared, even for this. The mage had been using his powers to sense forward. Aileron had guessed the army was here; it was why he'd been so adamant about not camping overnight against the mist of the Shadowland.

Even as he looked down, heartsick, upon what lay waiting for them, Paul felt a quick pride in the young war king who was leading them. Completely unruffled, Aileron took the measure of the army he would have to somehow try to defeat. Without turning around, his eyes ceaselessly scanning the plain below, he began to issue a string of quiet instructions.

"They will not attack tonight," he said confidently. "They will not want to come at us up this ridge, and at night they'll lose the advantage of the swans' eyes. We will have battle with the sunrise, my friends. I wish we had some way of fighting them for control of the air, but it can't be helped. Teyrnon, you'll have to be my eyes, for as long as you and Barak can do so."

"We can do so for as long as you need us to," the last mage in Brennin replied.

Paul noticed that Kim had gone pale at Aileron's last words. He tried to catch her eye but she avoided his glance. He didn't have time to find out why.

"The lios can help with that," Ra-Tenniel murmured. There was music in his voice still, but there was nothing delicate about it any more, nothing soothing. "I can post the most longsighted among us up on this ridge to overlook the battle."

"Good," said Aileron crisply. "Do that. Place them tonight to keep watch. They will stay there tomorrow as well. Ivor, assign pairs of auberei to stay with each of the posted lios, to carry their messages back and forth."

"I will," said Ivor simply. "And my archers know what to do if the swans come too low."

"I know they do," said Aileron grimly. "For tonight, all of you bid your men divide into three watches and keep their weapons to hand when they rest. As for the morning—"

"Wait," said Diarmuid, from beside Paul. "Look. We seem to have a guest." His tone was as effortlessly light as it always was.

He was right, Paul saw. The red light of the sunset picked out a single huge white-clad figure that had detached itself from the heaving mass of the army on the plain. Riding one of the monstrous six-legged slaug, it picked its way over the stony ground to a position carefully out of bowshot from those watching on the ridge.

An unnatural stillness descended. Paul was acutely aware of the breeze, the angle of the sun, the clouds scudding overhead. He reached, a little desperately, for the place within himself that would mark the presence of Mörnir. It was there, but faint and hopelessly far. He shook his head.

"*Uathach!*" Dave Martyniuk said suddenly. It was a snarl.

"Who is he?" Aileron asked, very calm.

"He led them in the battle by the Adein," Ivor replied, his voice thick with loathing. "He is an urgach, but much more than that. Rakoth has done something to him."

Aileron nodded but said nothing more.

Instead, it was Uathach who spoke.

"Hear me!" he cried, his voice a viscous howl, so loud it seemed to bruise the air. "I bid you welcome, High King of Brennin, to Andarien. My friends behind me are hungry tonight, and I have promised them warrior meat tomorrow and more delicate fare after that, in Daniloth." He laughed, huge and fell on the plain, the red sun tinting the mocking white of his robe.

Aileron made no reply, nor did anyone else on the ridge. In grim, repressive silence, stony as the land over which they rode, they looked down upon the leader of Rakoth's army.

The slaug moved restlessly sideways. Uathach reined it viciously. Then he laughed a second time, and something in the sound chilled Paul.

Uathach said, "I have promised the svart alfar meat for tomorrow and offered them sport tonight. Tell me, warriors of Brennin, of Daniloth, of the Dalrei, treacherous Dwarves, tell me if there is one among you who will come down alone to me now. Or will you all hide as the frail lios do, in their shadows? *I offer challenge in the presence of these armies! Is there one who will accept, or are you all craven before my sword?*"

There was a stir along the ridge. Paul saw Dave, jaw clamped tight, turn quickly to look at the Aven's son. Levon, his hand trembling, had half drawn his sword.

"No!" said Ivor dan Banor, and not only to his son. "I have seen this one in battle. We cannot fight him, and we cannot afford to lose any man here!"

Before anyone else could speak, Uathach's coarse laughter spilled forth again, a slimy flood of sound. He had heard.

He said, "I thought as much! Then let me say one thing more to all the brave ones on that hill. I have a message from my lord." The voice changed; it became colder, less rough, more frightening. "A year ago and a little more, Rakoth took pleasure in a woman of your company. He would do so again. She offered rare, willing sport. Black Avaia is with me now, to bear her back to Starkadh at his bidding. Is there one among you who will contest against my blade Rakoth's claim to her naked flesh?"

A sickness rose within Paul, of revulsion and of premonition.

"My lord High King," said Arthur Pendragon, as Uathach's laughter, and the howls of the svart alfar behind him, rose and fell, "would you tell me the name of this place."

Paul saw Aileron turn to the Warrior.

But it was Loren Silvercloak who answered, a knowing sorrow in his voice. "This plain was green and fertile a thousand years ago," he said. "And in those days it was called Camlann."

"I thought it might be," Arthur replied very quietly. Without speaking again he began checking the fit of his sword belt and the tilt of the King Spear in his saddle rest.

Paul turned to Jennifer—to Guinevere. What he saw in her face then, as she looked at the Warrior's quiet preparations, went straight to his heart.

"My lord Arthur," said Aileron, "I must ask you to defer to me. The leader of their army should fight the leader of our own. This is my battle, and I lay claim to it."

Arthur didn't even look up from his preparations. "Not so," he said, "and you know it is not. You are needed on the morrow more than any other man here. I told you all a long time ago, on the eve of the voyage to Cader Sedat, that I am never allowed to see the end of things when I am summoned. And the name Loren spoke has made things clear: there has been a Camlann waiting for me in every world. This is what I was brought here for, High King."

Beside him, Cavall made a sound, more whimper than growl. The red sun was low, casting a strange light upon all their faces. Below them, the laughter had ended.

"Arthur, no!" said Kimberly, with passion. "You are here for more than this. You must not go down there. We need *all* of you too much. Can't you see what he is? None of you can fight him! Jennifer, tell them it is foolishness. You *must* tell them!"

But Jennifer, looking at the Warrior, said nothing at all.

Arthur had finished his preparations. He looked up then, straight at Kimberly, who had summoned him. Who had brought him to this place by the binding of his name. And to her he made reply, in words Paul knew he would never forget.

"How can we *not* fight him, Seer? How can we claim to carry our swords in the name of Light, if we are cowards when we stand before the Dark? This challenge goes further back than any of us. Further back, even, than I. What are we if we deny the dance?"

Aileron was nodding slowly, and Levon, and Ra-Tenniel's eyes were bright with his agreement. Within his own heart Paul felt some deep eons-old force behind the Warrior's words, and as he accepted them, grieving, he felt another thing: the pulsebeat of the God. It was true. It was a dance that was not to be denied. And it seemed that it was Arthur's, after all.

"*No,*" said Guinevere.

Every eye went to her. In the windswept silence of that desolate place her beauty seemed to burn like some evening star brought among men, almost too fierce to look upon.

Motionless astride her horse, her hands twisted in its mane, she said, "Arthur, I will not lose you again like this. I could not bear it. Single combat is not why you were summoned, my love, it cannot be why. Camlann or no, this must not be your battle."

His face, under the greying hair, had gone still. He said, "We are caught in a woven doom of no escape. You know I must go down to him."

There were tears welling in her eyes. She did not speak, but slowly she shook her head back and forth in denial.

"Whose place is it, then, if not mine?" he asked, scarcely more than a whisper.

She lowered her head. Her hands moved in a little helpless, trapped gesture of despair.

And then, without looking up, she said, with sudden, terrible formality, "In this place and before these many people my name has been besmirched. I have need of one who will take this challenge upon himself and unmake it with his sword."

And now she lifted her head, and now she turned. To the one who had been sitting quietly upon his horse, not speaking, not moving, waiting patiently for what he seemed to have known was coming. And Guinevere said: "Wilt thou, who hast been my champion so many times before, be so yet again? Wilt thou take this challenge in my name, my lord Lancelot?"

"Lady, I will," he said.

"You can't!" Paul exclaimed, his voice crashing into the stillness, unable to stop himself. "Jennifer, he's wounded! Look at his palm—he can't even hold a sword!" Beside him someone made a curious, breathless sound.

The three figures in the center of the circle ignored him. Completely. It was is if he hadn't even spoken. There was another silence, laden with unsaid things, with so many layers of time. A stir of wind blew Jennifer's hair back from her face.

Arthur said, "My lady, I have known too many things for too long to ever deny Lancelot's claim to be your champion. Or that, healthy, he is far more worthy than I to face this foe. Even so, I will not allow it now. Not this time, my love. You have asked him, sorely wounded, to take this upon himself, not for your sake, or his, but for mine. You have not asked him in love."

Guinevere's head snapped back. Her green eyes went wide and then they blazed with a naked, dazzling anger. She shook her head, so fiercely that the tears flew off her face, and in the voice of a Queen, a voice that froze and bound them into the power of the grief it carried, she cried aloud, "*Have I not, my lord?* And shall *you* tell me so? Would you tear open my flesh that all men here might probe into my heart as Maugrim did?"

Arthur flinched, as if stunned by a blow, but she was not done. With icy, relentless fury she said, "What man, even you, my lord, *dares* in my presence to say whether I have spoken in love or no?"

"Guinevere—" Lancelot began, but quailed in his turn as her burning glance swung to him.

"Not a word!" she snapped. "Not from you or anyone else!"

Arthur had slipped down from his horse. He knelt before her, pain raw as a wound in his face. He opened his mouth to speak.

And in that moment, precisely then, Paul became aware of an absence and he remembered the slight, breathless sound at his elbow a moment before, a sound he'd ignored.

But there was no one beside him any more.

He turned, his heart lurching, and looked north, along the downward-sloping path to where Uathach waited on the stony plain.

He saw. And then he heard, they all heard, as a ringing cry rose up, echoing in the twilight air between the armies of Light and Dark:

"For the Black Boar!" he heard. They all heard. *"For the honor of the Black Boar!"*

And thus did Diarmuid dan Ailell take Uathach's challenge upon himself, riding forth alone on the horse his brother had brought for him, his sword uplifted high, his fair hair lit by the sunset, as he raced toward the dance his bright soul would not deny.

He was a master, Dave knew. Having fought beside Diarmuid at the winter skirmish by the Latham and then at the wolf hunt in Leinanwood, he had reason to know what Aileron's brother could do. And Dave's heart—halfway to his own battle fury—leaped to see Diarmuid's first swiftly angled engagement of the urgach.

And then, an instant later, battle frenzy gave way to chilled grief. Because he remembered Uathach too, from the bloody banks of the Adein in the first battle of Kevin's spring. And in his mind, replayed more vividly than such a memory should ever have been, he saw Maugrim's white-clad urgach swing his colossal sword in one scything blow from the slaug's saddle that had cleaved through Barth and Navon, both: the babies in the wood.

He remembered Uathach, and now he saw him again, and the memory, however grim, was less than the reality, far less. By the light of the setting sun, in that wasteland between armies, Diarmuid and his quick, clever horse, met, with a thunder of hooves and a grinding shock of blades, a foe that was too much more than mortal for a mortal man to face.

The urgach was too large, too uncannily swift despite his massive bulk. And he was shrewder than any such creature could ever have been had it not been altered in some way within the confines of Starkadh. Beyond all this, the slaug was a deadly terror in and of itself. Constantly ripping with its curved horn, seeking the flesh of Diarmuid's horse, running on four legs and lashing out with the other two, it was too dangerous for Diarmuid to do much more than evade, for fear that his own mount would be gored or trampled, leaving him helpless on the barren ground. And because he couldn't work in close, his slim blade could scarcely reach Uathach—though Diarmuid was a perilously easy target for the urgach's huge black sword.

Beside Dave, Levon dan Ivor's face was white with affliction as he watched the drama below. Dave knew how desperately Levon had wanted the death of this creature, and how adamant Torc—who feared nothing else that Dave knew—had been in binding Levon by oath not to fight Uathach alone.

Not to do what Diarmuid was doing now.

And doing, despite the horror of what he faced, with a seemingly effortless grace that somehow had, woven within its movements, the unpredictable, scintillant wit of the man. So sudden were his stops and starts, his reversals of direction—the horse seeming an extension of his mind—that twice, within moments of each other, he managed to veer around the slaug's horn to launch brilliant slashing blows at Uathach.

Who parried with a brutal indifference that almost broke the heart to see. And each time, his pounding counterstroke sent Diarmuid reeling in the saddle with the jarring impact of parrying it. Dave knew about that: he remembered his own first urgach battle, in the dark of Faelinn Grove. He had barely been able to lift his arm for two days after blocking one of those blows. And the beast he'd faced had been to Uathach as sleep was to death.

But Diarmuid was still in the saddle, still probing for an opening with his sword, wheeling his gallant mount—so small beside the slaug—in arcs and half-circles, random and disorienting, calculated to the hairsbreadth edge of sword or destroying horn, seeking an angle, a way in, a gap to penetrate in the name of Light.

"Gods, he can ride!" Levon whispered, and Dave knew that there were no words of higher, more holy praise that a

Dalrei could ever speak. And it was true, it was dazzlingly true; they were watching an exercise in glory as the sun sank into the west.

Then suddenly it became even more than that—for again Diarmuid scythed in on Uathach's right side, and again he stabbed upward for the heart of the beast. Once more the urgach blocked the reaching thrust, and once more, exactly as before, his counterstroke descended like an iron tree falling.

Diarmuid absorbed it on his blade. He rocked in the saddle. But this time, letting the momentum work for him, he reared his horse upward and to the right, and sent his shining sword slashing downward to sever the slaug's nearest leg.

Dave began a startled, wordless cry of joy and then savagely bit it back. Uathach's mocking laughter seemed to fill the world, and behind him the army of the Dark let loose a raucous, deafening roar of predatory anticipation.

Too great a price, Dave thought, hurting for the man below. For though the slaug had lost a leg, and so was much less of a danger than before, Diarmuid's left shoulder had been torn through by a ripping thrust of the animal's horn. In the waning light they could see his blood flowering darkly from a deep, raking wound.

It was too much, Dave thought, truly too inhuman a foe for a man to face. Torc had been right. Dave turned his head away from the terrible ritual being acted out before them, and as he did, he saw Paul Schafer, farther along the ridge, looking back at him.

Paul registered Dave's glance, and the pain in the big man's expression, but his own mind was a long way off, along the twisting paths of memory.

A memory of Diarmuid on the first night they'd arrived. *A peach!* he'd said of Jennifer, as he bent to kiss her hand. And then said it, and did it again, a few moments later, swinging lazily through a high window to confound Gorlaes sardonically.

Another image, another extravagant phrase—*I've plucked the fairest rose in Shalhassan's garden*—as he rejoined Kevin and Paul and the men of South Keep from within scented

Larai Rigal. Extravagance always, the flamboyant gesture masking so many deeper truths. But the truths were there to be seen, if one only knew where to look. Hadn't he shielded Sharra afterward, the day she'd tried to kill him in Paras Derval? And then on the eve of the voyage to Cader Sedat he had asked her to be his wife.

Using Tegid as his Intercedent.

Always the gesture, the deflecting glitter of style, hiding what he was, at root, behind the last locked doorway of his soul.

Paul remembered, hurting on that windy rise of land, unwilling to look down again, how Diarmuid had relinquished his claim to the throne. How in the moment when fate seemed to have come full circle, when Jaelle had been about to speak for the Goddess and proclaim a High King in Dana's name, Diarmuid had made the decision himself, flippantly speaking the words he knew to be right. Though Aileron had sworn he was prepared to kill him just moments before.

There was a grinding of metal on metal. Paul turned back. Diarmuid had somehow—the gods only knew what it must be costing him—managed to circle in again close to the monstrous urgach, and again he'd attacked, carrying the battle to his foe. To be beaten back one more with a bone-jarring force that Paul could feel, even up here.

He watched. It seemed necessary to watch: to bear witness and remember.

And one more set of memories came to him then, as Diarmuid's brave horse pirouetted yet again, just out of reach of slaug horn and urgach sword. Images from Cader Sedat, that place of death at sea. An island in all worlds and none, where the soul lay open, without hiding place. Where Diar's face, as he looked upon Metran, had shown the full, unshielded passion of his hatred of the Dark. Where he had stood in the Chamber of the Dead beneath the sea, and where—yes, there *was* a truth in this, a kernel, a clue—he had said to the Warrior, as Arthur prepared to summon Lancelot and so bring the old, three-sided tragedy into the world again: *You do not have to do this. It is neither written nor compelled.*

And Paul glimpsed then, with a shiver of primal recognition, the thread that led from that moment to this. Because it was for Arthur and Lancelot, and for Guinevere, that Diarmuid, in all the wild anarchy of his nature, had claimed this dance as his own.

It was against the weaving of their long doom that he had defiantly rebelled, and had channeled that rebellion into an act of his own against the Dark. Taking Uathach unto himself, that Arthur and Lancelot, both, might go forward past this day.

The sun was almost gone. Only the last long rays slanted low and red across Andarien. In the twilight the battle seemed to have moved farther away, into a realm of shadows like the past. It was very quiet. Even the loosely spilling, triumphant cries of the svart alfar had ended. There were flecks of blood staining Uathach's snowy robe. Paul couldn't tell if they were Diarmuid's or the urgach's own. It didn't seem to matter much: Diar's horse, fiercely gallant but hopelessly overmatched, was visibly tiring even as they watched.

Diarmuid backed it off a few paces, to try to buy it a moment's rest, but this was not to be allowed. Not in this battle, with this foe. Uathach, not laughing now, grim death in his black sword, came on, and Diarmuid was forced to cruelly spur his mount to motion again. Amid the silence along the ridge, a single voice spoke.

"There is one chance, only, left for him," said Lancelot du Lac.

Only one man understood and made reply.

"If you call it a chance," Aileron said, in a tone not one of them had ever heard him use before.

To the west, out beyond Linden Bay, the sun went down. Paul turned instinctively and saw its last dying light touch the face of the Princess of Cathal. He saw that Kim and Jaelle had moved to either side of her. After a moment he turned back to the figures on the plain. In time to see it end.

It was, on the whole, just a little bit ridiculous. This ugly, hairy monster, oversized even for an urgach, was as quick as he was himself. And it was swinging a sword that Diarmuid doubted he could even have lifted, let alone swung in those pounding, ceaseless blows. It was cunning too, unnaturally, viciously intelligent. By Lisen's river blood, urgach were supposed to be stupid! Where, the Prince thought, absorbing another blow like an avalanche on his sword, where was the sense of *proportion* in this thing?

He felt like asking the question aloud, but survival had become a matter of meticulous concentration these last few moments, and he had no breath to spare for even halfway witty remarks. A shame. He wondered, hilariously, what Uathach would say to a suggestion that this matter be settled with the gambling dice Diarmuid just happened to have in his—

Gods! Even with a leg gone, the slaug, twice the size of his own tiring horse, was death itself. With a movement of his sword as desperately swift as any he'd ever made, Diarmuid managed to block a thrust of the animal's ripping horn that would have disemboweled his own mount. Unfortunately that meant—

He resurfaced in the saddle, having passed clean under his horse on one side and up again on the other, with Uathach's annihilating slash a whistling sound in the darkening air where his own head had been an instant before. He wondered if Ivor of the Dalrei remembered teaching him how to do that so many years ago, when Diarmuid was a boy summering with his brother on the Plain. So many years, but for some reason it felt like yesterday, just now. Funny, how almost everything felt like yesterday.

The sweep of Uathach's last stroke had swung the urgach, grunting, sideways in his saddle and carried the slaug a few paces away with the shift of weight. Fresh, Diarmuid might have tried to use that to renew some kind of attack, but his horse was sucking air with desperate, heaving motions of its lathered flanks, and his own left arm was gradually growing cold, a weakness spreading from the deep tear of the wound, reaching across his chest.

He used the brief respite the only way he could, to buy time for the horse. A handful of seconds, no more than that, and it wasn't enough. He thought of his mother then. And of the day his father had died. So much seemed to have happened yesterday. He thought of Aileron, and of all the things left unsaid in all the yesterdays.

And then, as Uathach turned the slaug again, Diarmuid dan Ailell whispered to his horse one last time and felt it steady bravely to the murmur of his voice. Within himself he let a calm take shape, and from within that calm he summoned up Sharra's face, through whose dark eyes—doorways to a falcon's soul—love had entered into him so unexpectedly, and had stayed.

To carry him to this moment, her image in his mind, and the certain, sustaining knowledge of her love. To carry him forward across the darkened ground of that plain in Andarien, toward the last thing he could do.

Straight at the slaug he rode, his horse gallantly reaching for a last flourish of speed, and at the final second he veered it sharply left and launched the sternest blow he could at Uathach's side.

It was blocked. He knew it would be; they all had been. And now there came the huge, descending counterstroke of the urgach's sword. The one, like all the others, that would drive him, shuddering, back, when he parried it. That would numb his arm, bringing the inevitable end that much nearer.

He didn't parry it.

He wheeled his horse, hard, to gain just a little space, so Uathach's blade would not sever his body entirely, and he took that terrible blow on his left side, just under the heart, knowing it was the end.

And then, as white pain exploded within him in the darkness, towering, indescribable, as his life's blood fountained to fall among the stones, Diarmuid dan Ailell, with the last strength of his soul, almost the very last of his self-control, with Sharra's face before him, not Uathach's, did the final deed of his days. He rose up above his agony, and with his left hand he clutched the hairy arm that held that black sword, and with his right, pulling himself forward, as toward a long-sought dream of overwhelming Light, he thrust his own bright blade into the urgach's face and out the back of its head, and he killed it in Andarien, just after the sun had set.

Sharra watched as though from very far away. At the descent of dark, through a blurring mist of tears, she saw him take his wound, saw him kill Uathach, saw the beautiful, rearing horse gored hideously from below by the ripping horn of the slaug. The urgach fell. She could hear screams of terror from the svart alfar, the scream of the dying horse. Saw Diar fall free as the horse rolled on the ground and thrashed in its death agony. Saw the enraged, blood-maddened slaug turn to rip the fallen man to shreds of flesh—

Saw a spear, its head gleaming blue-white, flash through the dark and plunge into the throat of the slaug, killing it instantly. Saw nothing after that but the man lying on the ground.

"Come, child," said Arthur Pendragon, who had thrown the King Spear in a cast almost beyond belief, in this light and from so far. He laid a gentle hand upon her arm. "Let me lead you down to him."

She let him lead her down, through the rainfall of her tears. She was aware, distantly, of utter confusion among the ranks of the Dark. Terror at the loss of their leader. She was conscious of people on horseback beside her, but not of who they were, save for Arthur, who was holding her arm.

She went down the slope and rode across the dark, stony ground and came to where he lay. There were torches, somehow, all around them. She drew a choking, desperate breath and wiped away her tears with the loose sleeve of the robe she wore.

Then she dismounted and walked over. His head was cradled in the lap of Coll of Taerlindel, blood pouring and pouring from the wound Uathach's sword had made, soaking into the barren soil.

He was not yet dead. He breathed with quick, shallow motions of his chest, but every breath sent forth another torrent of his blood. His eyes were closed. There were other people there, but it seemed to her that she and he were all alone in a wide night world without stars.

She knelt on the ground beside him, and something, the intuitive awareness of her presence, caused him to open his eyes. By torchlight she met his blue gaze for the last time with her own. He tried to smile, to speak. But at the last there was too much pain she saw, he would not even be allowed this much, and so she lowered her mouth to his, and kissed him, and said, "Good night, my love. I will not say goodbye. Wait for me by the Weaver's side. If the gods love us—"

She tried to go on, tried very hard, but the tears were

blinding her and stopping her throat. His face was bloodless, bone white in the light of the torches. His eyes had closed again. She could feel his blood pouring from the wound, saturating the ground where she knelt. She knew he was leaving her. No power of magic, no voice of a god could bring him back from where this silent, terrible pain was taking him. It was too deep. It was final.

Then he opened his eyes, with a very great effort, for the last time, and she realized that words didn't matter. That she knew everything he would ever want to say. She read the message in his eyes and knew what he was asking her. It was as if, here at the very last, they had moved beyond all need for anything but looking.

She lifted her head and saw Aileron kneeling at Diarmuid's other side, his face laid open as if by a lash, distorted with grief. She understood something then, and could even find a place within herself to pity him. She swallowed and fought past the thickness in her throat to find words again: Diarmuid's words, for he could not speak, and so she would have to be his voice for this last time.

She whispered, "He wants you to set him free. To send him home. That it will not have been done by the urgach's sword."

"Oh, Diar, no!" Aileron said.

But Diarmuid turned his head, slowly, fighting the pain of movement, his breathing so shallow it was hardly there, and he looked at his older brother and he nodded, once.

Aileron was still for a very long time, as the two sons of Ailell looked at each other by the flickering torchlight. Then the High King stretched forth a hand and laid it gently against his brother's cheek. He held it there a moment, and then he looked at Sharra with a last question, asking dispensation with his own dark eyes.

And Sharra reached for all the courage that she had and granted it to him, saying, for herself and for Diar, "Let it be done with love."

Then Aileron dan Ailell, the High King, drew forth his dagger from a sheath that hung down at his side, and he laid its point over his brother's heart. And Diarmuid moved one hand, and found Sharra's, and Aileron waited as he brought it to his lips one last time. He was holding it there, and holding her eyes with his own, when his brother's knife, agent of love, set him free from his iron pain, and he died.

Aileron withdrew his blade and set it down. Then he buried his face in his hands. Sharra could hardly see, she was so blinded by her tears. It seemed to be raining everywhere, in that clear cool starry evening over Andarien.

"Come, my dear," said Jaelle, the High Priestess, helping her rise. She was weeping. The Seer came up on the other side, and Sharra went where they took her.

Diarmuid dan Ailell was borne back in his brother's arms from the place where he died, for the High King would suffer no man else to do so. Across the stony plain Aileron carried him, with torches buring on either side and all around. Up the long slope he went, the body cradled against his chest, and men turned away their heads so as not to have to look upon the face of the living brother as he bore away the dead.

They made a pyre that night in Andarien. They washed Diarmuid's body and clothed it in white and gold, hiding his terrible wounds, and they combed his golden hair. Then the High King took him up again for the last time and bore him to where they had gathered the wood of the pyre, and he laid his brother down upon it, and kissed him upon the lips, and withdrew.

Then Teyrnon, the last mage of Brennin, stepped forward with Barak, his source, and with Loren Silvercloak and Matt Sören, and all of them were weeping in the darkness there. But Teyrnon thrust forth his hand and spoke a word of power, and a single shaft of light flew forward from his fingers, blazing white and gold like the robes of the dead Prince, and the pyre roared suddenly to flame, consuming the body laid upon it.

So passed Diarmuid dan Ailell. So did his untamed brightness come in the end to flame, and then ash, and, at the very last, in the clear voices of the lios alfar, into song under the stars.

Chapter 15

A long way north of that burning, Darien stood in the shadows below the Valgrind Bridge. It was very cold, here at the edge of the Ice with the sun gone and no other living thing to be seen or heard. He looked across the dark waters of the river spanned by that bridge, and on the other side he saw the massive ziggurat of Starkadh rising, with chill green lights shining wanly amid the blackness of his father's mighty home.

He was utterly alone; there were no guards posted anywhere. What need had Rakoth Maugrim for guards? Who would ever venture to this unholy place? An army perhaps, but they would be visible far off amid the treeless waste. Only an army might come, but Darien had seen, as he walked here, countless numbers of svart alfar and the huge urgach moving south. There were so many, they seemed to shrink the vastness of the barren lands. He didn't think any army would be coming: not past those hordes he'd seen issuing forth. He had been forced to hide several times, seeking shelter in the shadows of rocks, swinging gradually westward as he went, so the legions of the Dark would pass east of him.

He was not seen. No one was looking for him, not for a solitary child stumbling north through a morning and an afternoon, and then a cold evening and a colder night. With pale Rangat towering in the east and black Starkadh growing more oppressively dominant with every step he took, he had come at last to the bridge and crouched down under it, looking across the Ungarch at where he was to go.

Not tonight, he decided, shivering, his arms wrapped

tightly about himself. Better the chill of another night outside than trying to pass into that place in the dark. He looked at the dagger he carried and drew it from its sheath. The sound like a harpstring reverberated thinly in the cold night air. There was a vein of blue in the sheath, and a brighter one along the shaft of the blade. They gleamed a little under the frosty stars. He remembered what the little one, Flidais, had said to him. He rehearsed the words in his mind as he sheathed Lökdal again. Their magic was part of the gift he was bringing. He would have to have them right.

The metal of the bridge was cold when he leaned back beneath it, and so was the stony ground. Everything was cold this far north. He rubbed his hands on the sweater he wore. It wasn't even his sweater. His mother had made it for Finn—who was gone.

And not really his mother, either; Vae had made it. His mother was tall and very beautiful, and she had sent him away and then had sent the man, Lancelot, to battle the demon in the Wood for Darien's sake. He didn't understand. He wanted to, but there was no one to help him, and he was cold and tired and far away.

He had just closed his eyes, there at the edge of the darkly flowing river, half under the iron bridge, when he heard a tremendous reverberating sound as some mighty door clanged open far above. He scrambled to his feet and peered out from under the bridge. As he did, he was hit by a titanic buffet of wind that knocked him sprawling, almost into the river.

He rolled quickly over, his eyes straining up against the force of the sudden gale, and far overhead he saw a huge, featureless shadow sweeping swiftly away to the south, blotting out the stars where it passed.

Then he heard the sound of his father's laughter.

Anger, for Dave Martyniuk, had always been a hot, exploding thing within himself. It was his father's rage, unsubtle, enormous, a lava flow in the mind and heart. Even here in Fionavar in the battles he'd fought, what had come upon him each time had been of the same order: a fiery, obliterating hatred that consumed all else within it.

This morning he was not like that. This morning he was ice. The coldness of his fury as the sun rose and they readied themselves for war was something alien to him. It was even a little frightening. He was calmer, more clearheaded than he could ever remember being in all his life, and yet filled with a more dangerous, more utterly implacable anger than he had ever known.

Overhead the black swans were circling, crying raucously in the early morning light. Below, the army of the Dark was gathered, so vast it seemed to blot out the whole of the plain. And at their head—Dave could see him now—was a new leader: Galadan, of course, the Wolflord. Not a blessing, Ivor had murmured, before riding off to receive Aileron's orders. More dangerous than even Uathach would have been, more subtle in his malice.

It didn't matter, Dave thought, sitting tall and stern in his saddle, oblivious to the diffident glances he was drawing from all who passed near to him. It didn't matter at all who led Rakoth's army, who they sent against him: wolves, or svart alfar, or urgach, or mutant swans. Or anything else, or however many. Let them come. He would drive them back or leave them dead before him.

He was not fire. The fire had been last night, when Diarmuid burned. He was ice now, absolutely in control of himself and ready for war. He would do what had to be done, whatever had to be done. For Diarmuid, and for Kevin Laine. For the babies he'd guarded in the wood. For Sharra's grief. For Guinevere and Arthur and Lancelot. For Ivor and Levon and Torc. For the dimensions of sorrow within himself. For all those who would die before this day was done.

For Josef Martyniuk.

"There is something I would ask," said Matt Sören. "Though I will understand if you choose to deny me."

Kim saw Aileron turn to him. There was winter in the High King's eyes. He waited and did not speak.

Matt said, "The Dwarves have a price to pay and atonement to make, insofar as we ever can. Will you give us leave to take the center today, my lord, that we may bear the main shock of whatever may befall?"

There was a murmur from the captains gathered there. The pale sun had just risen in the east beyond Gwynir.

Aileron was silent a moment longer; then he said, very clearly, so it carried, "In every single record I have ever found of the Bael Rangat—and I have read all such writings there are, I think—one common thread prevails. Even in the company of Conary and Colan, of Ra-Termaine and fierce Angirad from what was not yet Cathal, of Revor of the Plain and those who rode with him . . . even in such glittering company, the records of those days all tell that no contingent of the army of Light was so deadly as were Seithr and the Dwarves. There is nothing you might think to ask of me that I could find it within me to deny, Matt, but I intended to request this of you in any case. Let your people follow their King and take pride of place in our ranks. Let them draw honor from his own bright honor and courage from their past."

"Let it be so," said Ivor quietly. "Where would you have the Dalrei, High King?"

"With the lios alfar, as you were by the Adein. Ra-Tenniel, can you and the Aven hold our right flank between the two of you?"

"If we two cannot," said the Lord of the lios alfar, with a thread of laughter in his silvery voice, "then I know not who can. We will ride with the Riders."

He was mounted on one of the glorious raithen, and so too, behind him, were Brendel and Galen and Lydan, leaders of their marks. There was a fifth raithen, riderless, standing beside the others.

Ra-Tenniel gestured toward it. He turned to Arthur Pendragon, but he did not speak. It was Loren Silvercloak, no longer harnessing a mage's powers but still bearing a mage's knowledge, who broke the waiting silence.

"My lord Arthur," he said, "you have told us you never survive to see the last battle of your wars. Today, it seems, you shall. Although this place was once called Camlann, it carries that name no longer, nor has it for a thousand years, since laid waste by war. Shall we seek to find good in that evil? Hope in the cycle of years?"

And Arthur said, "Against all that I have been forced through pain to know, let us try." He stepped down from his horse and took the King Spear in his hand, and he walked over to the last of the gold and silver raithen of Daniloth. When he mounted up, the spear blazed for a moment with light.

"Come, my lord," Aileron said, "and my lord Lancelot, if you will. I bid you welcome into the numbers of Brennin and Cathal. We will take the left side of this fight. Let us seek to meet the Dalrei and the lios before the end of day, having curved our ranks inward over the bodies of our foes."

Arthur nodded, and so, too, did Lancelot. They moved over to where Mabon of Rhoden was waiting, with Niavin, Duke of Seresh, and Coll of Taerlindel, stony-faced, now leader of the men of South Keep, Diarmuid's men. Kim grieved for him, but there would be griefs and to spare this day, she knew, and there might be final darkness for them all.

It seemed that they had said what had to be said, but Aileron surprised her again.

"One thing more," the High King said, as his captains prepared to move off. "A thousand years ago there was another company in the army of Light. A people fell and wild, and courageous out of measure. A people destroyed now, and lost to us, save one."

Kim saw him turn, then, and heard him say, "Faebur of Larak, will you ride, in the name of the People of the Lion, at the forefront of our host? Will you join with the Dwarves today, at the side of their King, and will you take this horn I carry and sound the attack for us all?"

Faebur was pale, but not with fear, Kim saw. He moved his horse toward the black charger Aileron rode, and he took the horn. "In the name of the Lion," he said, "I will do so."

He rode forward and stopped at Matt's left hand. On the other side of Matt, Brock of Banir Tal was waiting. Kim's mouth was dry with apprehension. She looked up and saw the swans circling overhead, unchallenged, masters of the sky. She knew, without looking, how utterly lifeless the Baelrath was on her hand. Knew, as a Seer knew, that it would never blaze for her again, not after her refusal by Calor Diman. She felt helpless and a little sick.

Her place would be here on the ridge, with Loren and Jaelle and a number of others from all parts of the army. She still had her training, and they would have to deal with the wounded very soon.

Very soon indeed. Aileron and Arthur galloped quickly off to the left, and she saw Ivor cantering to the right beside Ra-Tenniel and the lios alfar, to join the Dalrei waiting there. Even at a distance she could make out the figure of Dave Martyniuk, taller by far than anyone around him. She saw him unsling an axe from where it hung by his saddle.

Loren came to stand beside her. She slipped her hand into his. Together they watched Matt Sören stride to the front of the host of the Dwarves, who had never fought on horseback and would not do so today. Faebur was with him. The young Eridun had dismounted to leave his own horse on the high ground.

The sun was higher now. From where Kim stood she could see the seething army of the Dark carpeting the whole of the plain below. To the left, Aileron raised his sword, and on the other side the Aven did the same, and Ra-Tenniel. She saw Matt turn to Faebur and speak to him.

Then she heard the ringing note of the horn that Faebur sounded, and there was war.

Cechtar was the first man Dave saw die. The big Dalrei thundered, screaming at the top of his voice, toward the nearest of the urgach as the armies met with a crash that shook the earth. Cechtar's momentum and his whistling sword blow knocked the urgach sprawling sideways in his saddle. But before the Dalrei could follow up, his mount was viciously speared by the horn of the slaug the urgach rode, and as the grey horse stumbled, dying, Cechtar's side was exposed and a svart alfar leaped up, a long thin knife in its hand, and plunged it into his heart.

Dave didn't even have time to cry out, or grieve, or even think about it. There was death all around him, bloody and blurred. There were svart alfar shrieking amid the screams of dying men. A svart leaped for his horse. Dave dragged a foot free of his stirrups, kicked at it viciously, and felt the ugly creature's skull crack under the impact.

Fighting for room to swing his axe, he urged his horse forward. He went for the nearest urgach then, and every time thereafter, with a hatred and a bitterness (cold, though, icily, calculatingly cold) that drove him on and on, the head of his axe soon red and wet with blood, as it rose and fell, and rose and fell again.

He had no idea what was happening even twenty feet away. The lios alfar were somewhere to the right. He knew that Levon was beside him, always, through everything that happened, and Torc and Sorcha were on his other side. He saw Ivor's stocky figure just ahead, and in all that he did he fought to stay within reach of the Aven. Again, as in the fight by the banks of the Adein, he completely lost track of time. His was a narrowed maelstrom of a world: a universe of sweat and shattered bone, of lathered horses and slaug horns, and ground slippery with blood and with the trampled flesh of the dying and the dead. He fought with a silent savagery amid the screams of battle, and where his axe fell, where the hooves of his horse lashed out, they killed.

Time warped and twisted, spun away from him. He thrust the axe forward like a sword, smashing in the hairy face of the urgach in front of him. Almost in the same motion he drove the axehead down, to bite through the flesh of the slaug it rode. He rode on. Beside him, Levon's blade was a whirling thing of ceaseless, glinting motion, a counterpoint of lethal grace to Dave's own driven strength.

Time was gone from him, and the morning. He knew that they had been advancing for a time, and then later, now, with the sun somehow high in the sky, that they were no longer pressing forward, only holding their ground. Desperately, they strained to leave each other enough room to fight, yet not so much space that the quick svart alfar might slip between, to kill from below.

And gradually Dave began to acknowledge, however hard he tried to block the thought, something that a part of him had known the evening before, when first they'd topped the ridge and looked down. It was the numbers, the sheer brutal weight, that would beat them.

It isn't even worth thinking about, he told himself, hammering the axe right through the blocking sword of an urgach on his right, watching Torc's sword slash into the creature's brain at the same moment. He and the dark Dalrei—his brother—looked at each other for one grim instant.

There was time for no more than that. Time and strength had rapidly become the most precious things in all the worlds and were becoming more rare with each passing moment. The white sun swung up the sky and paused overhead, balanced for an instant, as were all the worlds that day, and then began sliding down through a bloody afternoon.

Dave's horse trampled a svart alfar, even as his axe severed the raking horn of a dark green slaug. He felt a pain in his thigh; ignored it; killed, with a mighty blow of his fist, the dagger-wielding svart that had slashed him. He heard Levon grunt with exertion, and he wheeled just in time to crash his mount into the side of the slaug menacing the Aven's son. Levon dispatched the unbalanced urgach with a sweep of his blade.

There were two more behind it, and half a dozen of the svart alfar. Dave didn't even have room to stay with Levon. In front of him three more of the slaug pressed forward, over the body of the one whose horn he'd smashed. Dave fell back a couple of paces, sick at heart. Beside him, Levon was doing the same.

Then, disbelieving, Dave heard the ceaseless shrieking of the svart alfar rise to a higher pitch. The largest of the urgach advancing on him roared a sudden desperate command, and a moment later, Dave saw a space suddenly materialize on his left, beyond Levon, as the enemy fell back.

And then, even as it appeared, the space was filled by Matt Sören, King of the Dwarves, fighting in grim, ferocious silence, his clothing shredded, saturated with blood, as he waded forward over the bodies of the dead to lead the Dwarves into the gap.

"*Well met, King of Dwarves!*" Ivor's voice rose high over the tumult of battle. With a glad cry Dave thrust forward, Levon just ahead of him, and they merged with Matt's forces and began to advance again.

Ra-Tenniel, dazzlingly swift on the raithen, was suddenly beside them as well. "How are they doing on the left?" he sang out.

"Aileron sent us this way. He says they will hold!" Matt shouted back. "I don't know for how long, though. Galadan's wolves are on that side. We have to break through together and then circle back west!"

"Come on, then!" Levon screamed, moving past them all, leading them northward as if he would storm the towers of Starkadh itself. Ivor was right beside his son.

Dave kicked his own mount ahead, hastening to follow. He had to stay close: to guard them if he could, to share in whatever happened to them.

He felt a wind suddenly. Saw a vast, onrushing shadow sweeping across Andarien.

"*Dear gods!*" Sorcha cried, by Dave's right hand. There came a tremendous roaring sound.

Dave looked up.

At dawn Leila woke. She felt feverish and afraid after a terrible, restless night. When Shiel came to get her, she told the other priestess to lead the morning chants in her stead. Shiel took one look at Leila and went away without a word.

Pacing the narrow confines of her room, Leila struggled to hold the images that were flashing into her mind. They were too quick, though, too violently chaotic. She didn't know where they were coming from, how she was receiving them. She didn't know! She didn't want them! Her hands were damp and she felt perspiration on her face, though the underground rooms were as cool as they always were.

The chanting ended under the dome. In the sudden silence she became conscious of her own footsteps, the rapid beating of her heart, the pulsing in her mind—all seemed louder, more insistent. She was afraid now, more so than she had ever been.

There was a tapping at her door.

"Yes!" she snapped. She hadn't meant to say it that way.

Timorously, Shiel opened the door and peeped in. She did

not enter the room. Her eyes grew wide at the sight of Leila's face.

"What is it?" Leila said, fighting to control her voice.

"There are men here, Priestess. Waiting by the entranceway. Will you see them?"

It was a thing to do, an action to take. She brushed past Shiel, walking swiftly down the curving corridors toward the entrance to the Temple. There were three priestesses and a dun-robed acolyte waiting there. The doors were open, but the men waited patiently outside.

She came to the threshold and saw who was there. She knew all three of them: Gorlaes the Chancellor, Shalhassan of Cathal, and the fat man, Tegid, who had been so much in attendance while Sharra of Cathal had been here.

"What do you want?" she said. Again her voice was harsher than she meant it to be. She was having a hard time controlling it. It seemed to be a bright day outside. The sun hurt her eyes.

"Child," said Gorlaes, not hiding his surprise, "are you the one who is acting as High Priestess?"

"I am," she answered shortly, and waited.

Shalhassan's expression was different, more quietly appraising. He said, "I have been told about you. You are Leila dal Karsh?"

She nodded. Shifted a little sideways, to be in the shade.

Shalhassan said, "Priestess, we have come because we are afraid. We know nothing, can discover nothing. I thought it was possible that the priestesses might somehow have tidings of what is happening."

She closed her eyes. Somewhere, at some level, in the normal weaving of these things, this should be taken as a triumph—the leaders of Brennin and Cathal coming to the sanctuary thus humbly. She was aware of this but couldn't summon up the appropriate response. It seemed lifetimes removed from the brittle fevers of this day.

She opened her eyes again and said, "I, too, am afraid. I know very little. Only that . . . something is happening this morning. And there is blood. I think they are fighting."

The big man, Tegid, made a rumbling sound deep in his chest. She saw anguish and doubt in his face. For an instant longer she hesitated; then, drawing a deep breath, she said, "If you like, if you offer blood, you may enter within. I will share whatever I come to know."

All three of them bowed to her.

"We will be grateful," Shalhassan murmured, and she could hear that he meant it.

"Shiel," she said, snapping again, unable not to, "use the knife and the bowl, then bring them to the dome."

"I will," Shiel said, with a hardiness rare for her.

Leila didn't wait. Another inner vision sliced into her mind like a blade and was gone. She strode from the doorway, stumbled, almost fell. She saw the frightened eyes of the acolyte, as the young one backed away from her. *Young?* a part of her mind registered. The girl was older than she was.

Leila went on, toward the dome. Her face was bloodless now. She could feel it. And could feel a dark, cold fear rising within her, higher and higher all the time. It seemed to her that all around her as she went, the sanctuary walls were streaming with blood.

Paul tried. He wasn't a swordsman, nor did he have Dave's tremendous size or strength. But he had his own anger, and courage to spare, sourced in a driven nature, infinitely demanding of himself. He had grace and very fast reflexes. But swordsmanship at this level was not a thing one mastered overnight, not matched against urgach and Galadan's wolves.

Through the whole of the morning, though, he stayed in the heart of the battle on the western flank, fighting with a passionate, coursing renunciation.

Ahead of him he saw Lancelot and Aileron dismount, side by side, the better to wade, swords blurred with intricate flashing speed, among the giant wolves. He knew that he was seeing something never to be forgotten, excellence on a scale almost unimaginable. Lancelot was fighting with a glove on his burned hand, that the hilt of his sword might not dig into the wound. The glove had been white when the morning began, but already the palm of it was soaked through with blood.

On either side of Paul, Carde and Erron were fighting savagely, slashing through the svart alfar, battling the wolves, holding back, as best they could, the terrible mounted urgach. And, Paul was painfully aware, doing their best to guard him all the time, even as they fought for their own lives.

He did the best he could. Bending on either side of his horse's neck to thrust and cut with the sword he carried. Seeing a svart fall under one blow, a wolf draw back, snarling, from another. But even as that happened, Erron had been forced to whirl, with his lithe speed, to skewer another svart that had been leaping for Paul's exposed side.

No time for gratitude to be expressed, no time for any words at all. And only chance scattered seconds amid chaos in which to reach within himself and vainly seek some clue, some pulsebeat from the God, that might show him how to be more than a liability here, more than a source of danger to the friends guarding his life.

"Gods!" Carde gasped, in one brief respite some time later. "Why are the wolves so much worse than they were in Leinanwood?"

Paul knew the answer to that. He could see the answer.

Ahead of them and to the right, lethally fluid in all his movements, a palpable aura of menace hovering about him, was Galadan. He was battling in his animal shape, providing the guiding spirit, malevolent and subtle, for the onslaught of his wolves. For the whole of Maugrim's army.

Galadan. Whom Paul had so arrogantly claimed for his own. It seemed a mockery here, an act of fatuous hubris on the part of someone who couldn't even defend himself from the svart alfar.

In that moment, as he looked across the surging crush of the battle, a space opened up in front of Galadan, and then, with a hurtful twist of his heart, Paul saw grey Cavall move to confront, for a second time, the wolf with the splash of silver between its eyes. Memory slashed through Paul like a different kind of wound: a memory of the battle in the Godwood that had served to foretell the war they were fighting now.

He saw the scarred grey dog and the proud Lord of the andain face each other for the second time. Both were still for a frozen moment, coiling themselves in readiness.

But there was to be no reprise of that primal clash in the glade of the Summer Tree. A phalanx of mounted urgach thundered into the space between wolf and dog, to be met with a ringing crash of blades by Coll of Taerlindel and redheaded Averren, at the head of a score of the men of South Keep: Diarmuid's band. Fighting with a bleak savagery that day, each of them driving back heart's grief with the fury of war. Glad of the chance to kill.

On either side of Paul, Carde and Erron held their ground, covering his body as well as their own. The sight of the Prince's men struggling with the urgach just ahead decided him.

"Go join the others!" he shouted to the two of them. "I'm no help here! I'm going back up on the ridge—I can do more there!"

There was an instant to exchange a glance with each of them, an instant to know it might be the last. He touched Carde's shoulder briefly, felt Erron's hand grip his arm; then he wheeled his horse sharply and cut away, racing back to the high ground, bitterly cursing his uselessness.

To his left, as he rode, he saw another pair of figures break free of the press, galloping back toward the ridge as well. Angling his mount over, he intercepted Teyrnon and Barak.

"Where are you going?" he cried.

"Up above," Teyrnon shouted, sweat streaming down his face, his voice raw. "The fighting's too congested. If I try to throw a power bolt I'll hit as many of our own men as theirs. And Barak is hopelessly vulnerable when he has to source my magic."

Barak was weeping with frustration, Paul saw. They reached the slope and charged upward. At the top, a line of lios alfar stood, scanning the stretch of the battle. Mounted auberei waited beside them, ready to race down with word for the High King and his captains.

"What's happening?" Paul gasped to the nearest of the lios, as he dismounted and spun to look.

But it was Loren Silvercloak, striding forward, who answered him. "Too finely balanced," he said, his lined features grim. "We're being held to a standstill, and time is on their side. Aileron has ordered the Dwarves to drive east, toward the Dalrei and the lios alfar. He's going to try to hold the western flank and half of the center alone."

"Can he?" Teyrnon asked.

Loren shook his head. "For a time. Not forever. And see, the swans are telling Galadan everything we do."

Down below, Paul could see that the Wolflord had withdrawn to a cleared space toward the rear of the army of the Dark. He was in his mortal shape again, and every moment another of the hideous black swans would descend from the uncontested reaches of the air to give him tidings and carry away instructions.

Beside Paul, Barak began to curse, a stream of heartfelt, anguished invective. Below, to their left, a flash of light caught Paul's eye. It was Arthur, the King Spear gleaming in his hand, guiding his magnificent raithen all along the line of battle on the western flank, driving back the legions of Maugrim with the incandescent flame of his presence, shaping a respite for the beleaguered men of Brennin wherever he went. The Warrior in the last battle at Camlann. The battle he had not been meant to see. And would not have seen, had not Diarmuid intervened.

Behind Paul the embers of the pyre still glowed, and ashes drifted in the morning sun. Paul looked up: no longer morning, he realized. Beyond the circling swans the sun had reached its zenith and was starting down.

He jogged back toward the south. In a cleared space a handful of people, Kim and Jaelle among them, were doing the best they could for the wounded that the auberei were bringing up the ridge in frightening numbers.

Kim's face was streaked with blood and sweat. He knelt beside her. "I'm useless down there," he said quickly. "What can I do?"

"You too?" she answered, her grey eyes shadowed with pain. "Pass me those bandages. Behind you. Yes." She took the cloths and began wrapping the leg wound of one of the Dwarves.

"What do you mean?" Paul asked.

Kim cut the bandage with a blade and fastened it as tightly as she could. She stood up and moved on, without answering. Paul followed. A young Dalrei, no more than sixteen, lay in breathless agony, an axe wound in his side. Kim looked down on him with despair.

"Teyrnon!" Paul shouted.

The mage and his source hurried toward them. Teyrnon took one look at the wounded boy, glanced briefly at Barak, and then knelt beside the Dalrei. Barak closed his eyes and Teyrnon placed his hand over the jagged wound. He spoke, under his breath, half a dozen words, and as he did the wound slowly closed itself.

When he was done, though, Barak almost fell, fatigue etched into his features. Teyrnon stood up quickly and steadied his source.

"I can't do much more of this," the mage said grimly, looking closely at Barak.

"Yes, you can!" Barak snapped, glaring. "Who else, Seer? Who else needs us?"

"Go to Jaelle," Kim said tonelessly. "She'll show you the ones who are worst off. Do what you can, but try not to exhaust yourself. You two are all we have in the way of magic."

Teyrnon nodded tersely and strode off to where Paul could see the High Priestess, the sleeves of her white gown pushed back, kneeling beside the figure of a crumpled lios alfar.

Paul turned back to Kim. "Your own magic?" he said, pointing to the dulled Warstone. "What's happened?"

For a moment she hesitated; then she quickly told him the story of what had happened by Calor Diman. "I rejected it," she concluded flatly. "And now the swans have the sky to themselves, and the Baelrath is totally dead. I feel sick, Paul."

So did he. But he masked it and pulled her to him in a hard embrace. He felt her trembling against his body.

Paul said, "No one here or anywhere else has done as much as you. And we don't know if what you did was wrong—would you have gotten to the Dwarves in time if you'd used the ring to bind the creature in the Lake? It isn't over, Kim, it's a long way from over."

From not far off they heard a grunt of pain. Four of the auberei set down a stretcher they'd been carrying. On it, bleeding from half a dozen new wounds, lay Mabon of Rhoden. Loren Silvercloak and a white-faced Sharra of Cathal hurried to the side of the fallen Duke.

Paul didn't know where to look. All around them lay the dying and the dead. Below, on the plain of battle, the forces of the Dark seemed scarcely to have diminished. Within himself the pulsebeat of Mörnir seemed faint as ever, agonizingly far. A hint of something but not a promise; an awareness, but not power.

He cursed, as Barak had done, helplessly.

Kim looked at him, and after a moment she said, in a strange voice, "I just realized something. You're hating yourself for not being able to use your power in battle. You don't *have* a power of war, though, Paul. We should have realized that before. *I'm* that kind of power, or I was, until last night. You're something else."

He heard a truth, but the bitterness wouldn't leave him. "Wonderful," he snapped. "Makes me awfully useful, doesn't it?"

"Maybe," was all she said. But there was a quiet speculation in her eyes that calmed him.

"Where's Jen?" he asked.

She pointed. He looked over and saw that Jennifer, too, was dealing with the wounded as best she could. At the moment she had just risen from someone's side to walk a step or two north, looking down over the battlefield. He could only see her in profile, but as he gazed at her Paul realized that he had never seen a woman look as she did then, as if taking the pain of all the worlds onto herself. In the manner of a Queen.

He never, ever, knew what made him look up.

To see a black swan diving. Soundlessly, a terror against the sky, razored claws extended straight for Jennifer. Black Avaia, putrescent death in the air, returning to claim her victim for a second time.

Paul screamed a warning at the top of his voice and launched himself in a frantic sprint over the distance between. The swan was a black projectile hurtling down with annihilating speed. Jennifer turned at his cry and looked up. She saw, and did not flinch. She grappled bravely for the slim blade they'd given her. Paul ran as he'd never run before in all his life. A sob escaped him. Too far! He was too far away. He tried, reached for speed, for more, for *something*. A meaty stench filled the air. A shrieking sound of triumph. Jennifer lifted her blade. Twenty feet away, Paul stumbled, fell, heard himself screaming her name, glimpsed the raking teeth of the swan—

And saw Avaia, ten feet above Jennifer's head, smashed into a crumple of feathers by a red comet in the sky. A living comet that had somehow materialized, blindingly swift, to intersect her path. A horn like a blade exploded into Avaia's breast. A bright sword smote at her head. The black swan screamed, in pain and terror so strident they heard it on the plain below.

She fell, screaming still, at the feet of the woman. And Guinevere walked over then, not faltering, and looked down upon the creature that had delivered her unto Maugrim.

One moment she stood so; then her own slim blade thrust forward into Avaia's throat, and the screaming of the swan came to an end, as Lauriel the White was avenged after a thousand years.

The silence on the ridge was overwhelming. Even the tumult of war below seemed to have receded. Paul watched, they all watched in awe, as Gereint, the old blind shaman, climbed carefully down to the ground, to leave Tabor dan Ivor alone astride his winged creature. The two of them seemed eerily remote even in the midst of so many people, blood on his sword, blood on her deadly, shining horn.

The shaman stood very still, his head lifted a little, as if listening for something. He sniffed the air, which was foul with the corrupt odor of the swan.

"Pah!" exclaimed Gereint, and spat on the ground at his feet.

"It is dead, shaman," said Paul quietly. He waited.

Gereint's sightless eyes swung unerringly to where Paul stood. "Twiceborn?" the old man asked.

"Yes," said Paul. And stepping forward, he embraced, for the first time, the old blind gallant figure who had sent his soul so far to find Paul's on the dark wide sea.

Paul stepped back. Gereint turned, with that uncanny precision, to where Kim was standing, silent, inexplicable tears streaming down her face. Shaman and Seer faced each other, and no words at all were said. Kim closed her eyes, still weeping.

"I'm sorry," she said brokenly. "Oh, Tabor, I'm sorry."

Paul didn't understand. He saw Loren Silvercloak lift his head sharply.

"Was this it, Gereint?" Tabor asked, in a strangely calm voice. "Was it the black swan that you saw?"

"Oh, child," the shaman whispered. "For the love I bear you and all your family, I only wish that it were so."

Loren had now turned completely away, staring north.

"*Weaver at the Loom!*" he cried.

Then the others, too, saw the onrushing of the shadow, they heard the huge, roaring sound, and felt the mighty buffet of the wind that had come.

Jaelle clutched at Paul's arm. He was aware of her touch, but it was at Kim that he looked as the shadow came over them. He finally understood her grief. It became his own. There was nothing he could do, though, nothing at all. He saw Tabor look up. The boy's eyes seemed to open very wide. He touched the glorious creature that he rode, she spread her wings, and they rose into the sky.

He had been ordered to stay by the women and children in the curve of land east of the Latham, to guard them if necessary. It was as much for his sake, Tabor knew, as it was for their own: his father's attempt to keep him from leaving the world of men, which was what seemed to happen whenever he rode Imraith-Nimphais.

Gereint had called for him, though. Only half awake in that grey predawn hour in front of the shaman's house, Tabor heard Gereint's words, and everything changed.

"Child," the shaman said, "I have been sent a vision from Cernan, as sharp as when he came to me and named you to your fast. I am afraid that you must fly. Son of Ivor, you have to be in Andarien before the sun is high!"

It seemed to Tabor as if there was an elusive music playing somewhere amid the ground mist and the greyness that lay all about before the rising of the sun. His mother and sister were beside him, awakened by the same boy Gereint had sent with his message. He turned to his mother, to try to explain, to ask forgiveness. . . .

And saw that it wasn't necessary. Not with Leith.

She had brought his sword from their house. How she had known to do so, he couldn't even guess. She held it out toward him, and he took it from her hands. Her eyes were dry. His father was always the one who cried.

His mother said, in her quiet, strong voice, "You will do what you must do, and your father will understand since the message comes from the god. Weave brightly for the Dalrei, my son, and bring them home."

Bring them home. Tabor found it hard to frame words of his own. All about him, and more clearly now, he could hear the strange music calling him away.

He turned to his sister. Liane *was* weeping, and he grieved for her. She had been hurt in Gwen Ystrat, he knew, on the night Liadon died. There was a new vulnerability to her these days. Or perhaps it had always been there and only now was he noticing it. It didn't really matter which, not any more. In silence, for words were truly very difficult, he handed her his sword and raised his arms out from his side.

Kneeling, his sister buckled the sword belt upon him, after the fashion of the old days. She did not speak either. When she was done, he kissed her, and then his mother. Leith held him very tightly for a moment, and then she let him go. He stepped a little way apart from all of them.

The music had gone now. The sky was brighter in the east above the Carnevon Range, in whose looming shadows they lay. Tabor looked around at the silent, sleeping camp.

Then he closed his eyes and inside himself, not aloud, he said: *Beloved!*

And almost before the thought was fully formed, he heard the voice of his dreaming that was the voice of his soul respond, *I am here! Shall we fly?*

He opened his eyes. She was in the sky overhead, more glorious to see than even innermost knowledge remembered her to be. She seemed brighter, her horn more luminous, every time she came. His heart lifted to see her and to watch her land so lightly at his side.

I think we must, he answered her, walking over to stroke the glistening red mane. She lowered her head, so the shining horn rested on his shoulder for a moment. *I think this is the time for which we were brought together.*

We shall have each other, she said to him. *Come, I will take you up to the sunrise!*

He smiled a little at her eagerness, but then, an instant later, his indulgent smile faded, as he felt the same fierce exhilaration surge through him as well. He mounted up upon Imraith-Nimphais and even as he did, she spread her wings.

Wait, he said, with the last of his self-control.

He turned back. His mother and sister were watching them. Leith had never seen his winged creature before, and a far-off part of Tabor hurt a little to see awe in her face. A mother should not be awed by her son, he thought. But already such thoughts seemed to come from a long way away.

The sky was appreciably lighter now. The mist was lifting. He turned to Gereint, who had been waiting patiently, saying nothing. Tabor said, "You know her name, shaman. You know the names of all our totem animals, even this one. She will bear you if you like. Would you fly with us?"

And Gereint, as unruffled as he always seemed to be, said quietly, "I would not have presumed to ask, but there may yet be a reason for me to be there. Yes, I will come. Help me mount."

Without being asked, Imraith-Nimphais moved nearer to the frail, wizened shaman. She stood very still as Tabor reached down a hand, and Liane moved forward and helped Gereint up behind Tabor.

Then it seemed that there was nothing else to be said, and no time to say it, even if he could have managed to. Within his mind, Tabor told the creature of his dream, *Let us fly, my love.* And with the thought they were in the sky, winging north just as the morning sun burst up on their right hand.

Behind him, Tabor knew without looking, his mother would be standing, straight-backed, dry-eyed, holding his sister in her arms, watching her youngest fly away from her.

* * *

This had been his very last thought, his last clear image from the world of men, as they had sped through the morning high over the rolling Plain, racing the rising sun to a field of war.

To which they had finally come, and in time, with the sun high, starting over into the west. They had come, and Tabor had seen a black thing of horror, a monstrous swan diving from the sky, and he had drawn his sword, and Imraith-Nimphais, glorious and deadly, had reached for even greater speed, and they had met the diving swan and struck her two mortal wounds with shining blade and horn.

When it was over Tabor had felt, just as he had before, each time they'd flown and killed, that the balance of his soul had shifted again, farther away than ever from the world through which the people all around them moved.

Gereint descended, unaided, and so Tabor and Imraith-Nimphais stood by themselves among men and women, some of whom they knew. He saw the blood dark on his creature's horn, and heard her say to him, in the moment before he formed the thought himself, *Only each other at the last.*

And then, an instant later, he heard Silvercloak cry aloud, and he wheeled about and looked to the north, above the tumult of the battlefield where his father and his brother were fighting.

He looked, saw the shadow, felt the wind, and realized what had come, here, now, at the last, and knew in that moment why he had dreamt his creature, and that the ending was upon them.

He did not hesitate or turn to bid farewell to anyone. He was already too far away for such things. He moved his hands a little, and Imraith-Nimphais leaped into the sky to meet the Dragon.

The Dragon of Rakoth Maugrim in the sky over Andarien.

A thousand years before it had been too young to fly, its wings too weak to bear the colossal weight of its body. Most secret, most terrible of all Maugrim's malevolent designs, it had been another casualty of the Unraveller's untimely haste at the Bael Rangat—his Dragon had been able to play no part in that war.

Instead, it had lurked in a vast underground chamber hollowed out beneath Starkadh, and when the end had come, when the army of Light had beaten its way northward, Rakoth had sent his Dragon away, flying with awkward, half-crippled motions, to seek refuge in the northern Ice where no man would ever go.

It had been seen from afar, by the lios alfar and the longsighted among men, but they had been too distant, still, to discern it clearly or know what it was. There were tales told about it that became legends in time, motifs for tapestries, for nightmares of childhood.

It had survived, nurtured through the long, turning years of the Unraveller's imprisonment, by Fordaetha, the Queen of Rük, in her Ice Palace amid the Barrens. Gradually, as the years passed and then the centuries, its wings grew stronger. It began to fly on longer and longer journeys through that white and trackless waste at the roof of the world.

It learned to fly. And then it learned to harness and hurl forth the molten fire of its lungs, to send roaring tongues of flame exploding amid the white cold, far above the great ice floes that ceaselessly ground and crashed against each other.

Farther and farther it flew, its great wings beating the frigid air, the flame of its breath luridly lighting the night sky over the Ice where no one was there to see save only the Queen of Rük from her cold towers.

It flew so high it could see, at times, beyond the glacier walls, beyond the titanic prison of cloud-shouldered Rangat, to the green lands far away in the south. It was all Fordaetha could do, as the sweep of time pushed even the stars into newer patterns, to hold the Dragon back.

But hold it she did, having power of her own in the cold kingdom she ruled, and in time there came a messenger from Galadan, the Wolflord, and the message was that Rakoth Maugrim was free, and black Starkadh had risen anew.

Only then did she send it south. And the Dragon went, landing in a space prepared for it north of Starkadh, and Rakoth Maugrim was there. And the Unraveller laughed aloud to see the mightiest creature of his hate now full grown.

This time Rakoth had waited, savoring the malice of a thousand years, watching his own black blood fall burning from where his severed hand had been. He waited, and in the fullness of time he made the Mountain go up in flame, and he shaped the winter, and then the death rain over Eridu. And only when these were ended did he let his army issue forth in might, and only after that, saved for the very last, that its unforeseen coming might shatter the hearts of those who would oppose him, he sent out his Dragon to scorch and burn and destroy.

So did it come to pass that the sun was blotted out, and half the sky, over that battlefield in Andarien. That the armies of Light and Dark, both of them, were driven to their knees by the pounding force of the wind of the Dragon's wings. That fire blackened the dry ground of wasted Andarien for miles upon miles in a long, smoldering strip of twice-ravaged earth.

And so, also, did it come to pass that Tabor dan Ivor drew forth his sword, and the shining creature he rode lifted herself, wings beating in a blur of speed, even into the fury of that wind. They rose aloft, alone at the last, as both of them had known they would be from the very first, and they hovered in the darkened air, shining, gallant, pitifully small, directly in the path of the Dragon.

On the ground below, battered to his knees by the wind, Ivor dan Banor looked up for one instant only, and the image of his son in the sky imprinted itself forever onto the patterns of his brain. Then he turned away and covered his face with his bloodied sleeve, for he could not bear to watch.

High overhead, Tabor lifted his sword to draw the Dragon toward him. It was not necessary, though; the Dragon was already aware of them. He saw it accelerate and draw breath to send a river of flame toward them from the furnace of its lungs. He saw that it was vast and unspeakably hideous, with grey-black scales covering its hide and mottled grey-green skin below.

He knew that there was nothing, and no one, on the windswept ground below that could withstand this thing. He also knew, with an exquisite, quiet certainty—a last space of calm here in the teeth of the wind—that there was one thing and one thing only they could do.

And there was only a moment, this moment, in which to

do it, before the Dragon's flame burst forth to turn them into ash.

He stroked her shining, glossy mane. In his mind, he said, *So here it is. Be not afraid, my love. Let us do what we were born to do.*

I am not afraid, she sent back in the mind voice whose every cadence he knew. *You have named me your beloved, since first we saw each other. Do you know that you have been mine?*

The Dragon was upon them, blackness filling the sky. There was a roaring, a deafening noise of wind pushed to its outermost limits. Still, Imraith-Nimphais held steady before it, her wings straining as fast they had ever gone, her horn a point of blinding light in the roaring chaos of the sky.

Of course I know, Tabor sent to her, his last such thought. *Now come, my darling, we must kill it as we die!*

And Imraith-Nimphais forced herself higher then, somehow, and forward, somehow, directly into the maelstrom of the Dragon wind, and Tabor clung to her mane with all his might, letting fall his useless sword. Above the Dragon's path they rose; he saw it lift its head, open its mouth.

But they were hurtling toward it, angling downward like a shaft of killing light straight for the loathsome head. Making themselves, the two of them, having only each other at the last, into a living blade, that they might explode at this dazzling, incandescent speed, the sharp horn shining like a star, right into and *through* the skin and muscle, the cartilage and bone of the Dragon's brain, and so kill it as they died.

At the very edge of impact, the edge of the end of all things, Tabor saw the Dragon's lidless eyes narrow. He looked down and saw the first tongue of flame appear at the base of its gaping throat. Too late! He knew it was too late. They were going to hit in time. He closed his eyes—

And felt himself thrown free by Imraith-Nimphais in a tumbling, spiraling parabola! He screamed, his voice lost in the cataclysm. He spun in the air like a torn leaf. He fell.

In his mind he heard, clear and sweet, like a bell heard over summer fields, a mind voice say in the purest tones of love: *Remember me!*

Then she hit the Dragon at the apex of her speed.

Her horn sheared through its skull and her body followed it, truly a living blade, and just as Imraith-Nimphais had shone, living, like a star, so did she explode like a star in her dying. For the Dragon's gathered fire burst within itself, incinerating the two of them. They fell, burning, to the earth west of the battlefield and crashed there with a force of impact that shook the ground as far east as Gwynir, as far north as the walls of Starkadh.

And Tabor dan Ivor, thrown free by an act of love, plummeted after them from a killing height.

When the Dragon came, Kim was beaten to her knees, not only by the wind of its wings but by the brutal awareness of her own folly. *Now* she knew why the Baelrath had blazed for the Crystal Dragon of Calor Diman. Why Macha and Nemain, the goddesses of war whom the Warstone served, had known that the guardian spirit of the Dwarves would be needed, whatever the cost might be.

And she had refused. In her arrogance, her own imposed morality, she had refused to exact that price from the Dwarves, or to pay it herself. Had refused to accept, at the last test, the responsibility of the Baelrath. And so now Tabor dan Ivor, hopelessly overmatched, was rising into the sky, into the wind, to pay the price for her refusal.

If he even could. If they weren't *all* to pay that price. For the Dragon that was coming down upon them meant the end of everything. Kim knew it, and so did every person on the ridge or on the bloody plain below.

Stricken with a guilt that numbed her senses, Kim watched Imraith-Nimphais fight desperately to hold her place in the air against the annihilating whirlwind of the Dragon's approach.

There was a hand gripping her shoulder: Gereint's. She had no idea how the old shaman knew what she'd done, but nothing about Gereint could surprise her any more. It was clear that he did know and was seeking, even here at the end, to comfort her—as if she had any claim, or right, to comfort.

Blinking tears from her eyes, she saw the monstrous, jointed, grey-black wings of the Dragon pound the air. The sun was lost; a huge, rushing blackness lay over the land. The Dragon opened its mouth. Kim saw Tabor let fall his sword. And then, unbelieving, stupefied, she saw the glorious creature he rode, gift of the Goddess, shining, double-edged, begin to move forward into the maelstrom, straight toward the obliterating vastness of the Dragon of Maugrim.

Beside her, Gereint was still on his feet despite the force of the wind, stony-faced, waiting. Someone cried out in fear and awe. The horn of Imraith-Nimphais was a dazzling thing of glory at the edge of night.

And then it was a blur, moving almost too fast to be seen, as she found, from somewhere in her being, an even greater, more defiant dimension of speed. And Kim finally realized what was happening, and just how the price would be paid.

"*Teyrnon!*" Paul Schafer cried suddenly, at the top of his voice, screaming it over the wind. "*Quickly! Be ready!*"

The mage threw him a startled glance, but Barak, without questions asked, fought to his feet, closed his eyes, and braced himself.

And in that instant they saw Tabor thrown free.

Then Imraith-Nimphais met the Dragon and a fireball exploded in the sky, too bright to look upon.

"*Teyrnon!*" Paul screamed again.

"I see him!" the mage shouted back. Sweat was pouring down his face. His hands were outstretched to their fullest extent, reaching. Power surged from them in shimmering waves, as he struggled to break the fall of the boy tumbling helplessly earthward from so high.

The Dragon crashed to the ground with a sound like a mountain falling. All around Kim, people tumbled like dominoes to the trembling earth. Somehow Gereint kept his balance, staying upright beside her, one hand still on her shoulder.

And so, too, did Teyrnon and Barak. But as Kim looked up, she saw that Tabor was still falling, if slowly, spinning like some discarded toy.

"He's too far!" Teyrnon cried in despair. "I can't stop him!" He tried, though. And Barak, shaking in every limb, fought to source the magic that could break that terrible fall.

"Look!" said Paul.

Out of the corner of her eye Kim saw a flashing movement on the plain. She turned. A raithen of Daniloth was streaking westward over the ground. Tabor fell headfirst, slowed by Teyrnon's magic but unconscious, unable to help himself. The raithen shot over the ground like a golden and silver brother of Imraith-Nimphais herself. On its back, Arthur Pendragon let fall the King Spear and rose to stand in the stirrups. The raithen gathered itself and leaped. And as it did, Arthur stretched forward and up toward the boy spinning down out of the sunlight, and with his strong hands he caught Tabor as he fell and cradled him against his chest as the raithen slowed and stopped.

Racing in his wake, Lancelot leaned sideways in his saddle and reclaimed the fallen spear. Then together the two of them sped southward up the rise of land, to halt on the ridge where Kim stood, and Gereint, and all the others watching there.

"He is all right, I think," the Warrior said tersely. Tabor was ash white but seemed otherwise unhurt. Kim could see him breathing.

She looked at Arthur. There was blood all over his body; one deep gash above his eye was bleeding freely, partially blinding him. Kim moved forward and waited until he had handed Tabor down to be taken by a great many hands; then she made Arthur dismount while she tended his wound as best she could. She could see the ruin of Lancelot's palm, even through the glove he wore, but there was nothing, really, that she or anyone else could do about that. Behind her, Jaelle and Sharra were dealing with Tabor, and Loren had knelt beside Barak, who had collapsed. They would recover, she knew. They both would, though Tabor would carry an inner wound that only time might salve. If time were granted them. If they were allowed to go forward from today.

Impatiently, Arthur endured her ministrations. He was speaking constantly as she worked on him, relaying crisp instructions to the auberei gathered around. One of them he sent to Ivor, with word of his youngest son. Down on the plain the army of Light was battling again, with a passion and hope that the afternoon had not yet seen. Glancing down, Kim saw Aileron carving a lethal swath through the urgach and wolves with Diarmuid's men beside him, moving forward and to the east, struggling to link with the Dwarves in the center.

"We have a chance now," Teyrnon said, gasping with fatigue. "Tabor has given us a chance."

"I know," said Arthur. He turned away from Kim, preparing to race back down.

Then she saw him stop. Beside him, Lancelot's face had gone ashen, as pale as Tabor's was. Kim followed their gaze and felt her heart thud with a pain beyond words.

"What is it?" Gereint asked urgently. "Tell me what you see!"

Tell him what she saw. She saw, at this moment, even as hope seemed to have been reborn out of fiery death, an end to hope.

"Reinforcements," she said. "A great many, Gereint. A very great many coming from the north to join their army. Too many, shaman. I think there are too many."

There was a silence on the ridge. Then: "There must not be," Gereint said calmly.

Arthur turned at the quiet words. There was a passion in his eyes beyond anything Kim had seen there before. He said, in echo, "You are right, shaman. There *must* not be." And the raithen leaped down the ridge, bearing the Warrior back to war.

For one second only, Lancelot lingered. Kim saw him look, as if against his will, to Guinevere, who was gazing back at him. Not a word was said between them but a farewell was in the air, and a love that even now was still denied the solace and release of being spoken.

Then he, too, drew his sword again and stormed back to the battle down below.

Beyond the battlefield, north of it, the plain of Andarien was lost to sight, dark with the roiling movements of the advancing second wave of Rakoth's army: a wave, Kim saw, almost as large as the first had been, and the first had been too large. The Dragon was dead, but that hardly seemed to matter. It had only bought them time, a little time, shaped in fire to be paid with blood, but leading to the same ending, which was the Dark.

"Are we lost?" asked Jaelle, looking up from where she knelt by Tabor.

Kim turned to her, but it was Paul who made reply, among all the people gathered there.

"Perhaps," he said, in a voice that suddenly carried more

than his own cadences. "It is likely, I'm afraid. But there is one last random thread left for us, among all the weavings of this day, and I will not concede dominion to the Dark until that thread is lost."

Even as he spoke, Kim's own knowledge came sweeping over her, in an image like a dream. She looked at Jennifer for an instant, and then her gaze went north, beyond the battlefield, beyond the thunderous approach of Maugrim's reinforcements—they had been seen now, down below; there were cries of harsh, wild triumph rising everywhere—beyond the blackened line of fire-ravaged earth that marked where the Dragon had flown. Beyond all these, far, far beyond, Kim looked toward a place she'd only seen in a vision given her by Eilathen, rising from his lake so long ago.

To Starkadh.

Chapter 16

The laughter had frightened him. Darien passed a cold, fitful night, shot through with dreams he could not remember when the morning came. With the sun came warmth; it was summer, even here in the northlands. He was still afraid, though, and irresolute, now that he had come to the end of his journey. When he went to wash his face in the river the water was oily and something bit his finger, drawing blood. He backed away.

For a long time he lingered there, hiding under the bridge, reluctant to move. Movement would be such a decisive, such a *final* thing. It was eerily silent. The Ungarch ran sluggishly, without sound. Aside from whatever had bit him, there was no sign of life anywhere. Not since the Dragon had passed away to the south, a black shape in blackness. Not since the laughter of his father.

No birds sang, even on a morning in midsummer. It was a place of waste, of desolation, and across the river stood his father's towers, challenging the sky, so black they seemed to swallow the light. It was worse, somehow, in daylight. There were no obscuring shadows to blunt the impact of Starkadh's oppressiveness. Fortress of a god, with its huge, brutal, piled stones, blank and featureless, save for a scattered handful of almost invisible windows set far up. Crouching under the bridge, Darien looked at the exposed path leading up to the iron doors, and fear was within him like a living thing.

He tried to master it. To seek strength from an image of Finn, a vision of his brother dealing with this terror. It didn't work; however hard he tried, he couldn't even picture Finn in this place. The same thing happened when he tried to draw courage from a memory of Lancelot in the sacred grove. That didn't help either; it couldn't be superimposed.

He stayed there, lonely and afraid, and all the while, unconsciously, his hand kept returning to stroke the lifeless gem upon his brow. The sun rose higher in the sky. To the east Rangat gleamed, its upper shopes dazzlingly white, awesome, inaccessible. Darien didn't know why, but it was after he looked at the Mountain that he found himself on his feet.

He walked out from his hiding place to stand in the open under the brilliant sun, and he set foot on the Valgrind Bridge. It seemed to him that the whole world for miles around reverberated to the ringing of his tread. He stopped, his heart pounding, then realized that it was not so. The sound was small and slight, as he was; its echoes were only magnified in the chambers of his mind.

He went on. He crossed the River Ungarch and stood at last before the doors of Starkadh. He was not seen, though he was utterly unshielded there in the bleak flatness of that landscape: a boy in an ill-fitting if beautifully knitted sweater with a dagger in his hand, his fair hair held back by some circlet about his brow. His eyes were very blue in the sunlight.

A moment later they were red, and then the boy had gone. An owl, white as the vanished snows, flapped swiftly upward, to land on the narrow sill of a window slit, halfway up the black face of Starkadh. Had that been seen, there *would* have been an alarm.

It was not seen; there were no guards. What need had there ever been for guards about this place?

In his owl shape, Darien perched uneasily on the window ledge and looked within. There was no one there. He ruffled his feathers, fighting back a stifling apprehension, and then his eyes flared again and he was once more in his own form.

He slipped cautiously down from the window and so set foot at last in the fortress where he had been conceived. A long, long way below, his mother had lain in a chamber deep in the bowels of this place, and on a morning much like this one Rakoth Maugrim had come to her and had done what he had done.

Darien looked around. It was as if it was always night within these walls: the single window let in hardly any sunlight. The daylight seemed to die where it reached Starkadh. A green, fitful illumination was cast by lights set in the walls. There was an overpowering stench in the room, and as Darien's eyes adjusted to the baleful texture of the light he was able to make out the shapes of half-consumed carcasses on the floor. They were svart alfar, and their dead bodies stank. He understood, suddenly, where he was and why there was a window here: this was the place where the swans might return to feed. He remembered the smell of the ones he had killed. It was all around him now.

The foul putrescence made him gag. He stumbled toward the inner door. His foot squashed something soft and oozing as he went. He didn't look to see what it was. He opened the door and almost fell into the corridor, gasping, heedless if he was seen.

And he *was* seen. A single urgach, massive and sharp-clawed turned, five feet away from him. It grunted in disbelieving shock and opened its mouth to bellow an alarm—

And died. Darien straightened. His eyes receded back to blue. He lowered the arm he'd thrust forward at the urgach and took a deep breath. Power coursed through him, triumphant and exhilarating. He had never felt so strong. The urgach was gone; there was no sign it had ever even been there! He had obliterated it with one surge of his power.

He listened for the sound of footsteps. There were none. No alarm seemed to have been raised. *It wouldn't matter*, Darien thought.

His fear had vanished. In its place was a rushing sensation of might. He had never known how strong he was: he had never *been* this strong. He was in his father's fortress, the place of his own conception. The hearthstone, then, of his own red power.

He was a worthy son, an ally. Even an equal, perhaps. Bringing more than a Dwarvish dagger as a gift. He was bringing *himself*. In this place he could blast urgach to nothingness with a motion of his hand! How could his father not welcome him to his side in a time of war?

Darien closed his eyes, let his inner senses reach out, and

found what he was looking for. Far above him there was a presence infinitely different from Darien's awareness of urgach and svart alfar all through the fortress, a presence unlike any other. The aura of a god.

He found the stairway and began to climb. There was no fear in him now. There was power and a kind of joy. The sheath of the knife gleamed blue in his hand. The Circlet was dull and dead. His hand no longer went up to touch it, not since he'd killed the urgach.

He killed two more as he went up, exactly the same way, with the same completely effortless flexing of his hand, feeling the power course outward from his mind. He sensed how much more lay in reserve. Had he known about this, he thought, had he known how to tap into this power, he could have blasted the demon of the sacred grove into fragments all by himself. He wouldn't have needed Lancelot or any other guardian his mother sent.

He didn't even break stride at the thought of her. She was a long way off and had sent him away. Had sent him here. And here he was more than he had ever imagined he could be. He went up, tireless, climbing stairway after twisting stairway. He wanted to run, but he forced himself to go slowly, that he might come with dignity, bearing his gift, offering all he was. Even the green lights along the walls no longer seemed so cold or alien.

He was Darien dan Rakoth, returning home.

He knew exactly where he was going. As he climbed, the aura of his father's power grew stronger with every stride. Then, at the turning of a stair, almost the last, Darien paused.

A rumbling tremor rolled northward along the earth, shaking the foundations of Starkadh. And a moment later there came a cry from above, a wordless snarl of balked desire, of soul-consuming rage. It was too great, too brutal a sound. It was worse than the laughter had been. Darien's surging hope quailed before the hatred in that cry.

He stood still, gasping, fighting back the horror that rolled over him in waves. His power was still with him; he knew what had happened. The Dragon was dead. The fall of nothing else in Fionavar could have so shaken the earth. The trembling of the fortress walls went on for a long time.

Then it passed, and there was silence again, with a different texture to it. Darien stood rooted to the spot where he was, and a thought born of lonely hope bloomed in his mind: *He will need me even more now! The Dragon is lost!*

He took one step upon the last stairway, and as he did he felt the hammer of a god fall upon his mind. And with the hammer there came a voice.

Come! Darien heard. The sound became his universe. It obliterated everything else. The whole of Starkadh resonated to it. *I am aware of you. I would see your face.*

He wanted to go there, he had been going there, but now his feet were independent of his will. He could not have resisted however hard he tried, regardless of his rising power. In his mind, with bitterest irony, he remembered his own arrogance of the moments before: an equal to Maugrim, he had thought himself.

There were no equals to Rakoth Maugrim.

And on that realization he ascended the final stair of Starkadh and came out into a vast chamber, ringed about entirely with glass, though it had seemed as black as all the other walls when viewed from outside. Darien's mind rocked and spun, dizzily, at the perspective of that window.

He was seeing the battle in Andarien.

Beyond those high windows of Starkadh, the battle plain far to the south lay beneath his feet. It was as if he were flying over it: and a moment later he realized that this was exactly so. The windows—by exercise of a power he couldn't even begin to fathom—were showing the vision of the swans circling over Andarien. And the swans were the eyes of Maugrim.

Who was here.

Who turned now, at last, huge, mighty beyond the telling in this seat of his power. Rakoth Maugrim the Unraveller, who had entered into the worlds from outside the walls of time, from beyond the Weaver's Halls, with no thread of the Tapestry marked with his name. Faceless, he turned from the window to the one who had come, who had dared come, and Darien trembled then in every limb and would have fallen had his body not been held upright by the red glance of Maugrim.

He saw the blood drip, black and smoking, from the

stump of his father's hand. Then the hammer of before became as nothing, nothing at all, as he felt his mind battered by the probing of the Unraveller. He could not move or speak. Terror was a clawed thing in his throat. The will of Rakoth was all about him; it was everywhere, driving, pounding on the doors of his being. Demanding that he give way, hammering a single question over and over again until Darien thought he would go mad.

Who are you? his father screamed soundlessly, endlessly, beating about all the entrances to Darien's soul. There was nothing at all Darien could do.

Except keep him out.

And he did. Motionless, literally paralyzed, he stood in the presence of the darkest god in all the worlds and held Maugrim at bay. His own power was gone; he could do nothing, assert nothing. He *was* as nothing in this place, except for one single thing. He was strong enough, as none anywhere in any world had ever been, to hold to his mind in Starkadh: to keep his secret.

He could hear the question being screamed at him. It was the question he had come here to answer, to offer the knowledge as a gift. But because it was being demanded in this way, because Maugrim would strip it from him as a rag from a wound, leaving him raw and naked beneath, Darien said *no* within his soul.

Exactly as his mother had done within these halls. Though she had not been as strong. She was only mortal, if a Queen, and in the end she had been broken.

Or, not quite. *You will have nothing of me that you do not take*, she had said to Rakoth Maugrim. And he had laughed and set about taking everything from her. But he had not. She had been open to him, utterly. Maugrim had stripped and ravaged her soul, and when he was done he had left her, a broken reed, to be enjoyed and killed.

But she had not been broken. Somehow there had been a spar left in her soul to which the memory of love still could cling, and Kimberly had found her holding to that spar and had brought her out.

To bear the child who stood here now, refusing to surrender his mind or his soul.

Rakoth could kill him, Darien knew, as easily as he himself had killed the urgach or the swans. But there was something—he wasn't sure what, but there was *something* saved from the wreckage of his life in this resistance.

And then, as the Worldloom shuttled slowly about the axis of that chamber, with everything, all of time, suspended as in a balance, Maugrim stopped the whirlwind of his assault, and Darien found that he could move, if he wished to, and could speak.

Rakoth Maugrim said, aloud, "Not even Galadan, Lord of the andain, could hold his mind against my will in this place. There is nothing you can do to me. I can end your life in ten thousand different ways even as we stand here. Speak, before you die. Who are you? Why have you come?"

And so, Darien thought, dazed, there was still a way, still a chance. He thought he could hear respect, of a kind. He had proved himself.

He was very, very young, and he had no guidance here at all, and had not had any since Finn had gone away. He had been rejected by everyone and everything, even by the light he wore upon his brow. Cernan of the Beasts had asked why he'd been allowed to live.

Manning the walls of his mind, Darien whispered, "I have come to offer you a gift." He held out the sheathed dagger, hilt foremost.

And even as he did the hammer descended again, in an unspeakable, shocking assault upon his mind, as if Maugrim were a ravenous beast raging about fragile walls, bludgeoning away at Darien's soul, screaming in fury at being denied.

But denied he was, for a second time. And for a second time he stopped. He was holding the dagger, now, and had unsheathed it. He had come nearer to Darien. He was huge. He had no face. The talons of his one hand caressed the blue-veined blade. He said:

"I have no need of gifts. Whatever I want, from today to the end of time and beyond, I shall be able to take. Why should I want a bauble of the treacherous Dwarves? What is a blade to me? You have one thing only that I desire, and I shall have it before you die: *I want your name*."

Darien had come to tell him. To offer all he was and might be so that someone, somewhere, might be glad of his presence. He could speak now. He could move, and see.

He looked beyond Rakoth, out the windows of that place, and he saw what the black swans saw far to the south. He saw the battlefield, with such clarity that he could make out individual faces fighting there. His father had no face. With a shock of recognition he saw Lancelot, battling with blood all over his hand, swinging his sword at the side of a grey-bearded man who wielded a spear that shone.

Behind them, a phalanx of men, some mounted, some on foot, were struggling to hold their ground against stupefying numbers of the Dark. Among them—and Darien had to blink to be sure that he saw true—a man he knew gripped a rusty spear he remembered: Shahar, his other father. Who had been so much away, but who had swung him in the air and held him when he'd come home. He was not a fighter, Darien could see that, but he labored in the wake of his leaders with a desperate determination.

The vision shifted—the eyes of another swan—and he saw the lios alfar beleaguered in another part of the field. He recognized one of them from the morning beneath the Summer Tree. There was blood in the silver hair.

Yet another perspective: a ridge of land this time, south of the battlefield. And on the ridge stood his mother. Darien felt, suddenly, as if he could not breathe. He looked upon her, from so impossibly far away, and he read the sorrow in her eyes, the awareness of doom descending.

And he realized, a white fire igniting in his heart, that he did not want her to die.

He did not want any of them to die: not Lancelot, or Shahar, or the grey man with the spear, not the white-haired Seer standing behind his mother. He was sharing their grief, he realized; it was his own pain, it was the fire running through him. It was his. He was *one* of them.

He saw the innumerable loathsome hordes descending upon the dwindling army of Light: the urgach, the svart alfar, the slaugs, all the instruments of the Unraveller. They were foul. And he hated them.

He stood there, looking down upon a world of war, and he thought of Finn. In the end, here at the very end, it came back to Finn. Who had said that Darien was to try to love everything except the Dark.

He did. He was one of that besieged army, the army of

Light. Freely, uncoerced, he finally numbered himself among them. His eyes were shining, and he knew that they were blue.

And so there, in that moment, in the deepest stronghold of the Dark, Darien made his choice.

And Rakoth Maugrim laughed.

It was the laughter of a god, the laughter that had resounded when Rangat had sent up the hand of fire. Darien didn't know about that. He hadn't been born then. What he knew, terrified, was that he'd given himself away.

The window of the chamber still showed the high ridge of land above the battle. It showed his mother standing there. And Rakoth had been watching as Darien looked upon her.

The laughter stopped. Maugrim stepped very close. Darien couldn't move. Slowly his father raised the stump of his severed hand and held it over Darien's head. The black drops of blood fell and burned on Darien's face. He couldn't even scream.

Maugrim lowered his arm. He said, "You need not tell me anything now. I know everything there is to know. You thought to bring me a gift, a toy. You have done more. You have brought me back my immortality. *You* are my gift!"

It was to have been so, once. But not like this. And not now, not any more! But Darien stood there, frozen in his place by the will of Rakoth Maugrim, and heard his father say, "You do not understand, do you? They were all fools, fools beyond belief! I needed her dead, that she might never bear a child. I *must* not have a child! Did none of them see? *A child of my seed binds me into time! It puts my name in the Tapestry, and I can die!*"

And then came the laughter again, brutal crescendos of triumph rolling over him in waves. When it ended, Maugrim stood only inches away from Darien, looking down upon him from his awesome height, from within the blackness of his hood.

He said, in a voice colder than death, older than the spinning worlds, "You are that son. I know you now. And I will do more than kill you. I will thrust your living soul out beyond the walls of time. I will make it so that you have never been! You are in Starkadh, and in this place I have the power to do that. Had you died outside these walls I might have been lost. Not now. *You* are lost. You have never lived. I will live forever, and all the worlds are mine today. All things in all the worlds."

There was nothing, nothing at all, that Darien could do. He couldn't even move, or speak. He could only listen and hear the Unraveller say again, "All things in all the worlds, starting with that toy of the lios that you wear. I know what it is. I would have it before I blast your soul out of the Tapestry."

He reached forth with his mind—Darien felt it touch him again—to claim the Circlet as he had claimed the dagger and take it unto himself.

And it came to pass in that moment that the spirit of Lisen of the Wood, for whom that shining thing of Light had been made so long ago, reached out from the far side of Night, from beyond death, and performed her own last act of absolute renunciation of the Dark.

In that stronghold of evil, the Circlet blazed. It flared with a light of sun and moon and stars, of hope and world-spanning love, a light so pure, so dazzlingly incandescent, a light so absolute that Rakoth Maugrim was blinded by the pain of it. He screamed in agony. His hold on Darien broke, only for an instant.

Which was enough.

For in that instant, Darien did the one thing, the only thing, that he could do to manifest the choice he'd made. He took one step forward, the Circlet a glorious radiance on his brow, rejecting him no longer. He took the last step on the Darkest Road, *and he impaled himself upon the dagger his father held.*

Upon Lökdal, Seithr's gift to Colan a thousand years ago. And Rakoth Maugrim, blinded by Lisen's Light, mortal because he'd fathered a son, killed that son with the Dagger of the Dwarves, and he killed without love in his heart.

Dying, Darien heard his father's last scream and knew it could be heard in every corner of Fionavar, in every world spun into time by the Weaver's hand: the sound that marked the passing of Rakoth Maugrim.

Darien was lying on the floor. There was a bright blade in his heart. With fading sight he looked out the high window and saw that the fighting had stopped on the plain so far away. It became harder to see. The window was trembling, and there was a blurring in front of his eyes. The Circlet was still shining, though. He reached up and touched it for the last time. The window began to shake even more violently, and the floor of the room. A stone crashed from above. Another. All around him Starkadh was beginning to crumble. It was falling away to nothingness in the ruin of Maugrim's fall.

He wondered if anyone would ever understand what had happened. He hoped so. So that someone might come, in time, to his mother and tell her of the choice he'd made. The choice of Light, and of love.

It was true, he realized. He was dying with love, killed by Lökdal. Flidais had told him what that part meant, as well, the gift he might have been allowed to give.

But he'd marked no one's forehead with the pattern on the haft, and in any case, he thought, he would not have wanted to burden any living creature with his soul.

It was almost his last thought. His very last was of his brother, tossing him among the soft banks of snow when he'd still been Dari, and Finn had still been there to love him and to teach him just enough of love to carry him home to the Light.

Chapter 17

Dave heard the last scream of Rakoth Maugrim, and then he heard the screaming stop. There was a moment of silence, of waiting, and then a great rumbling avalanche of sound rolled down upon them from far in the north. He knew what that was. They all did. There were tears of joy in his eyes, they were pouring down his face, he couldn't stop them. He didn't want to stop them.

And suddenly it was easy. He felt as if a weight had been stripped away from him, a weight he hadn't even known he was bearing—a burden he seemed to have carried from the moment he'd been born into time. He, and everyone else, cast forth into worlds that lay under the shadow of the Dark.

But Rakoth Maugrim was dead. Dave didn't know how, but he knew it was true. He tooked at Torc and saw a wide, helpless smile spreading across the other man's face. He had never seen Torc look like that. And suddenly Dave laughed aloud on the battlefield, for the sheer joy of being alive in that moment.

In front of them the svart alfar broke and ran. The urgach milled about in disorganized confusion. Slaug crashed into each other, grunting with fear. Then they, too, turned from the army of Light and began to flee to the north. Which was no haven any more. They would be hunted and found, Dave knew. They would be destroyed. Already, the Dalrei and the lios alfar were racing after them. For the first time in that long terrible day, Dave heard the lios begin to sing, and his heart swelled as if it would burst to hear the glory of their song.

Only the wolves held firm for a time, on the western flank. But they were alone now, and outnumbered, and the warriors of Brennin led by Arthur Pendragon on his raithen, wielding the shining King Spear as if it were the Light itself, were cutting through them like sickles through a field of harvest grain.

Dave and Torc, laughing, crying, thundered after the urgach and the svart alfar. Sorcha was with them, riding beside his son. The slaug should have been faster than their horses, but they weren't. The six-legged monsters seemed to have become feeble and purposeless. They stumbled, careened in all directions, threw their riders, fell. It was easy now, it was glorious. The lios alfar were singing all around, and the setting sun shone down upon them from a cloudless summer sky.

"Where's Ivor?" Torc shouted suddenly. "And Levon?"

Dave felt a quick spasm of fear, but then it passed. He knew where they would be. He pulled up his horse, and the other two did the same. They rode back across the bloodied plain strewn with the bodies of the dying and the dead, back to the ridge of land south of the battlefield. From a long distance away they could see the Aven kneeling beside a body that would be his youngest son.

They dismounted and walked up the ridge in the late afternoon light. A serenity seemed to have gathered about that place.

Levon saw them. "He'll be all right," he said, walking over. Dave nodded, then he reached out and pulled Levon to him in a fierce embrace.

Ivor looked up. He released Tabor's hand and came over to where they stood. There was a brightness in his eyes, shining through his weariness. "He will be all right," he echoed. "Thanks to the mage and to Arthur he will be all right."

"And to Pwyll," said Teyrnon quietly. "He was the one who guessed. I would never have caught him, without that warning."

Dave looked for Paul and saw him standing a little way apart from everyone else, farther along the ridge. *Even now,* he thought. He considered walking over but was reluctant to intrude. There was something very self-contained, very private about Paul in that moment.

"What happened?" someone said. Dave looked down. It

was Mabon of Rhoden, lying on a makeshift pallet not far away. The Duke smiled at him and winked. Then he repeated, "Does anyone know exactly what happened?"

Dave saw Jennifer coming toward them. There was a gentle radiance in her face, but it did not hide the deeper well of sorrow in her eyes. Before anyone spoke, Dave had an unexpected glimmer of understanding.

"It was Darien," said Kim, approaching as well. "But I don't know how. I wish I did."

"So do I," said Teyrnon. "But I could not see far enough to know what happened there."

"I did," said a third voice, very gently, very clearly.

They all turned to Gereint. And it was the old blind shaman of the Plain who gave voice to Darien's dying wish.

In the soft light and the deeply woven peace that had come, he said, "I thought there might be a reason for me to fly with Tabor. This was it. I could not fight in battle, but I was far enough north, standing here, to send my awareness into Starkadh."

He paused, and asked gently, "Where is the Queen?"

Dave was confused for a second, but Jennifer said, "Here I am, shaman."

Gereint turned to the sound of her voice. He said, "He is dead, my lady. I am sorry to say that the child is dead. But through the gift of my blindness I saw what he did. He chose for the Light at the last. The Circlet of Lisen blazed on his brow, and he threw himself upon a blade and died in such a way that Maugrim died with him."

"*Lökdal!*" Kim exclaimed. "Of course. Rakoth killed without love, and so he died! Oh, Jen. You were right after all. You were so terribly right." She was crying, and Dave saw that Jennifer Lowell, who was Guinevere, was weeping now as well, though silently.

In mourning for her child, who had taken the Darkest Road and had come at last to the end of it, alone, and so far away.

Dave saw Jaelle, the High Priestess, no longer so coldly arrogant—it showed even in the way she moved—walk over to comfort Jennifer, to gather her in her arms.

There were so many things warring for a place in his heart: joy and weariness, deep sorrow, pain, an infinite relief. He turned and walked down the slope of the ridge. He picked his way along the southern edge of what had been, so little time ago, the battlefield whereon the Light was to have been lost, and would have been, were it not for Jennifer's child. Guinevere's child.

He was wounded in many places, and exhaustion was slowly catching up to him. He thought of his father, for the second time that day, standing there on the edge of the battle plain, looking out upon the dead.

But one of them was not dead.

Would the old estrangement never leave him? Paul was wondering. Even here? Even now, in the moment when the towers of Darkness fell? Would he always feel this way?

And the answer that came back to him within his mind was in the form of another question: *What right had he even to ask?*

He was alive by sufferance of Mörnir. He had gone to the Summer Tree to die, named surrogate by the old King, Ailell. Who had told him about the price of power during a chess game that seemed centuries ago.

He had gone to die but had been sent back. He was still alive: Twiceborn. He was Lord of the Summer Tree, and there *was* a price to power. He was marked, named to be apart. And in this moment, while all around him quiet joy and quiet sorrow melded with each other, Paul was vibrating with the presence of his power in a way he never had before.

There was another thing left to happen. Something was coming. Not the war; Kim had been right about that, as she had been right about so many things. His was *not* a power of war, it never had been. He had been trying hard to make it so, to find a way to use it, channel it into battle. But from the very beginning what he'd had was a strength of resistance, of opposition, denial of the Dark. He was a defense, not a weapon of attack. He was the symbol of the God, an affirmation of life in his very existence, his being alive.

He had not felt the cold of Maugrim's winter, walking coatless in a wild night. Later, his had been the warning of the Soulmonger at sea, the cry that had brought Liranan to their defense. And then again, a second time, to save their lives upon the rocks of the Anor's bay. He was the presence of life, the sap of the Summer Tree rising from the green earth to drink the rain of the sky and greet the sun.

And within him now, with the war over, Maugrim dead, the sap was beginning to run. There was a trembling in his hands, an awareness of growth, of something building, deep and very strong. The pulsebeat of the God, which was his own.

He looked down on the quiet plain. To the north and west, Aileron the High King was riding back, with Arthur on one side and Lancelot on the other. The setting sun was behind the three of them, and there were coronas of light in their hair.

These were the figures of battle, Paul thought: the warriors in the service of Macha and Nemain, the goddesses of war. Just as Kimberly had been, with the summoning Baelrath on her hand, as Tabor and his shining mount had been, his gift of Dana born of the red full moon. As even Dave Martyniuk was, with his towering passion in battle, with Ceinwen's gift at his side.

Ceinwen's gift.

Paul was quick. All his life he had had an intuitive ability to make connections that others would never even see. He was turning, even as the thought flared in his mind like a brand. He was turning, looking for Dave, a cry forming on his lips. He was almost, almost in time.

So, too, was Dave. When the half-buried feral figure leaped from the pile of bodies, Dave's reflexes overrode his weariness. He spun, his hands going up to defend himself. Had the figure been thrusting for his heart or throat, Dave would have turned him back.

But his assailant was not looking to take his life, not yet. A hand flashed out, precise, unerring, at this last supreme moment, a hand that reached for Dave's side, not for his heart or throat. That reached for and found the key to what it had so long sought.

There was a tearing sound as a cord ripped. Dave heard Paul Schafer cry out up on the ridge. He clawed for his axe, but it was too late. It was much too late.

Rising gracefully from a rolling fall ten feet away, Galadan stood under the westering sun on the bloodied ground of

Andarien, and he held Owein's Horn in his hand.

And then the Wolflord of the andain, who had dreamt a dream for so many years, who had followed a never-ending quest—not for power, not for lordship over anyone or anything, but for pure annihilation, for the ending of all things—blew that mighty horn with all the power of his bitter soul and summoned Owein and the Wild Hunt to the ending of the world.

Kim heard Paul shout his warning, and then, in that same moment, all other sounds seemed to cease, and she heard the horn for the second time.

Its sound was Light, she remembered that. It could not be heard by the agents of the Dark. It had been moonlight on snow and frosty, distant stars the night Dave had sounded it before the cave to free the Hunt.

It was different now. Galadan was sounding it: Galadan, who had lived a thousand years in lonely, arrogant bitterness, after Lisen had rejected him and died. Tool of Maugrim, but seeking ever to further his own design, his one unvarying design.

The sound of the horn as he sent his soul into it was the light of grieving candles in a shadowed, hollow place; it was a half-moon riding through cold, windblown clouds; it was torches seen passing far off in a dark wood, passing but never coming near to warm with their glow; it was a bleak sunrise on a wintry beach; the pale, haunted light of glowworms in the mists of Llychlyn Marsh; it was all lights that did not warm or comfort, that only told a tale of shelter somewhere else, for someone else.

Then the sound ended, and the images faded.

Galadan lowered the horn. There was a dazed expression on his face. He said, incredulously, "I heard it. How did I hear Owein's Horn?"

No one answered him. No one spoke. They looked to the sky overhead. And in that moment Owein was there, and the shadowy kings of the Wild Hunt, and before them all, unsheathing a deadly sword with the rest of them, rode the child on pale Iselen. The child that had been Finn dan Shahar.

And who now was death.

They heard Owein cry in wild, chaotic ecstasy. They heard the moaning of the seven kings. They saw them weave like smoke across the light of the sun.

"Owein, hold!" cried Arthur Pendragon, with all the ringing command his voice could carry.

But Owein circled over his head and laughed. "You cannot bind me, Warrior! We are free, we have the child, it is time for the Hunt to ride!"

And already the kings were swooping down, wildly destructive, invulnerable, the random thread of chaos in the Tapestry. Already it seemed their swords were shining with blood. They would ride forever and kill until there was nothing left to kill.

But even in that moment, Kim saw them falter, rein in their plunging, smoky steeds. She heard them lift their ghostly voices in wailing confusion.

And she saw that the child was not with them in their descent. Finn seemed to be in pain, in distress, his pale horse plunging and rearing in the reddening light of the sunset. He was shouting something. Kim couldn't make it out. She didn't understand.

In the Temple, Leila screamed. She heard the sound of the horn. It exploded in her brain. She could hardly form a thought. But then she understood. And she screamed again in anguish, as the connection was made once more.

Suddenly she could see the battle plain. She was in the sky over Andarien. Jaelle was on the ridge of land below, with the High King, Guinevere, all of them. But it was to the sky she looked, and she saw the Hunt appear: Owein, and the deadly kings, and the child, who was Finn, whom she loved.

She screamed a third time, aloud in the Temple, and at the summit of her mind voice in the sky far to the north:

Finn, no! Come away! It is Leila. Do not kill them! Come away!

She saw him hesitate and turn to her. There was white pain, a splintering all through her mind. She felt shredded into fragments. He looked at her, and she could read the distance in his eyes, how far away he was—how far beyond her reach.

Too far. He did not even reply. He turned away. She heard Owein mock the Warrior, saw the sky kings draw their burning swords. There was fire all around her; there was blood in the sky, on the Temple walls. Finn's shadowy white horse bared teeth at her and carried Finn away.

Leila tore desperately free of whoever was holding her. Shalhassan of Cathal staggered back. He saw her stride, stumble, almost fall. She righted herself, reached the altar, claimed the axe.

"In the name of the Goddess, no!" one of the priestesses cried in horror, a hand before her mouth.

Leila did not hear her. She was screaming, and far away. She lifted Dana's axe, which only the High Priestess could lift. She raised that thing of power high over her head and brought it crashing, thundering, echoing down upon the altar stone. And as she did she cried out again, building with the power of the axe, the power of Dana, climbing on top of them as upon a mighty wall to hurl the mind command:

Finn, I command you. In the name of Dana, in the name of Light! Come away! Come to me now in Paras Derval!

She dropped to her knees in the Temple, letting the axe fall. In the sky over Andarien she watched. She had nothing left; she was empty, a shell. If this was not enough it had all been waste, all bitterest waste.

Finn turned. He pulled his plunging horse, fought her around to face Leila's disembodied spirit again. The horse reared in enraged resistance. She was all smoke and fire. She wanted blood. Finn clutched the reins with both hands, battling her to a standstill in the air. He looked at Leila, and she saw that he knew her now, that he had come back far enough to know.

So she said, softly, over the mind link they had shared, with no power left in her, only sorrow, only love, *Oh, Finn, please come away. Please come back to me.*

She saw his smoky, shadowy eyes widen then, in a way that she remembered from before, from what he once had been. And then, just before she fainted, she thought she heard his voice in her mind saying one thing only, but the only thing that mattered: her name.

There wasn't even the tracest flicker in her ring, and Kim knew that there wouldn't be. She was powerless, empty of all save pity and grief, which didn't count for anything. A part of her mind was savagely, despairingly aware that it was she who had released the Hunt to ride, on that night at the edge of Pendaran. How had she not seen what would come?

And yet, she also knew, without Owein's intercession by the Adein River, the lios and the Dalrei would all have died. She would never have had time to reach the Dwarves. Aileron and the men of Brennin, fighting alone, would have been torn apart. *Prydwen* would have returned from Cader Sedat to find the war lost and Rakoth Maugrim triumphant.

Owein had saved them then. To destroy them now, it seemed.

So went her thoughts in the moment Finn pulled his white horse away from the others in the sky and began to guide her south. Kim put her hands to her mouth; she heard Jaelle whisper something on a taken breath. She couldn't hear what it was.

She did hear Owein cry aloud, shouting after Finn. The sky kings wailed. Finn was fighting his horse, which had reacted to Owein's cry. The horse was thrashing and bucking in the high reaches of the air, lashing out with her hooves. But Finn held firm; rocking on the horse's back, he sawed at the reins, forcing her southward, away from the kings, from Owein, from the blood of the coming hunt. Again Jaelle murmured something, and there was heart's pain in the sound.

Finn kicked at his balking horse. She screamed with defiant rage. The wailing of the kings was like the howling of a winter storm. They were smoke and mist, they had fiery swords, they were death in the reddening sky.

Then the wailing changed. Everything changed. Kim cried aloud, in helpless horror and pity. For in the distance, west, toward the setting sun, Iselen threw her rider, as Imraith-Nimphais had thrown hers, but not out of love.

And Finn dan Shahar, flung free from a great height, shadow and smoke no longer, becoming a boy again, mortal, even as he fell, regaining his shape, recaptured by it, crashed headlong to the plain of Andarien and lay there, very still.

No one broke this fall. Kim watched him plummet to the earth and saw him lying there, crumpled, and she had a vivid, aching memory of the winter night by Pendaran Wood when the wandering fire she carried had woken the Wild Hunt.

Do not frighten her. I am here, Finn had said to Owein, who had been looming over Kim on his black horse. And Finn had come forward, and had mounted up upon pale white Iselen among the kings and had changed, had become smoke and shadow himself. The child at the head of the Hunt.

No more. He was no longer Iselen's rider in the sky, sweeping between the stars. He was mortal again, and fallen, and very probably dead.

But his fall meant something, or it *might* mean something. The Seer in Kim seized upon an image, and she stepped forward to give it voice.

Loren was before her, though, with the same awareness. Holding Amairgen's staff high in the air, he looked up at Owein and the seven kings. The kings were moaning aloud, the same words over and over, and the sound of their voices whistled like wind over Andarien.

"*Iselen's rider's lost!*" the Wild Hunt cried in fear and despair, and for all her sorrow, Kim felt a quickening of hope as Loren cast his own voice over the sound of the kings in the air.

"Owein!" he cried. "The child is lost again, you cannot ride. You cannot hunt along the reaches of the sky!"

Behind Owein and his black horse the kings of the Wild Hunt were wheeling and circling in frenzy. But Owein held black Cargail motionless over Loren's head, and when he spoke his voice was cold and pitiless. "It is not so," he said. "We are free. We have been summoned to power by power. There is none here who can master us! We will ride and slake our loss in blood!"

He lifted his sword, and its blade was red in the light, and he made wild Cargail to rear back high above them, black as night. The wailing of the kings changed from grief to rage. They ceased their frightened circling in the sky and drew their own grey horses into place behind Cargail.

And so it was all meaningless, Kim thought. She looked from the Hunt away to the twisted body of Finn, where it lay crumpled on the earth. It had not been enough. His fall, Darien's, Diarmuid's, Kevin's death, Rakoth's overthrow. None of it had been enough, and it was Galadan, here at the last, who would have his long desire. White Iselen, riderless, flashed in the sky behind the riders of the Hunt. Eight swords swung free, nine horses lashed out with their hooves, as the Hunt readied itself to ride through sunset into the dark.

"*Listen!*" cried Brendel of the lios alfar.

And even as he spoke, Kim heard the sound of singing coming over the stony ground from behind them. Even before she turned she knew who it had to be, for she knew that voice.

Over the ruined plain of Andarien, covering ground with huge, giant strides, came Ruana of the Paraiko to bind the Wild Hunt as Connla had bound them long ago.

Owein slowly lowered his sword. Behind him the kings fell silent in the sky. And in that silence they all heard the words Ruana sang as he came near:

"The flame will wake from sleep,
The Kings the horn will call,
But though they answer from the deep
You may never hold in thrall
Those who ride from Owein's Keep
With a child before them all."

Then he was among them, chanting still in the deep, timeless voice. He strode to the forefront of the ridge, past where Loren stood, and he stopped, looking up at Owein, and his chanting ceased.

Then, in the wide silence, Ruana cried, "Sky King, sheath your sword! I put my will upon you! And I am one whose will you must obey. I am heir to Connla, who bound you to your sleep by the words you have heard me chanting, even now."

Owein stirred. He said defiantly, "We have been summoned. We are free!"

"And I shall bind you back!" Ruana replied, deep and sure. "Connla is dead, but the power of his binding lives in me, for the Paraiko have never yet killed. And though we are changed now and forever changed, that much of what we were I still command. You were only released from your long sleep by the coming of the child. The child is lost, Owein. Lost as he was lost before, when Connla first laid you to rest. I say it again: sheath your swords! *By the power of Connla's spell, I put my will upon you!*"

For one moment, a moment as charged with power as any since the worlds were spun, Owein was motionless in the air above them. Then slowly, very slowly, his hand came down, and he laid his sword to rest in the scabbard at his side. With a cold, sighing sound, the seven kings did the same.

Owein looked down upon Ruana and he said, half demanding, half in plea, "It is not forever?"

And Ruana said quietly, "It cannot be forever, my lord Owein, neither by Connla's spell nor by your place in the Tapestry. The Hunt will always be a part of the Weaver's worlds—all of them. You are the randomness that makes us free. But only in binding you to sleep can we live. To sleep only, Sky King. You will ride again, you and the seven kings of the Hunt, and there will be another child before the end of days. Where we will be, we children of the Weaver's hand, I know not, but I tell you now, and I tell you true, all the worlds will be yours again, as once they were, before the Tapestry is done."

His deep voice carried the cadences of prophecy, of truth that had mastered time. He said, "But for now, here in this place, you are subject to my will because the child is lost again."

"Only because of that," said Owein, with a bitterness that cut through the air as keenly as his unsheathed blade might have done.

"Only because of that," Ruana agreed gravely. And Kim knew then how narrow had been their escape. She looked to where Finn had fallen and saw that a man had gone over to that place and was kneeling beside the boy. She didn't know, at first, who it was, and then she guessed.

Owein spoke again, and now the bitterness was gone, replaced by a quiet resignation. He said, "Do we go to the cave again, Connla's heir?"

"Even so," Ruana replied from the ridge, looking up into the sky. "You are to go there and lay you down upon your stone beds again, you and the seven kings. And I will follow to that place, and weave Connla's spell a second time to bind you to your sleep."

Owein lifted his hand. For a moment he remained so, a grey shadow on a black horse, the red jewels in his crown gleaming in the sunset. Then he bowed to Ruana, bound to the Giant's will by what Finn had done, and lowered his hand.

And suddenly the Wild Hunt was flashing away, south toward a cave at the edge of Pendaran Wood, near to a tree forked by lightning thousands and thousands of years ago.

Last of them all, riderless, Iselen flew, her white tail streaming behind her like a comet, visible even after the horses of the kings were lost to sight.

Dazed by the intensity of what had just happened, Kim saw Jaelle going swiftly along the ridge to where Finn lay. Paul Schafer said something crisply to Aileron and then set out after the High Priestess.

Kim turned away from them and looked up, a long way up, at Ruana's face. His eyes were as she remembered: deeply, quietly compassionate. He gazed down upon her, waiting.

She said, "Ruana, how did you come in time? So narrowly in time?"

He shook his head slowly. "I have been here since the Dragon came. I have been watching from behind—I would not come nearer to war than that. But when Starkadh fell, when the war was over and the Wolflord blew the horn, I realized what had drawn me here."

"What, Ruana? What drew you here?"

"Seer, what you did in Khath Meigol changed us forever. As I watched my people set out for Eridu, it came to me that the Baelrath is a power of war, a summons to battle—and that we would not have been undone by it as we had been only to journey east, away from war, to the cleansing of the raindead, necessary as that might be. I did not think it was enough."

Kim said nothing. There was a tightness in her throat.

Ruana said, "And so I took it upon myself to come west instead of east. To journey to wherever the war might be and so to see if there was a truer part the Paraiko should play in what was to come. Something drove me from within. There was anger in me, Seer, and there was hatred of Maugrim, and neither of those had I ever felt before."

"I know that," Kim said. "I grieve for it, Ruana."

Again he shook his head. "Grieve not. The price of our sanctity would have been the Wild Hunt riding free, and the deaths of all living peoples gathered here. It was time, Seer of Brennin, past time, for the Paraiko to be truly numbered among the army of Light."

"I am forgiven, then?" she asked in a small voice.

"You were forgiven in the kanior."

She remembered: the ghostly images of Kevin and Ysanne moving among all the thronging dead of the Paraiko, honored among them, reclaimed with them by the deep spell of Ruana's song.

She nodded. "I know," she said.

Around the two of them there was silence. Kim looked up at the grave, white-haired Giant. "You will have to go now? To follow them to the cave?"

"Soon," he replied. "But there is something yet to happen here, I think, and I will stay to see."

And with his words a dormant awareness came back to life within Kimberly as well. She looked past Ruana and saw Galadan on the plain, ringed about by a great many men, most of whom she knew. They had swords drawn, and arrows trained on the Wolflord's heart, but not one of them moved or spoke, nor did Galadan. Near to the circle, Arthur stood, with Guinevere and Lancelot.

Off to the west, Paul Schafer, for whom they were waiting, at the High King's command, knelt by the body of Finn dan Shahar.

* * *

When Leila lifted the axe, Jaelle knew it. How could the High Priestess not know? It was the deepest sacrilege there was. And somehow it didn't surprise her at all.

She heard—every priestess in Fionavar heard—when Leila slammed the axe down on the altar stone and ringingly commanded Finn to come to her, a command sourced in the blood power of Dana's axe. And Jaelle had seen the shadowy figure of the boy on his pale horse in the sky begin to ride away, and she saw him fall.

Then the lone Paraiko came among them, and he put the binding of Connla's spell upon the Hunt, and Jaelle saw them flash away to the south.

Only when they were gone did she let herself go west to where Finn lay. She walked at first, but then began to run, wanting, for Leila's sake, to be in time. She felt the circlet that held back her hair slip off; she didn't stop to pick it up. And as she ran, her hair blowing free, she was remembering the last time this link had been forged, when Leila in the Temple had heard Green Ceinwen turn back the Hunt by the bloodied banks of the Adein.

Jaelle remembered the words she herself had spoken then, spoken in the voice of the Goddess: *There is a death in it*, she had said, knowing it was true.

She came to the place where he lay. His father was there already. She remembered Shahar, from when he had been home from war in the months after Darien was born, while the priestesses of Dana, privy to the secret, had helped Vae care for her new child.

He was sitting on the ground with his son's head in his lap. Over and over, his calloused hands were stroking the boy's forehead. He looked up without speaking at Jaelle's approach. Finn lay motionless, his eyes closed. He was mortal again, she saw. He looked as he had back in the days of the children's game, the ta'kiena on the green at the end of Anvil Lane. When Leila, blindfolded, had called him to the Longest Road.

Someone else came. Jaelle looked over her shoulder and saw that it was Pwyll.

He handed her the silver circlet. Neither of them spoke. They looked down at father and son and then knelt on the stony ground beside the fallen boy.

He was dying. His breath was shallow and difficult, and there was blood at the corners of his mouth. Jaelle lifted an edge of her sleeve and wiped the blood away.

Finn opened his eyes at the touch. She saw that he knew her. She saw him ask a question without words.

Very carefully, speaking as clearly as she could, Jaelle said, "The Hunt has gone. One of the Paraiko came, and he bound them back to the cave by the spell that laid them there."

She saw him nod. It seemed that he understood. He *would* understand, Jaelle realized. He had been one with the Wild Hunt. But now he was only a boy again, with his head in his father's lap, and dying where he lay.

His eyes were still open, though. He said, so softly she had to bend close to hear, "What I did was all right, then?"

She heard Shahar make a small sound deep in his chest. Through her own tears, she said, "It was more than all right, Finn. You did everything right. Every single thing, from the very beginning."

She saw him smile. There was blood again, and once more she wiped it away with the sleeve of her robe. He coughed, and said, "She didn't mean to throw me, you know." It took Jaelle a moment to realize that he was talking about his horse. "She was afraid," Finn said. "She wasn't used to flying so far from the others. She was only afraid."

"Oh, child," Shahar said huskily. "Spare your strength."

Finn reached up for his father's hand. His eyes closed and his breathing slowed. Jaelle's tears followed one another down her cheeks. Then Finn opened his eyes again.

Looking directly at her, he whispered, "Will you tell Leila I heard her? That I was coming?"

Jaelle nodded, half blind. "I think she knows. But I will tell her, Finn."

He smiled at that. There was a great deal of pain in his brown eyes, but there was also a quiet peace. He was silent for a long time, having little strength left in him, but then he had one more question, and the High Priestess knew it was the last, because he meant it to be.

"*Dari?*" he asked.

She found that this time she couldn't even answer. Her throat had closed completely around this grief.

It was Pwyll who spoke. He said, with infinite compassion, "He too did everything right, Finn. Everything. He is gone, but he killed Rakoth Maugrim before he died."

Finn's eyes widened at that, for the last time. There was joy in them, and a grieving pain, but at the end there was peace again, without border or limitation, just before the dark.

"Oh, little one," he said. And then he died, holding his father's hand.

There was a legend that took shape in after days, a tale that grew, perhaps, because so many of those who lived through that time wanted it to be true. A tale of how Darien's soul, which had taken flight some time before his brother's, was allowed by intercession to pause in the timelessness between the stars and wait for Finn to catch up to him.

And then the story told of how the two of them passed together over the walls of Night that lie all about the living worlds, toward the brightness of the Weaver's Halls. And Darien's soul was in the shape he'd had when he was small, when he was Dari, and the eyes of his soul were blue and Finn's were brown as they went side by side toward the Light.

So the legend went, afterward, born of sorrow and heart's desire. But Jaelle, the High Priestess, rose that day from Finn's side, and she saw that the westering sun had carried the afternoon well over toward twilight.

Then Pwyll also rose, and Jaelle looked upon his face and saw power written there so deeply and so clearly that she was afraid.

And it was as the Lord of the Summer Tree, the Twiceborn of Mörnir, that he spoke. "With all the griefs and joys of this day," Pwyll said, seeming almost to be looking through her, "there is one thing left to be done, and it is mine to do, I think."

He walked past her, slowly, and she turned and saw, by the light of the setting sun, that everyone was gathered on the plain about the figure of Galadan. They were motionless, like statues, or figures caught in time.

Leaving Shahar alone with his son she followed after Pwyll, carrying her silver circlet in her hand. Above her head as she walked down to the plain she heard the quick, invisible wings of his ravens, Thought and Memory. She didn't know what he was about to do, but in that moment she knew another thing, a truth in the depths of her own heart, as she saw the circle of men make way for Pwyll to pass within, facing the Wolflord of the andain.

Standing beside Loren, with Ruana at her other side, Kim watched Paul walk into the circle, and she had a sudden curious mental image—gone as soon as it came to her—of Kevin Laine, laughing carelessly in Convocation Hall before anything had happened. Anything at all.

It was very quiet in Andarien. In the red of the setting sun the faces of those assembled glowed with a strange light. The breeze was very soft, from the west. All around them lay the dead.

In the midst of the living, Paul Schafer faced Galadan and he said, "We meet for the third time, as I promised you we would. I told you in my own world that the third time would pay for all."

His voice was level and low, but it carried an infinite authority. To this hour, Kim saw, Paul had brought all of his own driven intensity, and added to that, now, was what he had become in Fionavar. Especially since the war was over. Because she had been right: his was *not* a power of battle. It was something else, and it had risen within him now.

He said, "Wolflord, I can see in any darkness you might shape and shatter any blade you could try to throw. I think you know that this is true."

Galadan stood quietly, attending to him carefully. His scarred, aristocratic head was high; the slash of silver in his black hair gleamed in the waning light. Owein's Horn lay at his feet like some discarded toy.

He said, "I have no blades left to throw. It might have been different had the dog not saved you on the Tree, but I have nothing left now, Twiceborn. The long cast is over."

Kim heard and tried not to be moved by the weariness of centuries that lay buried in his voice.

Galadan turned, and it was to Ruana that he spoke. "For more years than I can remember," he said gravely, "the Paraiko of Khath Meigol have troubled my dreams. In my sleep the shadows of the Giants always fell across the image of my desire. Now I know why. It was a deep spell Connla wove so long ago, that its binding could still hold the Hunt today."

He bowed, without any visible irony, to Ruana, who looked back at him unblinking, saying nothing. Waiting.

Once more Galadan turned to Paul, and a second time he repeated, "It is over. I have nothing left. If you had hopes of a confrontation, now that you have come into your power, I am sorry to disappoint you. I will be grateful for whatever end you make of me. As things have fallen out, it might as well have come a very long time ago. I might as well have also leaped from the Tower."

It was upon them, Kim knew. She bit her lip as Paul said, quietly, completely in control, "It need not be over, Galadan. You heard Owein's Horn. Nothing truly evil can hear the horn. Will you not let that truth lead you back?"

There was a murmur of sound, quickly stilled. Galadan had suddenly gone white.

"I heard the horn," he admitted, as if against his will. "I know not why. How should I come back, Twiceborn? Where could I go?"

Paul did not speak. He only raised one hand and pointed to the southeast.

There, far off on the ridge, a god was standing, naked and magnificent. The rays of the setting sun slanted low across the land and his body glowed red and bronze in that light, and there was a shining brightness to the branching tines of the horns upon his head.

The stag horns of Cernan.

Only an act of will, Kim realized, kept Galadan steady on his feet when he saw that his father had come. There was no color in his face at all.

Paul said, absolute master of the moment, voice of the God, "I can grant you the ending you seek, and I will, if you ask me again. But hear me first, Lord of the andain."

He paused a moment and then, not without gentleness, said, "Lisen has been dead this thousand years, but only today, when her Circlet blazed to the undoing of Maugrim, did her spirit pass to its rest. So too has Amairgen's soul now been released from wandering at sea. Two sides of the triangle, Galadan. They are gone, finally, truly gone. But you live yet, and for all that you have done in bitterness and pride, you still heard the sound of Light in Owein's Horn. Will you not surrender your pain, Lord of the andain? Give it over. Today has marked the very ending of that tale of sorrow. *Will you not let it end?* You heard the horn—there *is* a way back for you on this side of Night. Your father has come to be your guide. Will you not let him take you away and heal you and bring you back?"

In the stillness, the clear words seemed to fall like drops of the life-giving rain Paul had bought with his body on the Tree. One after another, gentle as rain, drop by shining drop.

Then he was silent, having forsworn the vengeance he had claimed so long ago—and claimed a second time in the presence of Cernan by the Summer Tree on Midsummer's Eve.

The sun was very low. It hung like a weight in a scale far in the west. Something moved in Galadan's face, a spasm of ancient, unspeakable, never-spoken pain. His hands came up, as if of their own will, from his sides, and he cried aloud, "*If only she had loved me! I might have shone so bright!*"

Then he covered his face with his fingers and wept for the first and only time in a thousand years of loss.

He wept for a long time. Paul did not move or speak. But then, from beside Kim, Ruana suddenly began, deep and low in his chest, a slow, sad chanting of lament. A moment later, with a shiver, Kim heard Ra-Tenniel, Lord of the lios alfar, lift his glorious voice in clear harmony, delicate as a chime in the evening wind.

And so the two of them made music in that place. For Lisen and Amairgen, for Finn and Darien, for Diarmuid dan Ailell, for all the dead gathered there and all the dead beyond, and for the first-fallen tears of the Lord of the andain, who had served the Dark so long in his pride and bitter pain.

At length Galadan looked up. The singing stopped. His eyes were hollows, dark as Gereint's. He faced Paul for the last time, and he said, "You would truly do this? Let me go from here?"

"I would," said Paul, and not a person standing there spoke to gainsay his right to do so.

"Why?"

"Because you heard the horn." Paul hesitated, then: "And because of another thing. When you first came to kill me on the Summer Tree you said something. Do you remember?"

Galadan nodded slowly.

"You said I was almost one of you," Paul went on quietly, with compassion. "You were wrong, Wolflord. The truth is, you were almost one of us, but you didn't know it then. You had put it too far behind you. Now you know, you have remembered. There has been more than enough killing today. Go home, unquiet spirit, and find healing. Then come back among us with the blessing of what you always should have been."

Galadan's hands were quiet at his sides again. He listened, absorbing every word. Then he nodded his head, once. Very gracefully, he bowed to Paul, as his father once had done, and moving slowly he walked from the ring of men.

They made way for him on either side. Kim watched him ascend the slope and then walk south and east along the higher ground until he came to where his father stood. The evening sun was upon them both. By its light she saw Cernan open wide his arms and gather his broken, wayward child to his breast.

One moment they stood thus; then there seemed to Kim to be a sudden flaw of light upon the ridge, and they were gone. She looked away, to the west, and saw that Shahar, only a silhouette now against the light, was still sitting on the stony ground with Finn's head cradled in his lap.

Her heart felt too large for her breast. There was so much glory and so much pain, all interwoven together and never to be untied, she feared. It was over, though. With this there had to have come an ending.

Then she turned back to Paul and realized that she was wrong, completely wrong. She looked at him, and she saw where his own gaze fell, and so she looked as well, at last, to where Arthur Pendragon had been standing quietly all this time.

Guinevere was beside him. Her beauty, the simplicity of it, was so great in that moment, that Kim found it hard to look upon her face. Next to her, but a little way apart and a little way behind, Lancelot du Lac leaned upon his sword, bleeding from more wounds than Kim could number. His mild eyes were clear, though, and grave, and he managed to smile when he saw her looking at him. A smile so gentle, from one unmatched of any man, living or dead or ever to come, that Kim thought it might break her heart.

She looked at the three of them standing together in the twilight, and half a hundred thoughts went through her mind. She turned back to Paul and saw that there was now a kind of shining to him in the dark. All thoughts went from her. Nothing had prepared her for this. She waited.

And heard him say, as quietly as before, "Arthur, the end of war has come, and you have not passed from us. This place was named Camlann, and you stand living in our presence still."

The Warrior said nothing. The heel of his spear rested on the ground, and both of his broad hands were wrapped about its shaft. The sun went down. In the west, the evening star named for Lauriel seemed to shine more brightly than it ever had before. There was a faint glow, yet, to the western sky, but soon it would be full dark. Some men had brought torches, but they had not lit them yet.

Paul said, "You told us the pattern, Warrior. How it has always been, each and every time you have been summoned. Arthur, it has changed. You thought you were to die at Cader Sedat and you did not. Then you thought to find your ending in battle with Uathach, and you did not."

"I think I was supposed to find it there," Arthur said. His first words.

"I think so too," Paul replied. "But Diarmuid chose otherwise. He made it *become* otherwise. We are not slaves to the Loom, not bound forever to our fate. Not even you, my lord Arthur. Not even you, after so long."

He paused. It was utterly silent on the plain. It seemed to Kim that a wind arose then that appeared to come from all directions, or from none. She felt, in that moment, that they stood at the absolute center of things, at the axletree of worlds. She had a sense of anticipation, of a culmination coming that went far beyond words. It was deeper than thought: a fever in the blood, another kind of pulse. She was aware of the tacit presence of Ysanne within herself. Then she was aware of something else.

A new light shining in the darkness.

"Oh, Dana!" Jaelle breathed, a prayer. No one else spoke.

In the east a full moon rose over Fionavar for the second time on a night that was not a full moon night.

This time she was not red, not a challenge or a summons to war. She was silver and glorious, as the full moon of the Goddess was meant to be, bright as a dream of hope, and she bathed Andarien in a mild and beneficent light.

Paul didn't even look up. Nor did the Warrior. Their eyes never left the other's face. And Arthur said, in that silver light, in that silence, his voice an instrument of bone-deep self-condemnation: "Twiceborn, how could it ever change? I had the children slain."

"And have paid full, fullest price," Paul replied without hesitation.

In his voice, now, they suddenly heard thunder. "Look up, Warrior!" he cried. "Look up and see the moon of the Goddess shining down upon you. Hear Mörnir speak through me. Feel the ground of Camlann beneath your feet. Arthur, look about you! Listen! Don't you see? It has come, after so long. You are summoned now to glory, not to pain. This is the hour of your release!"

Thunder was in his voice, a glow as of sheet lightning in his face. Kim felt herself trembling; she wrapped her arms about herself. The wind was all around them, growing and growing even as Paul spoke, even as the thunder rolled, and it seemed to Kim, looking up, that the wind was carrying stars and the dust of stars past her eyes.

And then Pwyll Twiceborn, who was Lord of the Summer Tree, turned away from all of them, and he strode a little way to the west, facing the distant sea, with the bright moon at his back, and they heard him cry in a mighty voice:

"Liranan, sea brother! I have called you three times now, once from the shore, and once from the sea, and once in the bay of the Anor Lisen. Now, in this hour, I summon you again, far from your waves. In the name of Mörnir and in the presence of Dana, whose moon is above us now, I bid you send your tides to me. Send them, Liranan! Send the sea, that joy may come at last at the end of a tale of sorrow so long told. I am sourced in the power of the land, brother, and mine is the voice of the God. I bid you come!"

As he spoke, Paul stretched forth his hands in a gesture of

widest gathering, as if he would encompass all of time, all the Weaver's worlds within himself. Then he fell silent. They waited. A moment passed, and another. Paul did not move. He kept his hands outstretched as the wind swirled all around him, strong and wild. Behind him the full moon shone, before him the evening star.

Kim heard the sound of waves.

And over the barren plain of Andarien, silver in the light of the moon, the waters of the sea began moving in. Higher and higher they rose, though gently, guided and controlled. Paul's head was high, his hands were stretched wide and welcoming as he drew the sea so far into the land from Linden Bay. Kim blinked; there were tears in her eyes, and her own hands were trembling again. She smelled salt on the evening air, saw waves sparkle under the moon.

Far, far off, she saw a figure shining upon the waves, with his hands outstretched wide, as Paul's were. She knew who this had to be. Wiping away her tears, she strained to see him clearly. He shimmered in the white moonlight, and it seemed to her that all the colors of the rainbow were dancing in the robe the sea god wore.

On the high ridge northwest of them, she saw that Shahar still cradled his son, but the two of them seemed to Kim to be alone on some promontory now, on an island rising from the waters of the sea.

An island such as Glastonbury Tor had once been, rising from the waters that had covered the Somerset Plain. Waters over which a barge once had floated, bearing three grieving queens and the body of Arthur Pendragon to Avalon.

And even as she shaped this thought, Kim saw a boat coming toward them over the waves. Long and beautiful was that craft, with a single white sail filling with the strange wind. And in the stern, steering it, was a figure she knew, a figure to whom she had granted, under duress, his heart's desire.

The waters had reached them now. The world had changed, all the laws of the world. Under a full moon that should never have been riding in the sky, the stony plain of Andarien lay undersea as far inland as the place where they stood, east of the battlefield. And the silvered waters of Liranan had covered over the dead.

Paul lowered his arms. He said nothing at all, standing quite motionless. The winds grew quiet. And borne by those quiet winds, Flidais of the andain, who had been Taliesin once in Camelot long ago, brought his craft up to them and lowered the sail.

It was very, very still. Then Flidais stood up in the stern of his boat and he looked directly at Kimberly and into that stillness he said, "*From the darkness of what I have done to you there shall be light.* Do you remember, Seer? Do you remember the promise I made you when you offered me the name?"

"I remember," Kim whispered.

It was very hard to speak. She was smiling, though, through her tears. It was coming, it had come.

Flidais turned to Arthur and, bowing low, he said humbly, with deference, "My lord, I have been sent to bring you home. Will you come aboard, that we may sail by the light of the Loom to the Weaver's Halls?"

All around her, Kim heard men and women weeping quietly for joy. Arthur stirred. There was a glory in his face, as understanding finally came to him.

And then, even in the very moment it appeared, the moment he was offered release from the cycle of his grief, Kim saw that shining fade. Her hands closed at her sides so hard the nails drew blood from her palms.

Arthur turned to Guinevere.

There might have been a thousand words spoken in the silence of their eyes under that moon. A tale told over so many times in the chambers of the heart that there were no words left for the telling. And especially not now. Not here, with what had come.

She moved forward with grace, with infinite care. She lifted up her mouth to his and kissed him full upon the lips in farewell; then she stepped back again.

She did not speak or weep, or ask for anything at all. In her green eyes was love, and only love. She had loved two men only in all her days, and each of them had loved her, and each the other. But divided as her love was, it had also been something else and was so, still: a passion sustaining and enduring, without end to the worlds' end.

Arthur turned away from her, so slowly it seemed the

weight of time itself lay upon him. He looked to Flidais with an anguished question in his face. The andain wrung his hands together and then drew them helplessly apart.

"I am only allowed you, Warrior," he whispered. "We have so far to go, the waters are so wide."

Arthur closed his eyes. *Must there always be pain?* Kim thought. Could joy never, ever be pure? She saw that Lancelot was weeping.

And it was then, precisely then, that the dimensions of the miracle were made manifest. It was then that grace descended. For Paul Schafer spoke again, and he said, "*Not so. It is allowed. I am deep enough to let this come to pass.*"

Arthur opened his eyes and looked, incredulous, at Paul. Who nodded, quietly sure. "It is allowed," he said again.

So there was joy, after all. The Warrior turned again to look upon his Queen, the light and sorrow of his days, and for the first time in so very long they saw him smile. And she too smiled, for the first time in so very long, and said, asking only now, now that it was vouchsafed them, "Will you take me with you where you go? Is there a place for me among the summer stars?"

Through her tears Kim saw Arthur Pendragon walk forward, then, and she saw him take the hand of Guinevere in his own, and she watched the two of them go aboard that craft, floating on the waters that had risen over Andarien. It was almost too much for her, too rich. She could scarcely breathe. She felt as if her soul were an arrow loosed to fly, silver in the moonlight, never falling back.

Then there was even more: the very last gift, the one that sealed and shaped the whole. Beneath the shining of Dana's moon she saw Arthur and Guinevere turn back to look at Lancelot.

And she heard Paul say again, with so deep a power woven into his voice, "*It is allowed if you will it so. All of the price has been paid.*"

With a cry of joy wrung from his great heart, Arthur instantly stretched forth his hand. "Oh, Lance, come!" he cried. "*Oh, come!*"

For a moment Lancelot did not move. Then something long held back, so long denied, blazed in his eyes brighter than any star. He stepped forward. He took Arthur's hand,

and then Guinevere's, and they drew him aboard. And so the three of them stood there together, the grief of the long tale healed and made whole at last.

Flidais laughed aloud for gladness and swiftly drew upon the line that lifted the white sail. There came a wind from the east. Then, just before the boat began to draw away, Kim saw Paul finally move. He knelt down beside a grey shape that had materialized at his side.

For one moment he buried his face deep in the torn fur of the dog that had saved him on the Tree—saved him, that the wheel of time might turn and find this moment waiting in Andarien.

"Farewell, great heart," Kim heard him say. "I will never forget."

It was his own voice this time, no thunder in it, only a rich sadness and a very great depth of joy. Which were within her too, exactly those two things, as Cavall leaped in one great bound to land at Arthur's feet even as the boat turned to the west.

And thus did it come to pass, what Arthur had said in Cader Sedat to the dog that had been his companion in so many wars: that there might come a day when they need not part.

It had come. Under the silver shining of the moon, that long slender craft caught the rising of the wind and it carried them away, Arthur and Lancelot and Guinevere. Past the promontory it sailed, and from that solitary height Shahar raised one hand in farewell, and all three of them saluted him. Then it seemed to those that watched from the plain that that ship began to rise into the night, not following the curving of the earth but tracking a different path.

Farther and farther it went, rising all the while upon waters of a sea that belonged to no world and to all of them. For as long as she possibly could, Kim strained her eyes to make out Guinevere's fair hair—Jennifer's hair—shining in the bright moonlight. Then that was lost in the far darkness, and the last thing they saw was the gleaming of Arthur's spear, like a new star in the sky.

PART V

Flowerfire

Chapter 18

No man living could remember a harvest like the one that came to the High Kingdom at the end of that summer. In Cathal, as well, the graneries were full, and the gardens of Larai Rigal grew more extravagantly beautiful—drenched in perfume, riotous with color—each passing day. On the Plain the eltor swifts ran over the rich green grass, and the hunting was easy and joyous under the wide sky. But nowhere did the grass grow so deep as on Ceinwen's Mound by Celidon.

Even in Andarien the soil had grown rich again—literally overnight, with the receding of the waves that had come to bear the Warrior away. There was talk of settling there again, and in Sennett Strand. In Taerlindel of the mariners and in Cynan and Seresh, they spoke of building ships to sail up and down the long coast, past the Anor Lisen and the Cliffs of Rhudh, to Sennett and Linden Bay. There was talk of many things as that summer came to an end, words woven of peace and a quiet joy.

Through the first weeks after the battle there had been little time to celebrate. The army of Cathal had ridden north under their Supreme Lord, and Shalhassan had taken charge, with Matt Sören—for the King of the Dwarves would not let his people rest until the last of the servants of Maugrim were slain—of cleaning out the remnants of the urgach and the svart alfar that had fled the Bael Andarien.

The Dalrei, badly ravaged by the wars, withdrew to Celidon to take council, and the lios alfar made their way back to Daniloth.

Daniloth, but no longer the Shadowland. Two months after the battle that ended the war, after the Dwarves and the men of Cathal had finished their task, men as far south as

Paras Derval had seen, on a night glittering with stars, a glow rise up in the north, and they had cried aloud for wonder and joy to see the Land of Light regain its truest name.

And it came to pass that in that time, with the harvest gathered and stored, Aileron the High King sent his messengers riding forth all through his land, and to Daniloth and Larai Rigal and Celidon, and over the mountains to Banir Lök, to summon the free peoples of Fionavar to a week of celebration in Paras Derval: a celebration to be woven in the name of the peace won at last, and to honor the three who remained of Loren Silvercloak's five strangers, and to bid them a last farewell.

Riding south with the Dalrei to what was to be his own party, Dave still had no clear idea of what he was going to do. He knew—beyond even his own capacity to feel insecure—that he was welcome and wanted here, even loved. He also knew how much he loved these people. But it wasn't as simple as that; nothing ever seemed to be, not even now.

With all that had happened to him, the ways he had changed and the things that had made him change, the images of his parents and his brother had been drifting through his dreams every night of late. He remembered, too, how thoughts of Josef Martyniuk had been with him all through the last battle in Andarien. There were things to be worked out there, Dave knew, and part of what he'd learned among the Dalrei was how important it was to resolve those things.

But the other thing he'd learned here was joy, a richness of belonging such as he'd never known. All of which meant that there was a decision to be made, and very soon—for it had been decided that after the celebration week was over, Jaelle and Teyrnon, sharing out the powers of Dana and Mörnir, would jointly act to send them home through the crossing. If they wanted to go.

It was beautiful here on the Plain, riding southwest over the wide grasslands, seeing the great swifts flash past in the distance under the high white clouds and the mild end-of-summer sun. It was too beautiful to be thinking, wrestling with the shadows and implications of his dilemma, and so he let it slip from him for a time.

He looked around. It seemed that the whole of the third tribe and a great many others of the Dalrei were coming south with him at the High King's invitation. Even Gereint was here, riding in one of the chariots that Shalhassan had left behind on his way south to Cathal. On either side of Dave, Torc and Levon rode easily, almost lazily, through the afternoon.

They smiled at him when he caught their eye, but neither had said much of anything on this journey: unwilling, he knew, to pressure him in any way. But such a realization took him right back to the decision he had to make, and he didn't want to deal with that. Instead, he let his mind return to images of the weeks gone by.

He remembered the feasting and the dancing under the stars and between the fires burning on the Plain. A dance of the ride of Ivor to the Adein, another of the courage of the Dalrei at Andarien. Other dances, still, intricately woven, of individual deeds of glory in the war. And more than once the women of the Dalrei shaped the deeds of Davor of the Axe in battle against the Dark. And more than once, afterward, all through the mild nights of that summer, with Rangat an unmarred glory in the north, there had been women who came to Dave after the fires had died, for another sort of dance.

Not Liane, though. Ivor's daughter had danced for them all between the fires, but never with Dave in his room at night. Once he might have regretted that, found in it a source of longing or pain. But not now, not any more, for a great many reasons. Even in this there had been a joy to be savored, amid the healing time of that summer on the Plain.

He had been honored and apprehensive, both, when Torc had come to him, a few weeks after the return to Celidon, to make his request. It had taken a long night of rehearsal, with Levon drilling him over and over and laughingly plying him with sachen in between sessions, before Dave had felt ready to go stand the next morning, with something of a hangover to complicate things, before the Aven of the Dalrei and say what was to be said.

He'd done it, though. He'd found Ivor walking amid a number of the Chieftains in the camp at Celidon. Levon had told him that the thing was to be done as publicly as possible. And so Dave had swallowed hard, and stepped in front of the Aven, and had said, "Ivor dan Banor, I am sent by a Rider of honor and worth with a message for you. Aven, Torc dan Sorcha has named me as his Intercedent and bids me tell you, in the presence of all those here, that the sun rises in your daughter's eyes."

There had been a number of marriages all over Fionavar that summer after the war, and a great many proposals were done after the old fashion, with an Intercedent—an act of homage, in a real sense, to Diarmuid dan Ailell, who had revived the tradition by proposing in this way to Sharra of Cathal.

A number of marriages. And one of them the third tribe celebrated not long after the morning Dave had spoken those words. For the Aven had given his consent with joy, and then Liane had smiled the secret smile they all knew so well and said, quite simply, "Yes, of course. Of course I will marry him. I always meant to."

Which was as maddeningly unfair, Levon commented afterward, as anything his sister had ever said. Torc didn't seem to mind at all. He'd seemed dazed and incredulous all through the ceremony in which Cordeliane dal Ivor had become his wife. Ivor had cried, and Sorcha too. Not Leith. But then, no one expected her to.

It had been a wonderful night and a wonderful summer, in almost every way. Dave had even ridden with the Riders on an eltor hunt. Again, Levon had tutored him, this time in the use of a blade from horseback. And one morning at sunrise Dave had ridden out with the hunters, and had picked an eltor buck from a racing swift, and had galloped alongside of it and leaped—not trusting himself to throw the blade—from his horse to the back of the eltor, and had plunged the blade into its throat. He had rolled, and risen up from the grass, and saluted Levon. And hunt leader and all the others had returned his salute with shouted praise and blades uplifted high.

A glorious summer, among people he loved, on the rolling

Plain that was theirs. And now he had a decision to make and he couldn't seem to make it.

A week later, he still hadn't made up his mind. In fairness to himself, there hadn't been much time for introspection. There had been banquets of staggering sumptuousness in the Great Hall of Paras Derval. There had been music again, and of a different sort this time, for the lios alfar were among them now, and one night Ra-Tenniel, their Lord, had lifted his own voice to sing the long tale of the war just past.

Woven into that song had been a great many things shaped equally of beauty and of pain. From the very beginning, when Loren Silvercloak had brought five strangers to Fionavar from another world.

Ra-Tenniel sang of Paul on the Summer Tree, of the battle of wolf and dog, the sacrifice of Ysanne. He sang the red moon of Dana, and the birth of Imraith-Nimphais. (Dave had looked along the table then, to see Tabor dan Ivor slowly lower his head.) Jennifer in Starkadh. Darien's birth. The coming of Arthur. Guinevere. The waking of the Wild Hunt, as Finn dan Shahar took the Longest Road.

He sang Maidaladan: Kevin in Dun Maura, red flowers at dawn in the melting snow. Ivor's ride to the Adein, battle there, the lios coming, and Owein in the sky. The Soulmonger at sea, and the shattering of the Cauldron at Cader Sedat. Lancelot in the Chamber of the Dead. The Paraiko in Khath Meigol, and the last kanior. (Across the room, Ruana sat by Kimberly and listened in an expressionless silence).

Ra-Tenniel went on. He encompassed all of it, brought it to life again under the stained glass windows of the Great Hall. He sang Jennifer and Brendel at the Anor Lisen, Kimberly with the Baelrath at Calor Diman, Lancelot battling in the sacred grove, and Amairgen's ghost ship passing Sennett Strand a thousand years ago.

And then, at the end, in shadings of sorrow and joy, Ra-Tenniel sang to them of the Bael Andarien itself: Diarmuid dan Ailell battling with Uathach, killing him at sunset, and dying. Tabor and his shining mount rising to meet the Dragon of Maugrim. Battle and death on a wasted plain. And then, far off in an evil place, alone and afraid (and it was all there, all in the golden voice), Darien choosing the Light and killing Rakoth Maugrim.

Dave wept. His heart ached for so much glory and so much pain, as Ra-Tenniel came to the end of his song: Galadan and Owein's Horn. Finn dan Shahar falling from the sky to let Ruana bind the Hunt. And at the very last, Arthur and Lancelot and Guinevere sailing away in gladness on a sea that seemed to rise until it reached the stars.

The tears of the living flowed freely in Paras Derval that night, as they remembered the dead and the deeds of the dead.

But it had been a week woven mostly of laughter and joy, of sachen and wine—white from South Keep, red from Gwen Ystrat—of clear, blue-sky days crammed with activity, and nights of feasting in the Great Hall, followed, for Dave, by quiet walks beyond the tents of the Dalrei outside the walls of the town, looking up at the brilliant stars, with his two brothers by his side.

But to settle the matter that was in his mind, Dave knew he needed to be alone, and so finally, on the very last day of the festival, he slipped away by himself on his favorite black horse. He looped Owein's Horn, on its new leather cord, about his neck and set out to ride, north and west, to do one thing and try to resolve another.

It was a route he had taken before, in the cold of the winter snows at evening, when Kim had woken the Hunt with the fire she carried, and he had summoned them with the horn. It was summer now, end of summer, shading toward fall. The morning was cool and clear. Birds sang overhead. Soon the colors of the leaves would begin to change to red and gold and brown.

He came to a curve in the path and saw the tiny jewel-like lake set in the valley below. He rode past on the high ridge of land, noting the empty cottage far below. He remembered the last time they had ridden by this place. Two boys had come out behind that cottage to look up at them. Two boys, and both of them were dead, and together they had acted to let all the peace of this morning come to be.

He shook his head, wondering, and continued riding northwest, angling across the recently harvested fields between Rhoden and North Keep. There were farmhouses scattered on either side. Some people saw him passing and waved to him. He waved back.

Then, around noon, he crossed the High Road and knew he was very near. A few minutes later he came to the edge of Pendaran Wood, and he saw the fork of the tree, and then the cave. There was an enormous stone in front of it again, exactly as there had been before, and Dave knew who lay asleep in the darkness there.

He dismounted, and he took the horn into his hand and walked a little way into the Wood. The light was dappled here, the leaves rustled above his head. He wasn't afraid though, not this time. Not as he had been the night he'd met Flidais. The Great Wood had slaked its anger now, the lios alfar had told them. It had to do with Lancelot and Darien, and with the final passing of Lisen, the blazing of her Circlet in Starkadh. Dave didn't really understand such things, but one thing he did understand, and it had brought him with the horn back to this place.

He waited, with a patience that was another new thing in him. He watched the shadows flicker and shift on the forest floor and in the leaves overhead. He listened to the sounds of the forest. He tried to think, to understand himself and his own desires. It was hard to concentrate, though, because he was waiting for someone.

And then he heard a different sound behind him. His heart racing, despite all his inward preparation, he turned, kneeling as he did so, with his head lowered.

"You may rise," said Ceinwen. "Of all men, you should know that you may rise."

He looked up and saw her again: in green as she always was, with the bow in her hand. The bow with which she'd almost killed him by a pool in Faelinn Grove.

Not all need die, she had said that night. And so he'd lived, to be given a horn, to carry an axe in war, to summon the Wild Hunt. To return again to this place.

The goddess stood before him, radiant and glorious, though muting the shining of her face that he might look upon her without being stricken blind.

He rose, as she had bade him. He took a deep breath, to slow the beating of his heart. He said, "Goddess, I have come to return a gift." He held out the horn in a hand that, he was pleased to see, did not tremble. "It is a thing too powerful for me to hold. Too deeply powerful, I think, for any mortal man."

Ceinwen smiled, beautiful and terrible. "I thought you would come," she said. "I waited to see. Had you not, I would have come for you, before you went away. I gave you more than I meant to give with this horn." And then, in a gentler tone, "What you say is not wrong, Davor of the Axe. It must be hidden again, to wait for a truer finding many years from now. Many, many years."

"We would have died by Adein without it," Dave said quietly. "Does that not make it a true finding?"

She smiled again, inscrutable, capricious. She said, "You have grown clever since last we met. I may be sorry to see you go."

There was nothing he could say to that. He extended the horn a little toward her, and she took it from his hand. Her fingers touched his palm, and he did tremble then, with awe and memory.

She laughed, deep in her throat.

Dave could feel himself flushing. But there was something he had to ask, even if she laughed. After a moment, he said, "Would you be as sorry to see me stay? I have been trying for a long time now to decide. I think I'm ready to go home, but another part of me despairs at the thought of leaving." He spoke as carefully as he could, with more dignity than he'd thought he possessed.

She did not laugh. The goddess looked upon him, and there was a strangeness in her eyes, half cold, half sorrowing. She shook her head. "Dave Martyniuk," she said, "you have grown wiser since that night in Faelinn Grove. I had thought you knew the answer to that question without my telling it. You cannot stay, and you should have known you cannot."

Something jogged in Dave's mind: an image, another memory. Just before she spoke again, in the half second before she told him why, he understood.

"What did I say to you that night by the pool?" she asked, her voice cool and soft like woven silk.

He knew. It had been hidden somewhere in his mind all along, he supposed.

No man of Fionavar may see Ceinwen hunt.

That was what she'd said. He *had* seen her hunt, though. He had seen her kill a stag by the moonlit pool and had seen the stag rise from its own death and bow its head to the Huntress and move away into the trees.

No man of Fionavar. . . . Dave knew the answer to his dilemma now: there was, had only ever been, one answer.

He was going home. The goddess willed it so. Only by leaving Fionavar could he preserve his life, only by leaving could he allow her not to kill him for what he had seen.

Within his heart he felt one stern pang of grief, and then it passed away, leaving behind a sorrow he would always carry, but leaving also a deep certitude that this was how it was because it was the only way it could ever have been.

Had he not been from another world, Ceinwen could not have let him live; she could never have given him the horn. In her own way, Dave saw, in a flash of illumination, the goddess too was trapped by her nature, by what she had decreed.

And so he would go. There was nothing left to decide. It had been decided long ago, and that truth had been within him all the time. He drew another breath, deep and slow. It was very quiet in the woods. No birds were singing now.

He remembered something else then, and he said it. "I swore to you that night, that first time, that I would pay whatever price was necessary. If you will see it as such, then perhaps my leaving may be that price."

Again she smiled, and this time it was kind. "I will see it as such," the goddess said. "There will be no other price exacted. Remember me."

There was a shining in her face. He opened his mouth but found he could not speak. It had come home to him with his words and hers: he was leaving. It would all be put behind him now. It had to be. Memory would be all he had to carry back with him and forward through his days.

For the last time he knelt before Ceinwen of the Bow. She was motionless as a statue, looking down upon him. He rose up and turned to go from among the shadows and dappled light between the trees.

"*Hold!*" the goddess said.

He turned back, afraid, not knowing what, now, would

be asked of him. She gazed at him in silence for a long time before she spoke.

"Tell me, Dave Martyniuk, Davor of the Axe, if you were allowed to name a son in Fionavar, a child of the andain, what name would your son carry into time?"

She was so bright. And now there were tears in his eyes, making her image shimmer and blur before him, and there was something shining, like the moon, in his heart.

He remembered: a night on a mound by Celidon, south of the Adein River. Under the stars of spring returned, he had lain down with a goddess on the new green grass.

He understood. And in that moment, just before he spoke, giving voice to the brightness within him, something flowered in his mind, more fiercely than the moon in his heart or even the shining of Ceinwen's face. He understood, and there, at the edge of Pendaran Wood, Dave finally came to terms with himself, with what he once had been, in all his bitterness, and with what he had now become.

"Goddess," he said, over the tightness in his throat, "if such a child were born and mine to name, I would call him Kevin. For my friend."

For the last time she smiled at him.

"It shall be so," Ceinwen said.

There was a dazzle of light, and then he was alone. He turned and went back to his horse and mounted up for the ride back. Back to Paras Derval, and then a long, long way beyond, to home.

Paul spent the days and nights of that last week saying his own goodbyes. Unlike Dave, or even Kim, he seemed to have formed no really deep attachments here in Fionavar. It was partly due to his own nature, to what had driven him to cross in the first place. But more profoundly it was inherent in what had happened to him on the Summer Tree, marking him as one apart, one who could speak with gods and have them bow to him. Even here at the end, after the war was over, his remained a solitary path.

On the other hand, there *were* people he cared about and

would miss. He tried to make a point of spending a little time with each of them in those last days.

One morning he walked alone to a shop he knew at the end of Anvil Lane, near to a green where he could see that the children of Paras Derval were playing again, though not the ta'kiena. He remembered the shop doorway very well, though his images were of winter and night. The first time, Jennifer had made him bring her here, the night Darien was born. And then another night, after Kim had sent them back to Fionavar from Stonehenge, he had walked, coatless but not cold in the winter winds, from the heat of the Black Boar, where a woman had died to save his life, and his steps had led him here to see the door swinging open and snow piling in the aisles of the shop.

And an empty cradle rocking in a cold room upstairs. He could still reach back to the terror he'd felt in that moment.

But now it was summer and the terror was gone: destroyed, in the end, by the child who'd been born in this house, who'd lain in that cradle. Paul entered the shop. It was very crowded, for this was a time of festival and Paras Derval was thronged with people. Vae recognized him right away, though, and then Shahar did, as well. They left two clerks to deal with the people buying their woolen goods and led Paul up the stairs.

There was very little, really, that he could say to them. The marks of grief, even with the months that had passed, were still etched into both of them. Shahar was mourning for Finn, who had died in his arms. But Vae, Paul knew, was grieving for both her sons, for Dari too, the blue-eyed child she'd raised and loved from the moment of his birth. He wondered how Jennifer had known so well whom to ask to raise her child and teach him love.

Aileron had offered Shahar a number of posts and honors within the palace, but the quiet artisan had chosen to return to his shop and his craft. Paul looked at the two of them and wondered if they were young enough to have another child. And if they could bear to do so, after what had happened. He hoped so.

He told them he was leaving, and that he'd come to say goodbye. They made some small conversation, ate some pastry Vae had made, but then one of the clerks called upstairs with a question about pricing a bale of cloth, and Shahar had to go down. Paul and Vae followed him. In the shop she gave him, awkwardly, a scarf for the coming fall. He realized, then, that he had no idea what season it was back home. He took the scarf and kissed her on the cheek, and then he left.

The next day he went riding, south and west, with the new Duke of Seresh. Niavin had died at the hands of a mounted urgach in Andarien. The new Duke riding with Paul looked exactly as he always had, big and capable, brown-haired, with the hook of his broken nose prominent in a guileless face. As much as anything else that had happened since the war, Paul was pleased by what Aileron had done in naming Coll to rank.

It was a quiet ride. Coll had always been taciturn by nature. It had been Erron and Carde or boisterous, blustering Tegid who had drawn out the laughter hidden in his nature. Those three, and Diarmuid, who had taken a fatherless boy from Taerlindel and made him his right-hand man.

For part of the way their road carried them past towns they had galloped furiously through so long ago with Diar, on a clandestine journey to cross Saeren into Cathal.

When the road forked toward South Keep they continued west instead, by unspoken agreement, and early in the afternoon they came to a vantage point from where they could look into the distance at walled Seresh and the sea beyond. They stopped there, looking down.

"Do you still hate him?" Paul asked, the first words spoken in a long time. He knew Coll would understand what he meant. *I would have him cursed in the name of all the gods and goddesses there are*, he had said to Paul very late one night, long ago, in a dark corridor of the palace. And had named Aileron, which was treason then.

Now the big man was slowly shaking his head. "I understand him better. And I can see how much he has suffered." He hesitated, then said very softly, "But I will miss his brother all the rest of my days."

Paul understood. He felt the same way about Kevin. Exactly the same way.

Neither of them said anything else. Paul looked off to the west, to where the sea sparkled in the bright sun. There were stars beneath the waves. He had seen them. In his heart he bade farewell to Liranan, the god who had called him brother.

Coll glanced over at him. Paul nodded, and the two of them turned and rode back to Paras Derval.

The next evening, after the banquet in the Hall—Cathalian food that time, prepared by Shalhassan's own master of the kitchen—he found himself in the Black Boar, with Dave and Coll and all the men of South Keep, those who had sailed *Prydwen* to Cader Sedat.

They drank a great deal, and the owner of the tavern refused to let any of Diarmuid's men pay for their ale. Tegid of Rhoden, not one to let such largess slip past him, drained ten huge tankards to start the proceedings and then gathered speed as the night progressed. Paul got a little drunk himself, which was unusual, and perhaps as a result his memories refused to go away. All night long he kept hearing "Rachel's Song" in his mind amid the laughter and the embraces of farewell.

The next afternoon, the last but one, he spent in the mages' quarters in the town. Dave was with the Dalrei, but Kim had come with him this time, and the two of them spent a few hours with Loren and Matt and Teyrnon and Barak, sitting in the garden behind the house.

Loren Silvercloak, no longer a mage, now dwelt in Banir Lök as principal adviser to the King of Dwarves. Teyrnon and Barak were visibly pleased to have the other two staying with them, if only for a little while. Teyrnon bustled happily about in the sunshine, making sure everyone's glass was brimming.

"Tell me," said Barak, a little slyly, to Loren and Matt, "do you think the two of you might be able to handle a pupil for a few months next year? Or will you have forgotten everything you know?"

Matt glanced at him quickly. "Have you a disciple already? Good, very good. We need at least three or four more."

"We?" Teyrnon teased.

Matt scowled. "Habits die hard. Some, I hope, will never die."

"They need never die," Teyrnon said soberly. "You two will always be part of the Council of the Mages."

"Who is our new disciple?" Loren asked. "Do we know him?"

For reply, Teyrnon looked up at the second-floor window overlooking the garden.

"Boy!" he shouted, trying to sound severe. "I hope you are studying, and not listening to the gossip down here!"

A moment later a head of brown unruly hair appeared at the open window.

"Of course I'm studying," said Tabor, "but, honestly, none of this is very difficult!"

Matt grunted in mock disapproval. Loren, struggling to achieve a frown, growled fiercely. "Teyrnon, give him the Book of Abhar, and *then* we'll see whether or not he finds studying difficult!"

Paul grinned and heard Kim laugh with delight to see who was smiling down on them.

"Tabor!" she exclaimed. "When did this happen?"

"Two days ago," the boy replied. "My father gave his consent after Gereint asked me to come back and teach him some new things next year."

Paul exchanged a glance with Loren. There was a genuine easing in this, an access to joy. The boy was young; it seemed he would recover. More than that, Paul had an intuitive sense of the rightness, even the necessity of Tabor's new path: what horse on the Plain, however swift, could ever suffice, now, for one who had ridden a creature of Dana across the sky?

Later that afternoon, walking back to the palace with Kim, Paul learned that she too would be going home. They still didn't know about Dave.

On the next morning, the last, he went back to the Summer Tree.

It was the first time he'd been there alone since the three nights he had hung upon it as an offering to the God, seeking rain. He left his horse at the edge of Mörnirwood, not far (though this he didn't know) from the place of Aideen's grave, where Matt had taken Jennifer early one morning in Kevin's spring.

He walked the remembered path through the trees, seeing the morning sunlight begin to grow dim and increasingly aware, with every step he took, of something else.

Since the last battle in Andarien—when he had released Galadan from the vengeance he'd sworn and channeled his power for healing instead, to bring the rising waters that ended the cycle of Arthur's grief—since that evening Paul had not sought the presence of the God within himself. In a way, he'd been avoiding it.

But now it was there again. And as he came to the place where the trees of the Godwood formed their double corridor, leading him inexorably back into the glade of the Tree, Paul understood that Mörnir would always be within him. He would always be Pwyll Twiceborn, Lord of the Summer Tree, wherever he went. He had been sent back; the reality of that was a part of him, and would be until he died again.

And thinking so, he came into the glade and saw the Tree. There was light here, for the sky showed above the clearing, mild and blue with scattered billowy clouds. He remembered the white burning of the sun in a blank heaven.

He looked at the trunk and the branches. They were as old as this first world, he knew. And looking up within the thick green leaves, he saw, without surprise, that the ravens were there, staring back at him with bright yellow eyes. It was very still. No thunder. Only, deep within his pulse, that constant awareness of the God.

It was not a thing, Paul realized then, from which he could ever truly hide, even if he wanted to, which was what he'd been trying to do through the sweet days of this summer.

He could not unsay what he had become. It was not a thing that came and then went. He would have to accept that he was marked and set apart. In a way, he always had been. Self-contained and solitary, too much so: it was why Rachel had been leaving him, the night she died on the highway in the rain.

He was a power, brother to gods. It was so and would always be so. He thought of Cernan and Galadan, wondering where they were. Both of them had bowed to him.

No one did so now. Nor did Mörnir manifest himself any

more strongly than through the beating of his pulse. The Tree seemed to be brooding, sunk deep into the earth, into the web of its years. The ravens watched him silently. He could make them speak; he knew how to do that now. He could even cause the leaves of the Summer Tree to rustle as in a storm wind, and in time, if he tried hard enough, he could draw the thunder of the God. He was Lord of this Tree; this was the place of his power.

He did none of these things. He had come for no such reason. Only to see the place for a last time, and to acknowledge, within himself, what had indeed been confirmed. In silence he stepped forward and laid one hand upon the trunk of the Summer Tree. He felt it as an extension of himself. He drew his hand away and turned and left the glade. Overhead, he heard the ravens flying. He knew they would be back.

And after that, there was only the last farewell. He'd been delaying it, in part because even now he did not expect it to be an easy exchange. On the other hand, the two of them, for all the brittleness, had shared a great deal since first she'd taken him down from the Tree and drawn blood from his face in the Temple with the nails of her hand.

So he returned to his horse and rode back to Paras Derval, and then east through the crowded town to the sanctuary, to say goodbye to Jaelle.

He tugged on the bell pull by the arched entranceway. Chimes rang within the Temple. A moment later the doors were opened and a grey-robed priestess looked out, blinking in the brightness. Then she recognized him, and smiled.

This was one of the new things in Brennin, as potent a symbol of regained harmony, in its own way, as would be the joint action of Jaelle and Teyrnon this evening, sending them home.

"Hello, Shiel," he said, remembering her from the night he'd come after Darien's birth to seek aid. They had barred his way then, demanding blood.

Not now. Shiel flushed at being recognized. She gestured for him to enter. "I know you have given blood," she said, almost apologetically.

"I'll do so again, if you like," he said mildly.

She shook her head vigorously and sent an acolyte scurrying down the curved corridors in search of the High Priestess. Waiting patiently, Paul looked beyond Shiel to his left. He could see the domed chamber and—strategically placed to be visible—the altar stone and the axe.

The acolyte came back, and with her was Jaelle. He had thought he might be kept waiting, or sent for, but she so seldom did what he expected.

"Pwyll," she said. "I wondered if you would come." Her voice was cool. "Will you take a glass of wine?"

He nodded and followed her back along the hallway to a room that he remembered. She dismissed the acolyte and closed the door. She went to a sideboard and poured wine for both of them, her motions brisk and impersonal.

She gave him a glass and sank down into a pile of cushions on the floor. He took the chair beside the door. He looked at her: an image of crimson and white. The fires of Dana and the whiteness of the full moon. There was a silver circlet holding back her hair; he remembered picking it up on the plain of Andarien. He remembered her running to where Finn lay.

"This evening, then?" she asked, sipping her wine.

"If you will," he said. "Is there a difficulty? Because if there—"

"No, no," she said quickly. "I was only asking. We will do it at moonrise."

There was a little silence. Broken by Paul's quiet laughter. "We really are terrible, aren't we?" he said, shaking his head ruefully. "We never could manage a civil exchange."

She considered that, not smiling, though his tone had invited it. "That night by the Anor," she said. "Until I said the wrong thing."

"You didn't," he murmured. "I was just sensitive about power and control. You found a nerve."

"We're trained to do that." She smiled. It wasn't a cold smile, though, and he realized she was mocking herself a little.

"I did my share of goading," Paul admitted. "One of the reasons I came was to tell you that a lot of it was reflex. My own defenses. I wanted to say goodbye, and to tell you that I have . . . a great deal of respect for you." It was difficult choosing words.

She said nothing, looking back at him, her green eyes clear and bright. Well, he thought, he'd said it. What he'd come to say. He finished his wine and rose to his feet. She did the same.

"I should go," he said, wanting to be elsewhere before one of them said something that was wounding, and so spoiled even this goodbye. "I'll see you this evening, I guess." He turned to the door.

"Paul," she said. "Wait."

Not Pwyll. *Paul.* Something stirred like a wind within him. He turned again.

She had not moved. Her hands were crossed in front of her chest, as if she were suddenly cold in the midst of summer.

"*Are you really going to leave me?*" Jaelle asked, in a voice so strained he needed a second to be sure of what he'd heard.

And then he *was* sure, and in that instant the world rocked and shifted within him and around him and everything changed. Something burst in his chest like a dam breaking, a dam that had held back need for so long, that had denied the truth of his heart, even to this moment.

"Oh, my love," he said.

There seemed to be so much light in the room. He took one step, another; then she was within the circle of his arms and the impossible flame of her hair was about them both. He lowered his mouth and found her own turned up to his kiss.

And in that moment he was clear at last. It was all clear. He was in the clear and running like his running pulsebeat, the clear hammer of his heart. He was translucent. Not Lord of the Summer Tree then, but only a mortal man, long denied, long denying himself, touching and touched by love.

She was fire and water to his hands, she was everything he had ever desired. Her fingers were behind his head, laced through his hair, drawing him down to her lips, and she whispered his name over and over and over while she wept.

And so they came together then, at the last, the children of the Goddess and the God.

They subsided among the scattered cushions and she laid

her head against his chest, and for a long time they were silent as he ran his fingers ceaselessly through the red fall of her hair and brushed her tears away.

At length she moved so that she lay with her head in his lap, looking up at him. She smiled, a different kind of smile from any he had seen before.

"You would really have gone," she said. Not a question.

He nodded, still half in a daze, still trembling and incredulous at what had happened to him. "I would have," he confessed. "I was too afraid."

She reached up and touched his cheek. "Afraid of this, after all you have done?"

He nodded again. "Of this, perhaps more than anything. When?" he asked. "When did you . . . ?"

Her eyes turned grave. "I fell in love with you on the beach by Taerlindel. When you stood in the waves, speaking to Liranan. But I fought it, of course, for many reasons. You will know them. It didn't come home to me until you were walking back from Finn to face Galadan."

He closed his eyes. Opened them. Felt sorrow come over to shadow joy. "Can you do this?" he said. "How may it be allowed? You are what you are."

She smiled again, and this smile he knew. It was the one he imagined on the face of Dana herself: inward and inscrutable.

She said, "I will die to have you, but I do not think it need happen that way."

Neatly she rose to her feet. He, too, stood up and saw her go to the door and open it. She murmured something to the acolyte in the corridor and then turned back to him, a light dancing in her eyes.

They waited, not for long. The door opened again, and Leila came in.

Clad in white.

She looked from one of them to the other and then laughed aloud. "Oh, good!" she said. "I thought this might happen."

Paul felt himself flushing; then he caught Jaelle's glance and both of them burst out laughing.

"Can you see why she'll be High Priestess now?" Jaelle asked, smiling. Then, more soberly, added, "From the moment she lifted the axe and survived, Leila was marked by the Goddess to the white of the High Priestess. Dana moves in ways no mortal can understand, nor even the others among the gods. I am High Priestess in name only now. After I sent you through the crossing I was to relinquish my place to Leila."

Paul nodded. He could see a pattern shaping here, only a glimmering of it, but it seemed to him that the warp and weft of this, followed back to their source, would reach Dun Maura and a sacrifice made on the eve of Maidaladan.

And thinking of that, he found that there were tears in his own eyes. He had to wipe them away, he who had never been able to weep.

He said, "Kim is going home or I would never say this, but I think I know a cottage by a lake, halfway between the Temple and the Tree, where I would like to live. If it pleases you."

"It pleases me," Jaelle said quietly. "More than I can tell you. Ysanne's cottage will bring my life full circle and lay a grief to rest."

"I guess I'm staying, then," he said, reaching for her hand. "I guess I'm staying after all."

She was learning something, Kim realized. Learning it the hardest way. Discovering that the only thing harder for her to deal with than power was its passing away.

The Baelrath was gone. She had surrendered it, but before that it had abandoned her. Not since Calor Diman and her refusal there had the Warstone so much as flickered on her hand. So, late last night, quietly, with no one else in the room, no one else to know, she had given it to Aileron.

And he, as quietly, had sent for Jaelle and entrusted the stone to the custody of the Priestesses of Dana. Which was right, Kim knew. She'd thought at first that he would give it to the mages. But the wild power of the Baelrath was closer, far, to Dana than it was to the skylore Amairgen had learned.

It was a measure of Aileron's deepening wisdom, one of the marks of the changing nature of things, that the High

King would surrender a thing of so much power to the High Priestess and that she would agree to guard it in his name.

And thus had the Warstone passed from her, which left Kimberly, on this last afternoon, walking with her memories amid the strand of trees west of Ysanne's cottage, dealing with loss and sorrow.

It should not be so, she told herself sternly. She was going home, and she *wanted* to go home. She wanted her family very badly. More than that, even, she knew it was right for her to be crossing back. She had dreamt it, and so had Ysanne, in those first days.

It is in my heart as well that there may be need of a Dreamer in your world too, the old Seer had said. And Kim knew it was still true. She had seen it herself.

So need and rightness had come together with her own desire to draw her back. This should have made things easy and clear, but it was not so. How, in truth, could it ever be, when she was leaving so much behind? And all her thoughts and feelings seemed to be complicated, made even more blurred and difficult, by the hollow of absence within her when she looked at the finger where the Warstone had been for so long.

She shook her head, trying to pull herself out of this mood. She had so many blessings to count, so many riches. The first, running deeper than anything else, was the fact of peace and the Unraveller's passing from the worlds, at the hands of the child whose name she had dreamt before he'd even been born.

She walked through the green woods in sunlight thinking of Darien, and then of his mother and Arthur and Lancelot, whose grief had come to an end. Another blessing, another place where joy might flower in the heart.

And for herself, she was still a Seer, and she still carried, and always would, a second soul within her as a gift beyond words or measurement. She still wore the vellin bracelet on her wrist—Matt had refused, absolutely, to take it back. It would serve no real purpose in her world, she knew, save for memory—which, in its own way, was as good a purpose as any.

Deep in the woods alone, reaching painfully toward an inner peace, Kim stopped and stood in silence for a time, listening to the birds overhead and the sighing of the breeze through the leaves. It was so quiet here, so beautiful, she wanted to hold this to herself forever.

Thinking so, she saw a flash of color on the ground off to her right and realized, even before she moved, that she was being given a final gift.

She walked over, following, as it happened, the steps that Finn and Darien had taken on their last walk together in the depths of winter. Then she knelt, as they had knelt, beside the bannion growing there.

Blue-green flower with red at its center like a drop of blood at the heart. They had left it, that day, gathering other flowers to take back to Vae but not this one. And so it had remained for Kim to take it for herself, tears welling at the richness of the memory it stirred: her first walk in this wood with Ysanne, looking for this flower; then a night by the lake under stars when Eilathen, summoned by flowerfire, had spun the Tapestry for her.

The bannion was beautiful, sea-colored around the brilliant red. She plucked it carefully and placed it in her white hair. She thought of Eilathen, of the blue-green glitter of his naked power. He too was lost to her, even if she had wanted to summon him, if only to bid farewell. *Be free of flowerfire, now and evermore*, Ysanne had said, at the end, releasing him from guardianship of the red Warstone.

The bannion was beautiful but powerless. It seemed to be a symbol of what had passed from her, what she could no longer do. Magic had been given to her that starry night by this lake, and it had rested in her for a time and had gone. It would be better for her, in every way, to be in her own world, she thought, to be removed from the sharpness of these images.

She rose and started back, thinking of Loren, who had to be dealing with the same withdrawal. Just as, she realized suddenly, Matt had dealt with it for all the years he'd spent in Paras Derval, fighting the pull of Calor Diman. The two of them had come full circle together, she thought. There was a pattern in that, more beautiful and more terrible than any mortal weaving could ever be.

She came out from the trees and walked down to the lake.

It was slightly choppy in the summer breeze. There was the hint of a chill; overture to the coming of fall. Kim stepped out onto the flat surface of the rock that jutted out over the water, just as she had done before, with Ysanne, when the Seer had summoned the water spirit under the stars.

Eilathen was down there, she knew, far down among his twining corridors of seastone and seaweed, amid the deep silence of his home. Inaccessible. Lost to her. She sat on the stone and wrapped her arms about her drawn-up knees, trying to number blessings, to shape sadness into joy.

For a long time she sat there, looking out over the waters of the lake. It had to be late afternoon, she knew. She should be starting back. It was so hard to leave, though. Rising up and walking from this place would be an act as lonely and as final as any she'd ever done.

So she lingered, and in time there was a footfall on the rock behind her and then someone crouched down by her side.

"I saw your horse by the cottage," Dave said. "Am I intruding?"

She smiled up at him and shook her head. "I'm just saying my goodbyes before this evening."

"So was I," he said, gathering and dispersing pebbles.

"You're coming home too?"

"I just decided," he said quietly. There was a calmness, an assurance in his voice she'd not heard before. Of all of them, Kim realized, Dave had changed the most here. She and Paul and Jennifer seemed to have really just gone further into what they'd already been before they came, and Kevin had remained exactly what he always was, with his laughter and his sadness and the sweetness of his soul. But this man crouching beside her, burned dark by the summer sun of the Plain, was a very far cry from the one she'd met that first evening in Convocation Hall, when she'd invited him to come sit with them and hear Lorenzo Marcus speak.

She managed another smile. "I'm glad you're coming back," she said.

He nodded, quietly self-possessed, looking at her in a calm silence for a moment. Then his eyes flickered with a certain amusement that was also new.

"Tell me," he said, "what are you doing on Friday night?"

A little breathless laugh escaped her. "Oh, Dave," Kim said, "I don't even know when Friday night *is*!"

He laughed too. Then the laughter passed, leaving an easy smile. He stood up smoothly and held out a hand to help her up.

"Saturday, then?" he asked, his eyes holding hers.

And bursting within her then like another kind of flower-fire Kim had a sudden feeling, a flashing certainty, that everything was going to be all right after all. It was going to be much more than all right.

She gave him both her hands and let him help her rise.

Here ends THE DARKEST ROAD
and with it
THE FIONAVAR TAPESTRY